DARK
UNIVERSE

EDITED BY
MILTON DAVIS
AND
EUGENE PETERSON

MVmedia, LLC
Fayetteville GA

MVmedia, LLC
PO Box 1465
Fayetteville, GA 30214
www.mvmediaatl.com

Publisher's Note: This is a work of fiction. Names, characters, places, and incidents are a product of the author's imagination. Locales and public names are sometimes used for atmospheric purposes. Any resemblance to actual people, living or dead, or to businesses, companies, events, institutions, or locales is completely coincidental.

Book Layout ©2017BookDesignTemplates.com

Ordering Information:
Quantity sales. Special discounts are available on quantity purchases by corporations, associations, and others. For details, contact the "Special Sales Department" at the address above.

Dark Universe. - 1st ed.
ISBN 978-0-9960167-8-0

Contents

To the descendants

We choose our own destiny. We create our own worlds.

—Samake

DARK UNIVERSE TIMELINE

2020-Earth

     The architects of slipstream tech and bio re-engineering are just entering higher education.

     Environ, a global rehabilitation corporation, develops patented green technology that forms the foundation for terraforming planets.

2030s-2100s

     Colonization of the solar system begins.

     Terraformable planets located beyond the system.

     Slipstream travel invented.

     Vast missions to the stars begin.

2100s-2300s

     Element "G" discovered.

     1st Gate built.

     Colony worlds established. Terraforming breakthroughs reduce time from centuries to decades. The first terraformed worlds cannot use the new tech.

     Mars…Titan…remain difficult to survive on without contained bio-domes…or vast bio re-engineering.

2311-Atlanta, Georgia

     The Cassad global business company is founded by Cornelius Cassidy.

     Earth economic blocs purchase planets and form network systems controlled by Earth bound governments.

January 25, 2411
> Cornelius Cassidy purchases M level terraformed planet. The planet is named 'Cassidy.'

September 8, 2416
> One million colonists arrive on Cassidy from Earth. They become known as The One Million, eventually evolving into the foundation of Cassad aristocracy.

May 15, 2427
> Environ, Inc. declares bankruptcy. Maintenance responsibility of terraformed planets revert to government blocs. The Bloc Wars begin.
> Cassidy declares itself an autonomous and neutral planet.

2427-3000
> The Bloc Wars. NAFTA and AFRICOM become the main combatants. Cassidy breaks diplomatic relations with all Bloc planets after converting its technology to an independently developed internet technology.

3000 - ?
> The Dark Age begins. Massive electromagnetic pulses render all tech useless for some 300 years. Technology is lost on most worlds; many collapse to Stone Age level existence. Most knowledge prior to the pulses is lost.

1 AD (After Dark)
> Cassidy becomes the first planet to emerge from the Dark Age due to its homegrown technology and the knowledge retained by the djele/historian AI, Samake. Ziara Cassad discovers the tombs of Cornelius Cassidy and reactivates Samake. She restores Cassad control as a kingdom and sparks the Afrocentric Renaissance.

110 AD

The Great Age of Discovery begins. Ziara Cassad dies, leaving a fully restored world as her legacy. Her son Shaka Cassad leads the first wave of Ziaran warships and diplomatic teams into the Known. The worlds of the Known begin to discover each other.

The Great space wars begin The Cassad Empire begins to take shape.

230 AD

The end of the Cassad Empires takeover.

The Reddeg, last holdouts against the Cassad Empire fall.

The Cassad Alifia begins. The Known Worlds prosper under Cassad rule.

1224-1273

The Cassad Alifia ends. The Wars of the Blade begin.

1275

Kujuinga Na Conference takes place. The participants form the New Regime and declare their independence from 'Cassad tyranny.' The Fall of the Cassads begins.

1298

The Trial and Conviction of Cassad.

1312

The New Regime dissolves. The Interregnum begins.

A SHORT HISTORY OF THE CASSAD EMPIRE

Part One: The One Million

When man finally took to the stars it was not for the purpose of scientific curiosity and knowledge but for the basic needs of survival and profit. Mother Earth's bounty was exhausted and those who robbed her set off to find more sources of wealth for the 20 billion inhabitants of Earth to consume. Though China had long ago eclipsed the United States as the prime world power, America still held the title in space exploration. The 'home of the free' sank its meager resources into exploring the galaxy to find new sources of wealth and hopefully prosperity. It was rewarded with the breakthrough of inter-dimensional travel, known as 'slipping' to its inventors. Slipping entailed passing into a dimension where the physical barriers of our dimension do not exist. In the case of space travel the important missing component was distance. The tenacity of the US to keep the secret of slip travel was amazing especially considering the porous security of the internet; it was 20 years after the discovery of slipping that the rest of the world became aware of America's advantage. America also held another advantage. The world's leading environmental recover company, Environ, Incorporated, was in the final stages of developing breakthrough terra-forming technology. By this time the world became aware of America's advantage ten planets had been rendered habitable and colonized, each adding immensely to America's wealth.

Once the secret was exposed America bowed to the financial and military pressures of the Middle Kingdom. The stars were opened to the world and Earth experienced a second

Renaissance. Goods and minerals streamed to Mother Earth from the newly terraformed worlds. Environ became the world's wealthiest corporation. Poverty became virtually non-existent as national competition diminished in view of such abundance. The dream of a global nation finally coalesced and the United Nations expanded into this new frontier. However as always, this wealth was not evenly distributed among Earth's inhabitants.

During the initial covert expansion, a small company with surprisingly deep pockets put in its bid for its own planet. This company, Cassidy Enterprises, was one of the few remaining African American corporations in America. Its founder, Cornelius Cassidy, was known as a generous man with a true empathy for his people, whose lot in America had decreased horribly during the country's economic decline. Cornelius saw himself as a modern-day Moses and was determined to deliver his people from their endless plight. He secretly established the Exodus Project, a plan to move every African American from America to his new world, Cassidy.

Cassidy was disappointed in the response. The fear of leaving the country and the planet was too much for the average black person. Of 50 million African Americans only 1 million answered Cornelius's call. These 1 million men and women were the foundation of the Cassad Empire.

Part Two: War

It is said that the only thing that can stop greed is death. For Earth the saying rings true, for despite the unlimited prosperity of every nation-state from the off-world plunder tensions grew. That tension reached the breaking point with the collapse of Environ. The corporation's collapsed brought terraforming to a halt, making a seemingly infinite opportunity suddenly finite and eventually scarce. Countries that sat in harmony at the UN table fought tenaciously for control of planets and asteroids. The conflicts of space finally spilled onto the planet and the First Intergalactic War began. The planets burned and the stars blazed as economic blocs fought for control of the resources that kept their populations in decadence. Throughout it all the inhabitants of Cassidy built their new home into a formidable economic and military powerhouse. Fearful of the racial retaliations that had destroyed black economic prosperity in the past, the Cassidites worked hard to preserve their future. Years, decades, and centuries passed but the war continued. The planet once known as Cassidy became Cassad and the family once known as benevolent corporate leaders became compassionate emperors.

But compassion ended at the rim of their atmosphere. The Cassads watched patiently as the planets fell from grace, drained by a war that lasted far too long and took too many lives. Their airspace buzzed with ambassador ships from every economic bloc seeking their assistance. Promises were made that would make Cassad a giant among equals but Cassad's emperors shrugged them away. The truth was clear to those who could see unobstructed by conflict. The fruit was ready to be picked.

But it was not to be. The Known was struck by a cataclysm which destroyed the technology of every single planet. The origins of the catastrophe have been debated continuously up to the time of the Interregnum, but the result went without question. The Known spiraled into a millennium of decline known as 'The Dark Age.'

Part Three: The Dark Age

A few hundred years after slipstream technology sends mankind from earth to the stars came the Dark Age; a cataclysmic event that spanned the full breadth of mankind's reach among the stars.

One after another, stars began emitting powerful electromagnetic pulses, disabling all electrical equipment. But there was something else embedded deep in the crust of the most heavily populated worlds that acted as a kinetic dampener. This rendered heavy powerful machines inert as well...even old ceremonial powder weapons were affected.

Worlds were so long adapted to their high level of tech that almost no "old world" tech existed. Who takes a paper book with them on a space voyage to a colony world?

Without the ability to use tech there was no way to maintain the infrastructures of the huge cities on the terraformed worlds. People were forced to abandon their high tech, wonderfully designed cities and flee into the tame wilderness...which on many worlds quickly became feral without human caretakers...

So many worlds had been colonized...so many new governments...only the strongest and most organized peoples were able to even keep a record or to preserve their histories. The rest...lost.

Lost their knowledge as the pulses continued for generations, lost their history as they were forced to start anew, and lost their technical knowhow because they had no use for it.

On some colony worlds there were vast numbers of genetically altered peoples. Their bodies had been changed, most intended to be only temporary changes, to survive in hostile environments. But with the pulses stopping them from recovering their natural bodies these people still could not deny the urge to procreate. They would re-enter the known later having forgotten they were ever human.

And genetically enhanced animals prospered in the Dark Age as well. Worlds of cetaceans and "modified" primates, dogs, cephalopods developed their own intelligent civilizations.

But then the pulses stopped as mysteriously as they began. Slowly the worlds began to redevelop their technical knowledge. On worlds with different challenges, different tech developed. Without being able to share with other worlds that only a few knew existed out among the stars...an amazing variety of solutions to common problems arose.

Because of the time the suns stopped pulsing was synchronous, the worlds re-established their tech at similar rates. Some worlds discovered each other before they managed to reach space via radio communications because their worlds were so close. Others met in space, discovering men like themselves amongst the stars.

And there of course were those that already knew. Some worlds fought hard to get to space before the others...they had managed to keep their historical records intact enough to know there were others out in the universe. They had a head start and began conquering worlds to establish system spanning empires. They remembered the time before and they saw their chance for power.

Then the Cassads reached space again...

...and the game changed.

Part Four: The Age of Discovery

After the Dark Age and the slow crawl back out of their individual worlds gravity wells, came the Age of Discovery, where the civilizations of the Known began to discover one another. Most worlds, having lost nearly all of their history, were ignorant to the fact that their own societies had not evolved on the planet on which they now lived. This gave rise to several "Origin" world wars. Even to this day, millennia later there is still conflict and debate over whose world is the original Earth.

The Age of Discovery was a wild time as worlds encountered each other both peacefully and violently. It is here that the seeds of the current Dark Universe begin, with the Cassads beginning their campaign to conquer all.

The vestiges of the Pre-dark age universe are clearer though they begin to fall away as worlds conquer worlds and re-write and erase histories.

However, the most significant discovery was made on Cassad. The Cassads still ruled the world despite the Dark Age but like others had lost most of what they once possessed. Ziara, daughter of the Alaafin, grew up on the stories of her ancestors which were told to her as fiction. She believed them to be true, and as a teenager set out to find the lost tomb of Cornelius Cassidy using an old map her father had hidden away. Two years later she found the mausoleum buried under dense vegetation on an island in an unnamed river. But there was more. Waiting within the crypt was Samake, AI djele/historian of the Cassad dynasty. The AI was reactivated by her touch, recognizing Ziara's lineage from her DNA spoor. It was then Ziara's true education began. For five years she studied under Samake, relearning what her people had lost. Ten years after leaving home she returned a different woman with one purpose; to resurrect Cassad and to claim its dominance of the Known. Ziara took over as Alaafin then immediately put her plan into action. She spent the remainder of her life rebuilding Cassad, yet passed away a few years before her plan was complete. That fell into the hands of her eldest son, Shaka Cassad, later known as Shaka the Conqueror. It was he who led the Cassad fleets into the stars to realize the dream his mother envisioned.

And thus, the Cassad Empire began.

Part Five: Ascendance and Decline

The conquest of the Known was a complex operation. For some planets, the Cassad arrival was considered a miracle, as the technology they brought with them lifted the worlds from Stone Age like conditions. For others, the Cassads negotiated alliances that would soon be betrayed. For others still, such as the Brython Theocracy and the Alien Worlds, it was all out war. In each case the Cassads prevailed due to their technological advantages, tenacity and deep resources. Soon most of the Known worlds were under Cassad control. Administrators selected from the One Million were placed in control of each world; each world was required to pay a 'rehabilitation tax' which paid the cost of the Cassad technological innovation. Soon the Known worlds possessed comparable technology but the payments were still required. This was the time of the Cassad Alifia, The Cassad Peace, which lasted for approximately one thousand years. The description was a misnomer. While the Core Worlds and worlds near the Gates experienced peace, those on the Rim of the Empire and near the Unknown existed in constant turmoil and served as a training ground for the Cassad military. Cassad, now called Ziara in honor of Ziara Cassad, experienced a prosperity that bordered on decadence. The One Million administrators, now generations into governing their worlds, began to despise the Empire as their Worlds deteriorated attempting to keep up with Ziara's increasing demands. The covert dissension culminated with Kujuinga Na Conference, during which the disgruntled worlds formed the New Regime and formally declared war against the Empire.

Logic would predict a long, bloody war. However, the Empire fell quickly. Ziara's Alaafin refused to take the rebellion seriously and continued to trust administrators that were now his enemies. The Cassad military was committed to fighting a growing conflict against the Alien Worlds which weakened the military response in the Core. The final blow was the coup on Ziara itself, in which the entire royal family was assassinated. Only Khalid Cassad survived. The heir to the Stool was leading a military operation against the Alien Worlds during the coup. He was captured by bounty hunter Pack Loren on his return to Ziara and made to stand trial for 'crimes' against the Known.

The New Regime's victory was short lived. Without a common enemy the Coalition weakened as the various Worlds broke away to fight for the spoils of the Empire and carve out their own empires from the disputed territories. And despite the New Regime's claims of victory, the Cassad Empire was not quite destroyed. A few Imperial worlds far from the Core continue to resist, clinging to the rumor and hope that Khalid Cassad still lives. The Interregnum begins.

LANDFALL

BY

MILTON DAVIS

May my words serve as enlightenment to those in darkness and nourishment to those in need. May the knowledge that I share strengthen the foundation that benefits us all.

There was once a man who had a dream, a dream that became a reality, and a reality that became an empire. His name was Cornelius Cassidy, and we are the descendants of his legacy.

-Samake, Cassad Djele/Historian

Cornelius Cassidy emerged from cryosleep in less pain than when he entered. His mouth was extremely dry, his joints ached, but he was anxious for the chamber to open. Ten years after spending a fortune he was finally going to see his dream realized.

"Mr. Cassidy?"

Cornelius's mouth ached when he smiled.

"Dr. Hanes?" he croaked.

"I see you survived. Congratulations."

"I hope that was meant as a joke."

Dr. Hanes laughed, her voice driving the chill from his body.

"So, when do I get to emerge from the crypt?"

"Soon. We're still running vitals. Everything seems to be stable but we have to be sure. We don't often have travelers your age."

"Too young, huh?"

Dr. Hanes laughed again. "If you say so."

Thirty minutes later the chamber opened. Cornelius squinted into the light as two nurses reached in; grasping him gently then lifted him up.

"I can do this myself," he fussed.

"I know, but I'm being safe."

Dr. Hanes appeared, her angelic brown face lifting his spirits. She clamped the exam pad to his wrist then looked at her holo-tablet.

"Vitals are good. You seem to travel well."

"I do a lot of other things well, too," he replied with a wink.

Dr. Hanes rolled her eyes as she smirked. "I'd kill you. Literally."

Cornelius chuckled. "I bet you would."

"Daddy?"

Yvonne Cassidy entered the room. She was the mirror image of her mother at the same age, dusky brown skin with high cheek bones and a dimpled smile.

"Hurry up and get on your suit. You need to see this!"

The nurses fitted him into his bionics. At one hundred and twenty-five he needed the assistance to travel long distances. After a few gestures he sprang to his feet then followed his daughter to the lift which took them to the observation deck. He was greeted by Oyewole Bamidele, ship's captain.

"Mr. Cassidy! Welcome to Cassidy."

The opaque walls turned clear. Cornelius felt as if he was standing in the sky as dense foliage rushed under his feet. Two bare rock columns protruded from the vegetation; in the distance a thunderstorm raged over a grassy plain.

"It's beautiful," he whispered. "Simply beautiful. And it's mine."

"Not quite."

Yuri Yamato strolled onto the deck, looking nonchalant as he gazed down on the planet. The Environ executive exuded the confidence of a man at the top of his game.

"We still have a few papers to sign, Mr. Cassidy."

"You didn't expect me to finalize this deal without inspecting the merchandise, did you?"

Yuri smiled. "Of course not. But this is a bit more than just merchandise, isn't it?"

Cornelius smiled. "Yes, much more. Do you know what this is, Yuri? This is a new start, a second chance, a Final Passage."

Yuri looked confused. "I don't understand."

Cornelius smirked. "Of course, you don't. When can we go planetside?"

"We'll have to wait until the storm passes," Oyewole said. "It's lingering in the vicinity of the compound."

"Your papers will have to wait until then," Cornelius said to Yuri.

The Environ executive walked to stand beside Cornelius. "I have to say you made a fine choice. This one went unnoticed. You're lucky none of the Blocs purchased this first."

"They don't know what to look for," Cornelius said. "Too much money to spend. They've made your company fat with their inefficiency. I estimate their cost overruns exceed 50% of projected costs due to additional terraforming."

"No comment," Yuri answered.

"No need to. I did my homework."

"Yes, you did. The solar deflectors were easy to place and the magnetic field boosters secured the atmosphere much sooner than we anticipated. Accelerated vegetation cycles progressed well and the transplanted fauna adapted rapidly as well."

They fell silent as the storm drifted east.

"Looks like we're ready for landfall," Oyewole said.

"Good," Cornelius replied. "Let's get to the shuttle. I'm ready to put my feet on solid ground."

The team took the lift to the shuttle bay. The shuttle was compact yet comfortable, holding Cornelius, his daughter and Yuri with ease. The craft dropped from the bottom of the ship, falling until it was far enough away to engage engines. It cruised low over the trees, giving a better yet swifter view of the landscape. They dropped low over the grasslands, scattering a herd of wild horses then entered a wide canyon. Cassidy Compound crowned a steep hill rising from the canyon floor, a graceful building promising an interesting tour inside.

"I see you didn't spare any expense," Cornelius groused.

"We treat our best clients like royalty," Yuri said.

"I'd feel better if it wasn't my money you were treating me with."

Yuri laughed. "Believe me, Cornelius; we threw this in pro bono."

"We'll see," Cornelius answered.

The shuttle came to a gentle rest on the upper landing pad. Cornelius stepped outside then took a deep breath. The air was sweeter than the ship, with a tinge of an organic smell that meant new life.

"This is pure air," Yuri commented. "I love the way a new world smells. Or should I say how it doesn't smell. Remember this moment, Mr. Cassidy. It goes downhill from here."

"Not if I can help it," Cornelius whispered.

"Shall we go inside?" Yuri said.

"Not yet." Cornelius took a moment longer to gaze on his gamble. If not one person ever migrated to Cassidy he would still feel successful.

"Okay, let's go inside."

Yuri led them through the functional structure to the main conference room. They spread out around the table as an Environ employee served them glasses of water.

Cornelius took a sip then grinned. "The water is as good as the air."

"Our work is first rate. It also helps when the heavenly body responds well to our handling."

Yuri's eyes studied Yvonne as he spoke.

"Let's get down to business," Cornelius said. "What do we have here?"

Yuri stood then activated the controls for the holoscreen. An image of Cassidy appears, spinning slowly on its axis.

"What we have is a class M-2 planet orbiting a G2V star. Our distance from the star is approximately 85 percent that of Earth, hence the solar defectors. Currently the temperature patterns are tropical to subtropical, but we are forming ice capes both north and south. The equatorial region is currently uninhabitable due to extreme heat but we expect that to moderate over the next twenty years."

"It there any chance the ice capes will expand to glaciers?" Yvonne asked.

"No," Yuri replied. "We provide climate monitoring at no charge for the next two hundred years. It usually takes that long for weather patterns to establish themselves."

The planet view zoomed in as Yuri approached the image.

"We've designated 30 initial sites for prime city development. We expect another 15 to come online once the patterns settle. For now, there is no threat of volcanic activity or earthquakes."

Cornelius eyebrow rose. "For now?"

"We're working on establishing a molten core," Yuri said. "It helps to anchor the atmosphere if the planet can generate its own magnetic field and a molten core is essential for it."

"I'm not sure I like that," Cornelius said.

"It's a necessary evil for a class M planet."

"How soon before we can start settling people," Yvonne asked.

"A year from now," Yuri replied. "How are your recruitment efforts going?"

Cornelius sagged in his seat. "Not good. So far, we have 750,000 signed. We'll probably lose half of those once we begin boarding on the ark ships."

For the first time since landfall Yuri looked displeased. "Our agreement called on an initial payment then a 100-year lease based on planet production. You'll need at least one million people to meet our requirements."

Cornelius took on a hard look. "Yvonne?"

His daughter handed Yuri a bank tablet. The screen displayed the Environ/Cassidy transaction data.

"Press enter," she said.

Yuri pressed enter. The remaining balance for Cassidy appeared in the Environ account.

"Oh my God!" Yuri whispered.

"You can verify it if you like. I think our business with Environ is done."

"Yes, I think it is."

"Can you deliver the other documents so we can make this deal final?"

Yuri was almost giddy. "Yes, I can. It will take a moment to download them."

Yvonne sat close to Cornelius.

"It's all yours now, daddy," she whispered.

"Yes, it is, baby girl."

"And we are now officially flat broke," she added.

"For now," he replied. "I've been here before. Don't I always rise again?"

Yvonne kissed his cheek. "Like a phoenix, daddy. Just like a phoenix."

* * *

Thomas Cassidy slumped in his office chair then moaned when he read the intertex from his sister. His forehead furrowed as he read the text again, hoping he'd got it wrong. But he hadn't. He pushed away from his mahogany desk then trudged to the window wall, looking down on the busy Atlanta streets. For the last 20 years he'd worked hard helping his father build Cassidy Enterprises into the most powerful company in the world. Now it was all gone, just like that.

He tapped his ear then waited for his mother to answer.

"Hello, Tommy," she said.

Her mellow voice eased his anger.

"Mamma, he did it."

There was silence for a moment.

"Tommy, I want you to close the office and come to the house right now. We have some things to discuss."

"We can talk right now," Tommy answered.

"Don't get fussy with me, boy," she replied sternly. "You come on down. I'll be in the garden."

"I might as well," he said. "It's not like we're solvent or anything."

"Quit sassing and come down," she said.

"Yes, mama."

Thomas sent a broadcast text to the office employees then cringed as a collective whoop went up. People hurried from their desk in a jubilant exodus to the elevators. He knew he wasn't as well liked as his father. He was considered a task master, which he was. Someone had to make up for all the money his father was spending lately. And now that he knew the reason he wouldn't be any better.

His personal sped him to the south Metro area to the house. "House" was an understatement; the Cassidy compound was a 2000-acre wooded nature preserve. The massive gate identified his personal and the gate opened. The small vehicle entered, proceeding up the paved driveway to the mansion. The driveway ended at the cul-de-sac; the personal stopped then Thomas jumped out, fast walking to the back of house. Mamma was tending her vegetable garden as always, wearing her dirty coveralls and large plantation hat. She looked up with her big smile, her smooth sepia face hiding her almost ninety years of life.

"Mamma, what's going on?" Thomas blurted.

"Give me a kiss, boy," she replied. "I ain't seen you all day."

Thomas rolled his eyes then kissed her on the cheek.

"You smell like earthworms," he said.

Mamma chuckled. "So, what's this about us being broke?"

"Daddy paid off the balance on Cassidy," he said. "He cleaned us out!"

Mamma walked away to her tomatoes. "All of it?"

"All of it."

She pushed back her hat. "I thought he would. No sense leaving things undone."

"What are you talking about?"

"Go get me my chair," she said.

Thomas hurried to the shed then brought back her folding chair. Mamma sat hard then wiped her brow.

"You know your daddy is dying, right?" she said.

Thomas looked solemn. "I know he's not in the best of health but..."

Mamma reached out then took his trembling hand. "No, son your daddy is dying. Soon. It's why he went to Cassidy and why he paid off the balance. He didn't want to leave us in debt."

"So, he's leaving us broke?"

Mamma smiled. "Cornelius spent all his money. He ain't spent any of mine."

Thomas was startled. "Your money?"

Mamma nodded. "Me and Cornelius always kept our money separate. Just in case he got in trouble."

Thomas cleared his throat. "Mamma if you don't mind me asking; how much money do you have?"

Mamma's eyes narrowed. "I ain't never told your daddy. Why you think I'm going to tell you? Let's just say I have enough to see things through."

She stood up then waved Thomas close.

"Come on. Let's walk to the house. We have some things to do."

* * *

Yuri grinned at the father and daughter.

"That seems to conclude our business," he said. "It' been a pleasure working with you."

Cornelius's smiled faded. "I don't think we're quite done yet, Yuri."

The Environ rep forced a smile. "Is there something else?"

"I believe there is," Cornelius replied. "A matter of something on 'my' planet that doesn't belong to me."

"What are you talking about?" Yuri maintained a rigid smile.

"Don't make me do this," Cornelius warned.

Yuri seemed dumbfounded, but Cornelius knew better.

"Let's take another ride," he said.

The trio returned to the main ship.

"Wole," Yvonne said. "Take us to the other site."

Oyewole nodded then the ship sped off. Yuri pulled at his collar.

"I don't see what this is all about."

Cornelius didn't reply. They streaked over a long stretch of forest before coming across a mountain range. Oyewole weaved the ship through the narrow passages until another building appeared.

"Ever seen that place before?" Cornelius asked Yuri.

"I can't say that I have," Yuri replied.

"I can say one thing about you. You stick to a lie until the end. It's an Environ monitoring station. It's got everything you need to keep close tabs on planet development. It also contains a big dose of Environ security tech just in case things don't go the way you planned."

"Cornelius, I had no idea..."

"Maybe you didn't, maybe you did. That doesn't matter. What matters is that this is my planet now and I want it gone."

"Just supposing this does belong to Environ. It would take years to dismantle and remove such a complex structure."

"Then I'll let you lease the land and tax your services until you can remove it," Cornelius said.

"You can't do that!"

"Yes, I can. It's my planet now and you're trespassing. An incident like this would give the Blocs just the evidence they need to extend government control over your operations."

Yuri dropped his act. "They couldn't if they tried."

"You're correct, but they'll try. Environ doesn't need the distraction. You have worlds to build."

"So, what do you propose?" Yuri asked.

"The deal I just offered."

"I'll contact my office," Yuri said. "You'll have an answer in the morning."

He stalked away to his cabin.

"Good work, Yvonne," Cornelius said. "Looks like we're not so broke after all."

Yvonne smiled. "I'll contact mamma and Tommy."

"Please do. That boy is probably pulling his hair out right about now."

Yvonne laughed. "Like father like son."

Cornelius smiled. "Unfortunately, true. But once he comes he'll change his mind. Too bad I won't be alive to see it."

Yvonne's smile faded. She walked away to carry out her duties.

Oyewole steered the ship away from the Environ facility.

Cornelius gazed at the pristine landscape, fighting a feeling of melancholy.

"Not much time left," he whispered. "None at all."

* * *

Thomas flinched from pain in his right thigh. He looked over at his mother, a frown on her face. He blinked his eyes then turned his attention to Reverend Charles Roy as he reached the climax of his stirring sermon. Half the congregation stood on their feet, shouting amen and holding up their hands in agreement and worship. Thomas almost rolled his eyes but remembered the painful pinch to his thigh just a moment ago. I swear that woman still thinks I'm eight, he thought.

"Get ready," mamma said. "You're up soon."

He couldn't believe he agreed to this. The fate of Cassidy Enterprises hung in the balance despite mamma's cash infusion and he was about to deliver a speech, the most important speech in his life if mamma was to be believed. But Thomas was never much on faith. His constant mantra was 'faith had nothing to do with it.' But it was mamma's money, so she made the rules. For now.

He suffered through five more minutes of sermonizing, the opening of the church doors then the obligatory collecting of the tithes. He was about to let the plate pass him by when mamma elbowed his ribs. He reluctantly dropped a twenty in the plate. Mamma gave much more, frowning at him all the while.

"We might need that money tomorrow," he whispered.

"Be quiet, boy. Your time is coming up."

After a few brief announcements by Bessie Lansbury, the church secretary, Reverend Charles took to the pulpit again.

"The Lord has blessed us with a good word today and I know y'all are ready to go home. But before we dismiss I seek your patience for a little bit longer. Cornelius Cassidy's boy, Thomas, has a few words to deliver on behalf of his father."

Reverend Charles turned to him. "Thomas?"

Thomas straightened his tie then took the podium. He looked out into the sanctuary and a hard knot formed in his stomach. He couldn't do this. He knew most everyone sitting before him. These were people that nurtured him from when he was a boy. To tell them what he was about to tell them, to convince these people who were like a second family to do what he proposed he had to believe it was the right thing to do. And that was the problem.

"Thank you, Reverend Charles. I'm not going to hold everyone long. I'm here to deliver a simple message and offer a life changing opportunity. A few days ago, my father accomplished a lifelong dream. He purchased a planet."

The sanctuary erupted in applause. Thomas waited until silence settled in the room again before speaking.

"But what's a world without people? My father is many things, but he's not The Almighty."

Laughter broke the tension and eased Thomas's mind.

"I come today to ask some of you to make a special commitment; a life changing commitment. Thousands of miles and five years away is a world waiting to be filled. It's a world ripe with new opportunities and it's waiting for you. Yes you. We are willing to transport anyone wishing to build a new future to our planet. We have ten ark ships waiting to take all of you who are willing to a new life, a life which all of us deserve without any restrictions. I know this is not for everyone. This is a one-way journey. You'll never see Earth again. But this is also the opportunity of a lifetime. A chance to build a society where second class does not apply, where racism doesn't exist. A chance to build a truly equal society. I would say more, but I'm not going to sell you. The opportunity speaks for itself. I appreciate your attention and I hope you think long and hard about this opportunity."

Thomas went back to his seat to modest applause. The congregation looked confused mostly.

"That was terrible," he whispered.

"You did just fine," mamma said. "Short and straightforward, just like your daddy."

Reverend Charles took the podium again.

"Thank you, Thomas. Your father is a good friend, a good deacon and a good brother. I hope everyone here today takes the time to consider this opportunity. Remember wherever God's people go, so shall He be. I'd also like to let everyone here know that when those ark ships lift off to Cassidy, I'll be one of the passengers."

Thomas gasped with the congregation.

"I told you it was going to work out," Mamma whispered.

* * *

Cornelius sat in the prep room of the ship, his daughter holding his hand. He looked at her nervous smile then patted her hand.

"Look at you. You'd think that you're the one going under the knife."

"Don't say that," Yvonne replied. "It sounds so terrible."

"So squeamish, just like your mother. Speaking of her, have you heard any word from them?"

"Their almost home," Yvonne said. "50,000 away from full capacity."

"Good, good. Looks like we have ourselves a viable planet."

"Not quite," Yvonne said. "Mamma said they're going to have to go abroad to get the last 50,000."

Cornelius pouted. "I was afraid of that. But they can do it. Thomas is a good son. He'll get it done whether he wants to or not."

Dr. Hanes entered the room with her usual bright smile.

"So, are you ready, Mr. Cassidy?"

"Ready as I'll ever be."

Dr. Hanes put the analysis band on his wrist then scanned the table. When she looked up her face was serious.

"You know we don't have to do this, don't you? There's technology that can perform the same function and be nowhere near as intrusive."

"I want this," he said. "We're making history and I want every bit of it recorded. Every bit."

Dr. Hanes looked at Yvonne. "Any chance we can bully him out of this?"

"I'm afraid not," Yvonne answered.

"Let me put it this way, Cornelius; this is a stressful operation. You could die."

"I'm already dying, Zarina. A lot faster than most. So, let's get this over with. We've missed too much already."

"Okay, then let's get started."

Dr. Hanes and Yvonne left the room. They activated the sealing sequence then initiated sterilization mode as she linked into the surgical robotics.

"How does this work again, Doctor?" Yvonne asked.

The Djele implant will be embedded into the cerebral cortex. Once it's in place a stimulant will be injected and the unit will merge with his brain. Its outer layer was constructed from your father's protein structure so there is no chance for rejection. From that point on it will record everything your father experiences. It will also enhance his memory."

Yvonne looked at her father lying on the operating table, surrounded by the surgery robots.

"And when he dies?"

"The unit will be removed. The data will be harvested for future reference."

Dr. Hanes performed a few preliminary motions to confirm complete synchronicity. A bot moved closer to her father then attached an IV filled with anesthesia. Yvonne could see her father's body relax.

"We're ready to proceed. Are you ready Yvonne?"

Yvonne cleared her throat. "Yes I am."

"Okay then. Here we go."

Yvonne said a prayer as Dr. Hanes made the first incision.

Thomas took off his jacket, rolled up his sleeves then loosened his tie as he gazed at the rows of sailboats in Durban mooring. He fidgeted as he waited for his contact, unhappy with the world. There was something strange about summer weather in December. He didn't care what hemisphere he was in, it just wasn't right. He wondered what odd conditions he would face on Cassidy, what strange weather patterns would set off his allergies after spending all that money to get them under control. So, when Angelica Buthelezi strode to his table with her statuesque looks and glowing smile he was not swayed.

"You're late," he said.

Angelica sat before him then took off her shades. "Good afternoon to you too, Thomas."

"So, what's the verdict?"

Angelica raised her palm to Thomas's face with a frown.

"Angelica, I don't have time for..."

"Silence," she commanded. "First things first."

A waiter glided to the table.

"Welcome, Ms. Buthelezi," he crooned. "Shall I bring you your wine?"

"Yes, Baxter, and bless you for remembering."

Baxter grinned. "How could I forget?"

The waiter glided away. Angelica leaned back in her seat.

"I'll have 30,000 ready in two weeks," she said.

"Thirty? That's all?" Thomas rubbed his head. "That's twenty thousand short."

"It's the best I can do with such short notice," Angelica replied. "Besides this is illegal. If the AU discovered what we're doing we'll both be thrown in prison."

"You think I don't know that?" Thomas wiped his sweaty forehead with a napkin, and then pulled a handful of rand from his pocket.

"You're leaving?" Angelica said.

"Of course, I am. I need to find 20,000 more people to take this trip, and I won't find them sipping wine and staring at your breasts."

Angelica smiled. "So, you did notice."

Thomas managed to smile. "Of course, I did."

The waiter arrived with Angelica's wine. She took a sip then nodded in approval.

"They'll be ready in two weeks," she said. "I've arranged a rendezvous in Natal."

"Make sure everyone is there and ready to go. We'll have a short window."

Angelica took another sip. "Don't worry. You should try Congo."

"For what?"

"For your other 20,000. Things are still unsettled there. You'll find plenty people willing to leave."

"But will they be the right people?" Thomas asked.

"Beggars can't be choosers." Angelica went into her purse then took out a Graycell™.

"Look at this when you're alone. He's a good contact."

Thomas took the chip then put it in his wallet. Angelica turned up her cheek; Thomas sighed then kissed it.

"We used to have so much fun," she said. "I miss the old Thomas."

"I miss him too," Thomas replied. "Goodbye, Angelica."

Thomas strode out the club to a waiting limo. One more stop then he was done.

"I hope you appreciate what I'm doing here, old man," he whispered. "I damn sure hope you do."

* * *

The ship followed the winding river, swaying with the turns. Cornelius stood before the window flanked by Yvonne and Dr. Haynes, his arms folded behind his back. Bandages still covered his head from the surgery, but he insisted that they take this trip as soon as possible. The doctor monitored his vital signs, the holoscreen hovering before her eyes.

"There," he said. "Do you see it?"

Yvonne nodded. "Yes, I see it."

The doctor glanced from the screen. "It's beautiful. You should sit down."

Cornelius gave her a sidelong glance. "I'll sit when I'm ready. Take us down closer."

The ship descended giving a better view of island.

"That's it. That's where I want to be buried," Cornelius said.

Yvonne was visibly upset. "That's why you brought us here? To show us where you want to be buried?"

Cornelius gave Yvonne a stern look. "Yes."

"The transports from Earth are arriving soon," she said. "We don't have time for this."

"Then make time!" The sudden emotion triggered a sharp pain in his head. Cornelius reached out then found his chair. He sat down hard. Yvonne was immediately at his side.

"Doctor?"

Dr. Haynes studied his scans. "He's still healing. The implant is still syncing. You'll have to keep your conversations friendly for now."

Cornelius waved Yvonne away.

"You're right. There are more serious things to attend to. I needed you to know just in case your mother wasn't able to..."

"She'll come, daddy," Yvonne assured him. "I don't know about Thomas, but I know mama will come."

"I hope so. I did this for her, too."

"Let get back to main base," Yvonne said. "We're the welcoming committee, remember?"

* * *

Ten huge transports circled Cassidy, each pregnant with 100,000 anxious passengers. The journey through the gates had been traumatic, especially for those who'd never experience jump space, which was most of them. No sooner had the ships established orbit did they begin filling the shuttles to take everyone planetside. A steady stream of the smaller ships descended single file through space then atmosphere, guided by skilled Environ controllers.

Cornelius watched the first shuttle touch down on the tarmac. Tears came to his eyes, as they did to Yvonne and even Dr. Haynes.

"Damn it, I hate crying," the doctor said. "But this is so beautiful. You must be so proud, Cornelius."

"You have no idea how much," Cornelius replied, his voice cracking.

The terminal could have been designed to release the passengers inside as was the norm, but Cornelius wanted each new resident to experience Cassidy as soon as possible. The ship taxied to fifty yards of them then came to a complete stop. The doors lifted then the stairway extended to the asphalt. The first to emerge was a young family; a husband, wife, two children and one infant. The report said the infant was born during transport, making her one of the first true citizens of Cassidy.

Two stewards guided the bewildered family to Cornelius and the others. Cornelius greeted them with a magnanimous smile. He shook the young father's hand then hugged his wife and children. This is what it was about, creating a new life for the young ones.

"Welcome to Cassidy," he said. "Welcome home."

Thomas took a long drag from his cigar then placed it on the holder beside the holobar on his coffee table. He glanced outside for a moment, savoring the Atlanta skyline. This was home. This right here. No matter what he was told, this was where he was meant to be.

The Environ technician had come earlier that day to install the bar. It was secret technology; he was not to let anyone know he possessed it. He had a mind to whisk it away to his R&D department to 'receive and duplicate' but he didn't want to cause trouble for anyone else. He'd done enough of that already.

He was officially banned from the African Continent by the AU for participating in illegal immigration. The company's assets had been seized and extradition orders filed with the US. But Thomas was a pro at getting in and getting out of trouble. As long as he stayed away from the continent he'd be fine. He had no intentions of going back. He had no intentions of going anywhere.

A piercing sound like the netline warning system filled the room. A blue light emerged from the Environ bar, halting about 12 inches above the device. A face appeared, an attractive female with red hair and freckles.

"Thomas Cassidy?" The woman said.

"That's me. And you are..."

"Catlyn Rogers, Environ Communications specialist. Please stand by."

The woman's face disappeared, replace by a 3D image of Yvonne.

"Vonne!"

"Hi Tommy!" Yvonne waved at him like a child. "It's so good to see you!"

"Same here. How is everyone?"

"They're good. Mama asked if you were keeping up her garden."

"Of course," Thomas lied.

Yvonne smirked. "Who did you hire?"

"Seasonal Landscapes," he answered. "You know I hate dirt."

They both laughed harder than they should have.

"How is everything?" Thomas finally asked.

"I can't imagine how it could be better," Yvonne answered. "We're keeping the settlers contained at the Environ cities for now while we begin construction on new cities. The planet is terraformed but there are still a few restricted areas."

"And how's daddy doing?"

"He's great. The change has done wonders for him."

And momma?

Yvonne chuckled. "Starting a new garden and bossing daddy around. The only thing missing is you."

Thomas slumped into his chair then picked up his cigar.

"Don't start, Vonne."

"Tommy, please come. We miss you and we're a family. You should be here with us."

"I'm a grown ass man," Thomas snapped. "I should be where I want to be."

"You're afraid," Yvonne said. "I know you are."

"Whether I am or not doesn't matter," he said. "I'm staying here."

"This is a new future, Tommy. A dream come true."

"I'm not a dreamer, Vonne. You know that. Besides, someone has to run the store."

"We don't need the store anymore. We have everything we need right here."

They were silent for a moment. Yvonne was right; he was afraid. It's one thing to go live in another country, but another planet? One built by human hands? Too many things could go wrong. He did miss his family, but not enough to make such a drastic change.

"I'm glad y'all are happy. I really am. But I can't come, Vonne. I can't."

Yvonne sighed. "Daddy said you wouldn't. This time I wanted him to be wrong. He wanted me to tell you that as of today Cassidy Enterprises, LLC belongs to you. You'll receive the paperwork within the week."

"Everything? To me?"

Yvonne nodded. "He's cutting ties completely."

Thomas put down the cigar. "Tell him I said thank you."

"You could tell him yourself," Yvonne said.

"No, it's best you did. We would only end up arguing."

Yvonne's eyes glistened. "Goodbye, Tommy. I love you."

Thomas felt a tear running down his cheek. "Goodbye Vonne. Love you, too."

Yvonne's image faded. The blue light descended into the bar then blinked out.

Thomas wiped his eyes as he sauntered to the window. So that was it. Just like that. It all belonged to him now. He looked out onto the city, the highway filled with traffic, jets filing into and flying out of Hartsfield like an airborne merry-go-round. Up there, out there somewhere his family was starting a new life without him. He never felt so alone in his life.

* * *

The ship cruised over the northern polar region, its third flyover in two days. The pilot checked her fuel reading then glanced at her solitary passenger. She was well aware of whom he was but it didn't make her job any easier. At some point the overtime didn't matter. She wanted to go home to her family.

"Seen enough?" she said, hoping her irritation didn't come across in her voice.

Thomas puffed his cigar.

"Yeah, I guess so. Can't avoid it any longer. Take me to Cassidy,"

The pilot grinned as she changed course south. Three hours later they cruised over the capital city. Thomas marveled at how normal it looked. He expected something different, better maybe. Though the cities were a disappointment, the planet was amazing. Yvonne was right. He should have come long ago.

The ship landed on the Cassidy compound pad. He was barely out of it when Yvonne rushed up to him and almost knocked him down as she hugged him.

"I'm so happy to see you, Tommy!" she said.

Thomas hugged her tight and let the tears flow.

"Looks like I'm home," he said.

Yvonne took his hand. "Let's get you settled."

"Not yet. I want to see them first."

Yvonne's smile faded. "You sure?"

Thomas wiped his eyes. "Yes. I'm sure."

They boarded a small shuttle then flew to the island. Thomas's eyes glistened as the mausoleum came into focus. He should have come sooner. His fear and selfishness kept him away. He had to watch both of them pass away in the holofeeds after awakening from cryosleep.

The shuttle landed near the entrance. Thomas followed Yvonne inside; he grinned when he saw the garden surrounding their tombs. There was bench opposite the tombs; Thomas sat down then folded his hands on his lap. Yvonne sat beside him.

"Now what?" he said.

"Now we run a planet," Yvonne said.

30

"This isn't like running a corporation," Thomas said. "We have to make laws, establish court systems, and maybe even fight wars. There's a planet grab happening as we speak. We might get caught in the middle of it."

"Daddy thought of that," Yvonne said. "We're way off the normal jump routes. We're also totally self-sufficient, unlike the other terraformed planets. By the time they find us, we'll be more than ready."

Thomas looked at Yvonne and smiled. She was so confident, but that was her way. She was just like Daddy that way.

"Are you sure about that?"

"I am, now that you're here," she said.

Thomas hugged her.

"Let's go then."

"So soon?" Yvonne said.

"I can always come back. The sooner we start the better. We have a world to run."

They stood then held hands as they left the gardens, both of them glancing back at the twin tombs. They wouldn't fail them. They couldn't.

* * *

The pilot circled the sacred island awaiting orders. Ziara Harriet Nzinga Cassad gazed down on the monument, a smile on her handsome yet stern face. So long she'd waited for this moment and now it was before her. It was a glorious time indeed.

"Take us down," she ordered.

The armed shuttle plunged through the clouds to the landing pad. Ziara was standing at the port before it touched down flanked by two Royal guardsmen, their red armor in sharp contrast to her black body hugging suit. A Cassad kente cloak hung from her shoulders matching the elaborate head wrap holding her flowing dreads in place. They strode from the shuttle as soon as the doors opened. What was once a small mausoleum was now the grand building it deserved to be. The guards snapped to attention as the trio entered the pyramid shaped structure. They crossed the expanded garden to the four tombs in the center. Ziara raised her hand and they halted.

She extended her left hand. The guard on her left handed her a gilded box. She took the box then walked to the tomb of the Matriarch. She opened the box, revealing a small shovel and seeds. Ziara knelt then dug a shallow hole in the rich soil. She placed the seeds into the hole then covered it.

She ambled back to the guards then extended her right hand. The other guard handed her a narrow wooden box. She took the box then sat on the bench before the tombs, the original bench Yvonne and Thomas Cassidy sat over five hundred years ago as they lay the foundation of what would become the Cassad Empire. She opened the box then took out the cigar and lighter. She placed the cigar in her mouth then lit it as she had practiced numerous times. The smoke did not choke her as it did her first time. She actually grew to like the custom, although she rarely indulged.

She took her time, smoking the entire cigar. After she finished she stood then bowed deeply.

"Thank you, ancestors, for what you have given us," she said. "Thank you for your vision. Thank you for your bloodline. I hope I do not shame you."

She turned then marched for the shuttle, the guardsmen falling in step. The shuttle waited, the port door open. Ziara settled into her seat.

"Take us up," she commanded.

The shuttle lifted then streaked upward through the clouds then out of the atmosphere into space. Ziara smiled as the war fleet came into view. Cornelius Cassidy had the foresight to create a planet away from the traffic of the other worlds, giving Cassad ample time to grow, develop and prosper. Because of his vision the planet suffered the least during the Dark Age and was the first to emerge from those terrible times. Now it was time for Cassad to take its rightful place, a light of hope among the devastation.

"Open the comm," she said.

She waited until the clear signal registered in her comm.

"Five hundred years we've waited," she said, her voice echoing in every ship. "Now is our opportunity to show our ancestors the honor they rightly deserve. Now is the time for us to claim what is ours. I expect the best of each and every one of you. Don't disappoint them. Most of all do not disappoint me. Ago!"

"Ame!"

Ziara leaned back into her chair, the faces of her baloguns appearing before her.

"Where do we go first?" Balogun Ojetade asked.

"Where it all began," she said.

MONSTERS OF EDEN

BY

RONALD T. JONES

As the Known emerged from the abyss of the Dark Age,
old technology was rediscovered. Before that time, many worlds
found their own ways to deal with the challenges and horrors,
ways that were cruel and questionable. The New Age brought
hope and change, but for many the old ways were not easily
abandoned...
     -Samake. Cassad djele/historian. From The Cassad
Chronicles

Gate 2212 glowed briefly before dimming to a steady,
ambient hue. A capsule emerged from the artificial wormhole,
vectoring toward the nearest planet. Gate 2212 made history
when it became the first wormhole to be initialized since the
cessation of the Dark Age.

Javaris Marshall, Skye Odele, and Cranston St. John, occupied the T5 landing capsule. The capsule's host vessel, a Deep
Space Recon cruiser, hovered on the other side of the gate some
125 light years away.

Skye, the pilot, kept the capsule on course while she
worked the instrument panel, pulling up data on the planet
ahead.

A revolving representation of the planet appeared on
screen, accompanied by the data she requested. A single continent wound half way around the planet like a massive green-
brown clasp. She nodded. "Twenty-five minutes to Cassadar."

"Eden," Javaris corrected. "That's what the inhabitants
have been calling it since well into the Dark Age. They weren't

exactly on the best of terms with the First Empire. You start referring to them as Cassadarans and you're liable to start an incident."

"I know what the place is currently called," Skye shot back. "I'm just staying consistent with the historical record."

"Our record, not theirs," Javaris emphasized with a goading smirk. "Don't get too caught up in it and start throwing 'Cassadar' in their faces."

Skye turned her head, half facing Javaris who sat behind her, alongside Cranston. "Seriously," she said tightly. "Do you really think I'd be that crass?"

Javaris smiled, exuding his usual charm and good humor. He nudged Cranston with an elbow. "I don't know. What do you think Crans?"

With his finger, Cranston pushed his spectacles from the tip to the bridge of his nose. The spectacles, of course, were a holdover from the Dark Age when corrective eye tech did not exist. On Cranston's world, eye lenses had followed a curious trajectory from optical necessities to fashionable accessories.

"I think I'm going to avoid being pulled into this latest spat of yours and grab a quick nap." Cranston shifted his large bulk as best he could in his narrow seat. "Wake me when we're planetside." He shut his eyes.

"Coward," Skye murmured.

Cranston opened a single eye. "With you two, that's the safest course."

***

The capsule's nose glowed red-hot with friction as it knifed into Eden's cloud- drenched atmosphere. A city sprawled below, coated in somber shades of sun-deprived gray. The buildings were quite short. But new construction dotted this largely somnolent urbanscape. Huge assemblers worked sites where partially erected towers, much taller than the ancient buildings around them, were being built. The rediscovery of high technology meant that elevators would be installed in these budding skyscrapers. The sky became the literal limit for Edenite architecture.

Skye landed the capsule five miles north of the main district. The city was called Cresthill, a name predating the Dark Age. The inhabitants never changed it.

She swept a gaze across the port. The vast majority of the vehicles parked on docking plates were aerial. The few space capable craft she identified were incapable of travel beyond Eden's two moons…a sign that Cassadarans…uh…Edenites were in no hurry to reconnect fully with an awakening universe.

"You think Eden will sign the treaty…willingly?" Skye asked, though she wasn't expecting a definitive answer from either of her partners.

Cranston shrugged. "I suppose that'll depend on the outcome of our mission." He unsnapped his safety harness and shook his head, his brow furrowed in pessimism. "I don't think that'll matter. Edenites got a good dose of independence during the Dark Age and they're loving it more than most worlds. They value their isolation."

Skye shut down the capsule's control, which gave her a brief moment to think. "Isolation is no good for them." She leaned back in her seat, staring contemplatively ahead. "I'm hoping they'll come to the realization that no world can go it alone in a galaxy that just got its utilities turned back on."

Javaris gave Skye a pat on the shoulder. "Well, why don't we let the politicians and diplomats sort out that issue while we do what we came here to do?"

Skye wanted to argue that point, but sighed a concession and unsnapped her harness.

***

An Edenite delegation of five arrived at the port to greet the visitors from afar. A short thin man with a golden crew cut and blade sharp features stepped forward. He was dressed, like the others who accompanied him, in a dark blue tunic that fell just below the waist. His matching blue slacks were tucked into a pair of polished, maroon ankle boots.

Skye recognized the Chairman of the Eden Planetary Authority before he extended a hand of introduction.

"Welcome to Eden," the man addressed with a gracious smile. "I am Chairman Ward Johansen."

Skye, Javaris, and Cranston shook the Chairman's hand as the latter introduced his aides.

Skye in turn introduced herself and her partners and the group headed for the port facility building.

"We don't receive many off-worlders," said the Chairman. "You will encounter some who won't exactly be amenable to your presence."

"We understand," said Javaris, shooting a subtle glance Skye's way.

Skye caught the look and stuck out a mental tongue at him.

When they entered the building, three individuals in gray military uniforms approached.

"Speak of the devil," Chairman Johansen whispered.

The tallest of the trio strode to the forefront and halted, pinning flint-hard eyes on the Chairman. "Greetings Chairman Johansen." He brushed the visitors with a cool gaze. "So, these are the esteemed Investigators."

"I don't know how esteemed we are," Skye returned with a not so genuine smile. "But we are Investigators."

The military man stared at Skye and Johansen jumped in. "Investigators, this is General Ran Corvin, Defense Command…"

Before the Chairman could finish the introductions, General Corvin interjected. "I'm told that you Investigators can help us with our infestation problem." Corvin made the belligerency in his tone unmistakably obvious.

Skye looked squarely into the dark-haired general's hawkish blue eyes. "You were told correctly."

Corvin shifted his gaze to the Chairman. "I've been trying to tell our good Chairman that we have the situation well in hand."

"A little help never hurts," said Skye.

"As long as your help does not impede our efforts." Corvin lifted his chin, pivoted and walked away with his officers in tow.

***

Thunder boomed. Lightning flashed. A heavy downpour lashed the city as a four-vehicle motorcade pulled into a wide lane leading to Vigilance Hall, the governing headquarters of the Planetary Authority.

Chairman Johansen and the Cassad investigators emerged from the middle car. Security officials with parasols escorted the chairman and his guests through a gated side entrance into the building.

Once inside, the Cassads met First Inspector Clement Abdil, head of the Continental Police. Afterward, they settled in the Hall's main conference room.

"It would have been nice if General Corvin were here," Johansen remarked, walking to the head of a hard wood table with a mirror-glossed surface. "Unfortunately, he declined due to pressing issues."

"Not more pressing than the matter at hand I hope," Javaris said dryly.

The chairman's mirthful look conveyed more than words ever could. When everyone was seated, he got down to business. He gestured and an aide moved to the other end of the table with a large paper map that he unfurled on top.

Johansen removed an adjustable pointer from a compartment beneath the table, extended it, and used it to tap a location on the map. "This is Tolliver Province, the site of the worst Goehlem attack in a century. Goehlems…pure bloods…overran this city." The Chairman slid the pointer's tip until it stopped on a black dot representing a city called Hedleyville. "They wiped out a third of a population numbering little over half a million before our forces moved in to contain and neutralize them."

Horrific as the story was, Skye could not help but to be mildly distracted by the quaintness of a hard copy map. Maybe I'll suggest to the chairman that he upgrade with a visual screen. It'll put far more pep in his presentations. Just as quickly she thought better of the idea and refocused on Johansen.

"I wish I could say our response eliminated the problem," said Johansen. "Most pure blood Goehlems have been exterminated. Most, not all. The biggest problem we're dealing with is human-appearing Goehlems who blend into the population. It's terribly difficult to root them out since their genetic structure mimics our own. As a result, the whole of Tolliver is under Quarantine Level martial law. That means no residents are allowed to leave the province and no one other than containment specialists are allowed in."

"How long has this quarantine been effect?" asked Cranston.

"Two years," the Chairman replied.

Skye frowned. "Two years? That's a long time for that implementation to be active, especially when Cassad assistance was readily available."

Johansen nodded with a grimace, his tone taking on a measure of distaste. "I agree. Unfortunately, it took that long for me to get my colleagues in the Planetary Authority to agree to that assistance. As for the quarantine, Tolliver is afflicted by more Goehlem activity than the rest of Eden."

"From my understanding," said Javaris. "The entire planet is under a state of emergency."

"To an extent," Inspector Abdil grimly confirmed. The gray coloring his thick mop of curly hair was not entirely a result of aging. "It's an ongoing struggle combating an enemy that more often than not resembles the people we're trying to protect. There have been too many instances where we couldn't tell friend from foe until it was too late."

Johansen leaned forward, placing his elbows on the table. He swept an earnest gaze from Investigator to Investigator. "I'll be brutally honest. Cassads are not popular on Eden. If it were put to a vote whether this world should be integrated into this Second Empire your government is forming, the overwhelming majority would reject it. I don't share that sentiment. In my view, existing beneath the parasol of empire is the key to Edenite survival and ultimately, prosperity."

"Obviously, General Corvin disagrees," Skye stated coolly. "Will he be a problem?"

The Chairman steepled his fingers. "I'll do what I can to prevent him from interfering with your work. Mind you, it won't be easy. He's backed by powerful anti-Cassad factions in the Authority."

"And the factions who back you," wondered Skye. "How strong is your support?"

Johansen dipped his head and chuckled. "Well, Investigator Odele, the strength of my support depends upon your performance in the field. You have access to better resources than we do to aid us in our efforts against the Goehlems. My expectation for success is high."

"What the chairman is trying to say," Abdil cut in. "Is that we're putting the three of you up front. This conflict needs fresh eyes, a fresh perspective, and new tools. You'll devise the strategy, the tactics. The forces I command will follow your lead. And if there's anything you need from us, just ask and we'll do our utmost to accommodate you."

"In that case," said Cranston. "I do need one thing."

The chairman extended a hand for the Investigator to continue.

"I need a pure blood Goehlem body, preferably alive or very freshly dead." Cranston nodded to Skye and Javaris. "My colleagues and I can do the bagging; we just need transportation to an active Goehlem site. From what you've presented to us, Tolliver Province qualifies."

Johansen drew himself up as if a world-crushing weight had been lifted from his shoulders. "That can be easily arranged, Investigator."

***

Javaris looked over at Cranston as he checked his Regency Special assault blaster. "You may want to give a heads up next time before volunteering us to rush our happy asses into a situation where we could get...oh I don't know...killed, slaughtered, wiped out." He slung the blaster across his shoulder and pulled a duel edge Orisha blade from the capsule's weapons rack and slid it into his thigh sheathe.

Cranston surveyed the rack and selected a short, thick barreled carbine along with a semi-auto beam pistol. "Sorry. I let my enthusiasm get the best of me. But rest assured, from this point on I will duly warn you."

Despite being the smallest of the trio, Skye detached the largest weapon from the rack: a Toussaint 20 grenade launcher/plasma rifle. She cocked a wry grin. "What's wrong, Javaris? Nervous?"

Javaris made a scoffing noise. "Are you kidding me? I was in the Grayhorn campaign. Anything after that is a walk in the park."

"I respect your history, Javaris," cautioned Cranston. "But don't let it lead you to underestimate our opponent. A pure blood Goehlem possesses strength ten times that of the strongest human. They are incredibly fast and their skin is dense as armor."

Javaris slipped on a battle vest. "You don't have to worry about me, Crans. Scary as those things are, I won't hesitate to blast heads from shoulders." He pressed a tab on the chest portion of his vest and its gel-soft material solidified to steel hardness. The rest of his field wear, like that of his companions, consisted of a form fitting top, pants, and blast-proof helmet, all interwoven with durable composite links.

"Just a reminder," said Skye. "Cranston wants one alive."

"Or freshly dead," Cranston reiterated. "But preferably alive."

Javaris scrunched his face. "You guys can try to catch one alive if you want. Me, I'm more of a 'freshly dead' type of guy. It's what I do best."

Skye gazed at Javaris and shook her head. She clamped a pair of grenades to her belt and closed and secured the hatch leading to the weapons rack. "All right, Cranston, Mr. 'Freshly Dead.' We've got some hunting to do. Let's move out."

***

Skye peered out the window of the rapid transport aerial vehicle. Hedleyville was laid out below like a neat arrangement of blocks. There existed none of the feverish renovation and construction characterizing Cresthill. It may in large part have been the Goehlem crisis that kept progress at bay in this small city. Either way, the place had an idyllic look that hardly screamed threat. All the more reason for caution. Tranquil places were the most dangerous because they had a tendency to lull one into a false sense of security.

Inspector Abdil accompanied the Investigators on this trip. Thirty Edenite para officers were on board as well.

The easy manner in which the inspector interacted with the paras suggested that he made frequent visits to the field. Skye respected a commander who shared the same dangers and privations as his soldiers.

Abdil pointed at an area below. "There, the Western district, where Goehlem activity is heaviest. It's deserted, no human presence."

"Perfect." Skye stood and Javaris and Cranston came to their feet as well.

The transport swooped ground-ward, hovering several feet above a wide street. The side door slid open, ushering in a gust of warm wind.

Javaris gave Abdil a pat on the shoulder. "Thank you, Inspector."

"You sure you don't need us to accompany you?" Abdil asked with a look that almost begged the Investigators to consider otherwise.

"No, Inspector," said Javaris. "That won't be necessary."

"We reserve the risk for ourselves on this one," Skye added. "We'll be fine. We'll contact you when we're ready for extraction."

Abdil's gaze shined admiration. "Good luck, Investigators."

The Investigators jumped out of the transport and the craft soared away. The three activated their helm respirators and the metallic taint of contaminated air filtered out. Something in a

Goehlem's biological makeup altered the environment. Humans breathed in oxygen and exhaled carbon dioxide. Whatever a Goehlem exhaled, it was a sharp, eye-watering toxicity that lingered in the air with the stubbornness of a persistent chemical agent.

Since this operation was Cranston's brainchild, he took point, leading his comrades toward a cluster of abandoned buildings his location finder identified as housing units. Cranston withdrew a mini-probe from his field pouch and tossed it up. Once airborne, the probe took flight and darted toward the units, shrinking with distance.

As the investigators skulked amid a forest of low rise buildings, a pinging noise filled their helmets.

"Contact," said Skye, pulling up a radar grid on her helm HUD. A red dot flashing incessantly at the bottom right corner of her display represented the probe.

"Thirty yards north, twelve west," Cranston called out, increasing his pace.

"We don't need to rush," said Javaris. "They'll come to us."

A heavy patter of footfalls eerily confirmed Javaris's prediction.

Cranston held up a hand, bringing his comrades to a halt in front of a dilapidated unit.

The pinging in their helmets increased in frequency and intensity until a group of Goehlems burst from the building's corner.

Initially, the investigators hesitated. They were briefed on Goehlems before coming to Eden. They knew that at one extreme, Goehlems were huge lumbering monstrosities not far removed from the nightmare images of human imagination. At the opposite extreme, most appeared as normal humans.

The sight of a mob coming at them comprised of individuals that looked like mothers, fathers, sisters, brothers, aunts, uncles, nephews and nieces jarred the Investigators.

Until now, those briefings were academic and Skye had to remind herself that beneath human masquerades lay the biology of creatures that were anything but. She leveled her Toussaint upon the ravening mob.

"Let 'em have it!" she shouted.

The Toussaint flared. Rapid bolts of white hot light swept across the charging Goehlems, burning front, second, and a portion of their third rank in a broiling furnace of fire.

Cranston and Javaris took out the rest of the group, rupturing Goehlem heads and bodies with precisely aimed shots.

Ear piercing screeches no humans could come close to imitating rippled from the creatures' throats. Wounded Goehlems flopped and twisted on the ground like fish out of water. The investigators blasted the creatures, putting them out of their misery and moved on.

They came upon smaller units grouped close enough that little more than a yard of walkway separated the structures.

The mini-probe detected more Goehlem activity. Cranston led the way down the narrow sidewalk.

A pair of wild-eyed Goehlems burst from the side door of a house and came bounding down the walkway in a blood lusting frenzy.

Calmly, Cranston triggered two bolts from his carbine, hitting the lead Goehlem in the chest. The second received a bolt to the face. Both attackers tumbled lifelessly at Cranston's feet. He stepped over their bodies and continued to the end of the walkway.

Skye and Javaris followed close behind.

The probe kept pinging, but the tone grew deeper, indicating more than the presence of Goehlems, but a specific kind of Goehlem. A full blood. According to the radar grid, three full bloods resided in a house at the end of the walkway.

"Our quarry is not far," Cranston announced with a touch of excitement. He quickened his stride.

"Slow down, big man…" said Javaris, before he noticed that the blinking dot had vanished from his HUD. "Guys, we're no longer receiving probe readings."

"Malfunction?" Skye speculated.

"More likely a Goehlem spotted the probe and knocked it out," said Cranston.

"What?" Javaris and Skye exclaimed at the same time.

"Full bloods are more intelligent than their lesser evolved brethren," Cranston stated calmly. "I wouldn't put it past them. Be on guard."

'You don't have to tell me twice," Skye murmured.

When the Investigators reached the house, they didn't hesitate. They held the advantage in weapons, armor, training, and smarts. They would utilize the full brunt of that advantage by going in strong. No stealth, no subtly, just plain, brute force.

Skye increased the yield on her Toussaint and delivered a highly potent, combustible beam that blew a gaping hole in the side of the house.

The Investigators dashed through the smoking aperture.

Human-appearing Goehlems lay sprawled on the floor, some dead, others wounded from the entry blast. No full bloods in sight.

Uninjured Goehlems leapt to the attack. The investigators pumped streams of bolts, ripping a dozen of the howling creatures apart.

Suddenly, two full bloods charged through the aperture. The creatures were massive in girth and height. Close to seven feet of rippling musculature, they possessed large malformed heads with deep set rheumatic looking eyes, a nub nose and gaping shovel-toothed mouths. Their dense hides were mottled beige and clawed hands and feet were webbed as if adapted for an aquatic environment.

Javaris turned and fired a burst from his Regency Special that chewed a bloody furrow across the first Goehlem's torso.

Javaris took in the sight of the second Goehlem. He started to shoot the full blood, but changed his mind and lowered his weapon. "Ah, what the hell." He whipped out his Orisha blade and started toward the Goehlem.

The creature lunged, swinging a rangy arm at the human's head.

Javaris dove beneath the swing and rebounded to his feet close enough to flash his ion-edged blade, hamstringing the creature's left leg.

The Goehlem roared in pain and toppled sideways. Before it crashed to the floor, Javaris plunged his Orisha twice through the Goehlem's back, penetrating the spine.

A third full-blood pounded through the hole.

"Down!" Skye yelled.

It took a flicker of a second for Javaris to realize he was in Skye's line of sight. He dropped to the floor and Skye launched a spear of high energy that hammered the Goehlem off its feet, sending its instantly dead carcass flinging ten yards backwards.

Javaris rose and stood triumphantly over the full-blood he incapacitated.

The growling Goehlem lay on its back thrashing its head and arms, struggling to move its paralyzed legs.

Javaris brought the butt of his blaster down on the Goehlem's head multiple times, putting an end to its tantrum.

Skye regarded Javaris teasingly. "Had a change of heart I see."

Javaris scowled. "Silence." He turned to Cranston. "Alright, you've got your trophy. Let's call for a pickup and get the hell out of here."

The Investigators transported the wounded Goehlem to a medical research building in Cresthill. Edenites considered it one of the top science facilities on the planet.

Cranston brought his equipment from the capsule and set it up in a laboratory on the building's top floor. Current Edenite tech was insufficient for the work he had to do. As Cranston labored away, Skye, Javaris, and Inspector Abdil rode to the perimeter of Cresthill in an official rover car. It was one of the more conspicuous paradoxes of Eden that a planet familiar with all stages of ion propulsion relied on something as rudimentary as steam to fuel its lesser vehicles. She looked forward to the day when Edenites would eschew the primitive and speed up their return to pre-Dark Age tech. It made her insides knot in frustration at the thought of where humanity would be had the stars not turned against civilization.

What new knowledge would the First Empire have discovered? How much of the galaxy would have fallen under its rule?

Skye cringed at that unbidden upsurge of imperial impulse. She was well aware of the iron that lurked beneath the First Empire's benevolence. She observed Cresthill's residents through the car's blue tinted side window. Their pale faces and mostly light, straight hair reflected their descent from ancient Earth's Northern European branch. Their ancestors migrated to the stars two centuries after the first Cassad world was settled. It was doubtful Edenites would have taken kindly to outside authority no matter the level of its moderation. But the Edenites had no choice. It was either submit to Cassad protection (ultimately rule) or face subjugation, even extinction at the hands of hostile alien races. Eden's current trouble with the Goehlems was a holdover from an age when the first empire fought tooth and nail against alien interlopers.

In one particularly savage war, a species called the Ch'erdin launched a biological attack on Eden. They seeded the planet with spores that infected humans on contact. The spores gained access into human bodies through inhalation or ingestion. Over a period of time, the spores altered a human's genetic structure, remolding physiology, turning its unwilling host into a creature of pure instinct and terror, motivated by an unquenchable lust for violence. Edenites called these creatures Goehlems, the name being traced to mythical monsters associated with an old religion that existed long before humans stepped into space.

Fortunately, the Cassads defeated the Ch'erdin before the latter could launch similar attacks against other Cassad worlds. Cleansing Eden of the alien infection took the best biohazard specialists the First Empire had to offer. In time, through intensive research and plenty of trial and error, the specialists managed to disarm residual spores. They were also able to cure humans who had not advanced to full blood stage of infection which entailed a total loss of all physical human characteristics. The Cassads were well on their way to expunging the infection completely when night fell upon the Known like an unexpected, unwanted curtain call.

Stars throughout the Known began emitting peculiar electromagnetic pulses which disabled all forms of high technology. Machines from the largest space going vessels to the smallest appliances died in sustained bursts of EM activity. Sentients, humans and aliens alike that thrived on advanced tech were suddenly plunged into a harsh and brutal darkness both literally and figuratively.

Star spanning civilizations fragmented, trans-space communication ceased; the flow of space travel halted like water from a faucet being turned off. Signal traffic between worlds vanished in a heartbeat. Chaos and bloodshed consumed cutoff worlds as distraught inhabitants struggled to come to grips with their sudden and inexplicable transformation from the luxuries and conveniences of high tech life to the dirt scratching drudgeries of a primitive existence.

In time, knowledge of high technology disappeared from the collective memories of formerly advanced species.

The Cassad Empire was as adversely affected by this disaster as its alien rivals. But it didn't lose all of its knowledge. Rumors spread like wild fire that the Cassads knew the stars would turn rogue before the event occurred. The most vehement anti-Cassad elements even accused the first empire of complicity in the stellar catastrophe…as if the Cassads were stupid enough to cripple themselves in so spectacular a manner. It was unlikely the Cassads would have tampered with so many suns, even if they had the technology and the will to do so. Regarding foreknowledge, the evidence was not concrete, yet not totally dismissible. Someone in the first empire began recording as much human knowledge, particularly technical knowledge, as could be compiled in a four-year period leading to the EM deluge. And that knowledge was recorded on hardcopy and stored in an underground vault.

When the EM pulses stopped, the core Cassad worlds relied on that reserved knowledge to climb out of the Dark Age's pit faster than the extraneous planets it once ruled, faster than many alien civilizations.

That didn't appear coincidental to the reasonably suspicious.

The Cassads reconstituted much of their tech base, becoming among the first of the pre-Dark Age powers to return to space. That achievement enabled the Cassads to begin the process of piecing together a broken empire. But the process of reunification had to be conducted with a gentle touch. Former Cassad worlds had been out of contact with the center for far too long. They had become long accustomed to independence, and in several cases showed little interest in returning to the status quo. The Cassads sent advisors to these worlds, armed with the gift of high technology. Planets with populations suffering from diseases, malnutrition and a host of other debilitating ailments benefited from the wonders of restored advanced medical science.

Good deeds won back a growing number of worlds to the Cassads, enough to form the Second Empire.

Skye was hopeful that Eden could be won back in similar fashion. If not, well, the velvet glove would have to come off...

***

The car approached an area of block shaped structures surrounded by a barbed fence. Watchtowers overlooked the buildings, each one occupied by an armed soldier.

Guards at the entrance check point waved the car past when they recognized Inspector Abdil.

"What is this place?" Javaris asked.

"Internment camps for those infected by the Goehlem gene," replied the Inspector.

As the car pulled deeper into the camp, Skye and Javaris studied the prisoners moving about under the watchful gazes of armed guards. Not one exhibited signs of aggression associated with Goehlem behavior.

"They don't appear to be infected," Skye commented. "In fact, they're not acting any different from you or me."

"And me," Javaris emphasized with a mock wounded frown.

Skye cut a dry look glance at Javaris before continuing. "How many of these camps exist?"

"Thousands across the planet," said Abdil. He leaned forward. "There's General Corvin." The inspector's expression hardened at the sight of the man, barely masking his enmity.

Skye noticed the look but refrained from commenting on it.

The car glided to stop along the edge of a large open space.

General Corvin and a mixed gathering of guards, military officers, and soldiers stood about observing a curious looking construct in the middle of the yard.

Abdil and the Cassad Investigators stepped out of the car.

General Corvin turned to the new arrivals with a smile. "Inspector Abdil, Investigators. Welcome. Thank you for joining us today."

Skye and Javaris traded glances, both caught a bit off balance by the General's friendly demeanor in contrast to the venom he displayed during their first meeting.

The General pointedly ignored the Inspector.

"Good day, General," Skye greeted in turn, then cut to the chase. "You requested our presence here."

"Indeed, I did." Corvin squinted. "Where is your comrade?"

"He's studying a Goehlem we picked up," Javaris answered tersely.

The General raised a brow. "Oh. Quite an impressive operation procuring your prize I might add."

"Thank you, General," said Skye. "Of course, that operation will only be a success when Investigator St. John's research reveals how we can best combat this foe."

The General's face went blank for a split second before livening up. "Well let's get on with this shall we?" He threw up a signal gesture and camp prisoners dressed in light blue coveralls emerged from one of the blockhouses on the opposite side of the square. Guards escorted the prisoners to the construct, prompting Javaris to point to it.

"What is that thing?"

The construct was approximately six feet high, twelve yards across. It resembled an extra wide speaker's platform. A beam ran across the top of the platform connecting to two poles on both ends. The beam was elevated at a height of eight feet. Anchoring the platform was a round slot with a lever protruding from it. The most curious feature regarding the construct were eight ropes hanging from the beams, spaced about three feet apart, each one arranged in a noose.

"That, Investigator, is our standard method for dealing with Goehlems," Corvin explained all too proudly.

The guard marched over twenty prisoners to the platform and coaxed eight of them up steep steps leading to its surface.

Fear radiated from the prisoners' faces. A few tried to resist, receiving baton blows from the guards for their efforts.

The guards positioned the prisoners beneath the ropes and placed the nooses around their necks.

A queasy sensation formed in Skye's gut. She wasn't sure what she was seeing, but she definitely had a sinking feeling about the outcome. "General, what's going on?"

A guard seized the lever and wrenched it back.

The surface beneath the prisoners' feet retracted with a clank that echoed across the yard.

The prisoners dropped through the holes in the surface, their fall arrested by suddenly taut ropes.

Skye flinched, her jaw unhinged in shock. She was certainly not unaccustomed to violence, having observed it, and inflicted it on a few occasions. But this manner of death she witnessed deeply unsettled her. The sound of snapping necks was not likely to vacate her memory anytime soon.

She glanced at Javaris, his expression grim and tight-lipped. Then she shined an angry spotlight on the general. "How do you know those people were Goehlems?"

"We have our ways of spotting a Goehlem out of a crowd." the general sneered. "Certain movements, gestures, facial expressions betray their nature."

"What if you're condemning innocents?" Javaris demanded. "What you've listed is not much to go on."

"It's enough for us," Corvin replied icily. "We've been fighting these abominations for a very long time. We've kept them from taking over this planet. We don't need Cassads coming here telling us how to fight a war that we are winning."

The guards quickly removed the bodies of the executed prisoners and prodded another row of victims up the steps to stand beneath those terrible nooses. They placed the nooses around the prisoners' necks. Resigned to their fate, the prisoner's offered no resistance, exhibited little trepidation.

"As you can see, Investigators." Corvin waved an arm toward the doomed prisoners. "We have the situation well in hand. There's really no need for your presence here. I believe there is something on the order of a hundred planets far less fortunate than Eden that desperately require Cassad attention."

"Until the Planetary Authority decides otherwise, we will maintain our presence here until our work is done," Skye said testily. "In the meantime, I'll recommend to the Authority that a moratorium be placed on executions until we're able to better determine who is infected and who isn't."

Corvin shrugged, though it was immediately obvious from the burn in his eyes that he wasn't as nonchalant as he tried to appear. "Recommend away, Investigator. I'll just continue in my endeavor to make this planet safe for humans...Edenite humans."

A clank, followed by the snapping of multiple necks, seemed to punctuate the General's words.

Skye looked over at the row of freshly hung bodies and her anger elevated, threatening to spill out of her like lava bursting from a volcano.

Javaris sensed his partner's mood and intervened. "We should be going. Thank you for the demonstration, General." He shot Corvin a smile that bore not a hint of amicability.

Abdil picked up the queue and jerked a stiff nod to Corvin. "Yes, thank you indeed for the demonstration." He headed to the car without another word.

Inside the car, silence hung heavy between Abdil and the Cassad Investigators until Skye broke it. "Inspector, I'm appalled at what we just witnessed. Is that what the Planetary Authority sanctions?"

"Those executions have been part of an ongoing Goehlem-eradication policy for centuries," said a subdued looking Inspector. "The Authority, long ago, left the military in charge of all anti-Goehlem efforts. The military controls the camps and they, in concert, with Intelligence, determine who occupies them. Only in the last five years has the legitimacy of the camps been called into question. Like you, I and a growing number of people inside and outside of the government, feel that we are killing innocents along with the infected on a mass scale. We've called for a review of our anti-Goehlem policy on many occasions, but there are never enough votes in the Authority to bring about that review and the military vehemently opposes the slightest measure that alters how they fight Goehlems. The military and its supporters in the authority are even opposed to the research undertaken to cure infected humans of the Goehlems gene. It's ridiculous."

"You and the Chairman must do something to put an end to this butchery," Skye said, still smarting from the memory of bodies dangling from ropes.

"I'm sure the Inspector and the Chairman realize that, and are doing what they can to bring reform to this process," Javaris pointed out with high formality. The look he gave Skye brimmed with rebuke.

Immediately, Skye realized her transgression and dropped her eyes. She was coming off like a typical Cassad imperialist, lecturing to the natives. She didn't mean to be condescending. Javaris could not have been more right. Of course, Johansen, Abdil and their like-minded supporters were doing what they could to end the military's madness. They wouldn't have called in Cassad Investigators if they were less than determined to solve this problem.

"My apologies, Inspector."

"None required," Abdil replied graciously. "With your help we may get the military and its supporters to see the error of their ways."

Cranston called Skye and Javaris to the laboratory early the following morning. From his reddened eyes to the unshaven growth shadowing his broad face, it was clear he received little to no sleep. Yet, the pep in his voice advertised an enthusiasm for his work.

The Goehlem was laid out on a chrome pallet when Skye and Javaris entered the white walled lab. The creature's wrists and ankles were bound with restraints, though it was unconscious. Cranston kept it under constant sedation.

Javaris scrutinized Cranston with a lopsided grin. "You look like hell. Did you get any sleep?"

Cranston stood in front of a lab counter examining readings on his bio sensor tablet "Sleep is a distraction."

Javaris took that as a no and left it alone.

Cranston beckoned his two comrades over. "Take a look at this."

Skye glanced warily at the restrained Goehlem as she walked past the palette.

"Don't worry," said Cranston. "Our friend won't be waking up anytime soon and those restraints are strong enough to keep ten Goehlems down." He held up his bio-tablet, presenting an image on the screen. "These are two DNA strands, the Goehlem's and my own. Both look remarkably similar, practically identical, don't they?"

Javaris nodded.

Skye took an extra few seconds to study the screen. "Very much so, but then again that..." she pointed to the sedated goehlem, "...thing was once a human being."

"The operative word being 'once'," Cranston emphasized. He tapped an adjustment on his tablet and held it for his viewing audience. A series of red dots speckled the Goehlem DNA strand. "I was able to uncover these markers on the Goehlem strand, referencing research performed by Cassad scientists before the blackout. It took high resonance optics at a maximum setting to bring those markers to light. The scientists actually devised a treatment to reverse the Goehlem effect."

"Meaning that humans who transformed could become human again?" Skye asked with heightened interest.

Cranston sobered. "For the most part. I don't know how reversible the effect is for full-bloods. The Dark Age arrived and the results of that research never reached the core worlds...at least not in the fullest detail. So, what I've been doing is conducting an intensive analysis of our Goehlem here in hopes that its body reveals something that I can use as a basis to formulate a cure."

"That's good," Skye ventured thoughtfully. "That's very good. How long will it take for you to come up with that cure?"

Cranston rubbed the back of his neck with uncertainty. "I'm only scratching a surface here, but I'll know for sure if I'm making a dent in a week's time."

Skye had no doubt Cranston would devise something. As a graduate of the prestigious Science and Technology Institute she expected him to work miracles. Unfair? Yes. Did Cranston mind? Not at all. Nothing stimulated his prodigious scientific intellect like a complex challenge.

"Cranston, I need you to do something for us in the short term," said Skye.

The big man was all ears.

"You've discovered...or rediscovered a way to detect Goehlems. I need you to build a portable detector for purposes of scanning individuals. These Edenites are using shoddy ass guess work to determine who is or isn't affected by the Goehlem gene and in the process, I know they're condemning innocents."

"The worse thing is Corvin clearly doesn't give a damn if his low tech, intuition-based screening process is completely accurate," Javaris chimed in with snarling distaste.

Cranston nodded thoughtfully and his comrades could almost see his mental gears whirring into motion. "Give me a couple of hours; I should have a device put together by then. It'll be rather crude and rudimentary, but I can guarantee it'll be an effective detector."

"As long as it can prevent unnecessary loss of life that's all we can ask for," Skye said gratefully. She gave Cranston a pat on the arm and headed toward the lab exit.

"Good luck," said Javaris.

"Luck is based on a random flow of events." Cranston went to his tool kit resting on a lab counter. "I seek to minimize the random."

As Cranston dug into his kit, taking out an assortment of components, Javaris' brow wrinkled in puzzlement. "Whatever," he commented. "Do your thing." He followed Skye out of the lab.

It took little more than an hour for Cranston to craft a Goehlem scan. It was a flat plastic oval with an inlaid display that took up most of its surface space. When Cranston waved the scan over the restrained Goehlem, the screen pulsed red, indicating a positive reading. He withdrew the scan from the Goehlem and held it a few inches above his own forearm. The screen pulsed a green light, meaning his body contained negative Goehlem indicators.

It worked. Anyone else would have been flush with accomplishment at having created a complex bio-detector with a minimum of parts. For Cranston, the task was elementary engineering. Nothing to brag about. He took out his com and contacted his fellow Investigators.

With the bio-detector in hand, Skye walked briskly to the nearest block house where the internees where being held. Revulsion and anger etched a scowl into her features at the word 'internee.' Prisoner was a far more fitting term to describe the wretched souls languishing in what was essentially an extermination camp. She and Javaris wasted no time coming to this place after receiving Cranston's detector. Skye made sure to contact Inspector Abdil so he could meet them at the camp entrance.

The Inspector was indeed on site when Skye and Javaris arrived at the camp. A squadron of fully geared para-officers accompanied Abdil, which pleasantly surprised Skye. She had been counting on Abdil's rank as Head of the Continental Police to get the Investigators into the camp. And while she entertained a nibble of concern that the guards, being regular military, might be less-than-compliant regardless of Abdil's position, she kept quiet. Advising that the Inspector bring back up in case of trouble might have been perceived as her trying to throw her imperialistic weight around...even if all she did was offer a non-patronizing suggestion.

She blamed Javaris for her restraint. Him and his soft-handed, sensibility-soothing diplomacy. She was happy Abdil brought along the extra guns. But even if he hadn't, she and Javaris were getting back into that camp one way or another. Bet on it.

A slouched guard standing post outside the blockhouse drew erect when he saw that Abdil and his dark-skinned Cassad guests had returned. The camp warden, a large, jowl-faced woman named Hertan, shuffled along beside them.

"Please, Inspector, Investigators," Hertan practically pleaded. "With due respect, I need to know what you are doing, why you want access to the internees."

Stop calling them that! Skye wanted to scream.

"We're just doing examinations to determine who's infected and who's not," Javaris calmly explained.

The Warden's face reddened with fluster. Her eyes flashed between Javaris and Abdil. She wanted to stop and talk, but that damnable female Investigator was walking in the lead toward the blockhouse and she would not slow her pace.

"Now hold on," Hertan insisted, trying to gain some measure of control. "We already know who is infected. Our own examiners have determined that."

"Your examiners' methodology is fatally flawed," Skye said, every word in that sentence a hammer blow of indictment.

Hertan drilled resentful eyes into the female Investigator's back before turning to Abdil. "Inspector, they do not have authorization."

"As long I'm here they do," Abdil stated, daring the Warden to test that claim.

"Until General Corvin says otherwise," Hertan countered with a budding, challenging smile. "I've already placed the call."

Abdil flashed a matching smile. "Good for you, Warden. I made a call of my own: to the Chairman." The Inspector looked straight ahead, ignoring the Warden.

The Cassad Investigators were on their third blockhouse by the time General Corvin arrived in the camp, accompanied by a pair of soldiers. The blockhouse's occupants were lined up outside the structure as Skye tested each one with the bio-detector. Perhaps in a deliberate show of rudeness, the General neither acknowledged Inspector Abdil nor the Investigators. He brushed past Abdil's para-officers as if they did not exist and stood before the Warden, annoyance simmering just beneath the veil of his professional poise.

"Warden," he addressed tightly. "Why are those internees not confined to their quarters?"

"My apologies, General," the Warden quickly replied with an implicating glance at Abdil. "The Inspector ordered me to make these individuals available so the Investigators can run their tests."

"You're infringing on the military's jurisdiction." Corvin regarded the Inspector gravely. "That is unacceptable."

"It's no more or less acceptable than your people storming into districts, superseding local law enforcement which, by the way falls under my purview, to snatch persons you suspect of being Goehlems," Abdil shot back evenly.

Skye continued scanning internees as Javaris watched the exchange between the top ranking Edenites with seeming casual indifference. He kept a surreptitious eye, however, on Corvin's soldiers. Though the soldiers had their magazine-fed assault rifles shouldered, the weapons were capable of doing tremendous damage, particularly in skilled hands. From the files Javaris studied prior to making planetfall, Edenite soldiers were nearly as deadly and proficient as Cassad Imperial Marines.

"And what does she think she's doing?" Corvin queried, casting a contemptuous eye Skye's way.

"Investigator Odele is testing these people with a device that detects Goehlems," said Abdil. "It was developed by their colleague and it is a proven success. Over two hundred have been tested so far. One hundred and eighty-six do not have the Goehlem gene. I've ordered their release. The ones showing signs of Goehlem contamination have been placed in isolation until a cure can be found for their condition. Their colleague has been very busy working to find that cure, and given the state of

Cassad medical knowledge relative to our own, I have no doubt he will succeed."

Corvin's forced calm gave way to a roiling blend of amusement and annoyance. "You ordered the release of internees? Based on what? Results from some hand held, makeshift tech of dubious quality?"

"I can assure you, General," said Javaris, cutting into the conversation. "There is nothing dubious about this tech."

Skye paused from her scanning to hold up the detector. "General, this detector catalogs all analysis results, which we are willing to share with Eden's top medical and disease specialists. We'll also provide past and current Cassad research on the precise nature of a Goehlem infestation. Such data will broaden their understanding; bring them up to date on what we know about this alien weapon and its lingering and malevolent effects on the human body. So please, General, until then, trust the detector results." She indicated a group of interned persons standing near the corner of the blockhouse that the detector confirmed to be Goehlem-free. "Trust that those people are fully human."

"I will trust nothing but the tried and true results of Edenite screening," Corvin snapped. He looked to Abdil. "This charade ends now, Inspector."

"You can say that, General," said Abdil with a smirking arrogance he'd wanted to throw in Corvin's face for an achingly long time. "But the Chairman would disagree. He lends his full support and authorization to this effort. There will be no more killing of innocents."

"The Chairman!" Corvin scoffed. "This is a military-run camp, and this planet is still in a state of emergency!"

"Who do you think controls the military and who has the power to declare or lift a state of emergency, General?" Abdil's eyes bored into the General like welding lasers. "This is still a civilian-run planet. Or have you forgotten?"

The General leveled a seething stare at the Inspector. Finally, he turned and walked toward the blockhouse. Without warning he took out his sidearm and triggered a spatter of solid rounds into the group that passed the detector tests.

Carbon-jacketed bullets ripped through flesh and bone with frightful ease. Five men and two women were hit, their bodies plopping to the ground. Most of them died before they could register alarm.

Javaris reacted with trained swiftness. His own sidearm was out and pointed at the General before his brain could process the action.

Corvin's escorts unlimbered their rifles, training them on Javaris.

The internees screamed in terror and crouched low.

Skye had her blaster in one hand, the detector in the other. She leveled her weapon on the soldiers.

Warden Hertan backed away, steering clear of a possible shootout between Corvin's soldiers and the Investigators.

Abdil's para-officers clustered around him, but their weapons were not drawn, though their hands hovered threateningly close to the grips.

"Lower your weapon, General!" Javaris shouted, not unmindful of the guns on him.

Javaris felt little worry. Skye had him covered. Besides, as good as those soldiers were, he was ex-Space/Ground Assault. Even without Skye's help, he could end their world in a blink...and would do so if they twitched the wrong way.

"General, what are you doing?" Abdil yelled in shock and indignation.

"I said lower your weapon," Javaris warned the General.

"Are you going to shoot me, Investigator?" Corvin asked, his expression hard as ice-frosted steel. "You would be willing to kill me, a full-blood human to protect them, monsters?" He gestured with his chin to the surviving internees clustered together in a trembling, terrified huddle. "No. You lower your weapon. Not to worry. I won't kill any more of your monsters. I've made my point."

Skye looked around. Guards from across the camp were scrambling and running toward the scene. She spotted the barrel of a sniper rifle pointing in their direction from the firing port of the nearest watchtower.

She calculated odds that came up pitifully short in favor of her and Javaris. She lowered her blaster. "Javaris. Stand down."

Javaris kept his weapon on Corvin, enraged at the internees' senseless deaths. He felt his cool professionalism melting away beneath the lapping flames of his fury. "I only see one monster, General."

"Javaris!" Skye called out.

Slowly, reluctantly, Javaris holstered his blaster.

Corvin nodded to his soldiers and they lowered their rifles in turn.

Corvin slid his pistol back into his holster, turned and walked away. He paused to cast a malignant gaze at Javaris, and then eyed Abdil with a smile that conveyed illicit anticipation. "This isn't over, Investigator." He craned his head toward Skye. "Your mission on Eden has concluded, Investigator. I'll see to that."

Skye rushed to check the bodies and her heart sank. Every person the general shot lay dead.

Javaris shook his head in disgust. "Murdering bastard."

"We need to leave," Abdil urged. "I have a feeling he'll be back. In force."

"You can leave, Inspector," Skye said with venom in her tone. "My colleague and I are staying. I still have people to test. I won't let that butcher harm anyone else in this camp."

Abdil wanted to sway her, but the implacable look in her eyes told him that any argument he offered would fall on deaf and stubborn ears. Against his better judgment, for which he harbored absolutely no regret, he came to a decision. "So be it. I'll stay too."

Skye put a hand on the Inspector's arm. "As appreciative as I am, you don't have to do this."

"Nonsense. You need backup and I'm only too happy to provide it." Abdil turned to the Warden. "Effective immediately, this camp is now under Continental Police jurisdiction. You and your guards will report to me."

The Warden's face turned sour at the announcement. "Inspector, this is highly irregular."

"Nevertheless," Abdil said coldly. "I've given the order and you will obey."

Hertan fluttered a nervous nod and stomped away.

As Abdil began consulting with his para-officers, Javaris approached Skye with a wry expression. "You and Cranston seem to have a knack for putting me in life-threatening situations."

"Well, we have to keep you on your toes," Skye quipped.

Javaris grinned at that. "With the prospect of facing an onslaught from the military, consider my toes firmly planted. What's the play?"

Skye took out her com and held it up. "I'm going to alert Cranston and then prepare a surprise for Corvin if he chooses to escalate this matter."

Javaris didn't have to ask what the surprise was. He knew all too well and as he glanced at Corvin's dead victims, the blood in his veins solidified to ice. "I'm sure he'll be foolish enough to do just that."

***

"This government is broken," Corvin said as his driver rushed to open the ground cruiser's door. The General climbed into the large, combat-fortified vehicle, his soldiers following.

"Johansen is broken, the system is broken." Corvin's jaw clenched, his face reddening with fury. "The safeguards that have kept the Goehlem infestation at bay are unraveling thanks to those meddling Cassads and our incompetent government aids and abet them like mewling puppets!"

The General's soldiers settled on either side of their ranting superior, not sure whether to offer verbal agreement or just keep silent and let him rant. Both opted for the latter.

The General reached for the overhead radio. "The idea that aliens infected this world, that they're responsible for what happened to us...no. Cassad propaganda. Cassad lies. We lapped up that lie all those centuries ago and we're still blindly accepting it. Aliens didn't curse us with this Goehlem disease, the Cassads did. They're the ones responsible and they're going to pay for their misdeeds, along with anyone foolish enough to support them!"

The General opened a channel and spoke into the radio. "This is General Corvin. Execute Protocol Delta. Repeat, Protocol Delta." Corvin placed the receiver back in its slot and nodded to the driver. "Take us back to Headquarters. It's time to make preparations. It's time to save this world."

***

Chairman Johansen was at a dedication ceremony on the other side of the world when a message arrived from Inspector Abdil warning of trouble. Johansen initially thought the Inspector was referring to trouble of a Goehlem nature. Still, he wasn't surprised when Corvin's name came up. In fact, Johansen all but expected the General to make a move at any moment. All he needed was the right pretext, a catalyst to act. The Cassad Investigators may have been a perfect combination of both.

Johansen considered canceling the ceremony speech he was scheduled to give in a stadium complex. But the situation with Corvin was not serious enough to warrant that course of action. He would operate as if nothing were out of the ordinary. In the meantime, he ordered Abdil to place the Continental Police on alert. He sent no such order to Defense Command. The military was a hotbed of Corvin supporters.

The Chairman's eight car motorcade wound swiftly through the city of Gallo, eventually merging onto a four-lane avenue leading to a massive silver domed venue.

The avenue was clear of vehicular and pedestrian traffic to expedite the motorcade's journey.

Johansen gazed out of his backseat window admiring Gallo's skyline. New buildings were springing up here as quickly as they were in Cresthill. Eden's rebirth was proceeding with vigor. For a heady moment, Johansen visualized a fully developed Eden once again taking its rightful place in the community of stars. That effervescent moment of optimism exploded in a boil of light. The first three cars in the motorcade burst into flaming wreckage.

Johansen's car was the fourth vehicle. Shock waves from the blasts pummeled it like battering rams, sending it swerving and spinning and colliding with the shattered remnants of the cars in front of it. Portable-launched missiles streaked toward the motorcade's rearward vehicles from opposite directions. The cars were well protected against small arms projectiles, but stood no chance against armor piercing missiles. Enormous flame-laced explosions marked the catastrophic demise of those vehicles. Fresh shockwaves rippled outward, sweeping up the chairman's car in a violent eddy and flipping it end over end.

The vehicle landed on its wheels and slid to a scraping halt.

Johansen's ears rang loud as thunder. His head and body ached to high hell and his vision blurred. He squeezed his eyes shut and opened them. No improvement in his sight. He could barely make out his driver and bodyguard in the front seat. They began to stir. His aide squirmed beside him groaning in pain. Shakily, Johansen unlatched his seatbelt and fumbled with his aide's belt.

His bodyguard twisted toward him, his face smeared with blood. "Ch... Chairman, are you alright, sir?"

Johansen tried to shake off a wave of delirium. "Call for help..."

Suddenly, three figures in civilian garb ran to the car, slapped disks on all four door locks and scurried to a safe distance.

Four deafening pops stripped away what little hearing Johansen had left. His door fell open, smoke pouring ravenously into the vehicle, smothering the occupants.

Rough hands tugged at his body, pulling him out of the car and hurling him to the pavement.

Johansen tried to rise, anger dulling his pain. He saw blurred outlines of armed assailants pulling the others out of the car.

One of the assailants, stomped Johansen in the gut, and kept his foot there, applying enough pressure to pin him. The blow knocked the wind out of Johansen. He lay sputtering for breath while witnessing the other assailants line up his driver, bodyguard, and severely wounded aide.

One of the assailants raised a snub nose assault weapon. The muzzle flared and horror seized the Chairman as three methodically-placed bullets ruptured the heads of his subordinates. Blood and brain matter splattered the vehicle as their bodies crumpled to the ground.

"You're coming with us, Chairman," the assailant with his foot on Johansen declared with glittering cruelty.

But Johansen heard nothing. Even if he did, he was too fixated on the bleeding corpses of his people to take notice of his captivity.

***

Heavily armed soldiers, members of the elite Hard Strike Brigade, stormed Vigilance Hall. With the rapid precision and ferocity for which they were known, the HSBs easily overpowered Vigilance Hall's security force, taking no prisoners. Afterward, they surged into the assembly chamber. Alarmed legislators made an outcry, but otherwise remained in their seats under HSB guns.

Moments later, a group of men and women in formal blue suits entered the chamber. Members of the Intelligence Bureau, the grim-faced agents sifted through legislators, separating Johansen supporters from the rest. A detachment of HSBs escorted the Johansen supporters to a plaza behind Vigilance Hall where they were promptly executed.

***

Pummels were the most advanced fighter jets in Eden's arsenal. Like the rest of Eden's sub-orbital as well as its few orbital craft, the flat, sleek, swept-winged jets were liquid fueled. They also traveled five times faster than sound.

Five Pummels dove toward the Continental Police headquarters building on the outskirts of Cresthill. Each jet released a pair of air-to ground Mallet missiles and veered upward, their afterburners blazing with effort. The missiles slammed into the roof and upper and lower sections of the twenty-story diamond-shaped building. Intensely bright explosions sprouted from points of impact, followed by billowing sheets of flame that surrounded the structure like a crimson shroud. Mallets were fuel/air explosives and it showed as the very air fed into a raging conflagration, scorching everything and everyone inside the shattered building to charred husks.

The Pummels came around for a second pass, bombarding the headquarters' campus. A gale force storm of collateral damage reduced an eight square block radius, beyond ground zero, to a sweltering disaster zone.

***

Eight soldiers in visor helmets and bulky body armor barged into the laboratory of the medical research facility.

Cranston glanced up, barely taking notice of the intruders, and returned to his task of extracting blood from the sedated Goehlem with a quantum extractor.

One of the soldiers, presumably the ranking officer, stepped forward, pointing his rifle at the investigator. "Investigator Cranston St. John, you will stop what you are doing and come with us."

Cranston waved a dismissive hand. "Not now, I'm busy." He detached a blood-filled beaker from the extractor and settled it inside an analyzer slot.

The soldier flipped his helmet visor up, revealing a puzzled face. "Did you not hear me, Cassad?"

"I heard you," Cranston replied impatiently as he studied the analyzer's display screen. "Now go away. What I'm doing here is very critical."

The soldier's puzzlement heightened to exasperation. He flipped his visor down and made an emphatic gesture. "Grab him!"

Without hesitation, the other soldiers advanced toward Cranston. Had they been more perceptive, they would have noticed a mild sheen of distortion in front of them, producing a lens effect. The first three soldiers to come within twelve feet of Cranston and his work space bounced painfully off of that distortion and tumbled on their backs.

The ranking soldier let out an astonished "What the hell?" He reached out tentatively, running a hand along the invisible barrier's electro-static surface. Then he opened fire on the barrier, his soldiers following suit. A hail of bullets deflected off the barrier, hitting walls, ceiling and four soldiers. Luckily, their body armor protected them form serious injury. Still, they yelled out in pain and shock.

Cranston blew out a breath, relieved, though he hid it well. Thanks to Skye's warning, he managed to hastily construct a kinetic nullification shield emitter from parts he kept in his trusty tool kit. It was a crude assembly, more so than his Goehlem detector, but it worked...for the moment.

***

A helicraft flew into the internment camp and landed several yards from where Skye, Javaris, Abdil and his para-officers were located.

Thirty heavily armed Continental Police Rapid Tactical Responders emerged from the vehicle, its duel top mounted propellers whipping up a miniature windstorm.

The Responders' lead officer approached Abdil, his face ashen. "CP headquarters is gone, Inspector, wiped off the map."

Abdil snapped his head around, giving the Investigators a sharp look. They had already informed Abdil of an attack on CP HQ. Soon after Corvin's departure, Skye sent a transmittal to their explorer capsule's computer, initiating the launch of a surveillance probe. Expecting Corvin's return, she intended for the probe to monitor forces under his command. Instead, the probe picked up signal traffic and images bespeaking far more sinister activity than she could have ever anticipated from the General.

Corvin had blanketed Eden in a worldwide communication blackout. Abdil could not contact anyone via radio. The Investigators' communicators became his only link to the outside. Still, he did not want to believe it when Skye told him of the HQ attack. The Responder's horrific confirmation cut sharp and deep like a knife through his heart. Abdil's eyes glazed over in shock. He turned back to the Responder. "The Chairman?"

"No word, Inspector. Tightbeam transmissions report that his motorcade was hit. Our listening posts near Gallo are trying to cut through the static to get more details. Vigilance Hall is completely blacked out."

"I'm sorry, Inspector," Skye said softly.

Abdil rubbed his eyes as the magnitude of what was transpiring began to sink in like thorns embedding in his flesh. "That son of a bitch. I never thought he'd go this far. I should have known. I damned well should have known. I should have read him better!"

"If it's any consolation, Inspector, I should have seen this coming, too," Skye admitted, not at all pleased with herself. Her deep understanding of history informed her of countless conflicts and unrest caused by individuals who stopped at nothing to maintain a sliding grip on an outmoded idea or a rotting status quo. From the dreadful developments unfolding on Eden, Corvin was turning out to be no different and she failed to see that.

"We're about to have company," Javaris called out, his hand resting on his blaster's grip.

Skye turned to see Warden Hertan approaching, accompanied by a dozen camp guards. The Investigator briefly regarded the large crowd of prisoners she just tested. They were assembled around a block house, their faces lit with fear and uncertainty. Skye vowed to protect those innocents with her life. She and Javaris traded determined glances. She was happy to know that he had her back, even if her stance did exceed their mandate as Investigators.

The Warden brushed the Cassads with a disdainful eye before focusing on Abdil.

"Inspector, I just received orders from General Corvin. He says you have no authority over this camp. He orders you and your officers to disarm and surrender to us. We are to detain you until the General arrives to receive you into his custody."

The Warden pivoted sneeringly to Skye and Javaris. "Investigators, the General advises you to leave Eden immediately. If you refuse, he will take punitive action."

Javaris cocked his head. "You tell your General he can kiss our..."

"Only the Chairman can issue that kind of advice," Skye interrupted. "We will only listen to Chairman Johansen."

"I concur," said Abdil. "I answer only to the Chairman. I'm not making a single move without his consent. I would advise you, Warden, to take no more orders from the General. He is a murderer and a traitor. It's best you jump off his sinking ship now while you still have a chance."

The Warden's face morphed from smug to irate. "Don't talk to me about the General being a traitor. You and your precious Chairman betrayed us all the moment you allowed those Goehlem-loving Cassads in our midst. I will enjoy watching you die!" She turned abruptly and walked away, her procession in tow.

Skye watched the Warden's departure with a cool gaze before taking out her com and speaking into it. "Cranston, what's your status?"

***

Cranston ran a micro-scan over a spot of Goehlem blood sample. All the while, more Edenite soldiers entered the lab with guns drawn. They stood before the containment shield Cranston erected, trying to figure a way to get through or around it.

"I'm good so far," he replied to Skye's query. At that moment, a soldier walked in with a portable launcher. The commanding officer ordered the rest of his soldiers to evacuate the lab.

The soldiers filed out quickly leaving the soldier with the launcher behind.

Cranston eyed the weapon, doing his best not to let his wariness seep through the imperturbable face he was presenting to would-be killers.

The soldier propped the launcher on his shoulder, triggered a rocket and darted from the lab just as the projectile struck the shield.

The resulting blast whiplashed through the lab, blowing equipment and furnishing to splinters. When the smoke cleared, the nullification shield remained firmly in place.

Cranston raised a brow. He wasn't quite ready to pat himself on the back, but he was pleased the shield held.

***

Rose Installation, located in a suburban district north of Cresthill, was the largest military base on the planet as well Defense Command's central headquarters. General Corvin walked into his office in the base administration building and was satisfied to see Chairman Johansen in the custody of two stern-faced soldiers.

A prominent bruise colored part of the chairman's face. His wrists were tightly bound with handcuffs, and his dark gray suit was wrinkled and torn in places.

"Criminal!" Johansen yelled, his eyes flaring with rage at the sight of Corvin. "You have lost your mind! The people of Eden will never stand for this coup!"

Corvin walked up to Johansen until he was mere inches from the Chairman's face. He smiled.

"The people will welcome this, Chairman." Corvin pivoted toward the audio/visual cam resting on his desk. He nodded to a soldier operating the cam and the latter flicked a prompt on the device, activating its broadcast mode.

Corvin looked into the cam's clear optic, took a breath and spoke.

"Citizens of Eden. I am General Ran Corvin. Do not be alarmed by recent developments. All is secure. A few hours ago, I uncovered a massive conspiracy, initiated by Chairman Johansen and his disreputable cronies, to seize absolute control of our constitutionally-sanctioned government and impose a dictatorship. Johansen planned to enlist the aid of Cassad Investigators in his dastardly undertaking. Worse, he intended to unleash

Goehlems upon us in a campaign of terror designed to pacify resistance to his illegal action. But worry not, citizens. The Chairman's plot has been foiled by the brave and patriotic efforts of our armed forces. He is presently in our custody and those who supported him in his evil scheme are being apprehended and dealt the punishment they deserve." Corvin paused, allowing the soldier to direct the cam in Johansen's direction. The Chairman stiffened, glaring defiantly into the cam.

"As we continue tracking down more conspirators," Corvin continued. "I must, in the name of public safety, elevate our current state of emergency to Level Five until this crisis is abated. Until then, God bless Eden and may He smite our enemies."

Corvin signaled with a downward swipe, ending the broadcast. He looked at Johansen with eyes cold as frozen venom. "Now, if you'll excuse me, Chairman. It's time for me to pay a visit to your Cassad friends. Afterward, you'll go on trial."

"Mock trial, you mean," Johansen said disdainfully.

"However, you wish to term it, Chairman." Corvin exited his office with a mirthful expression.

***

Skye continued testing camp internees. She smiled at a toddler whose test result certified the little bright-eyed girl as Goehlem free. The child's mother grabbed Skye's hand and squeezed, her eyes an overflow of tears, relief, and gratitude. "Thank you, Investigator!"

Skye offered a slight nod tinged with worry. The detector picked up not a trace of Goehlem contamination in the mother and child. Skye wished she could have guaranteed their safety from a human menace with equal, absolute certainty.

"The General's on the move," Javaris reported, looking at probe-fed data on his com display screen. "Shit. They're headed our way with large ground transport vehicles."

Abdil peered at the crystal-clear display images radiating from Javaris' com. "Those are Rragnars. They're used for delivering artillery. I would guess Omniex guns."

"I perused your military database before our arrival on Eden," said Javaris. "These Omniex guns appear to be your heaviest artillery."

"And most dangerous," Abdil confirmed grimly. "They fire thermal shells. A single salvo from enough of them will turn this camp into an inferno."

Javaris raised a sardonic brow to match his tone. "Well now, from the looks of it, I'd say they're bringing in more than enough."

Skye pointed to a mobilization of camp guards and almost reached for her weapon. But they were not mobilizing for an attack, they were withdrawing. Air and ground vehicles packed with camp personnel sped and soared away from the camp.

"They clearly know what's coming," Javaris remarked casually.

Skye gave Abdil her most earnest look. "Inspector, again, words cannot express my appreciation for you staying with us. However, I strongly advise you to leave while you still can. I only wish I could evacuate these prisoners."

"There's nowhere for us to go," Abdil replied, waving an arm at his Responders and para-officers, who were as vociferous about not departing the camp as their leader. "The military controls the air and ground. All approaches are covered by Corvin's goons. And even if we could slip through their net somehow, we're not going anywhere. So, whatever you have planned now is the time to implement it. Otherwise..." the Inspector gave a nihilistic shrug: "we die together."

"Certainly not my idea of a bonding experience" said Javaris.

Skye cocked an eye at her insouciant colleague, suppressing a grin. She sighed heavily. "So be it, Inspector."

***

General Corvin observed as support crews offloaded dozens of Omniex guns from shell-shaped Rragnar transport vehicles. Gun positions were set up a half mile from the camp's perimeter, at fifty-yard intervals, along a stretch of an overpass highway. Perfect elevation and distance from which to rain down fire and death.

Corvin's gaze intensified with battle-lust. He could not have been more pleased when Warden Hertan informed him that those arrogant Cassads were still in the camp, along with Abdil and his CPs. My two most pressing problems eliminated in addition to a camp full of Goehlems and potential Goehlems, he thought. The hell I'm sending them to will be a relief compared to what they're about to receive.

He took out his radio and spoke into it. "General Corvin to Unit Leader. What's your progress?"

"General. We're unable to break that Cassad force field," an angst-ridden voice responded. "Rockets and charges have had no effect."

Corvin's jaw tightened, his teeth clenching. "Find a way to neutralize that Investigator. I don't care about force fields. Level the building if you have to. I do not..."

"General Corvin."

The general blinked at the sound of a female voice interrupting his transmission. Instantly, he recognized that voice and could not help but to be a tad unnerved at the ability of the Investigator to cut through his com blackout. He wasn't about to ask how she tapped into his private frequency.

Corvin masked his unease with a display of posturing. "Investigator, I wasn't expecting your call. If you're begging for mercy then I regret to inform you that you're too late. You should have been long gone by now."

"No General, I did not call you to beg for mercy. I called to ask you to reconsider your actions. There is no victory for you in this wave of terror you've initiated."

"You can't intimidate me, Investigator." Corvin smirked. "If you you're referring to a Cassad response then know this, your precious empire isn't the only force with high technology. The Dark Age had not completely wiped Eden's memory. Unbeknownst to you, we've retained some pre-Dark Age tech, enough to construct a string of anti-orbital batteries across the planet. Those weapons will erase any Cassad warship foolish enough darken our skies. You will never have this planet. Eden will never submit to Cassad rule. You have lost, Investigator!"

"The only thing I've lost is my patience, General. Pull back. Demobilize your forces, release the Chairman and surrender. That is a demand, not a request and I will only make it once."

Corvin gawked at his radio, convinced that this bloody Cassad had gone certifiably mad.

"I hope you don't die too quickly, Investigator." He cut the transmission and gestured to the artillery commander. "Don't wait for my command. The very second those guns are set up, open fire and don't stop until that camp is glazed flat, understood?"

The artillery commander straightened. "Understood, General!"

Corvin walked a short distance to the edge of the overpass. He moved parallel to the waist high railing in search of an ideal vantage point from which to view the coming bombardment.

Suddenly, a thunderous boom quaked the ground beneath his feet, its force nearly vaulting the general over the railing. He looked up and his eyes widened. He snatched his weapon out of his holster and backed away. His first instinct was to run. Instead, he held his ground and cursed as hell erupted around him.

A boiling mass of black smoke rose from of a churning column of fire where an Omniex gun once existed.

A small gray craft soared overhead, releasing a series of missiles at a rapid-fire rate. The missiles speared into the remaining artillery positions, shattering guns as if they were made of fragile glass. Successive blasts ignited munitions, generating calamitous secondary explosions that burned with hellish fury. Flame-smothered remnants of Omniex guns hurtled over the edge of the overpass, plunging toward the ground in a ninety-yard drop. Over a hundred soldiers were swept into scorching oblivion by the blasts. Clumps of burning bodies lay scattered across a charred surface. Uninjured, but deeply rattled survivors pointed their rifles at the sky, discharging them.

The mysterious craft made an impossibly sharp turn and flew back for another pass. The soldiers fired on the vessel, their shots ineffectual. Quad barrel turrets popped from beneath the craft and began spitting crimson energy. Lethal, high explosive iridescence sliced into soldier after soldier with horrific accuracy, each hit a kill, each hit ripping a body apart in a wet plume of gore. The craft slowed to a hover. Soldiers that had not been cut down by beam fire bravely or foolishly, depending on perspective, continued firing on the intruder. The craft's impregnable hull shrugged off a litany of assault rifle rounds. Portable-launched projectiles slammed into the craft in flaring impacts, barely nudging it.

The craft's turrets swiveled full circle, dousing hostile positions in a deluge of hot energy. More explosions rang out. Several soldiers were turned into bonfires and flailed about, screaming in agony and panic until they could scream no more. A group of soldiers burst from the cover of overturned vehicles in a desperate attempt to flee. One of them launched an RPG. The projectile impacted the craft's underbelly, producing a blast that would have holed a vehicle of Edenite construction.

Undamaged, the craft rotated. A turret trained on the soldier with the RPG. A straight line of radiance caught the soldier square in the chest rapidly immolating him. Though the other soldiers scrambled to escape the craft, its turrets whirred in their direction, targeting them with unsparing, almost malevolent intent for a machine. The quad-barrel vomited fury, dissecting twenty more of Corvin's finest troops. Resistance to the craft withered to an impotent silence.

The craft hovered in place a few more seconds, its onboard tactical computer scanning for additional targets. When the computer confirmed that all threats had been neutralized, the craft turned and glided away, leaving behind a seething ruin.

***

Skye used her com to switch the T5 landing capsule from Autonomous Combat Mode to manual operation. In ACM, the capsule maneuvered with graceful, unencumbered fluidity, like the flight of a valley eagle. Under Skye's control, to her mild chagrin, it became almost comically haphazard. The vessel wavered and dipped its way forward until she managed to set it down none-too-gently a few yards from where she stood.

Skye scrunched her face. "Cranston is much better at this than I am. I prefer piloting these things from the cockpit."

"You did all right," Javaris said with a wry backhanded smile to match the compliment. "I've seen worse."

Skye gave her colleague a mock stern stare. "I don't think so."

Abdil stood next to the investigators, oblivious to their banter as he gazed in slack-jawed awe at the fiery destruction wrought by such a minuscule, unassuming vessel. Skye's remote piloting skills could not have been further from his mind.

"That little vehicle of yours packs a powerful punch," he said, almost at a loss for words."

It would have taken a squadron of heavy helo-gunships, each amassing five times the Cassad vessel's size, to affect that kind of devastation on an equivalent scale. Perhaps twice that number to do so within a similar timeframe.

"That was a moderate demonstration," Javaris offered lightly. "You should see what it can do at optimum engagement."

Abdil crinkled a puzzled look at the Investigator. "There had to have been a thousand soldiers, in addition to twenty Ominex guns on that overpass. All eradicated. How optimum could it get?"

Javaris grinned mischievously but never elaborated.

A boarding ramp extruded from the vessel. Skye headed toward it, turning partially to beckon the Inspector. "Let's check on our handiwork."

***

Skye landed the capsule with ease on the overpass. She, Javaris and Abdil immediately exited. The CP helicraft settled beside the capsule and disgorged its complement of Responders.

Twisted metal heaps that were once artillery guns sweltered white hot like nightmarish abstract sculptures in the blazing aftermath of their destruction. Corpses, whole and in pieces, littered the surface, interspersed with smoldering debris. The sickly-sweet pungency of burnt flesh blended with the bitterly sharp tang of slagged alloy.

Skye breathed with her mouth to spare her nostrils aromas that assailed nasal passages with the virulence of acid coated spores. Heavy smoke stung the eyes, producing a shimmering gray haze.

Investigators and Responders waded through this smoky murk, scanning bodies in their search for General Corvin.

They came across few survivors. Of that remnant, most were so grievously wounded that they could barely move under their own power.

Skye walked past those moaning, broken wretches without a sliver of sympathy. What those soldiers were about to inflict on hundreds of innocent civilians sickened her more than the cloying, prevailing stench of injury and death. It did not matter that they were following orders. Corvin's actions were illegal and any soldier that still followed him wallowed neck deep in a shit hole of criminal culpability.

Abdil bent, turned over a body and moved on. He cast concerned glances toward the distance. "We shouldn't be here any longer than necessary. Enemy reinforcements may be en route."

"Not immediately," said Skye. "I had the capsule jam communications. If anyone tried to transmit, I guarantee you they weren't successful."

Abdil nodded his admiration. "Another wondrous Cassad technical capability."

Skye cracked a wry smile. "Eden had those wondrous capabilities before the blackout. Your world can easily regain them."

At the cost of our independence, Abdil added in thought. Reinstatement in the empire would surely diminish Eden's autonomy. The Inspector wasn't sure how he felt about that. But if it meant a cure for the Goehlem disease, a lifting of the state of emergency, and an end to internment camps and mass murder, then a loss of independence seemed a proper enough cure for a brutalized, traumatized society.

"Inspector!" One of the Responders called out from the other end of the kill zone.

Abdil headed in that direction with Skye and Javaris close behind.

General Corvin lay next to the overpass railing. He still lived, though not much beyond a wisp of life remained to animate the contorted shrapnel-riddled wreck of his battered body. His face was a splotched mass of blistered flesh, leaving nothing of its original make up save a portion of nose and a single functional eye. His lips were burned away, his exposed teeth locked in a hideous rictus grin.

Skye, Javaris and Abdil stood over the General, staring down at him with coldly judicious eyes.

Corvin stared back through his one good eye with unflinching, defiant, hatred. His lipless mouth opened and closed in a jittery attempt to form words. "Y... y... you...d... die!"

Skye's hand drifted to the grip of her holstered blaster, stopping just short of drawing it. "It wouldn't be right for me to do what I'm aching to do at this very second would it?"

"No, it wouldn't," Javaris replied, his tone regretful. "As Investigators, it's not our place."

Abdil pulled out his pistol and shot Corvin in the forehead, killing the General instantly. The Inspector calmly holstered his weapon and regarded the astonished Investigators with ruthless satisfaction.

"As an Edenite, the place is mine."

***

Skye dispatched a message beacon through the Gate requesting assistance from the Deep Space Recon cruiser. Two hours later, the Cassad ship exited the Gate and fell into a synchronous orbit above Cresthill. Based on the Investigators' report, the cruiser's captain sent Tac Teams, supported by an Infantry Brigade, to the surface.

Beforehand, he ordered Eden's anti-orbital defenses disarmed. This was accomplished by means of an override code inserted into the defense system's computer. General Corvin's boast to the contrary, Eden's anti-orbital weapons never posed an actual threat to a cruiser that was a product of a highly advanced post-Dark Age empire. The non-violent means employed by the captain to shut down Eden's defenses attested to the empire's unmatched capability. And if the captain ordered those defenses destroyed, a single volley from the cruiser's planet-pounding weapons banks would have achieved that objective in a matter of seconds.

The Tac Teams' first priority was to secure the Investigators.

Black-garbed Tac Operatives dropped from hovering stealth personnel carriers like obsidian rain. With rapid precision, they established a protective perimeter, encompassing the internment camp, extending to the overpass.

Skye and Javaris approached the Tac Team leader. "Glad to see you guys," Javaris greeted.

The Tac operator's armor glistened like a moonlit tar pit. His black visor retracted, revealing a cheerful, strong jawed face almost as dark. "Always a pleasure to bail out Investigators."

"I hope you're bailing out the third member of our party," said Skye.

The operator nodded confidently. "That situation is being handled."

***

Edenite soldiers, undoubtedly demolitions experts, placed triangle shaped devices on the charred floor just beyond the shield.

Cranston watched the soldiers for a moment, and turned to the window when a large helo-gunship dipped into view, its missile racks cycling to launch mode. Cranston surmised that the demolition soldiers were going to synchronize the detonation of their explosive charges with a missile attack from the gunship.

He grimaced. The shield likely would not hold. If channeled detonations could not neutralize it, the gunship's sustained firepower would. And if, by some incredible miracle, the shield weathered the overwhelming storm of those attacks, Cranston held little hope for the surrounding structure. He faced the prospect of dropping so many lower levels down, and being buried beneath tons of rubble to make matters worse. How long would the shield last then? How much of his valuable research would be so disrupted that he would be forced to start over? If he survived...

A searing flash like red lightning pierced one side of the ponderous gunship and exited out the other. A follow-up beam of light struck the vehicle's aft engine. A raging fuel-fed explosion consumed the gunship, tearing it into a constellation of flaming, plummeting pieces.

The demolitions soldiers looked to the window and wilted in a storm of blaster beams before they could react.

Cassad Tac operatives poured into the lab, their weapons pulsing deadly accurate fire until every target in the room was down.

At the sight of them, Cranston smiled, relieved. When the massacre ceased, he tapped a prompt on his com, deactivating the shield.

"Just in the nick of time."

One of the operatives acknowledged the Investigator with a crisp nod as his comrades checked the bodies of their victims. No survivors.

Cranston threw up a thankful wave and went back to his work.

***

A month later...

Skye and Chairman Johansen strolled leisurely across Vigilance Hall's inner plaza. Towering statues of historical personages from Eden's past loomed like sentinels throughout the plaza's vast space. Floral gardens along the fringes added a vibrant touch of nature. The gem-inlaid surface shone bright enough to cast the illusion that the pair were walking on a still pond.

Skye found it difficult to envision the violence committed in this place a month earlier when three hundred and twelve legislators were gunned down by Corvin's death squads.

Armed guards stood post at various sections of the plaza, just conspicuous enough to be a deterrent. Up until two weeks ago, the guards were Cassad Infantry soldiers. The Cassad force that secured the Investigators also rescued the Chairman and stormed Vigilance Hall, killing and capturing Corvin loyalists. This enabled the Continental Police and elements in the military opposed to General Corvin an opportunity to rally and takes back their planet.

A Cassad troop presence was necessary to usher in stability. When order was restored, the Cassad military force was immediately withdrawn before they could become an eyesore to the populace.

In that time, Cranston developed a serum designed to temporarily reverse the effects of the Goehlem affliction, at least for those who had not reached the full blood stage.

With the Investigators leaving Eden in a few hours, Cranston could not wait to return home so he could continue work on creating a permanent cure. Imagine what he'll accomplish in a fully equipped Cassad research facility, Skye thought optimistically.

"I appreciate what you have done for us," Johansen said, interrupting Skye's reverie. "You and your people have averted us from a path this planet most certainly did not need to tread. You saved us from monsters and mad men."

"You and your people had a tremendous hand in saving yourselves, Chairman," Skye remarked modestly. "The vast majority of your population could have fallen behind the General. That didn't happen."

Johansen shrugged. "Well something about self-appointed despot wannabes overthrowing a legitimate government simply does not sit well with the average Edenite."

"I can imagine being reinstated into a large starfarring entity would be similarly off putting to an Edenite," Skye submitted, regarding the Chairman closely.

After a thoughtful pause, Johansen nodded. "It would be...still is. And yet, what you have done for us should be a mitigating factor in easing us toward what's to come. Our Goehlem problem is solved. Now, we can channel maximum effort into developing our world, even if it has to be within the framework of an empire."

Skye extended her hand. "On that note, Chairman, I want to wish you and the people of Eden good fortune."

Johansen took the other's hand and shook it. "Good fortune to you, Investigator. So, do you get to go home or is there another crisis for you and your colleagues to tackle?"

"In my case, I won't find that out until I return to the ship." Skye's mouth parted in a weary grin. "There are plenty of worlds with problems hindering their reintegration into the empire and not enough Investigators to solve those problems."

"Hopefully not all of those problems will be as pressing as what you encountered here," said Johansen with a sympathetic smile.

Skye could not have agreed more. "Hopefully."

The two parted ways after a final farewell.

THE QUIET BLACK

BY

MALON EDWARDS

*The Dark Age saw the collapse of the First Great Age.
Even now its origin is still debated. The science binding worlds
was obliterated; for some worlds the effect was crippling, for
others it was fatal. But for the sentient species inhabiting all
worlds one basic rule prevailed; adapt or die.*

*-Samake. Cassad djele/historian. From The Cassad
Chronicles*

You keep swimming, even though you know you will
not escape the fifty-foot-long trulluk. But you were pulse-bred
for this.

You are faster than all of the young women and all of the
young men in Aggregation Four of your mating shoal. Your sail
fin retracts quicker. Your musculature is sleeker. Your gill plate
is wider. Your caudal secretions bond stronger. Your sirenomelia lasts longer. Your determination to find enjoyment in new
and different ways each day is unmatched.

Which is why you are in this predicament now.

The trulluk has been pursuing you for the better part of
the last three hours. Your gills burn. Your lungs burn. Your caudal secretions are loosening. In ten minutes, your legs will separate. Your speed will decrease. The trulluk will spear you. And
the trulluk will eat you.

You cannot let this happen. We will not let this happen.
But we cannot help you unless you first help yourself.

Up ahead, you see the shelf of the Blue Coral Reef. The
outer reef and the reef edge are not far. The drop-off extends

hundreds of feet down into the deep, dark, black water of the Marijani Sea. This is your only chance. There is where you must go if you wish to escape. There is where you must hide if you wish to live. There where you must stay if you wish to see Dawud again.

A school of bumblefish flit and scatter as you approach. Within seconds, they disappear into the darker blue mottles of open water. Bumblefish are small. You are not. They can do that. You cannot.

But you can feel the trulluk getting closer. The electroreceptors in your fluke place it about one hundred yards behind you. Never before has a trulluk come this close to you in flat out blue water pursuit. Never again, you vow.

And then, you feel your fluke cleave. The secreted mucus there gives way. Seawater passes between the two halves. Not much. Enough to tickle. Enough to cause drag. Enough to slow you down. Enough to get you eaten.

For the first time in your life, you are afraid. The warm tropical water now feels cold. Your caudal region is blind. You have never been without that sense before. Your fluke has never split before. Not like this. Not while being pursued by a trulluk. Not during such a marathon of a chase.

You have no idea how close the trulluk is now. But you do not dare look back to see where it is. You know it is there. You know it is gaining. You know it is angry. Worst of all, you know you do not have much left.

This just may be your death. This just may be the end.

***

You believe this planet is trying to kill you.

We are not surprised.

But you are wrong.

This planet is not trying to kill you.

We are.

Who are we, you ask?

We are the double star your ocean world revolves around. We are the source of the powerful, unending electromagnetic pulses that have been bombarding your ocean world for millennia.

Our pulses are the reason your ancestors could not establish a technological foothold when they landed here thousands of years ago. Our pulses are the reason your people cannot build man-made structures upon the islands of your ocean world. Our pulses are the reason you and your ancestors have evolved into an efficient, water-dependent, human-fish hybrid.

That may come as a shock. Yes, we bred you. You are the decisive result of hundreds of years of careful genetic modification. You exist because we want you to exist.

But we have become exasperated with your people. You are unambitious. You are lazy. You are complacent. We expected your collective intelligent quotient to be much higher than it is now.

As such, we have not diminished the power of our pulses. We have not ceased their transmission. We will continue at this rate and at this strength. We will ensure survival of the fittest.

Today, your colony has less than one thousand people. Your colony is on its way to extinction. Soon, your colony will be no more. And then, we will start over.

We may keep you. But only you. You have responded well to our machinations (and let's be honest; that is what they are). You are better than the others. You are faster than the others. You are stronger than the others.

However, we are not so certain you are smarter than the others. Just look at you. Just look at this situation in which you have found yourself. That trulluk is not very smart. But you have yet to outlast her. You have yet to outpace her. You have yet to outwit her.

Prior to three hours ago, we would have said you are well on your way to peak evolutionary fitness. We had thought you would be the first of your people to do so. Until now, none of your people has survived the level of difficulty and the variety of challenges you have experienced with your foolishness. We had high hopes for you. We looked forward to swelling with pride as your intelligence increased.

And yet, you disappointed us. You should not have been confused by that shiver of female trulluks. Yes, it was nine leagues beyond the Blue Coral Reef. And yes, at this depth and in this water column adolescent female trulluks frolic and play in shivers of twenty or less. But you only needed to use your eyes.

Now, we will admit, we did not make it easy for you. We never do. We obscured the size of the shiver. We did not want you to gauge how many trulluks there were on first glance. With well-timed pulses, we made visibility poor. We made the trulluks to play with such vigor the water churned. We made their attacks on each other swift and brutal.

At that moment, you should have known something was wrong. You should have vacated the area. You should have used that speed of yours you take so much pleasure in bragging to everyone about and continued on to your tryst with Dawud. You would have been early for once. Dawud would have been pleased.

But you stayed. You were fascinated. You could not help but watch.

Their long bills speared. Their curved tails whipped. Their sharp, triangular teeth snapped. Thick, ragged, torn, white and blue and silver chunks of their flesh floated to the ocean floor. Red clouds of blood fogged the water.

You could taste it through your gills. You could taste it on your tongue. It was sharp. It was heady. It was delicious.

You had never seen adolescent female trulluks in such frenzy before. And then, after far too long, realization struck: these were not adolescent female trulluks. This was not play. This was no game.

These female trulluks had just reached maturity. These female trulluks were establishing the dominance hierarchy for their shiver. These female trulluks were determining the alpha, the strongest female, down the ranks to the omega, the weakest female.

And yet, you still did not flee.

You wanted to play. You wanted a game. You wanted danger. You wanted a thrill. So, you swam into their midst. All fifty of them. You wanted to aid the omega female. You wanted to give her a fighting chance of surviving the ritual.

You went about it in your usual flashy way. You somersaulted over the thrusts of their long, pointed bills. You twisted away from slaps of their curved tails. You twirled beneath the chomps of their sharp teeth. You were enjoying yourself. But you were also infuriating the alpha female.

We are not surprised she pursued you for more than three hours. We are not surprised her stamina has not yet flagged. We are not surprised her determination has not yet wavered. You meddled where you should not have.

But we admire your foolhardiness. It will one day get you killed, no doubt, but we like it. You are entertaining to watch.

But you are also arrogant. You are immature. You are conceited. And that we do not like.

You believe this ocean world is your playground. You believe this ocean world is at your beck and call. You believe this ocean world flows its currents and blows its winds to meet your needs and satisfy your desires.

That does not sit well with us. This ocean world is ours. It revolves around us. Its currents flow and its winds blow because of our gravity well. Because of our push and pull. Because of our electromagnetic pulses. We are the twin stars. We regulate life in this solar system. We are the reason for this Dark Age. Do not forget it.

Look, now you have upset us. We did not think our creation, as almost perfect as you are, would turn out this way. You are selfish. You are stupid. You are haughty. You are reckless.

No prospector in your mating shoal swims faster than you do. No prospector in your mating shoal ventures farther or deeper into the Marijani Sea than you do. No prospector in your mating shoal discovers more expansive, virgin coral reefs than you do. And no prospector in your mating shoal stalks, catches, and feasts on larger fatfish or more succulent clawfish than you do.

You are an exceptional specimen of human-fish hybrid. You could be your colony's leader.

You know where the largest fatfish run and the most succulent clawfish crawl. You could provide your colony with the choicest meat. But you won't.

You know where a series of atolls stand with beautiful coral encircling untouched, lush islands. You could relocate your colony to a better coral reef habitat the trulluks cannot penetrate. But you won't.

You know where to find secluded, stress-free coral mating lagoons with no threat of trulluks. You could save your colony from extinction. But you won't.

You refuse to share any of this information with your colony. You refuse to fulfill your role as a prospector. You refuse to propagate.

All because you do not want to be a mature adult. All because you do not want to take on responsibility. All because you do not want to marry Dawud and have children with him.

All because you only want to frolic and play in the ocean.

We are not pleased. We are not pleased with any of that. In fact, we are disappointed.

***

The reef edge comes up fast. You go over the side. You free fall down the drop-off. Deep, dark, black water waits below. You want the darkness to snatch you. You want the darkness to hide you. You want the darkness to comfort you. You want the darkness to love you. You want to nestle in the bosom of the darkness and sleep. Forever, if you must.

But you will have no such luxury.

Your legs fly apart. The mucus has dissolved. The force of the sudden separation flings you sideways. Heels overhead. Over and over and over again. With a deliberate, slow-motion patience. Down into the deep, dark, black water.

It is a calm, peaceful descent.

And then, the trulluk shatters your tranquility.

You feel her surge before you see her. She is above you. She is coming for you. Her mouth is open. Her jaws are pushed forward. Her teeth are ready. Seawater rushes into her gorge. You can feel its pull. Your legs flail and kick and thrust and—

—then the deep, dark, black water swallows you whole.

You do not know how long you fall. Perhaps one minute. Perhaps one hour. You do not mind. You do not fret. You do not panic. You enjoy the quiet. You enjoy the black.

You blackout.

It is the oddest feeling to blackout while conscious. But that is what the deep, dark, black water does. It snatches memory. It snatches time. It snatches body. It snatches soul.

And when the deep, dark, black water is done with you, it gives you back. Not all of you. Some of you it keeps. Some of your time. Some of your memory. Some of your body. Some of your soul.

The bit of you the deep, dark, black water does not return it adds to the quiet. It adds to the black. Forever you will mingle. Forever you will exist.

But you will not know you are within the quiet. You will not know you are a part of the black. Not until you die.

You do not want to die.

So, you fill both of your lateral swim bladders with gas. Your descent is halted. You float, weightless, embraced by the deep, dark, black water. Your skin shifts from silvery blue, matching the sunlit water far above, to matte black, matching the quiet, matching the black.

You can see nothing. Not even the webbed hand before your face. A familiarity tugs at the liminal space between your subconscious and conscious. This must have been how it was in the womb.

More time passes. Perhaps ten minutes. Perhaps ten days. You feel rested. You feel relaxed. You feel sleepy. But you stay alert. You heighten your senses.

You extend your sail fin through a groove in your back. We have designed you well. Your sail fin is covered with hundreds of sensory cells. These cells feel the trulluk's displacement of water. She is out there. She is searching for you. She is here with you. She wants to devour you.

So, you prepare.

You re-secrete the super-tacky mucus through the skin of your caudal region. Your thighs fuse together. Your calves fuse together. New scales regenerate and seal the cleft. This is your slinky tail.

The mucus triggers a chemical reaction within your body. Your feet fuse together. Your toes stretch and bend. This is your curved fluke.

In three seconds, your sirenomelia form is complete.

And now, it is time for you to have some fun.

Your skin flares with a quick succession of color—brown, red, orange, yellow, blue, silver—ending in a brilliant flash of white. The trulluk is blinded by the after-image of your bright form. She is disoriented. She has no infrared vision now. She thrashes—tail, head, fin, teeth—flailing in the black.

She hopes to find you. She hopes to grab you. She hopes to rip and tear and smash and rend you and your once again matte black skin.

But you avoid every strike. You feel the pressure shifts in the deep, dark, black water long before they reach you. You spin and whirl and turn and flip. You laugh at her clumsiness. You whoop at her wild misses. She cannot see you. She cannot touch you. She cannot eat you.

And then, she touches you.

The trulluk smashes her broad, heavy tail against the drop-off. She is a clever girl. Hard, rock-like coral cascades down upon you, striking you on your head and your shoulders and your back and your tail. Instinct takes over. You retract your sail fin. You empty your swim bladders. You flatten your fluke. And—

—then, as you two are so very fond of saying, I dive further into the black.

My forehead is bleeding. I do not stop. My back is bruised. I do not slow. I see a white pinprick of light far below.

My head, just beneath my skull, feels swollen and tight. My sinuses, just behind my nose, feel pinched and compressed. Touch is distant. Light is absent. Except for the pinprick.

It is getting closer. It is getting larger. It is getting brighter. This must be how it is when you die.

But I will not die. I will not die today. I will not die tomorrow. I will not die before I reach Dawud.

You two search for me. My twin stars. Jata and Nyota. My god and my goddess. My creators. My destroyers.

You look and you look in the black. But you do not see me. You do not see the trulluk. You cannot believe we have eluded you. You are frustrated. You are flabbergasted. You are gob smacked. You are blind. Just like the trulluk.

I enter the bright and wind my way through the underwater tunnels beneath the Blue Coral Reef. Bright, glowing sea creatures line the walls and guide my way. The trulluk will not be able to enter once she regains her sight. The cave opening is too small. I designed our new city this way. It seems I am not stupid after all.

It does not take me long to reach the underground lake. I surface. I take a deep breath. My lungs fill with cavern air. The air triggers a chemical reaction within my body. My legs separate. My feet harden. My scales smooth out. My webbing retracts. My matte black skin shifts three shades lighter.

I climb out of the lake. Dawud stands on the cavern shore. He looks at my forehead. He takes me in his arms. He kisses me. I kiss him back.

"They will come," I tell him, after I have had my fill of him. "All of them."

He smiles. He is proud of me. "When?"

"Tomorrow. They will migrate here over the next few days." I touch my forehead. There is not much blood. But it is tender.

Dawud places a hand on my belly. "And how is our little one?"

"She is fine." I cover his hand with mine.

He barks a laugh. It echoes off the rocky cavern walls and the high ceiling. "She, you say?"

"Yes." A playful smile touches my lips. "She, I know." It seems I can propagate.

I want to kiss him again, but the others are coming. They stream in from an endless series of underwater caves. This is our new city. It seems I can relocate to a better habitat.

The others want news of our old city. They want news of their families and their friends and their loved ones. I take Dawud's hand and lace our fingers. They will be pleased to hear our people will be one again.

You won't.

I am surprised by you two. You have yet to realize your electromagnetic pulses do not travel well through seawater at this depth. Or you don't care.

This is what happens when you become bored with us. This is what happens when you turn your full attention away from us. This is what happens when you favor the other planets in your precious system.

We plot against you. We take back our lives. We propagate. We survive.

A TRYST THAT CUTS BOTH WAYS
BY
K. CERES WRIGHT

The New Regime formed and declared independence from the Cassad Empire, which has begun to weaken from within. As the Perimeter worlds expand, so do the ambitions of their inhabitants. Families whose interests include investments and banking form alliances, spy out rivals, and map out their own agendas. The games begin; beware the players.
-Samake. Cassad djele/historian. From The Cassad Chronicles

Kalinda ran her fingers down the frayed cover of the Wayfarer prayer book. The black leather was dry and cracked, curling tan at the edges. The book contained just eight pages, the rest having been lost long ago to the ravages of time, war, and relocation. She could only read a few paragraphs. The Wayfare language hadn't thrived among the descendants of the One Million after settlement on distant planets, and she had forgotten most of what she had been taught as a child. She opened to the first page and read.

"Father of the heavens, stars, and galaxies, watch over our journey and deliver us to solid ground. Let our daily bread be sufficient, our fuel abundant, and water overflowing. Guide us by Thy hand among the beacons of the eternal night, until Your light leads us to our future."

Her reading was interrupted by Kobe, her butler, whose voice sounded overhead, through the speakers.

"Oba Jakande, your cousin, Mr. Okeke, is on the line."

"Thank you, Kobe. Please put him through."

After a moment, Kalinda said, "Zuberi, to what do I owe the pleasure?"

"Cut the shit, Kal. I heard you've been making a deal with the Kur Dak behind my back. Is that true? I thought we signed a truce."

"The terms of our agreement are, and I quote, 'Neither party will engage in business transactions or mergers that infringe upon the core business of the other party.' But this deal doesn't have to do with investment banking, stocks, or commodities. It's for a ...different type of product," Kalinda said.

"Oh, yeah? What is it? Weapons? Winter wheat? Woolly mammoths?"

"How'd you guess?" she said drily.

"I swear, if you've violated our agreement, I'll file suit, and once your new client get wind of that news, I wonder how long they'll stick around."

"Your desperation is showing, cousin. And I must say, it's quite unbecoming," Kalinda said.

"Damnit, Kal, is it true or not?"

She paused, considering what to tell him. "Remember, oh, about six months ago, you lent money to the Global Bank of The Tennance and wouldn't tell me what it was for?"

An audible sigh sounded overhead. "Fine. It was for repairs to the Hampton Gate."

"Ah...don't tell me...the Perimeter Worlds want to keep it hush-hush that they're being attacked by the Green Federation."

"Bad for business," Zuberi said. "They officially said the gate was down for maintenance. But there are rumors to the contrary, which I'm actively trying to suppress. So...what's your story?"

"The Kur Dak want to dip their toe into Cassad investments, but are ignorant of the ways of humans. I'm just a teacher of human customs...and investment strategy.

Zuberi let out a long, low whistle. "Mbutu said they were getting money from somewhere and were looking for somewhere to put it. I was wondering when they'd come sniffing around. I don't know about you, Kal, but I'm starting to think these events are not unrelated. Kur Dak new-found money, gate sabotage by the Federation. I wouldn't be surprised if the Brythons were behind it."

"You always suspect the Brythons. Of everything. It's getting tiresome."

"There've been rumors, Kent and his father, Percival, are up to something more than usual Brython ambition. I think it has to do with what we're talking about, especially the attacks on the gates."

Kalinda paused. She didn't pay much attention to gate shutdowns since she rarely traveled to other planets. Most of them were backwater wilderness on which families had carved out some small oasis of civilization. And the Clusters were noisy with the constant din of construction.

"For once in your life, you may have a valid opinion," she said.

Zuberi guffawed. "Love you, too, cuz."

"How about dinner, say, tomorrow? My place. Five."

"Grat with hoka nuts?"

Kal chuckled. "And pear clafouti for desert."

"You're on. See you then."

As soon as the line closed, an arm encircled her waist. She gasped in surprise and twisted around to confront the culprit.

"Kent! What are you do—"

An urgent kiss interrupted her, and she melted into it, surrendering to the warm wetness of it. He pulled her closer, the bulge in his pants meeting her mons. Kalinda moaned and sank further into his embrace. They broke, both panting heavily. She looked up into dark brown eyes and a mop of black hair that fell just below the eyebrows.

"How'd you get in?" she said.

"Old habits."

"Old habits?"

"Yeah, you didn't bother hanging the door code on the sentry bot. I keep telling you to be more mindful of security," he said.

She smiled. "No point in arguing. "How much did you hear?"

"Ever vigilant. Something about, oh, repairs to the Hampton Gate, Kur Dak investments. Oh, and Brython conspiracies."

Kal leaned back in surprise. "That much?"

"Don't worry, darling." He kissed her on the nose. "Your secrets are safe with me. And now, enough talk."

He picked her up and carried her to the bedroom.

***

A shaft of sunlight streamed through the heavy burgundy curtains and landed on Kalinda's eyes. She awoke and turned her head to shield her face from the intruding illumination. The sight of Kent's black hair and muscled torso greeted her. She smiled as she ran a hand along his shoulder, noting the contrast of his pale skin and her terracotta. He stirred, and then settled back into sleep. It usually took a Cassad army to wake him, so she slid out of bed, closed the curtain to complete darkness, and stepped into the bathroom.

A tub stood on a dais against a backdrop of four columns that opened onto the Red Forest, named for its abundance of red-leafed trees.

"Open curtain and run water," she said. The gauzy teal curtains drew back, allowing the sun to break through onto the white porcelain tile. A long, thin faucet that ran the length of the tub protracted from the top edge and poured forth steaming water. In minutes, the tub was filled, with a layer of bubbles sitting atop.

Kalinda stepped gingerly into the hot water and slowly sat. The fragrance of laressa flowers wafted up. She closed her eyes and relished the perfumed warmth.

"Mind if I join you?"

Kalinda opened her eyes and tilted her head back to see Kent leaning over her. He placed a kiss on her lips, and then dipped his tongue behind her teeth as he reached a hand into the water and cupped her left breast, running a thumb along her nipple. Her breath caught and he grinned.

"So, what garden path are you going to lead the Kur Dak down?" He stepped around the tub and climbed inside.

"Kur Dak? And what line have you been feeding the Green Federation? Getting them to do your dirty work?" She pulled him closer as he nestled between her legs.

"They're just malicious rumors." He buried his head in the curve of her shoulder and bit her neck.

"Bullshit," she moaned. "You're up to something." She ran her fingers through his hair and breathed in his scent.

"This is the only thing I'm up to." He slid inside her and rocked his hips back and forth. The water undulated with his movements, lapping against the walls of the tub. Kalinda bit his ear and dug her fingertips into the firm muscles of his back.

"I must say…it's a brilliant plan…your only mistake…was to allow the Kur Dak…to find out." She spoke between gasps.

"Who's to say…we didn't want…them to know?"

Realization and orgasm dovetailed, culminating in enlightened ecstasy. She cried out, satisfied in both mind and body. Kent soon followed, locking his stride and tensing his body. A low groan vibrated his chest, and he shuddered, and then stilled.

"You want the Kur Dak involved in local investments, to throw Cassad suspicion on them, not the Federation, while the Brythons insert themselves into the Perimeter Worlds. You're letting the Kur Dak blackmail you." She heaved a sigh and kissed his cheek.

"You make a great Brython," he whispered.

"You mean you make a great Jakande." They both laughed.

***

"The projected commissions from the Kur Dak investments are netting abut twenty million Kwacha a month." Abena was Kalinda's executive assistant, and was organized where Kalinda was not.

"What about our terraforming? The planets along the Perimeter Worlds? And Jakande II in the Cluster?"

Abena sat in a chair clustered with a sofa and a loveseat in front of a fireplace. Kalinda stood in front of a large picture window that overlooked Dakarai Park, named after her father.

"Jakande II and III are pretty much complete with final touches being performed as we speak. Jakande IV is in phase two, with animals being introduced, and Jakande V is still in the first phase, with soil sample studies."

"Soil samples? I thought we were preparing for plantings."

"We were, but scientists found anomalies, which they refuse to explain at the moment."

"Refuse to explain?" Kal turned and stared at Abena as if she were one of the scientists.

"Said they needed more time."

"Tell the group leader I want to see him in my office in an hour." She didn't have time for their games, and it wasn't on their dime. It was her money funding the project, and she was going to wring every Kwacha out of it.

"Will do. That it?"

"Send in Jabari on your way out. Thank you, Abena."

Abena nodded and left. Kal sat behind her desk, erect, trying to look as imposing as possible. After a moment, a man walked in. He was 6'3", 230 pounds, and sported shoulder-length dreads that matched Kalinda's.

"You wanted to see me?"

"Yes, the Brythons are paying the Green Federation to destroy the gates of the Perimeter Worlds and allowing the Kur Dak to blackmail them. I need you to find out who the players are on all sides."

Jabari put his hands on his hips and scowled at her. "Why don't you just ask your husband?"

Kalinda's eyes narrowed. "Keep your voice down. And I suppose if I asked him, I wouldn't need you. If you don't want the money..." She trailed off, shrugging her shoulders.

Jabari heaved a sigh. "All right. But one day, I'll get a straight answer out of you."

Kalinda ignored his comment. "How long will it take to do the job?"

"If I call in a few marks, couple hours."

"Do it. Report back as soon as possible. Thank you, Jabari."

He nodded, and then left without a word. As soon as the door shut behind him, Kalinda called a number and spoke cryptically to the person on the other end.

"I'm requesting a meeting. Tonight, 5:30, Red Leaf Forest, under the oak tree."

***

Kalinda gazed at the table before her, spread with flowered plates, gold chargers and silverware, and crystal glasses. A flower centerpiece that matched the plates completed the look.

"Excellent, Kobe. Thank you," Kalinda said. She turned to her butler, who bowed his head slightly in acknowledgment.

"Thank you," he said.

A chime sounded, and Zuberi and his wife, Yejide, walked in. The butler made a discreet exit as the group greeted each other and sat at the table.

"Still without a husband, I see," Yejide said.

"One day, Yejide. One day," Kalinda replied. She had long ago become inured to Yejide's veiled insults. Kalinda made a slight hand gesture of twisting her ring around her finger. It looked innocuous to the casual viewer, but told Kobe to hurry dinner along by bringing out the dishes as quickly as possible and clearing them as soon as the last bite was swallowed. He and the chef momentarily brought out the main dish and the wine.

"Mmm, my favorite," Zuberi said, breathing deeply over his plate.

"Well, you requested it." Kalinda took a deep draught of her wine, waiting for it to kick in.

"So, tell me, how are your investments going?" Yejide said.

"I'm terraforming four planets and just discovered today that one of them holds a reserve of verenge ore," Kalinda replied.

Zuberi stopped chewing and stared at her.

"Verenge ore. That's for…" Yejide trailed off, waiting for Kalinda to fill in the blank. She obviously didn't know what it was used for.

"For coating spaceships to protect the passengers from cosmic radiation. Rather rare. In fact, my head scientist was reluctant to tell me about it. I had to threaten to throw him off planet before he would admit it."

"Really?" Yejide said. "He thought he would take it all for himself?"

"Oh, I'm sure he would have let me have a 20 percent stake."

"In your own planet," Zuberi said, chuckling. He had finished the grat and was working on the hoka nuts.

"Exactly," Kalinda said. "How generous of him."

"It's so hard to find good help nowadays," Yejide said.

As Kalinda took a bite of grat, the stone on her ring blinked twice. She cursed under her breath, then stood up. Zuberi and Yejide looked up at her, surprised.

"My apologies. I'm suddenly not feeling very well, but I don't want to ruin your dinner. Please, finish, and accept an invitation to a future dinner." With that, Kalinda turned and left.

Once out of sight of her guests, she hurried down the long hallway to a side door that led to the Red Leaf Forest. Kalinda placed her hand on the bio-ident and the door slid noiselessly open. She ran along the dirt trail to an oak tree that had been planted there when her family first arrived, 30 years ago. They had brought several acorns with them on the long journey, but only one had survived.

A hooded figure stood under the tree. At the sound of Kalinda's steps, the figure pulled a weapon and trained it on her. Kalinda threw up her hands.

"It's me, Oba Kalinda Jakande," she whispered loudly.

The figure relaxed and withdrew the weapon, then pulled back the hood. It revealed a short woman with a closely cropped afro and large eyes that shone like the full moon.

"My name is Makena. I represent Alaafin Nala Cassad, ruler of the empire."

Kalinda nodded. "Okay. I have information."

"What kind of information?"

"Well, you swear to secrecy?"

"Of course. I have been a Representative since I was 13 sun turns."

"Sun turns, eh? You sure speak differently on the Cluster Worlds. Okay, I'll make this quick. I'm secretly married to Kent Penry, of the Brythons. I found out that they're looking to insert themselves into the Perimeter Worlds while paying the Federation to sabotage gates and letting the Kur Dak blackmail them. With these funds, the Dak will invest in Cassad bonds, which will throw suspicion on the Dak that they're getting a toe hold in the area, but don't let that fool you. It's the Brythons you have to be worried about. And something else you should be worried about."

"What?" Makena said.

"The Alaafin's son, Mosi, is leading the saboteurs."

"Impossible!"

"Oh, it's more than possible. Here, look at these holo-crystals." Kalinda pulled out the crystals that Jabari had given her. She activated the first one, which showed Mosi and five other members of the Federation setting explosives on the Hampton Gate and then running off, just before it blew.

"This was obviously tampered with," Makena said.

"My information source is impeccable. But I would suggest you have your people do some digging. If this gets out, the Alaafin would surely be blackmailed or forced out of office."

Makena didn't say anything, but just stared at Kalinda.

"You're welcome," Kalinda said.

"Why are you sacrificing your life being married to a Brython?"

"It's not a sacrifice. I love Kent. And he loves me. Of that I'm sure. Of course, his family wouldn't approve, and mine would be looked on with suspicion, so we kept it quiet. And there's the added bonus of not having to see each other every day and getting tired of one another. But it's bigger than us. I want to ensure the descendants of the One Million thrive, no matter what."

"But how do you know he isn't using you the same way? Giving the Brythons information on the One Million?"

"He likely is," Kalinda said. "But it's a chance I'm willing to take. I think I'm the better spy, but it's hard to say, for sure. It's…complicated. But it's worth it."

Makena nodded.

"I'll call when I get more information. I also have four planets that can be used as bases when it all goes down. Let the Alaafin know."

"I will."

"All right. See you next time." Kalinda turned and walked back down the dirt trail, hoping Zuberi didn't eat all the grat, and wondering who Kent was eating dinner with.

ONCE SPOKEN

BY

BALOGUN OJETADE

During the Dark Age isolation and deprivation sparked unique evolution. For some the mutations were biological; for others they manifested in technical manipulations. But for a small population of humans on the planet of Atunbé, an adaptation occurred that could not be defined. It made them desirable, dangerous... and hunted.
-Samake, djele/historian. From The Cassad Chronicles

I. Slaughter at Once Spoken

The strangers came under a red half-moon to Once Spoken, a tiny village in Buruku State on the planet Atunbé. They wore strange clothes – stiff-looking black and red jumpsuits of foreign design, with red hats with wide brims. Their weather-beaten faces were half-concealed under carefully-manicured beards. On their belts they carried guns, all but the one woman among them, who walked a few paces ahead of the rest. She carried no weapons and seemed to wear a perpetual easy smile.

Ogunlana Dako and his sister, Koya, watched the strangers as they approached.

"He is so handsome," Koya said nodding toward one of the men. They were watching the strangers sit high upon their bikange as they rode past the Once Spoken – effigies that gave the village its name. The stone statues, ancient guardians of this small, distant place, stared at the men without seeing. Their power had weakened over generations: Now they were little more than mute stone and no one in the village could remember ever hearing them speak.

Dako felt a tingling at the tip of his fingers. He saw with his inner eye: The leader rode unarmed because her power was great. The aura of ashé around her was unmistakable. Unease made Dako close his fingers into a fist. The woman, passing close to them, glanced casually their way. He could smell the foul breath of her ekange – a large, spotted creature not unlike the hyenas of earth he learned about in Earth History class. The leader's eyes locked on Dako's for one long, uncomfortable moment. Then her gaze shifted to Koya and his smile flared up like a small sun.

* * *

There was a celebration that night in the center of the village as the elders welcomed the strangers. Fires burned and the strangers ate bowls of noodles made from the eggs of the nocturnal angile turtle and roasted Biped. The strangers complained about the heat of the Atunbéan spices. But not their leader, whose skin seemed to glow with an internal fire no chili could ever match. There was a fire in her eyes, too, and it flamed brighter when she watched Koya.

She had eyes for no one else.

"Who are these strangers?" Dako pondered. "Why have they come to Once Chosen?"

Nobody came to Once Chosen 'just because'. They also never came to cause trouble. The village was small but very wealthy and also of great importance to the military dealings of Atunbé, so most of the villagers felt safe that they would never be attacked by outsiders. No one would dare incur the wrath of the most skilled tacticians and martial artists in the Known.

Had anyone been aware of Atunbé's most guarded secret – that everyone on the planet possessed psionic abilities – they would have also been viewed as the greatest threat to Cassad.

But unlike the rest of Atunbé, Once Spoken's focus was making money, not war.

When the Iwuje, or Galaxy-Stone fell from the sky one clear night half a century before, a small but prosperous mining industry formed in Once Spoken. The village dug for and then sold talismans of the ashe-rich stone to high-ranking Research and Development officers in the Divisions of Atunbé, who used the talismans in the creation of weapons and machines that channeled ashe and enhanced psionic ability.

The visitors were greeted by the village elder, Lieutenant Mohan Abacha. A Petty Officer stood at Lieutenant Abacha's rear and at both flanks.

"Greetings!" Lt. Abacha said, bringing his fingertips to his brow in salute. "I am Lieutenant Mohan Abacha, elder of the three Companies that comprise our beautiful village. Welcome to Once Chosen!"

"My name is Dey Valu," the leader of the visitors said.

"Her voice is as deep and rich as the fresh water ocean of our moon," one of the villagers whispered. He was about to say something else, but someone nearby shushed him.

"We are members of an expeditionary mission seeking investment opportunities in Buruku State," Dey Valu continued. "We are forming a New Regime that will soon rule the planets beyond the Known."

"And since Atunbé is at the fringes of the Known, it is easier to do business with us, as we are the closest planet with enough wealth to give you a good return on your investment, is that correct?" Lt. Abacha said.

"That is correct," Dey Valu replied.

Lt. Abacha was silent. He locked his gaze on Dey Valu's chest.

Dako knew the elder was reading Dey Valu's surface thoughts.

From the time he could understand words, Dako's father had taught him the history of Atunbé and how its people came to develop psionics:

Atunbé lay on the outskirts of the Cassad Empire. Rich in minerals, but – due to its harsh, arid environment and sandy terrain – lacking any flora or fauna, the Cassad Empire deemed the planet invaluable for habitation and dispatched a small colony of miners, geologists, engineers and chemists (and their families) to the planet to mine and gather her resources.

Unknown to the Cassad, Atunbé was plagued by a severe alien infestation. The colony on Atunbé called for help and the

Empire dispatched their elite, brutal "Swick" – Special Warfare Combatant, Craft Crewman – Division to quell the infestation and then to hold the planet until the infestation in that sector of the Empire was put down.

Upon arrival on Atunbé, the Swicks found most of the male population dead or severely injured, thus the all-male Swicks eventually took wives among the colonists.

Food soon became scarce on the planet and the population of Atunbé resorted to eating the flesh of their alien enemies in order to survive.

The citizens of Atunbé began to notice that eating alien flesh enhanced their senses and increased their intelligence. Soon, the Atunbéans began to develop permanent enhancements to their senses and mental capacities at incredible levels. These enhancements made them more capable of protecting themselves from the infestation and, indeed, made them the deadliest opponents of the aliens. They called the manifested powers Psionics and the fuel for that power, the energy found in all things, ashe. But ashe depletes with use. Psionics and other manifestations of ashe's power weakens. Thus, men must seek new sources of power.

"You may stay the night and we will discuss business matters in the morning," Lt. Abacha said. "I will send a Petty Officer or two to escort you to your quarters. Do not wander off. We have strict protocols in Once Chosen."

"We are well aware of Atunbé's military structure," Dey Valu said with a slight bow. "We would not dare violate your rules and regulations."

Dey Valu performed feats of prestidigitation and illusion for the children, making coins appear out of nowhere, fire dance, and changing tadpoles from a nearby stream into a five-toed chicken. She also read fortunes using four sandfish shells.

While Dey Valu put on her show, her eyes remained fixed on Koya, who was not oblivious to the attention, and whose pretty face had turned as red and warm as fire. Dako left the other children, using psionics on them to mask his passing. Though he had just reached puberty, he knew his ashe was strong. He inhaled it; breathing ashe in like it was air. He let it guide him, until he found himself, at last, standing below the three Once Spoken.

The Once Spoken towered above him, their gentle, wind-swept faces staring into nothingness. He put his hand against one of the statues. The stone was warm; pulsing. The statue's pulse spread into Dako's fingers, causing them to tingle. After a few moments, the tingling in his fingers increased, growing into a pain that spread up his arm.

Dako wailed in agony. He pulled his hand away from the stone.

A crimson mist rose in the distance, over the roofs of the village. Dako stared up at the statues. Something was happening to them. Their shapes softened, their color changed from gray to pitch black. They seemed to move, to sway in an invisible wind. Dako stared – in horror? Excitement? He did not know – as the blind faces turned and their stone mouths opened. For the first time in centuries, the Once Spoken had come alive.

They screamed.

Dako covered his ears, but the screams dug into his nerves like great spears. He cried out in pain, running away from the Once Spoken, towards the village. The crimson mist was growing, but Dako was nearly half-way back before he realized what he saw:

The entire village was in flames.

He heard shouts, panicked cries. Gunfire pierced the night. A bright light rose above the village. Dako squinted at it, studying it. The light was a fireball, which hovered for almost a full minute before swooping down upon the village and the villagers.

People ran, screaming. But there was nowhere to hide.

The fireball engulfed the villagers, smothering their screams.

The strangers rode through the burning alleyways and roads, their snarling bikange blocking escape.

Dako watched in horror as the strangers gathered the young and the fit while they let the elderly burn. He watched his cousins and friends being herded and roped together like cattle.

"Koya!" He thought.

Dako ran, wrapping himself in shadow to avoid detection by the strangers.

He arrived at a clearing of packed earth in the center of the village.

There, he saw Dey Valu standing in a circle of flame. Her hands burned unharmed, and from her fingers, fire streamed forth, engulfing the entire village.

Standing beside her, as mute as iron, was Koya. Flames were in her eyes. She did not move.

Crying, Dako charged toward his sister and the leader of the strangers who had destroyed his village. The shadows fell away from him.

Dako raised his hands. A ball of green energy formed before him. He cast it at Dey Valu.

Dey Valu turned, laughing. She extended her hands and caught the green ball of energy. In her hands, the ball of ashe formed by Dako's mind turned black. It then crumbled and then floated away, like black steam rising from Dey Valu's palms.

"You think you can take me, boy? You?" Dey Valu sounded amused, not angry. "You think your people are the only ones who can focus and control their ashe?"

"My sister!" Dako shouted. "What have you done to her?"

He felt his ashe rise all around him, power such as he had not ever known – not even dreamed of – before it surged within him. Dako reached out with his mind, sending out invisible, thread-thin tendrils that searched the scorched ground around him. He felt the presence of a fist sized, jagged stone behind Dey Valu. He focused, causing it to rise. Dako forced the stone to rocket toward the back of Dey Valu's head.

Dey Valu ducked, just before the stone struck her, evading the blow.

Dako clutched his fists. The stone exploded above Dey Valu. Shards of stone rained down upon her.

Dey Valu released a low gasp. She returned her gaze toward Dako. Blood poured from a gash in her cheek. She no longer looked amused.

Dey Valu raised her hand. A green javelin seemed to form out of nowhere between her fingers.

Dako knew he could not stop it. Moving the stone and making it explode had temporarily depleted his ashe and had physically fatigued him. He stood his ground, preparing to die.

Dey Valu paused. "Do you fear for Koya's life after you die?" she said. Some of the amusement had crept back into her voice. "You shouldn't. I will look after her; Make her my wife...on a planet that is amenable to such things. Who would have thought to find, on this Gods-forsaken planet of Biped eaters, a girl almost more beautiful than ashe?'

"I won't let you take her!" Dako shouted

"Brave words," Dey Valu said with a shrug. "And futile."

"Please," Koya said. Her voice was muffled. Her words, slurred. Her lips barely moved, enslaved by flame. "Don't hurt him. Let him go."

"I'm afraid that I can't do that," Dey Valu said, still aiming the psionic spear at Ogunlana Dako. "Your people are well trained in mining for ashe, and will make valuable workers, but your brother is too headstrong to serve me."

Dey Valu turned her attention back to Ogunlana Dako. "On my planet, we call a skilled wielder of ashe an ndoki – a sorcerer – and our abilities kindoki – magic. Do you consider yourself a sorcerer, boy? Or are you simply a soldier like the rest of your people"

Dey Valu did not wait for an answer. "Since you are my brother-in-law, I will give you a chance. Live as a sorcerer, or die as a soldier."

Dey Valu lifted a large shell, which hung from a leather strap at her waist, to her lips. She blew into it and a deep howl echoed across the night sky.

A few seconds later, her ekange padded up to her. In one swift motion, Dey Valu was on her steed's back with Koya behind her in the saddle.

Dako tried to move, but his fatigue and Dey Valu's powerful "magic" immobilized him.

Dey Valu's men appeared, dragging with them the remnants of Ogunlana Dako's people. One of the men drove a cart pulled by three bikange. The cart was loaded with iron chests. Each chest was packed full of Galaxy-Stone talismans – an entire autumn's work.

"We ride," Dey Valu said, trotting away from the village center. Her men followed him.

Dako struggled to reach out with his mind. To find one last stone to hurl.

The sight of Dey Valu riding back toward her, grinning as she raised the psionic javelin above his shoulder, brought Dako's thoughts to a screeching halt.

Dey Valu hurled the javelin. It streaked through the air, landing between Dako's feet.

A moment later, flames engulfed him.

"Live as a sorcerer!" Dey Valu's voice came through the smoke, growing distant. "Or die as a soldier...."

Dako was trapped in the flames. He closed his eyes, forcing himself to breathe deeply, to slow the beating of his heart. The flames were the product of Dey Valu's thoughts; an expression of her will, so Dako knew that he could control the flames; render them harmless, if his will was strong enough. He tried to calm himself; to beat back the searing pain of the flames.

The Once Spoken effigies visited him in the midst of the flames. They sang to him an ancient song in a more ancient tongue that Dako had never heard before.

He closed his eyes again and sang along, whispering words he had not known until that very moment.

II. The Cradle

Ogunlana Dako sat alone before the fire. A small ring of blackened stones served to hold the fire in check. Noodles and meat and some wild garlic boiled within a pot that hanged over the fire. He added a few drops of pepper from a small bottle and then stirred the food with a wooden spoon. As he stirred the stew, he observed the night and waited.

After a while, he heard footsteps. He listened for a moment and then relaxed, removing the pot from the fire and served the food into two bowls. The footsteps came closer and then stopped.

"You're a lousy cook," a voice said.

Dako snapped his head toward the voice. An old man, rail thin, with leathery skin heavily wrinkled with age, stood before him.

"Lieutenant Abacha," Dako said. "You took your time."

"I had to be careful, didn't I?" The old man replied. "And how many times do I have to tell you, call me Mohan. Lieutenant Abacha died with his village.

"Even though it has been thirteen years since Once Chosen fell, I am still Ogunlana Dako," Dako said.

He nodded toward the fire. Mohan sat down on the other side of it.

Dako studied Mohan. An eye-patch covered his left eye, and his hair grew long at the back. Over the years, Mohan had taught him much – about psionics; how to kill efficiently and effectively and how to survive in the wasteland created by Dey Valu and her men. But Dako never allowed himself to get too close to the old Lieutenant, which was just fine with Mohan. Until the Atunbéans were able to take back their planet, a man made his own way in life. But at least Mohan was someone he could trust. Within reason.

They ate in silence, shoveling stew into their mouths. When they were done, Dako stretched, leaned back, and then drew a cigar from the inner pocket of his jacket.

Mohan stared at the fire for a moment, and then snapped his fingers. A flame danced between his thumb and forefinger. He brought it to the tip of Dako's cigar. Dako inhaled.

A cloud of indigo smoke escaped from his lips and into the atmosphere. "Well?" he said.

"The mine lies two days' ride away," Mohan replied. "Just as the mapmaker said. It's heavily guarded."

"As could be expected," Dako said.

"And you can't use psionics," Mohan said.

"Oh?" Dako said.

"It is the biggest deposit of ashe to be discovered in nearly a century," Mohan said.

"At the Cradle."

"Yes," Mohan said with a nod. "Any use of psionics there is amplified beyond the user's control.

The place was called the Cradle because it was where the Galaxy-Stone had landed so many decades ago.

"The ashe in the Cradle is too concentrated," Mohan said. "I have never felt such power! The miners dig it out and the artificers shape it into coins and talismans and these are taken away by the soldiers of the Bandoki. I tracked their path. They go across the border, into the wild lands and into Fort Toure. The mine never stops running. The overseers are Bandoki. But the workers are Atunbéan."

"Not being able to use psionics might be a problem," Dako said.

"It could also be an advantage," Mohan said. "They can't use it against you, either."

"They have guns?'

"Of course."

"And beyond the impact area?"

"Traps; patrols," Mohan replied. "Nothing we can't handle."

"They're very confident."

Mohan shrugged. "And why shouldn't they be? They conquered us and the rest of the Known has no clue."

"And they won't until five years from now, when they make their customary twenty-year supply run and inspection," Dako said.

"And when they do, the Bandoki will destroy them," Mohan said.

Dako slipped his shotgun into the sheath on his back and then shrugged. "Guess we gotta destroy them, first."

"Guess so," Mohan replied.

III. Recompense in Scarlet

To make it this far Dako had had to make a deal; and deals made by and with an ndoki was unbreakable. He didn't like what he had had to do, and what he still needed to do. There was always a price to pay.

They rode at dawn. Far in the distance, mountains loomed and giant shapes rose so high they appeared as birds in flight. It was said the legendary Atunbéan dragons dwelled in those mountains; Dako would have liked to have seen one.

They rode upon their three-wheeled ATVs in silence. Mohan hummed tunes from time to time while drumming slow rhythm on the assault rifle that lay across his lap.

Dako psychically scanned the surrounding countryside for signs of psionic activity. He could feel the ashe level slowly rise the farther they advanced. Once, when he turned his head, Dako thought he saw a plume of smoke rising far in the distance, at their back. He checked, but Mohan didn't seem to have noticed it.

They rode until sunset and then set up camp in an abandoned mine.

"Only a day's ride, now," Mohan said.

Dako nodded.

"You could still go back," Mohan said.

Dako smiled. There was an old burn mark on his chest from when Dey Valu left him to die in the psionic flames as a boy. He scratched at it absentmindedly. "Not gonna happen."

Dako laid his head on a rolled-up blanket and then pulled the collar of his poncho over his eyes, shielding them from the brightness of their campfire. After a short while, he nodded off to sleep.

A sliver of sunlight kissed his nose, awakening him.

"Mohan, time to get up," he said, rising to his knees.

Mohan didn't answer.

"Mohan!" Dako called as he peered into the darkness of the mine.

No answer.

Mohan was gone.

Dako rode alone, which suited him.

The ashe rose in the area and with it, his awareness. He focused his mind, probing for the unseen defenses he knew must be present. At noon he came to a village. It was as Mohan had described it. Nothing much remained but blackened foundation stones.

Hanging from one tree he saw a skeleton, strung up with a rope around its neck. It had been dead a long time.

As he stared at the swaying skeleton, he felt a tingling at the tips of his fingers.

The skeleton began to kick its legs, the old bones making a clicking, clattering din with each movement.

Dako jerked his hand upward, pointing his palm at the skeleton. He snapped his fingers and the skeleton crumpled into a cloud of alabaster dust that drizzled onto the burned ground. It had been imbibed with a bit of ashe to act as an alarm system; unable to find peace even in death.

Dako did not dally in the dead village after that.

* * *

The Bandoki knew what they were doing. One of the most powerful conductors for ashe was blood. In fact, in some regions of Atunbé, a woman's menstrual cycle was referred to as 'ashe'.

By shedding blood, they were able to erect walls of solid psionic power around the Cradle. Dako found his progress slowing as he negotiated tapestries of tightly woven psionics. Men and women had died violently on this land, and their ghosts remained, enslaved by the foreigners' "sorcery." They had made a payment in blood. Where he could, Dako released the trapped spirits. His progress was slow. His spirit was muddied by the work. It felt as if his mind was wading through thick, grayish-brown syrup.

Perhaps that was why he did not notice the ambush until it was too late.

IV. A Fistful of Galaxy-Stone

There were four of them, two mounted on bikange with mottled, reddish-brown fur; the other two stood on opposite sides, hands raised; lips moving silently.

Out of nowhere, the wind howled. Dako squeezed the breaks on the handlebars of his ATV, bringing him to a screeching halt.

From the fingertips of the standing men, a wire mesh seemed to erupt, unfolding in the air above Dako.

The mesh descended upon him.

Cursing, Dako closed his eyes, raising his fists above his shoulders to the height of his brow. He spread his fingers as he spread his arms wide.

The wire mesh tore into several pieces and then dissipated into nothingness.

There was much ashe here – too much. Dako heard one of the standing men shout a warning. They drew their pistols, training them on him. The one on the left raised his hands in a universal gesture of calm. "The guns are loaded with Galaxy-Stone," he said. "Come without a fight and you won't be harmed."

"I doubt that," Dako said. He drew his shotgun from the leather sheath on his back with blistering speed. He fired, blowing a chunk out of the skull of one of the bikange. The creature fell over on top of the man who tried to negotiate with Dako, pinning the man under its tremendous weight. It rider rolled in the scorched dirt, landing in a twisted heap. He did not move.

The remaining foreigner on foot and the one atop the surviving ekange opened fire. Dako rolled to his right, evading the shots.

He took cover behind a boulder.

The Bandoki fired a volley of Galaxy-Stone rounds into the boulder. The boulder shook violently and then disintegrated, leaving Dako exposed.

He let loose another blast from his shotgun, hitting the standing Ndoki in the chest.

The Ndoki flew backward, landing on the ground with a dull thud. Smoke billowed from the hole in his chest.

The mounted Ndoki took aim with his pistol.

Dako focused on the man's trigger finger, forcing it backward at an odd angle.

The man screamed in agony.

Dako focused again, raising his hands before his face. He felt the Ndoki's chin and the crest of his head between his palms, even though they were several yards apart. Dako jerked his hands in a circular motion, as if he was untwisting the lid of a large jar.

The Ndoki's head twisted with a loud snap. He fell from his ekange, landing on his chest. His dying eyes gazed at the sky.

Dako saw the shadow of a rifle rising towards him. He whirled toward it, but was too late. He had been careless; too focused on the enemies before him. Mohan had taught him better.

The butt of the weapon slammed into his face with a sickening crunch

Dako did not have time to feel pain, however. There was only blackness.

* * *

"That was foolish."

The voice was familiar.

Dako opened his eyes. He was in a dark room. There were no windows; the only illumination was the scented candles burning in the corners. The room carried the heavy scent of frankincense, lavender and chaisimmon, a fragrant plant found only on Atunbé.

Both of Dako's hands and feet were bound by iron shackles. He sat on his haunches, with his back against a cold stone wall.

Dako could only make out the silhouette of the person standing above him.

"Did you really think you could approach undetected? This mine belongs to Her Majesty, Queen of the Bandoki."

Dako spat blood onto the concrete floor.

The voice above him chuckled. "You may have thought to pass through undetected by magic; what you call psionics," it said. "Which is possible. The concentration here is such that magical defenses are difficult to erect. However, where magic fails a pair of binoculars might suffice."

Dako could feel the pulse of ashe everywhere. In the air within the room; in the aching of his bones.

"The Cradle," he thought. "I must be right at the source."

"You are still alive," the voice said, "because I am, I must confess, curious. Did you come here for this?" The figure knelt before him. He saw a face he could never forget – older, now, but with the same mocking grin, and flames dancing in her eyes – Dey Valu.

A handful of smooth discs fell from Dey Valu's fist onto the floor. "Did you come for the Galaxy-Stones? My Galaxy-Stones?"

"She does not recognize me," Dako thought.

"I thought the Galaxy-Stones belonged to your queen," he said.

Dey Valu laughed. "She is far away," he said. "Here, I am the only law."

"I didn't come to rob you," Dako said.

Dey Valu arched an eyebrow. "Oh? Why then?"

"Did you think I came alone?" Dako said. "Old age has made you stupid, Dey Valu. You are trespassing on Imperial ground. Your presence here is an act of war against Cassad."

"Atunbé," Dey Valu hissed. "Who cares about Atunbé?"

"All of the Cassad Empire is one," Dako replied. "And you are like a mosquito landing on its flesh. Sooner or later the hand of the Emperor is going to reach down and scratch."

"Charming analogy," Dey Valu said. "But I don't believe you. You come alone, where the Emperor would have sent an army. And you look like no government agent I have ever seen."

"No one wants a war," Dako said. "Take your soldiers; take your sorcerers; take your loot and go, now. You have one day to vacate this planet."

Dey Valu laughed. Then she punched Dako in the mouth. She stood and walked out of the room.

When the door closed behind her, Dako leaned back against the cold stone wall. It, too, pulsed with raw energy. So much ashe! And he could not use it to free himself.

But there was more than one kind of ashe in the world.

* * *

Once, several years after leaving his burned village, Dako, when he was still a boy, had found shelter from the rain in a barn on the outskirts of Once Chosen. There had been other itinerant travelers there and one – an old, one-eyed man – gave them a demonstration of his powers.

There had been no ashe in that place for a long time and none that he could detect, yet the old man-made scuttle-slugs appear out of a freshly poured glass of water, pulled streamers of colored silks out of thin air and made coins disappear. He cut a rope clean in half and then joined it as if it had never been broken. The other men there laughed and clapped, but Ogunlana Dako just stared, and then said, almost accusingly: "This isn't psionics."

"No," the older man agreed. He had a reedy, though not unpleasant, voice. "It is illusion, boy. Most magic is."

Dako had made a disgusted sound; such illusions reminded him of the ones performed by Dey Valu just hours before she destroyed his life. "Then what good is it?" he said. "Smoke and mirrors; tricks to entertain children."

"I use no smoke, nor mirrors," the one-eyed magician said. "And you are little more than a child yourself. You might care to show more respect to your elders."

Dako had laughed, but later that night a force of the local constabulary came and rousted them, saying that the farmer in whose barn they took shelter had complained. They were taken into the city and locked up in jail, behind thick bars and sturdy locks. Most of the men found it more comfortable than the barn, and did not complain. But the old, one-eyed magician only smiled when they locked the gate behind them.

"Can you magic these locks and bars away?" Dako had hissed.

The old man admitted that he could not.

Dako ran his finger along the bars, he could sense the faint power running through them – ashe-reinforced metal, impervious to psionic, or "magical" tampering.

Without another word, the old man removed one shoe. He pulled aside a hidden compartment in the sole, from which he brought out a small, strangely-shaped metal wire. Rummaging through his thin hair, another curious item appeared. Whistling softly, the old man approached the locks and set to work.

The next morning, they were found missing from the jail, though no one was certain how they had escaped.

"Vanished," one of the other prisoners told the bemused jailers, "like ghosts in the night."

The jailers had chalked it up to magic and gave thanks that the sorcerers they had unwittingly locked up had not harmed them. Life was hard enough without incurring the wrath of a sorcerer.

Dako traveled for a few years with the old magician, learning his secrets in exchange for scrounging and stealing food and water and building shelters when none could be found.

* * *

When Dey Valu returned to Dako's cell, her face was troubled.

"My watchers have spotted smoke in the distance," she said. "Did you have anyone following you?"

"As I said before," Dako replied. "Did you really think I came alone?"

"I cannot risk a war."

"There was a village," Dako said.

"What?"

"There was a village. It was only a small one; far from here. A star had fallen there, centuries before and it was relatively prosperous."

"What are you talking about?" Dey Valu hissed.

"You probably don't even remember it," Dako said.

His hands slipped out of the unlocked shackles.

He sprang to his feet, clutching a long, thin blade in his fist.

Dey Valu stumbled backward. "What the hell!"

Dako exploded forward, pressing the blade against Dey Valu's throat.

"You came to that little village in friendship," Dako said. "But you looted it of its two greatest treasures."

"Once Spoken," Dey Valu croaked. When she spoke, her Adam's Apple bobbed against the blade.

Dako smiled grimly in the darkness. "I've come for my sister."

"There was a boy," Dey Valu said. "In the flames...you?"

"Where is she?"

"Would it matter if I told you I loved her?" Dey Valu's voice was low, bitter. "If the elders had let us, we would have been married there and then. But they would not have a woman marry one of her own; especially not the flower of that damned village."

Dako pushed the blade forward a little.

Dey Valu winced. Blood poured from the wound.

"Where is she?"

Dey Valu stood very still. "She died," she said softly. "The fever took her, three years ago now. We were happy..."

Dako thrust the point of the blade deep into the side of Dey Valu's neck. "I wasn't."

Dey Valu didn't make a sound as she dropped, softly, to the floor.

V. Now, Comes the Dawn

"You did well," Fleet Admiral Bundu Yaka said.

The reformed Atunbéan forces had moved in through the night. Now, with dawn peeking over the horizon, the Cradle was fully occupied. In the dim light, Dako could see the deep shafts leading into the mines, and already the grimy, dusty workers were lining up for their first shift. The soldiers kept order. The

Bandoki, lacking their leader, were unable to stand against the onslaught of the Atunbéans, who were determined to take back their planet. No one wanted a war., so the Bandoki retreated, evacuating Atunbé with great haste.

And the Fleet Admiral now held the mine.

"What will happen to them?" Dako asked.

Fleet Admiral Yaka looked surprised. "Who?"

"Them." Dako gestured at the miners.

"They will continue to work," Fleet Admiral Yaka said. "The mine must remain open."

"Life, mining ashe, is short and hard," Dako said. "And when they die?"

"Others will take their place."

"I see."

"Come see me next week," the Fleet Admiral said. "As we rebuild Atunbé, I want you and others like you at my side. I will train you, personally and help you to develop your psionics to levels never before imagined."

"For what purpose?"

"If you survive your training, you'll find out."

"I see."

With that, the Fleet Admiral had two of his Lieutenants escort Dako away from the mine.

When they had traveled a few miles away from the Cradle, Dako stopped his ATV.

"You did well," one of the Lieutenants said. "The Fleet Admiral is grateful."

Dako smiled, then, pulled a cigar from inside his jacket. "I'll be grateful if one of you got a match," he said. But before the Lieutenant could reply he said, "Never mind," and snapped his fingers.

THE INITIATIVE ON EUPHRATES

BY

PENELOPE FLYNN

*On February 12th, the twenty-third year of the New Regime I
was convicted of mass murder by a jury of my so-called peers.
As the only surviving member of the ruling Cassad family, I
would pay for the thousands of years of "oppression" inflicted
on the three hundred and fifteen planets, asteroids and dust
chains of the Regime. Deggar Prison, once the depository of enemies of the Regime, had been 'liberated'. It was to be my future
home until the sentence could be carried out. The revolutionaries were ecstatic. I was neither happy nor sad. As my sentence of
death was announced the judgment hall filled with cheers and
curses. I was unmoved, for I knew that what seems like victory
to some was interpreted as a mere set back to others. I smiled at
the angry crowd, ignoring their spittle running down my bruised
face. The revolutionaries had underestimated me.*

    ~Khalid Cassad

CALL ME PROTEA

    On the 12th of February I sat in the judgment hall of the
Capitol packed cheek to jowl with the revolutionaries who
shouted and cheered at the sight of the last Cassad heir bound
battered and awaiting judgment. I envied them. I wished that I
could have joined in their revelry, wished that I was as naive as
they were. As they congratulated themselves and each other they
never asked themselves why this man was still alive... the last
heir to an alleged tyrannical dynasty who should have been

executed without fanfare. They failed to understand the simple truth... that true power buys the most precious commodity of all... time. And in their desire to show off their prisoner and gain political capital from the carnival display, his enemies had provided him that aforementioned item which he needed to ensure that he would not be held captive for long. They had to know that his forces were mobilizing even as they shouted, jeered and spat at him. He never made a sound and barely acknowledged their existence. But I knew that he was taking it all in. I knew what kind of man he was. I learned the ways of the Cassad during their landing on Euphrates.

PARADISE

Euphrates was one of the least traveled outposts of the Empire and was never a hub of great industry remaining lush, fertile and peaceful. My grandfather General Saidu Tawiah had been a highly decorated general in the Cassad Fleet and one of the previous Emperor's close friends and confidantes. My grandfather's loyalty and constancy had earned him a wealthy and comfortable existence as an Ambassador for the sovereign world of Euphrates. My mother, a decorated fighter pilot, military hero during the Alien Insurgencies and arguably one of the most beautiful women to grace the sands of Euphrates was in her youth hotheaded, tactless and determined by the Council of Elders to lack the requisite diplomatic aplomb to take the helm of the Ambassadorship which in a perfect world would have been bestowed upon her by default, as my grandfather's eldest child. Disappointed at what he knew to be the obvious outcome of her candidacy my grandfather made alternate plans. At all times aware of my mother's tastes and proclivities my grandfather was shrewd enough to encourage her relationship with a young officer from the Diplomatic Corp, a man he thought would be worthy of the Ambassadorship post, who would understand the expectation of familial loyalty and who would have the diplomacy to rein my mother in when necessary. The Elders approved of him and my mother desired him. The two were joined in wedded union within a year of their meeting. I am one of the three products of that union.

My brothers and I grew up with one foot in the Military and the other in the Diplomatic Corps. We had the opportunity to become learned and sophisticated while living in a tranquil, erudite society where the greatest unrest included commercial disputes and grumblings now and then about the tribute which was paid to an Empire that barely recognized the planet's existence. And me, well I was a woman in love. My partner, Dariel was dark, well-built and had the mischievous nature of an imp, a nature that served him well in his post as one of the up-and-coming scientific minds in Euphrates.

Dariel like many of the Cassad Euphraten was part native. The natives of Euphrates were absorbed almost immediately into the burgeoning Cassad imperial colonization initiative. Of course, the native bloodline was evident in anyone bearing their genes. So strong was the gene that the trait of the double iris that ran from near black to pale pink was held by anyone who carried even a drop of native blood. The double iris was not a trait held by anyone in our family, however. We generally married and intermarried with those from the first Cassadite wave – the First One Million. It was tradition. My parents were both descendants of the First Wave as were their parents, and their parents' parents. I had already seen thirty-two winters as they would be counted on the old world and being on such a far-flung outpost made me an unlikely candidate for marriage to the more ambitious First Wave descendants.

Relationships and marriage were obviously the last thing on my mind when I was dispatched to monitor repairs on the fusion reactor in the main science lab. I had risen through the ranks as a successful diplomat and was ordered through the Diplomatic Corp to make certain that the scientific unions and labor unions were of one accord with regard to what repairs should have been made and whether they were sufficient to the needs of the scientific community. That was the day I met the overconfident and infinitely charming young scientist, Dariel. We struck up a conversation. He had a way of getting beyond my practiced diplomatic mode into the fiery side of me that gave no doubt that I was my mother's daughter. It didn't take long before we became inseparable. More than anything it was his openness and vast knowledge on any number of issues that I found enchanting.

But for the double irises, Dariel looked much like any other Cassadite. We made quite the pair as we strolled the parks of Cygnus, the first city of Euphrates and as I stood one hand higher than my beau, he would jokingly but lovingly refer to me as his "Amazon goddess" a reference he said to a warlike civilization of women who purportedly lived on the Earth home world millennia ago. He would wink and say that I was perfect for breeding. It was a joke – a joke which it appears was lost on the Cassad heir.

It came as a shock to me and all my family when the Cassad heir came for me, as he claimed he had a right to do under the terms of my grandfather's appointment and my position as a direct descendant on both sides, of the First One Million. Again, thirty-two winters had come and gone and I was no virgin – not by any stretch of the imagination, but these facts did not seem to concern the Cassad. Even when I insisted through the Ambassador's envoy that I was already involved in a very serious relationship which undoubtedly would lead to marriage, the Cassad heir's representative was not dissuaded.

My father who had accepted the probability of my union with Dariel to the point where they referred to each other as "father and son," attempted to negotiate with the Cassad, to offer access to females with similar genetic sequencing. I even offered my own genetic material for artificial conception. The Cassad refused. His envoy indicated that it was not only the use of the genetic material but the necessity of a familial alliance. Euphrates apparently was to become a staging area for an Imperial military exercise and I was to be the linchpin – an Imperial consort and Euphraten dignitary charged with convincing the Euphraten people of the benefits of this incursion. I listened to the quietly whispered gossip and rumors within the Diplomatic Corp staff. The rumor was that the Cassad intended to build upon the mythology of the First One Million. Certainly, there were many worlds where the head of the Cassad Empire was considered a god but the deification of the First One Million implied a movement of socio-political proportions not seen since the Cult of Empress Claudia swept the colonies.

It was the Cult of Empress Claudia that wiped out the native Euphraten population in less than three generations. Empress Claudia, a geneticist and renowned priestess of Vudun or one of the other old religions brought over during the First Wave, personally visited nearly a thousand planets in her lifetime that supported humanoid native populations. When it was determined by her staff that a race was appropriate for interbreeding, her temples would be built in those colonies. Claudia employed science, sorcery and diplomacy to seduce the seed carrying members of these humanoid populations. She knew well how to make anyone fall in love with her and they were all in love with her. When she decreed that their seed should be offered as tribute to the Empire there was nearly universal compliance. The seed-bearing members of the populations left off impregnating their own and for generations only Cassadite women who offered themselves as proxies for the Empress Claudia gave birth in the colonies. It was ingenious. The Cult of Empress Claudia converted entire sectors to the Cassad cause without as much as the blast of cannon. However, the deification of the First One Million would have consequences so far reaching that the Cult of the Empress Claudia would seem to be a footnote in the annals of history by comparison.

PLANS

Dariel was incensed when he was finally made aware that the Cassad heir rejected my father's most recent offer and was instead insisting upon my appearance. But Dariel wasted no time attempting to vent his anger. When the last offer to the Cassad was rejected we immediately stole away and left Cygnus for Sophia, the hamlet where Dariel was raised. The Cassad heir was not amused when the news of my absconding reached him. We were on the train racing toward Sophia and then onto the uncharted wilderness when the Euphrates Public Address System issued an alert. I saw my father's face, dispassionate, ashen and gray as he read out the warrant for Dariel's arrest for my kidnapping. I knew that he had been forced to do it, as did Dariel. Even though the address was published throughout Euphrates we were undaunted. We had planned carefully and took little used by-ways until we finally arrived at our destination, the Immoryte temple in Sophia. According to the rites necklaces, earrings, bracelets, rings, vows and kisses were exchanged. We drank and sang and left the temple, wed.

Our attempt to flee into the countryside however was thwarted by well-meaning citizens who believed the false kid-napping reports and who informed on us. We were stopped at the border then taken into custody and brought before the Cas-sad in chains.

The Cassad heir and his entourage had temporarily taken up residence in the Regent's Palace outside of Cygnus and it was there in the Regent's receiving room that I first met the newest arbiter of Cassad power in Euphrates, the Regent, Safara Aristide. She was nearly as tall as I and strode the room taking account of me and Dariel as if we were cattle. She stood before me appraising me. I did the same with regard to her. The Regent was not what I would call a beautiful woman but she was what we would call stunning. She was a bit slighter than me and wore her hair in a manner that was severe and only softened by her doe-ish eyes and pouty lips. She had the bearing of a soldier and her military training had not taught her to hide her contempt, the way my diplomatic training had taught me to hide mine.

For a moment the Regent said nothing as both Dariel and I were held fast before her by armed guards. She regarded me for a moment then spoke directly to Dariel.

"You are aware that the Cassadite female you have ab-ducted is promised by contractual obligation to the Cassad heirs?"

"The female," Dariel hissed, "Is my wife bound to me this life and into the next by the rites of the Immoryte temple."

I could almost *see* the Regent thinking this comment through. One of the primary diplomatic issues dealt with by the Cassad Empire was the right of religious freedom. The Cassad had learned early on that almost every sin committed against a native people was forgivable if you gave them license to pray to the god of their choice from whom this forgiveness could flow. The Cassad always made a great show of how they maintained a *laissez faire* attitude with regard to the religions of native cultures. So, the Cassad's Regent was in a quandary. If she took me against my will after a duly performed Immoryte ceremony there could be a backlash in Euphrates that might send ripples throughout the Empire.

"Dariel," the Regent finally said, "Descendants of the First One Million at birth are by our laws at the disposal of the Cassad Empire. I am sure you know this."

"Yes," Dariel responded, "But once a descendant of the Cassadite First Wave achieves thirty winters the descendant cannot be called by obligation – they must voluntarily submit to the call."

Again, the Regent was deep in thought. She looked to the guards who held Dariel and nodded.

Without warning they fell on him, kicking, punching, and beating. Dariel refused to cry out and after several minutes the Regent held up her hand and the beating ceased.

For the first time the Regent spoke to *me*. She demanded, "Submit to the call of the Cassad."

Admittedly Dariel and I had anticipated this. We knew that the Cassad would attempt to extract a concession from us and we had decided to resist at all costs. This was however much easier to say than do. But I persisted in the plan and was resolute in saying, "I will not submit."

The Regent nodded again, and this time two more guards appeared bearing weapons. Like before they set on Dariel without warning. I heard the sickening sound of bones crushing when they smashed his jaw and slammed the butts of their weapons against his hands, ankles and feet. My knees became weak but I stood my ground as Dariel had asked, had demanded. But then came the fire. Though he could barely see or speak the inhuman scream when they applied the white-hot metal brands to his feet wrenched all prior thoughts of stoicism and rebelliousness from my head. I was pulling off my rings, all my wedding jewelry and robe, everything before I was even conscious of it. The Cassad Regent raised her hand and the torture stopped.

"Submit to the call of the Cassad," she said to me.

"I have conditions," I responded.

"Name them," the Regent replied.

It took all my discipline to block out Dariel's voice as he tried to beg and plead with me crying, "No, no!" the only intelligible thing he could say with his mouth and body so shattered. But I continued my negotiation relying upon my hostage situation training to guide me.

"Dariel will be taken to the hospital at Cygnus and cared for until he is rehabilitated. These two," I said pointing at two of the guards "will be charged with insuring his care and thwarting any saboteurs and will stay with him until such time as I believe he is safe. And you will have my father announce that the kidnapping alert was based upon false information, that Dariel is innocent of any wrongdoing."

"And what do we receive in return?" The Regent asked.

"I will revoke and renounce my marriage vows and submit to the authority of the Cassad," I said.

"Very well," the Regent replied with smirk, "You have my word."

"No." I replied, "I don't want your word. I want you to swear on the blood and bones of the First One Million that this will be made so."

The guards all raised their eyes to the Regent. The Oath was serious. My even asking her to make it bordered on blasphemy but I was desperate. I was gambling Dariel's life on this move and had no margin for error.

"I swear on the blood and bones of the First One Million that the word and spirit of our agreement will be made so," the Regent said.

I managed to stay on my feet as the wave of relief flooded through me. I continued to block out Dariel's sobs as he was lifted up and taken away. I couldn't look at him. I knew I had done the right thing but all I could feel was shame.

"Take our guest to her rooms," the Regent said to the remaining guards as she focused her attention on information that was being streamed to her console, "We will have an opportunity to converse, later."

I couldn't feel my feet, my legs or arms as I followed the guards down the hallway on the path to fulfill my traditional responsibilities to the Cassad.

ENGAGEMENT

The servants of the Regent had laid out the gown I was to wear during my engagement with the Cassad heir. Two of them monitored my bathing not so much because they were there to assist but because they were charged with insuring that I did not take my own life. Two additional women came to wash and dry my hair which they braided close to my scalp in front and let billow out in a halo framing my face, from the crown. I was provided the gown and the robe of a consort. The gown chosen for me was translucent white with strategically placed decorative elements. It left little to the imagination. In the first five minutes the Cassad heir would see more of me than Dariel had seen in the first five months. But this was not a romance. This was an obligation, an obligation I brought upon myself. I looked at my reflection, one that only hours ago belonged to a married woman, but now belonged to the Empire.

As I sat waiting to be called, the door opened and without request for entry the Cassad's Regent stepped into the room. She was dressed in uniform, but no longer in full regalia. She wore no cape and her service boots were replaced with sensible shoes but the contemptuous scowl was ever present.

"So, this is how you will present yourself to the Cassad heir?" She asked.

"Have you provided me any other options?" I responded surlier than I intended, not because I didn't want to offend her, but because I had no intention of giving her the satisfaction of believing that any words from her made a difference to me at that juncture.

"You know you are not the first candidate considered to wed the Cassad heir… far from it," The Regent said matter-of – factly.

"I was a married woman before you tortured and coerced this decision. My life was fine before you arrived. Dariel is a wonderful man. He would have been a wonderful husband and father."

"There is no question in my mind that you are

undoubtedly insane. No one in their right mind would choose that... *male* over the Cassad heir," she scoffed.

"Without knowing more, it appears to me that you have probably spent your entire career chasing this Cassad fantasy of repairing the Empire to its former glory, knowing as any *sane* person would, that once the Empire was fragmented it would take godlike power, godlike effort and a godlike resolve to mend. And with all due respect these are qualities that your Cassad heir has yet to demonstrate that he possesses in great abundance."

The expression that flashed across her face was nothing short of homicidal rage. Her gloved hands clenched and balled into fists. I know she wanted to hit me... but certainly not as much as I wanted her to try. She took a deep breath, relaxed her hands, then turned on her heels and left the room as three similarly dressed servants entered.

After reviewing my outfit for appropriateness, two of the servants led me from the room. Even though the consort's robe was opaque and beautifully embroidered, the guards were not permitted to look upon me when I was wearing it. The servants and I walked the empty corridors until we arrived at the Cassad heir's suite of rooms. As soon as I entered the servants left. I made my way in through the receiving area and followed the sound of voices into the main chamber. The Cassad heir was standing in the center of the room conducting a meeting with his advisors and other dignitaries. I stood in the doorway just out of view of the holographic projectors. He acknowledged my presence with a glance then informed his advisors that he was late for another engagement and would contact them soon. The advisors all bid their farewells and for a brief moment among the assembled group I saw my father's face. I fought the compulsion to step into the projection area – just so he could see that I was there and know that I was all right. But he quickly disappeared like the others and I was left alone with the Cassad heir.

Before I could think of words of introduction a servant entered with a carafe and two glasses. He placed them on a bedside table then approached the Cassad heir and removed his robe.

If I were to speak honestly, I would have had to admit

that if this situation had occurred five years earlier… before I knew of the existence of Dariel, before I became a woman in love, the Cassad heir would have been precisely the type of engagement I would have sought out and been interested in. He was even more heavily muscled through the shoulders and back than I had formerly surmised and had a well-chiseled abdomen. Purely from force of habit based upon our heights and body types I had quickly identified the nine positions I believed would be most effective in a coital engagement between the two of us. I immediately chastised myself.

"It has been a very long day. Would you like a drink?" he asked as he approached me with a glass filled to the brim with a purple liquid with green highlights.

The drink was called "ease" a level 3 intoxicant. I took the glass and drank slowly looking to put off meeting my obligation as long as possible. But the evening did not unfold quite as I thought. The Cassad heir instead of being amorous summoned up the relief maps of Euphrates and questioned me on terrain, obstacles and vegetation. I had drunk down three glasses of the purple liquid and was actually feeling more relaxed… more at ease. It must have been apparent as the Cassad heir then asked if I would like him to take my robe. I nodded in the affirmative and he slipped the robe off my shoulders. He made no comment once he disrobed me but I saw the flicker in his eyes as he assessed my considerable assets which were accentuated by the provocative design of the translucent gown.

The drink had done its job. I was feeling sultry and aroused and it was evident that the Cassad heir was as well. His hands and lips were on my body with the same fervor that mine were on his. I slipped the knot on his bottoms right before he slipped the gown off over my head. Intoxicated by the liquor and spurred on by arousal we crashed onto the bed. And as my mind spun through the various positions I intended to experience with the Cassad heir an image of Dariel flashed through my mind. As the Cassad heir's hands kneaded and pressed me to submit I recalled the sound of the weapons cracking the bones in Dariel's hands and his stoic silence throughout the brutality. I scrambled off the bed and stood shaking at its foot.

"What is it?" The Cassad heir asked.

When I opened my mouth to respond, what emerged was a gut-wrenching sob followed by successive sobs. I did what I had not done since five years out of my mother's womb. I cried. I wailed and gasped it seemed for an hour. My eyes streamed tears and my nose bubbled. Each time I tried to take hold of myself I would think of Dariel and how he suffered for the sake of our relationship and it only made matters worse. I finally rushed into the bath and splashed cold water on my face, but it still took several more fits and starts before I was able to re-enter the chamber, my eyes red and swollen. I was finally prepared to meet my obligation. The Cassad heir however was gone.

I sat for the remainder of the evening and woke up the next morning in the heir's bed, alone. When I returned to my rooms, my clothes and breakfast were set out but there was no message with regard to the Cassad heir. A week passed and still no word from him though the household functioned normally in his absence. When I asked the servants, they indicated that he was unavailable. I waited another week trying to keep my ear to the ground so to speak, listening for any rumors or gossip that might give me any idea as to what my fate was to be.

On more than one occasion I had considered simply slipping away from the palace and getting back to my family in Cygnus. But this proved impossible as I did not have the access and egress codes to the facility and thought it best under the circumstances not to ask. A particularly chatty servant charged with cleaning the bedchamber recounted in lurid detail the news story of a Euphraten scientist found in Crescent Park the victim of a vicious attack and robbery attempt. He had been rushed to the hospital in Cygnus for critical care. The officials of Cygnus were increasing patrols in the parks as a result.

At least the Regent has kept her part of the bargain... which was more than what I could say for myself. I had greatly underestimated the impact that Dariel's suffering would have on my ability to discharge my obligation and I was fairly certain that the Regent took great joy in the fact that I had buckled under the burden of my guilt and despair.

Three days later the Regent again paid me a visit. She

could barely contain her smugness as she entered the room.

"I have received a message from the Cassad heir's envoy that he was travelling in Euphrates within the uncharted wilderness and will speak with you upon his return."

"When do you expect that might be," I asked.

"It might be a week, possibly a month... but no more than a year," she said, her voice saturated with officiousness.

"You believe I will fail in consummating my portion of our agreement," I said to the Regent.

"Success or failure is probably irrelevant, now. Your little display has most likely insured that the Cassad heir will want nothing to do with you."

"Then am I excused?" I asked gazing at her expectantly.

"You will be excused when the Cassad heir excuses you," she replied coolly.

At least, may I return to my family while he is away? I could be taking on assignments, earning time toward my Diplomatic Corp credentials," I said.

"That would not be advisable," the Regent said, "You have history as a flight risk. We would not want a repeat of your previous activities."

"But I gave my word. I renounced my vows," I replied.

"At this juncture you have done nothing toward fulfilling your portion of the agreement. You will therefore remain until the Cassad heir says otherwise."

There was nothing left to say as she turned on her heels leaving me to further consider my fate. I had heard the servants speaking among themselves. The Regent was an Aristide, one of the fringe members of the First Wave. Though I had never interacted with any of them, they reputedly have questionable ethics. I was amazed that one of them had risen to such a vaunted position in the Cassad heir's entourage. I could only presume that her positioning was due to the financial might of the family. The Aristides remained wealthy despite the shifting political tides over the last millennium and maybe it was that necessity for stability that made her a perfect fit in the Cassad heir's campaign to resurrect the Empire.

OBLIGATION

It was a full month after I received the message however before the Cassad heir returned and even upon his return he did not send for me.

I had been held at the Regent's palace for nearly two months before I was informed that the Cassad heir would see me. I entered his chambers with trepidation. Again, I entered the main chamber where he was in communication with someone wearing a uniform I didn't recognize. He quickly concluded the communication and turned his attention to me.

"I gather you are feeling better," he said.

"Yes, sir I am," I replied taking my cues on how to proceed from the formality of his approach.

"I have seen quite a bit of Euphrates and it is as you stated, lush terrain dotted with picturesque natural landscapes. We have located bases of operation for our staging area and are committed to retaining as much of the natural condition of the land as we can," he said.

"I am happy that you were able to achieve both goals."

"I have news for you," the Cassad heir said as he activated the communications screen.

I was awestruck as there on the screen was Dariel. He appeared to be in a medical unit. I presumed that it was the one in Cygnus. I knew that his internal injuries and broken bones would be best mended there as I had been a patient on two occasions to repair severe fractures. I could tell that his fingers had already been reset and that the damage to his jaw had been attended to. He looked wonderful. Tears of joy began to well in my eyes.

"I wanted you to see that we are fully involved in meeting obligations under the Agreement made with the Imperial Regent," the Cassad heir said. But I was oblivious to his commentary as I watched Dariel focusing on working through manual dexterity exercises.

"Time grows short," the Cassad heir said as I watched rapt.

"Are you ready for your sponge down, sir?" A woman's voice cooed from the screen. A woman dressed in hospital worker garb then slipped into the frame and pressed the panel which raised the translucent barrier around the bed. I couldn't help but notice how Dariel's mood brightened.

"Ahhh," he said as she sat down beside him, "The most beautiful therapist in all of Cygnus."

The woman laughed. So did Dariel. My heart began to thump loudly in my chest. I no longer cared what the Cassad was saying. I was focused on the screen, on Dariel and this woman.

"How is the work coming along?" The woman asked as she began to watch him work through the exercises.

"Good I think. But I seem to be having some problem with my grip," Dariel answered with a twinkle in his eye.

"Oh really?" The woman asked sounding quite a bit like I would have when Dariel and I were playing some of our *special* games.

"Well what are you having problems gripping?" She asked as if it were a well-rehearsed line.

Dariel lifted the bed covers with an impish grin and both he and the woman assessed his problem.

"Oh dear!" She said with her obviously well-practiced look of surprise, "Well this will never do. Let me see what I can do to help you with that."

The woman's hand disappeared under the covers and not long afterward Dariel lay back with his eyes closed biting his lip to keep his moans of pleasure quieted.

"Turn it off!" I said.

The Cassad heir switched off the screen then called up his maps of Euphrates.

"This area here in the mountains may be the best location for what we have in mind," the Cassad heir said pointing to the image, "or here in the lowlands between the mountains and the uncharted areas beyond."

It took all my discipline not to grab the heaviest item in the room that I could lift over my head to beat the Cassad heir to death with. Instead I calmly asked, "Were you paying attention to what just occurred?"

"Yes," the Cassad heir answered, "Your friend, Dariel is recovering from his injuries. I predict that he will make a full and complete recovery."

"Did you happen to notice the woman in the room with him?" I asked doing my best to keep my anger at bay.

"As I am neither blind nor deaf I fully experienced the fact that there was a female person of native descent in the room with him," the Cassad heir continued while reviewing the map images.

Then it struck me …this was probably their plan from the beginning, to appear to comply with the terms of our Agreement only to have everything I traded for sullied and warped.

"Before you begin spinning off conspiracy theories," the Cassad heir said while reviewing another set of maps, "I had nothing to do with the woman being assigned to your friend – not directly, not indirectly."

"Well certainly at least indirectly," I replied angrily, "If you had not come for me, none of this would have happened and he would not have been at the medical facility to encounter her."

"*You* chose the Cygnus facility, and I, or any of the other Cassad heirs could have come for you at any time. That was always a given. The producing cause of your current situation is your betrayal of your husband."

"My betrayal?" I repeated dumbfounded.

"You and your husband obviously had a pact that neither of you would submit to the authority of the Cassad. According to the Regent, he suffered extreme physical torture in support of his vows. However, *you* immediately bowed to pressure and relented."

"So I was supposed to allow her to torture and kill him?" I asked incredulous.

"He was prepared to be tortured and killed in support of his marriage, in support of his faith."

"What good would our marriage or his faith be if I let him die?" I asked at the point of pulling my hair out by the root.

The Cassad heir smiled exhibiting an expression that was almost sympathetic, "You understand that the Immoryte believe death is not the end. Once you took your vows you committed to Dariel for all eternity. Can you imagine how he must have felt…battered, broken, standing at death's door then hearing his beloved wife reject him then give herself to the Cassad? For all he knew his life could have ended at any moment and his beloved wife, for whom he risked everything renounced him and cast him adrift for all eternity."

"That's not what happened," I said, my chest tightening so much I could hardly breathe, "I did it for him, to save him."

"For all he knew, you did it to save *yourself*," the Cassad heir replied. "If as you say, you did what you did for *him*, then why would you begrudge him in this time of abandonment someone to bring him solace... to help him forget?"

My head began to swim; I clutched the edge of the console for support. Everything grew dark and my world suddenly seemed reduced to a black tunnel where my former happy life was beyond my reach, moving farther and farther away with increasing speed. The Cassad heir again focused his attention on the map and asked, "As far as the Euphraten populace is concerned, which of these locations will garner the least amount of opposition as an installation?"

My voice came out wooden and halting, "The area in the lowlands would garner the least opposition."

For the next few hours I was an automaton answering the Cassad heir's questions regarding Euphrates, its people, politics and culture. My emotions and resistance had drained away. I was a husk. He had embarked upon questions regarding the local water systems when a servant entered the room and spoke to the Cassad heir in hushed tones. He nodded to the servant then glanced at me and said, "We will continue this later."

Without another word to me, the Cassad heir left with the servant in tow. After several minutes my body robotically propelled itself down the corridor and into my suite of rooms where I sat for the remainder of the day, my mind reeling as I replayed the sequence of events from the past two months over and over trying to make sense of it all. I ignored the comings and goings of the servants. My dinner went untouched. Night fell but I was unaware of it as I mulled my fate - my thoughts always finding their way to Dariel. In my mind the horror of *his* torture was replaced with the horror of the images from the medical facility that had become *my* torture. The dark tunnel of my despair was at the point of overwhelming me when suddenly everything became clear.

Resolutely, I rose from my seat and helped myself to

remnants from my uneaten dinner then entered the bath. I washed and perfumed my body then arranged my hair letting it loose, the hair now wild and untamed in an arcing halo reaching upward and out to my shoulders. I called for the Cassad heir's servants. By the time the servants arrived at my suite I had chosen and pulled on a provocative blue gown. It lacked the elegance of the white gown from the first encounter, but left no question as to intention. It dipped low in the back and front giving a view of cleavage both advancing and retreating.

"Has he returned?" I asked the first servant.

"Yes ma'am, but he has not called for you."

"Then announce me," I said moving past him and walking into the corridor.

The second servant was frantically attempting to keep up with my long strides. The guards had not been warned to exit the hallway and were clearly unsure as to what to do. I knew they were forbidden to touch me in my current role as the Cassad's consort and in fact would suffer extreme punishment if they even admitted to having seen me dressed as I was. Those who did not rush from the corridor averted their eyes.

By the time we arrived at the Cassad heir's suite, a third servant met us at the door carrying a carafe and a single glass. The first servant entered and we all filed in behind him.

When we entered the bedchamber the Cassad was completing his evening rituals. I stood behind the first servant as the second hurriedly threw a robe over my shoulders. The third servant slipped past and deposited the tray with the carafe and glass on the Cassad heir's bedside table then quickly left the room with the second servant in tow. The first servant cleared his throat but before he could speak the Cassad heir said, "Leave us."

I could see the relief on the servant's face as he turned and quickly left. I walked to the center of the room and let the robe fall then swept about slowly to give the Cassad a complete view of what I had to offer. The Cassad heir regarded me for a moment then said with a smirk, "This is much more 'you,' isn't it?"

I ignored what I took to be a slight and said, "I am here

to fulfill my obligations under our agreement."

"Is that a fact?" He asked. "What makes you believe that I am even desirous of such an engagement especially in light of our last encounter?"

Then it was my time to smirk as his lower third append-age rose precipitously making it abundantly clear that the sought-after engagement was indeed welcomed.

"How do I know that there will not be a repeat of your previous performance?" He asked.

I indicated toward the carafe. He raised it then poured the bright pink liquid into the glass and nodded knowingly, "So now you're experimenting with Lethe?" He asked.

"After your revelation today about Dariel, I was admit-tedly taken aback," I said, "I was filled with doubt. But then I remembered that before Lethe was made into a cocktail and drunk in the high Cassadite palaces, it was medicinal. The medi-cal grade of Lethe was used as part of the treatment plan for trauma victims… trauma victims like Dariel."

"So you're suggesting that your friend, Dariel may have been under the influence of Lethe? After-all you are so unforget-table that the only way he could carry on would be through the administration of a high-level intoxicating drug."

The Cassad heir's snide comment was meant to sting but it only made me more insistent.

"She was a therapist. She may have prescribed it— "

"—Or he may have requested it," the Cassad heir inter-jected.

"Regardless," I said, "Lethe will help to temporarily for-get the root of your trauma."

"And is that your intention;" he asked as I took the glass from his hand, "to forget?"

"My intention is to make good on my obligation. There was a saying on the old world which I believe is fitting for such an occasion," I said as I raised my glass, "'Whatever gets you through the night.'"

I drank the liquid down then stretched out on the bed to wait for the rush. From the corner of my eye I watched the Cas-sad heir pour the remaining liquid into the glass and down it in one gulp. I closed my eyes and felt him lay down next to me right before the rush kicked in. There would be no Dariel, no therapist, no torture, no Euphrates, no Regent, no Empire that night.

My recollections of that night amount to a collage of sensory images…the Cassad heir's lips on my neck, my back, my inner thighs; the sounds of moaning, sighing, panting ; dirty, filthy words contrasted with sweet, tender ones, sharp pinches and slaps being received and given; the cold stone of the floor of the bath against my back, my legs encircling the rise and fall of the Cassad heir's hips, the taste of his seed; and slow deep kisses as I rode him slowly guided by his hands on my derriere. I fell asleep spent and exhausted before daybreak not concerned about obligations or agreements but feeling strangely safe in the arms of the Cassad heir.

When I finally awoke the Cassad heir still lay beside me, awake and deep in thought, his arm wrapped around me. He began to speak as though we were already involved in conversation.

"Plus or minus three standard deviations from the mean is an acceptable variance in predictability. You are being calculated at plus or minus six."

"Protea," he said looking into my eyes and for the first time addressing me by name, "it is unfortunate that your unpredictability has made you unfit for the original role selected for you, but you will nevertheless be useful to the cause of the Empire."

I was unsure as to what I should do, so I remained where I was as he continued, "You know of the Santé?" He asked.

"Yes sir, I do," I responded in a formal tone that seemed out of place with the circumstances.

"There is the daughter of a Hene, Cresala Damte. Do you know her?"

"No sir," I replied.

"Then you will get to know her," he said, "You will be sent to Santé' as a special envoy. You will learn her likes and dislikes. You will make certain that she is unattached. You will become her friend and when I come for her you will have used your considerable diplomatic skills to make certain that she is more than willing. I will not have a repeat of what happened, here."

"But what if she is already attached…as I was," I asked.

"Then you must use your other skills – the ones taught to you by your mother – to remove any of those impediments. Do you believe you have the wherewithal to carry out this mission?"

"Do I have a choice?" I asked.

The Cassad heir laughed then rolled on top of me pinning my body with his. Without his making request, my knees of their own accord bent and spread giving him access. My arms wrapped around his neck, pulling him close. I almost wept with shame when he entered me. I was sopping wet, snug, my body begging for him. There was no Lethe to blame.

He whispered in my ear as his strokes became rhythmic, "You feel you are betraying Dariel. He had you make a promise which you could not keep, which I knew you could not keep. He was your lover but he could never understand you the way that I do. The blood of the First One Million flows through our veins, our common heritage of intrepidness, brilliance, brutality and the unceasing quest for peace he could never understand."

My tears began to flow unabated as he continued, "I should have been angry that you fell in love with him but you were raised here on this far flung planet with few choices, but I am here now."

The sound of the Cassad's voice was hypnotic and I found myself meeting his thrusts with my own. His kisses were so sweet and probing that they felt sincere.

"Like no other beings in this universe, we were made for each other," he said, "the blood of our ancestors ordained these unions millennia ago. There is no shame in them. They should be treasured, cherished."

I had no idea what to think anymore. Everything was in a whirl but somewhere at the core, everything he said seemed to make sense. I knew I could never put it all together in his presence. I needed time and space to consider it all, to make logical decisions. But that would come later.

CONSEQUENCES

The two of us lay in bed all day taking our meals, discussing Euphrates, his travels and mine, ancient military battles and the diplomatic successes and failures of the Empire and our lives growing up as descendants of the First Wave. With the knowledge that I would no longer be required to marry and produce an heir, we simply enjoyed each other's company... debating, laughing and fulfilling each other's erotic fantasies.

We were entangled in the sheets laughing hysterically as we unsuccessfully attempted to replicate an impossible erotic position we viewed in a contraband Dalian sex manual when the door to the chamber opened and the Regent entered. Our laughter subsided as the Cassad heir pulled on his robe and quickly approach the Regent where she stood near the door. I remained wrapped in the sheets as they spoke *sotto voce*.

My instincts as a Diplomat suddenly drew everything clearly into focus. It made sense that the Regent would enter *my* chamber unbidden. It was an imposition, a show of power. But she had no such hierarchical dispute with the Cassad heir. She was his functionary. She would never have entered his personal chambers without invitation – unless she had a *standing* invitation. *Fool!* I had been so wrapped up in my own anger and sense of loss that I misread a critical cue, a fatal flaw for any Diplomat. This Aristide, this militarily trained Regent was not simply a staunch traditionalist vying for position within the Empire. This was a woman in love. I saw the look on her face. I could only imagine that it rivaled the expression the Cassad heir saw on my face when he provided me the view of Dariel at the Medical Center at Cygnus. There it was... the face of a woman in love who was powerless to argue or prosecute her cause. Earlier I might have been pleased to see her look as miserable as I had been when she directed the torture of my beloved Dariel. I *should* have been pleased, but I wasn't.

As she spoke with him she was focused and professional. I knew that she didn't blame him for our entanglement. She blamed *me*. She had relied upon my conviction as a woman in love, a sister in this perverse war of intimacy and hierarchy and I had betrayed her.

She finished her conversation then left the room without making eye contact with me.

The Cassad heir immediately accessed his communication console and I took this as a cue that I should be on my way. The Cassad heir's servants appeared with my clothing and I bathed in his chambers as he dealt with issues of the Empire. When I was done bathing, the Cassad heir had already left, so I returned to my rooms where all my belongings had been packed and made ready for travel. The Cassad heir's second servant entered with the uniform of an official Envoy of the Empire flung over his arm.

"You are to wear this during your journey," he said.

It made no sense to ask questions. I took the uniform and changed. My life as a member of the Euphrates Diplomatic Corps had ended. I was no one's mate, no one's consort. Now I was a messenger and functionary. I wondered how deeply this relationship between the Regent and the Cassad heir ran. Maybe his sending me to court Cresala Damte was his attempt to safeguard the Regent's emotions in this search for a proper, well-connected, mate. I asked what time we were set to leave for Santé. The servant indicated that the Cassad heir's guard would come for me at the appropriate time. True to his word, the guard came for me and escorted me to the docking area where the vessel for Santé' was preparing to board.

Under heavy guard, the Cassad heir and the Imperial Regent for Euphrates arrived at the port. I was surprised that he planned to see me off. The Cassad heir and I stood at the port, he in his robes and I in the uniform of an official envoy of the Empire. My bags and equipment were taken onboard as we stood together looking out on Euphrates below. He turned and took my hands and said, "My beloved Protea, I have complete faith that this mission will be accomplished, now that it has been entrusted to your very capable hands."

"I will perform to the best of my abilities, sir."

"That is all I can ask," he said.

Then he took my face in his hands and kissed my forehead tenderly whispering, "Now to the Protea contained somewhere within that plus or minus six standard deviations, that unpredictable Protea who is her mother's daughter. Know well that the only person I care about on this forsaken planet will be off-world during your mission. If for any reason you fail, a failure I know would be intentional; know this, my unpredictable beloved. I will destroy every living thing on this planet. I will raze Euphrates down to its barren soil and light its waters aflame – a fireball lighting the heavens to be seen from every corner of this sector. Do you understand me?"

I was stunned. This man with whom I had shared confidences and camaraderie. He had admittedly enjoyed the fruits of a land and people who he now threatened with annihilation.

"You're threatening to destroy Euphrates?"

"Believe me Protea if the enemies of the Empire are allowed to continue their path, there probably will not be much of Euphrates left for you to return to," he whispered in a measured cadence.

"But to threaten an entire world?" I asked, incredulous.

"There are those in the Known who would pay any amount, do anything, and take any risk to have had the opportunity to save their worlds from the mayhem that has destroyed them. You are being provided precisely this opportunity yet you show no gratitude. I'm disappointed," he said as he stepped back and away from me.

"I do not mean to disappoint, sir."

"Then don't." He said, and then added, "Now, am I understood?"

"Yes sir. I understand," I said. Then, from the corner of my eye I saw the Imperial Regent flash a predatory smile and my blood ran cold. She had no ties to Euphrates and had no interest in my completing the mission set for me. If there was even one vengeful bone in her body, I had foolishly created a fearsome enemy who was to be left as trustee and commander over all I held dear.

So, as I sat among the throng of the rebellious, for a moment fantasizing that I could be free of my obligation, I knew it was not to be. This circus was simply a detour. I was bound to find my way to the Santé to complete my mission. I feared for and envied Cresala Damte. But I knew that I had no choice either way. I would complete my mission. All of Euphrates hung in the balance.

THE END OF THE KNOWN
BY
MILTON DAVIS

*Khalid Cassad was nothing like his father. He was con-
servative rather than opulent; compassionate rather than ruthless; cautious rather than impetuous. Some said he was not the
man his father would have chosen to take the Stool and many
agreed Khalid would not have suffered from the slight. But
sometimes life and circumstances give few choices and fewer
freedoms. ...*

*-Samake. Cassad djele/historian. From The Cassad
Chronicles*

Khalid Quentin Cassad threw the covers aside and sat up
on his cot. He gripped his head and clinched his teeth, a mixture
of pain and fear filling his mind. The headaches were not new;
they were known among the imperial physicians as 'The Cassad
Curse.' There was no effective treatment, only the gnashing of
teeth and gripping something durable for the duration of the attack. The only consolation was that they were infrequent and
brief.

But this attack was particularly violent. Khalid felt as if
he was experiencing physical damage, as if his mind was being
ripped apart. He wanted to cry out but he would not; he was a
Cassad, heir to Ose XXIV, Balogun of the Sons of War and
commander of eight hundred ships streaking across the Telian
Gap to confront the latest alien insurgence. He had no time for
this. He tried to stand but vertigo sent him back to his cot. He
would have to ride it out as he had the others. If that was not

possible, he would resort to other means, means that would compromise his actions and jeopardize his mission.

The Known burned. The colonies were in rebellion, led by the very families granted title and status by the Stool now armed and calling for Cassad blood. The aliens had also risen, finally putting their deep hatred of one another aside to unite against a common enemy. Cassad forces battled throughout the Empire, fighting foes that had once been friends while Empire intelligence sifted through millions of cryptic signals to discover who would betray The Stool next.

But the alien threat was clear. Emboldened by the revolt, the aliens rose to shake off the imperial yoke, led by Gendala, a half-Cassadite claiming lineage to the Stool. According to Khalid's father her claims were legitimate. So it was only appropriate that the future heir of the Stool deal with the threat of an unruly sister.

Khalid gritted his teeth as his door slid open. Thomas Keel, his bridge captain, stepped into his room.

"Sir, long range scanners have detected the alien fleet," Thomas said.

Khalid stood, forcing himself not to sway. "Good. Let's end this thing once and for all."

His headache subsided as they walked to the helm. Khalid studied Thomas, trying to dampen the suspicion rising in his head. Thomas was descended from the First. His family accepted an off-world appointment reluctantly but had managed Thrace well, always meeting the quota while increasing the prosperity of the locals. They'd trained together with the Royal Guard and entered the secret rituals of the Oshun society, emerging as brothers. If there was anyone he could trust, it was Thomas. Or so he thought. The rebellion had changed everything.

As they reached the helm Khalid reasoned away his fear. Every man, woman and A.I. in his fleet had been evaluated and screened down to their genotype. Every last one of them was capable of commanding their own fleets and signed on voluntarily to deliver what was to be the deathblow to the alien insurgence. Once the alien threat was eliminated the Stool could concentrate once again on the betrayers. Despite his logic, a hint of doubt remained. His headache increased.

The crew stood as he entered and he waved them back to their stations.

"Warriors,' he said calmly. "We've been here before. You know what you have to do. You know what I expect. When we leave these stars, there will be no alien threat. The end of the war begins today."

He settled onto his command chair. Alien holograms appeared in his vision. They were outnumbered three to one, impossible battle odds under conventional military thought. But this war was anything but conventional. One of his ships possessed twice the firepower of the alien attack ships and three times the hacking capacity. In addition, the aliens, while united in theory, were still separate entities. He saw each fleet as an individual segment of an uncoordinated whole, their distinct ship configurations revealing their distrust of each other.

"Sir, we have a problem," Thomas said.

Khalid turned to look at his scanner officer.

"An unidentified fleet has emerged from the Gate."

"Give me visuals," Khalid commanded.

The fleet appeared before him. His eyebrows rose as he clutched the arms of his chair.

"Rebels," he said.

It was a credit to the discipline of his crew that no one responded. Their mission was to be secret. Apparently, it was not.

"Battle analysis suggests we are in an unfavorable position," Thomas said. "The alien fleet won't disperse unless we attack. Our calculated losses would reduce our odds against the rebel fleet considerably."

"Decrease our speed," Khalid said.

"Sir?" Thomas asked.

"I'm not in the habit of repeating orders," Khalid replied. "Our odds are favorable. "

"Sir, begging your pardon, I disagree."

Khalid grinned. "You depend on your toys too much, my friend. Your analysis is correct. The odds are not in our favor.

But our system fails to include the fact that the aliens do not know that the fleet emerging from the Gate has come to destroy us. To them, the rebel fleet is reinforcements."

Thomas grinned. "Excellent."

"We'll let them come close enough. It will seem as if we are merging. Keep them on the edge of bolt range."

"Yes, sir," the helmsman replied.

"Rheem?"

The hacker commander's image appeared before Cassad. "Sir?"

"Focus your attack on the center of the alien force. I need control of their navigation programs."

Rheem was silent for a moment. "That will take some time, sir. Navigation is usually flooded with reactive counter hacks."

"You have ten minutes," Cassad replied.

"Ten minutes is ..."

"...not enough time," Cassad finished. "It's all you have."

"Yes sir." Rheem's disgruntled face disappeared.

He wiped Rheem's holo image away then replaced it with Sundiata's hard stare.

"Weapons assessment," he said.

"The rebel force skews our advantage as you know," Sundiata replied.

"Program ninety percent of our defensive array to the rear," he said. "Concentrate aggressive fire forward. Wait to fire until the rebel force is within attack range."

Sundiata's stare broke. "Our range?"

"Their range," Khalid replied.

"Sir, there is a high probability we will suffer considerable losses if the rebels decide fire upon us."

Khalid hesitated before answering. He knew every person under his command. His plan put a considerable number of them at great risk, but he had no other choice. If a rebel fleet was here, it meant the situation among the core worlds was not going well. He had to save as many of his ships as possible to return to the core to assess the situation. But he had one more tactic in his bag that might delay any assault.

"Adjust the weapons array," Khalid confirmed.

Sundiata's hard countenance returned. "As you wish, sir."

Khalid wiped him away then summoned Aria, his communications commander.

"Aria, open a line to the rebel fleet."

Aria looked away for a second then back to him.

"They are refusing connect," she said.

"Hack it," Khalid replied.

Aria's eyebrows rose. "We might expose secret technology if we..."

"Hack it," Khalid repeated.

"Yes sir," Aria replied.

Her face melted away, replaced by the face of the rebel fleet commander. Khalid controlled his anger as he looked upon her face. She was One Million, no doubt. Ntanga bloodline, which mean she was descended from the first group of administrators sent to rule over newly subdued planets after the end of the consolidation.

"Identification," Khalid said.

"Commander Folasade Agani," Aria replied.

"Open vocal communication."

A low ping echoed in the command bridge.

"Commander Agani, what is the meaning of this?" Khalid said.

The commander jumped as a chorus of curses broke out in the rebel ship. The commander looked around as if looking for annoying bug.

"They're applying counter measures," Aria said.

"Keep the link," Khalid replied. "Open visuals."

Folasade finally focused on his face.

"Khalid Cassad," she said, bitterness in her voice.

"Sade," Khalid answered. "How is your father?"

Sade's expression became more severe. "By the Authority vested in me by the New Regime Council I demand you surrender your fleet to me. We are awaiting link procedures."

"The Authority of the New Regime?" Khalid smiled. "The New Regime has no authority. You are rebels, nothing more. And as you can see, I have a situation to deal with."

"I suggest you update your information feeds," Folasade replied. "You'll discover the political situation of the Known has changed."

A piercing pain emerged at the base of Khalid's skull. He tried his best to mask it, closing his eyes slowly as in thought.

"Your threats are useless," Khalid replied. "The Empire stands. It will never fall."

Folasade grinned. "It already has."

Thomas touched his shoulder. "The aliens have launched their attack."

Khalid broke communication with the rebels.

"Begin evasive formation," Cassad commanded. "Rheem?"

"We're guiding the alien LMF through the pattern. Impact on the rebel fleet in two minutes."

"Keep them cloaked until impact," Khalid ordered. "Retaliatory assessment."

"The rebels are close," Rheem replied. "We will suffer damage."

Khalid frowned. He was not the type of commander that factored loss into his strategy. He calculated on bringing everyone back from an operation, but this was his first time leading such a large operation. Loss was expected; as a matter of fact, it was inevitable. Still, it did not sit well with him.

"How much?" he finally asked.

"Twenty-eight percent," Rheem answered.

"Increase attack speed," he said. "I want to be as close to the alien force as possible when the rebels retaliate."

Thomas leaned in close. "What are you planning?"

"I'm trying to reduce our losses," Khalid replied.

"I thought our purpose was to defeat the alien force."

"That was our operation until the rebels appeared. You know as well as I do that the odds are not in our favor. Rebel tech is either slightly below or equal to ours. That decreases our battle factor considerably."

Thomas smiled. "Now who's being too analytical?"

"I trust every last one of my comrades," Khalid replied. "But ferocity and skill will not get us out of this situation. This is a time for calculations."

The mass of alien missiles appeared on visual, a swarm of metallic death approaching at near light speed. Rheem's hacking proved almost perfect; the missiles weaved through the Imperial fleet then slammed into the rebels' ships.

"Damage assessment!" Khalid shouted.

"Fifteen percent to our fleet, thirty-eight percent to the rebel force!" Rheem shouted back. "The rebels are arming their weapons."

"What's there target resolution?"

"They're changing formation," Rheem answered. "Fifty percent of the ships are focusing on the alien fleet. They're hailing them, sir."

"Can you override them?"

"On it, sir. I'm changing the message to an ultimatum."

"When the aliens refuse, send them a gift," Khalid answered.

Rheem smirked. "Yes, sir."

Thomas touched him on the shoulder.

"Sir there seems to be a disturbance in the engine complex."

Khalid's eyes rose. "Disturbance?"

Thomas face took on a worried look. "Yes sir."

He handed Khalid his earpiece. Khalid held it close to his ear.

"Is that gunfire?"

The ship lurched to the left. Khalid grasped the arms of his command seat as the other lurched to the side.

"Report!" he shouted.

The first to respond was Aria.

"Sir, we've been hit by a massive virus," she said. "It's attacking our systems on every level. But that's not the worst of it."

"What's going on, Aria?"

"Our A.I.s have been compromised. They been given an imperative command to shut down this ship...and kill you."

"Hack the A.I.s?" Thomas said. "That's impossible!"

"Apparently not," Khalid replied. "Seal off engineering and medical. Prepare an assault team. We'll enter engineering through the Shute."

"They'll be waiting," Thomas said.

"I know," Khalid replied. "We'll send a surprise to clear the way."

"You should stay here," Thomas advised.

Khalid shook his head then almost passed out.

"Are you alright, sir," Thomas asked.

"Yes, and I'm going with the team. They expect me to either be here or attempting to leave this ship. Rheem!"

"Sir!" Rheem replied.

"The alien navigation?"

"Is ours," Rheem replied.

"I want a hole in their center large enough to get our fleet through," Khalid said. "If my memory serves me right there's a Gate three parsecs ahead of us. When we're in the midst of the alien fleet, we jump. Every last one of us."

Rheem's smile was joyous. "Excellent, Balogun!"

Khalid looked at Thomas, whose smile was just as wide.

"You're mad. You know that, right?"

Khalid managed to smile back despite the increasing pain. "Let's take care of the engine room."

Thomas and Khalid rushed over to the chute hatch. The pathway led directly to engineering, a barely used portal for emergency response and evacuation. Two other assault members joined them draped in shock armor and carrying throwing knives.

The ship shuddered from a nearby blast. Khalid wanted desperately to survey the battle but he had to retake his ship first. He tapped the comm on the side of his helmet, linking him to the team.

"Make a hole," Khalid ordered.

The swoosh of the pods echoed through the chute. The first explosion shook the ship; the second was less violent but more effective.

"Vital monitors indicate all engineering personnel are down," Aria reported.

"Okay!" Khalid shouted. "Let's..."

A cloak of blackness swallowed him. He fell, his mind spinning like a damaged fighter ship in freefall. Had the drop pods destroyed the ship? Was he in the lasts moments of consciousness before joining the ancestors?

Khalid opened his eyes to his father's meeting chamber. Sitting before him was a group of men and women that should be impossible for him to see. They looked upon him with grim countenances.

"So, the rebels have succeeded," he said. "I'm dead."

A woman stood, her stern face just as familiar to Khalid as his own. Ziara approached him then placed a firm hand on his shoulder.

"You are not dead, son. But the possibility is imminent. What you see before you was planted inside you during your initiation. It is an emergency protocol which none of us hoped you or any of your family would ever see."

Khalid knelt before the elder, totally submitting to her authority.

"How can I serve you, Elders?" Khalid asked.

"If you are seeing us, the Empire is lost, at least for now," the woman said. "Your family is most likely dead and the New Regime in the process of consolidating its control of the Core worlds."

Grief threatened to overwhelm him. He clinched his fists.

"The One Million can no longer be trusted," the woman continued. "This was inevitability."

Khalid raised his head. "If this was such a certainty, why did you not prevent it?"

The woman's expression remained unchanged.

"That which is fated to be cannot be altered," the woman said. "Every calculated scenario led to the same conclusion."

Calculated. Khalid's grief was tempered by anger.

"Human nature cannot be calculated," he said. "Is this a plan based on statistical probabilities?"

The woman said nothing.

Khalid stood. "This is flawed. I will not..."

The searing pain burned through his mind. He felled back to his knees.

"This is not an option, Khalid Quentin Cassad," the woman said. "Failure to follow this plan will result in the total collapse of the Empire and the sacrifice of your life."

"If I die there will be no one to continue the legacy," Khalid said.

"There are others," the woman replied.

Others? Gendala was known, but she had been compromised. He knew of no others.

"In order to proceed, you must acquire Djele," the woman continued. "The griot contains information that is vital to the next step."

"That's impossible," Khalid said. "Djele is on Ziara. If what you say is true and the New Regime has prevailed, Ziara is occupied."

"Djele is necessary," the woman said. "You will acquire him."

"I don't have the forces to retake an entire world," he said.

"We are not ordering you to retake a world," the woman replied. "We are ordering you to acquire Samake."

The pain increased hi Khalid's head.

"I will do it," he said, succumbing to the threat. "I will acquire Djele. And then what?"

"We will return to give you further instructions."

"I wish to know now," Khalid demanded.

"You will not," the woman replied. "In order to protect the plan, it will be revealed to you in stages."

Khalid grinned. "You don't expect me to succeed?"

"Failure is always a possibility," the woman answered.

The pain diminished with the ancestors' images. When Khalid opened his eyes, he lay on his cot. Emergency lights doused him in a blue hue. The ship vibrated with an erratic pulse. He sat up slowly, hanging his head as he rubbed his head. Blood splattered on his boots; he touched his nose and smeared blood on his hand.

His room door swished open and Thomas and Rheem entered. Thomas looked relieved; Rheem looked annoyed.

"What's our situation?" Khalid asked.

"Not good," Rheem replied. She was about to continue but Thomas cut her off with a wave of his hand.

"What is your situation, Khalid?" he asked.

Khalid looked up at his friend and managed to smile.

"If you are assessing my ability to lead this mission I can assure you that I am fully capable to fulfill my duties," he answered.

"I'm asking you as a concerned friend," Thomas replied.

"I could be better," Khalid said. "I will be. Now get me up to speed."

Thomas nodded to Rheem.

"We're currently in the Shona Quadrant beyond the Sundiata Gate," Rheem said. "Fleet effectiveness is down sixty-five percent."

Khalid closed his eyes. "That many?"

"Yes, sir," Rheem answered. "It was the jump. We only sustained ten percent due to it. It was the debris shower afterwards. We dragged the alien fleet with us. Our shields failed. Of our remaining ships ninety percent are damaged."

"Enemy assessment?" he asked.

"The alien fleet was completely destroyed," Thomas said. "The Regime fleet refused to pursue us through the Gate."

"That was blessing," Khalid said. "Rheem, I need a complete evaluation of the remaining ships as soon as possible. We need to be prepared to move in two hours."

Thomas eyes widened. "Begging my pardon sir, we'll need more than two hours!"

Khalid looked past Thomas to Rheem. "You have my orders."

Rheem smirked as she saluted. "Yes sir. I'll have your report in an hour."

"Excellent," Khalid replied.

Thomas and Rheem turned to exit his room.

"Thomas, stay," Khalid said.

Thomas turned, a curious look on his face as Rheem went about her duties.

"What is it?" he asked.

"Have we had a chance to confirm what Folasade said was true?"

"No," Thomas replied. "We've been out of communication since we jumped the Gate. We remained so to avoid detection while we repair."

"What do you think?" Khalid asked.

"I don't know, sir," Thomas replied. "It's possible, but it would have to be from some sort of betrayal. The Core is well defended, especially Ziara. It would have had to come from within and based on circumstances could most like have occurred that way. There's also the matter of the size of fleet sent to apprehend you. I don't think the rebels would have sent such a large force unless they felt they were secure on other fronts. But then the message may have been a ploy to convince you to surrender. They then could use you as leverage in negotiations with the High Family."

"I believe she tells the truth," Khalid replied. "I believe the rebels have captured Ziara."

"How can you be so sure?" Thomas asked.

A flash of pain was his reason why, but he could not reveal his condition to Thomas, at least not yet.

"I have my reasons, but I need to be sure," he said.

Thomas's eyebrows rose. "We're going to the Core. We're going to Ziara."

"Yes," Khalid said. "At least some of us are."

"Sir, we're not strong enough for such a mission."

Khalid stood. "We have to be. We'll go in covert."

"And how will we accomplish that?" Thomas asked. "We don't have any cloak ships in our fleet."

"Pick your men," Khalid said. "Be ready to depart in an hour."

Thomas stared at Khalid for a moment before answering.

"By your command, Oba." He touched his fingers to his chest then exited.

Oba. Khalid let the word simmer in his mind. Everyone in the fleet assumed the worst was true and he was now ruler of the empire, at least what was left of it. He'd imagined his coronation as a splendid affair, an event that would go down in history for its extravagance. Not that he would have wanted it that way, but he knew his father well and the old man would not miss an opportunity to display Cassad wealth and power. It was those displays that raised the anger of many in the empire, the anger that eventually led to the revolt.

The familiar pain registered and he closed his eyes to let the ancestors speak.

"You have made arrangements to acquire the djele?"

"Yes, I have."

"Good. We will inform you of the next stage after completion."

Khalid opened his eyes then reached for a napkin, wiping away the blood that trickled from his nose.

The men were assembled on the deck when Khalid entered. He took a quick glance and smiled. Thomas chose well.

"I don't know if you were informed, but we have a mission to complete. We're going to Ziara to retrieve a valuable item. Since we are at this point wanted men, our approach must be discreet. We will therefore travel to the Uhuru Belt to obtain merchant ships for our journey to the Core."

The men looked among each other. They were not happy.

"I know what you're thinking," Khalid continued. "We'll be traveling into what will be enemy territory with unarmed ships. To top it off you'll have the most wanted man in the empire among you. Not the best situation, I agree."

The men grinned. Thomas did not.

"We'll pack as many weapons necessary for our mission. Although we're going in unarmed, it doesn't mean will return that way."

"If we return," Thomas said.

Khalid's eyes narrowed as he looked at his friend.

"We will return," Khalid replied. "Are the ships ready?"

Thomas nodded.

"Then let's do it. May the ancestors guide our way."

The men prostrated then hurried to their duties.

"Thomas, a word," Khalid said.

Thomas strode to Khalid. "Sir?"

"Never question my authority before the men," Khalid said. "I shouldn't have to say this to you."

"My doubt was not for them," Thomas replied. "It was for you. This is a dangerous mission that may fail. If it does, you'll be either killed or executed if captured. You should not go with us."

"I have to," Khalid said. "No one can retrieve the djele unless they are of Cassad blood. Since I am the only one among us that fits the qualification I must go."

"Then we should come up with an alternate plan."

"There is no other plan!" Khalid immediately regretted his outburst. Thomas's eyes went wide.

"I ask you again, Khalid, is everything okay?"

"No Thomas, it's not. But there is nothing either of us can do about it. I need you focused on the mission, not me. You understand?"

"I understand, oba."

"And stop calling me that," Khalid said.

"Yes...commander."

Thomas turned on his heels then marched away.

Three gate jumps brought them to the outskirts of the Uhuru Belt. Khalid joined the others on the bridge as the main station came into view. Soon afterwards they received hailing inquiries.

"Open communication," Khalid ordered.

The smooth face of the docking officer came into view. He smiled as he brushed back his hair.

"Welcome, Jamal," the officer said.

"Hello Jad," Khalid replied.

"It's so good to see you," Jad said. "Things have been crazy. I guess you heard."

"Yes, we did," Khalid replied. "Is it as bad as they say?"

Jad nodded. "They said the entire royal family was killed. Coalition forces are scouring the planet for Khalid Cassad, but the rumor is he's hiding in the Unknown."

"I see," Khalid said, hiding his anger. "Permission to dock?"

"Of course," Jad said. "The more security teams here the better."

Khalid turned over the ship's control to the docking tug.

"Remember why we're here," he said to his men through the intercom. "We'll gather as many weapons as we can. Try to gather as much intel as possible without being conspicuous. You have three hours."

The ship docked and Khalid exited into Uhuru station. The massive ring was one of the oldest stations in the Known, built during the Empire's first wave. Khalid was very familiar with Uhuru; he relaxed as Jad walked to him, a grin on his face.

"How long are you here?" Jad asked.

"Not long," Khalid replied. "We're here to replenish supplies then we're heading to Njaro."

Jad frowned. "Are you sure you want to do that? Rumor is Njaro's hot."

"That's why we're going," Khalid replied. "You forget who we are?"

Jad shrugged. "Better you than me. Need some help?"

"No, we're good," Khalid replied. "But you can fill me in on what's going down on Ziara."

"I don't know much more than I already shared," Jad said. "I can't believe the Empire got caught flat-footed. It's not as if…"

Uhuru station went dark. Emergency lights kicked in immediately, filling the station with a dim blue glow.

"What the fek?" Jad exclaimed.

An amplified voice boomed.

"Khalid Cassad, you are hereby ordered to surrender to the Authority of the New Regime. Any resistance to our order will result in deadly force!"

"Everyone back in the ship now!" Khalid shouted.

Jad looked bewildered. "The Regime? Here? How did they..."

Pulse fire erupted throughout the station. Jad flinched then his face went slack. He fell aside, revealing a squad of armored men running toward Khalid, pulse rifled lowered. Khalid dropped to one knee as he snatched his shongo from his waist. He twisted the handle to activate the blade then threw it sidearm. Three more shongos flew over his head. The blades appeared simultaneously as they streaked toward the squad then attacked with coordinated precision, burning through the reactive armor and cutting the men down in seconds. Khalid opened his palm and the shongo returned to him, slapping into his palm. Thomas stood before the carnage, staring down at the smoking heap.

"Hurry, Thomas!" Khalid shouted.

Thomas bounded over the men and ran to the ship with a provision box bouncing on his shoulders. Khalid and the guardsmen who joined his shongo attack formed a rearguard as the others returned. There were very few.

They backed into the ship. The crew was at work, cutting any physical and programmed links to the dock.

"Get us out of here hot," Khalid ordered.

Rheem nodded. The ship lurched backwards, throwing everyone not seated to the floor.

They were throwing into the midst of scrambling ships and attacking fighter drones. The Regime mothership sat off a distance, discharging its lethal cargo in waves.

"Strap up!" Rheem shouted. "I'm going to jump!"

"Fek!" Khalid said. He managed to reach his seat and strap in just before jump. The jolt caused him to black out for a moment, and then he stood before a sight that was becoming familiar.

The ancestors studied him with disapproving eyes. They were no longer obscure figures, he could recognize them all. Standing at the forefront was Ziara Cassad, her severe expression well known to all Cassads. Beside her was her son, Shaka Cassad. He smirked as he sat on his stool, his confidence still prominent as a spirit. The third spirit confirmed what he had heard and hoped not to believe. Ose XXIV, his father, sat on his stool with a solemn gaze.

It was Ziara who finally addressed him.

"You have been betrayed," she said.

"Yes," Khalid replied.

"You know the culprit. You must set an example," Shaka said.

"Yes," Khalid replied.

His father stood and approached him.

"You would not have been my choice," he said.

Khalid didn't reply.

"Be the man I tried to make you," Ose continued. "Take back our Empire!"

The ancestors faded and Khalid's vision cleared to the bridge of his ship. They were in empty space, the crew and others looking about with uncertainty. Khalid unbuckled then stood.

"Rheem, I need an assessment of what we were able to salvage. I also need a head count."

"Yes sir," Rheem said.

Khalid's eyes fell on Thomas.

"Come with me," he said.

Khalid proceeded to his cabin, Thomas close behind. The door opened this swished close behind them.

"Sit," Khalid said.

Thomas took a seat.

Khalid folded his arms across his chest. He studied his friend for a moment before speaking, knowing his next words would destroy everything.

"Why?" he finally asked. "Why did you do this?"

"What are you talking about, Khalid?"

Thomas's denial angered him.

"Fek, Thomas! If you're going to stab me in the back at least be honest about it. The Regime troops were waiting for us at Uhuru because you told them we were coming! Good men died because of you!"

Thomas looked away. When he looked at Khalid again his expression was resolved.

"I'm One Million Khalid, but I am Thracian first."

"Since when did Thrace become part of the Regime?"

"Three years ago, when it became obvious to our leaders that the Empire would fall."

"Obvious?"

Thomas stood. "The Alien Wars have drained Cassad resources to a dangerous level. In addition, the energy spent identifying and eliminating covert threats within the Empire have diminished Empire intelligence. The only way a takeover could have been aborted would be employing extreme measures. In other words, wiping out those worlds considered central to the Regime's efforts. Ose would not allow that."

A bitter taste formed in Khalid's mouth. "My words."

"Yes," Thomas replied.

Both men pulled their shongos. Khalid kicked Thomas over the chair before arming his knife. He swung down; Thomas blocked with his blade and they sparked. Thomas rolled to his feet then attacked, striking at Khalid desperately. Khalid parried his attacks easily, fighting the sadness that threatened to overtake him. The Empire was mad. The Known had become chaos. His family was dead, and his best friend was trying to kill him.

He sidestepped Thomas's knife thrust then sliced his blade across Thomas's neck. Thomas jerked then gurgled. He collapsed, blood flowing from the razor thin gash across his neck. Khalid turned off the shongo then re-attached it to his belt. He went to his desk then pressed the button to his comm.

"Rheem, I need you to come to my cabin. Bring a medic."

Moments later his door slid aside. Rheem strode in, followed by Cerilius.

"What's the mat...by the ancestors!"

Cerilius dropped to his knees then examined Thomas. He looked up, his face a mix of shock and certainty.

"He's dead," he said.

"Get rid of him," Khalid said. "Make sure no one else sees you."

Both men looked at Khalid as if waiting for an explanation.

"The Regime will no longer know where to find us," he said.

Anger twisted Rheem's face. She looked down at Thomas then spat on him.

"I'll do it," he said.

"No," Khalid said. "I need you back on the bridge. We need to go to Ziara immediately."

"We don't have the fuel to make it all the way," Rheem said. "We'll have to stop at Njaro."

"Understood," Khalid said.

Cerilius sealed Thomas's wound. Together with Rheem he lifted the body onto his shoulder then carried it from the cabin. Khalid sat on his bed then covered his face with his hands. He yelled, letting out the frustration and rage in those few moments. Then he lowered his hands and adjusted his clothing. He stood before his mirror and inspected himself. A slight pain crept into his head; behind his reflection he could see Ziara, Shaka and his father looking on in approval.

"You are Khalid Nkrumah Cassad, twenty-seventh emperor of the Known," Ziara said. "We stand behind you."

Khalid nodded his head. He opened his cabinet then took out a small cup then filled it with water. He took the cup in both hands then poured it into the base of the ficus tree in the corner of his cabin.

"I pour libations in your honor," he said. "I am, because you were. I shall not fail you."

He replaced the cup, inspected himself once more, and then left his cabin.

KING'S HUNT

BY

HOWARD NIGHT

The war between the Cassad Empire and the New Regime drew indistinct lines across contested space.
Lawlessness.
Violence.
Death.
These became the tenants of the worlds in between. But for those that were strong enough, or fast enough...or guileful, contested space became a place to thrive.
-Samake. Cassad djele/historian. From The Cassad Chronicles

Chapter One
The Indo Bar

"Just a piece of fek dive bar, Pack," my pops once told me. "They're the same everywhere in the known." He'd just pulled me and Drez out of "Jags", the local hole in the wall back in Buckets Hollow. I remember how terrified we were when he popped up in front of us at that filthy corner table where we were sitting and freaking out because we couldn't pay our tab.

"Look at you now..." he'd said more annoyed and disappointed than anything else. Ten Arcadian cycles, an eye, an arm and All knows how many "piece of fek" dive bars later and I understand why. We were young and looking to get in on all the action the adults were hiding in that little after hours spot but Pops told us better. There's nothing in these dark little watering holes worth wasting anyone's time.

Of course, here I am...again.

Third bar on this world, the seventh straight night here and I'm beginning to think the intel I bought ain't worth fek. The only thing I'm finding is the same thing my old man told me to expect; nothing.

The Last Ship Out is what remains of a nearly five-hundred-year-old gunboat and sits down deep in the lower levels of Passieun City; third biggest port city here on Indo. Ownership and the name has changed dozens of times since it was first dragged into the old city and opened but since then it's pretty much always been a dive bar. It's a big space but dark, even to those with optic upgrades. Most places like this fill the air with the standard privacy invasion counter measures. So the booths, the alcoves and the far corners of the room remain cloaked in shadow. The bar is lit up, of course, as well as the tables in the center of the floor. The servers are illuminated by little balls of light that orbit their bodies to allow the patrons to see them coming. Wouldn't do to have one of them walk up unnoticed and hear something they shouldn't.

One makes her way back around to my table. Most places still use live servers because they can offer more than a droid or bot. She asks me if I want another drink, hoping that the ink I'm sipping on will get me chambered up enough to zip her some cred. But I'm not interested in binding with some wage slave when it might cost me finding my mark.

I flash two fingers at her, ordering another ink. Got to be careful with that though; "gunks" are the most ridiculous looking addicts.

The big door at the end of the bar collapses open and lets in a gust of cool air that doesn't smell of alcohol, burnt sugar or body funk. A small group of Indo workers shuffle in bringing the funk of a hard day's work with them. They work salvage out in the dead plains where the electromagnetic field is still up on this world. A hold over from the Wars of the Blade, an area about a quarter of the planet is a tech dead zone. Thousands of war ships fell to this planet's surface during a particularly nasty battle. Usually the wrecks would have been long since plundered but somebody forgot to turn off the EMF over that one fourth of the planet and whatever's generated it is still running ten cycles later. Conventional salvage can't be done even with the best faradon gear but the wrecks are way too valuable to be left out there. So, by hand, the Indo workers work the dead plains, dragging the debris clear of the EMF and manually picking the wrecks clean.

Hazardous work, I don't envy them even with the big coin they're pulling in.

The Indo workers find a quiet corner of the bar and turn it into a loud one. Servers come rushing up to take advantage of the coin in their pockets and the hard-worked salvagers are eager to give it. I watch the negotiations for a bit, growing more restless. By the time a few of the group disappear into the dark recesses of the private booths I'm ready to leave myself. Seven straight nights and seven straight no shows means that…whoa now.

He's big, like I expected, as most of them are, but older than I would have thought. There's more gray in his spiky stubble than black now. Even so he moves with a grace that I would never have noticed if I didn't already know what he was. The clothes on his back are pretty commonplace and don't mark him as being from anywhere in particular. But they're roomy enough to hide a good-sized weapon.

Maybe two.

He crosses the room at an odd angle, as if he's so tired he doesn't notice where he's going, and then he catches himself and cuts back across the room.

Nice.

Without giving himself away he's just gotten a good look at everyone in the bar. And he wouldn't have bothered if he didn't have military grade optics so he knows what everyone in the bar is packing. That includes me.

Anything more serious than a bladed weapon would have set off all the bells and whistles of his security gear. Course there's plenty of ways to beat military grade optics. Next gen military grade camo, for one, would deny him a peek at what you've got. If you've got the coin the upgrade will even make him think he's seeing an unarmed man.

I do not have the coin.

There's a sweet V.I. hacking matrix that will render his optics unable to read specific weapon signatures but you have to know exactly his optical manufacturer. Now I know where this guy got his originals but I really doubt he's still using those.

No, I have to beat his optics the only way left to me; I have to actually be unarmed.

But not too unarmed. A small blade won't look as out of place as being completely unarmed in a pit like this would look suspicious and I don't want him looking at me any longer than he looks at anybody else. I slump in my seat to shorten my long twenty decimeter frame. I'm nowhere near as tall as this guy but Arcadians grow pretty big so I tend to stand out just a bit. Right now, we're the two biggest guys in the bar and I'm hoping that doesn't draw his eye.

Surprisingly he takes a seat in the well-lit center of the room, with his back to the door. He's either not worried about who's coming in behind him, which I doubt, or he's got it covered somehow. Either way I settle in and begin my recon.

Two fingers again call the server over with another ink. I just want to look like another beat up Indo scavenger dulling away the day's pain. But I watch him, try and figure out exactly how he's armed and what allies, if any, he has. He's probably got one of the servers or even the owner on his payroll to keep him updated on newcomers. Hopefully the fact that I've been coming here for over a week will give me enough of a pass that they won't bring it up to him.

To my surprise though he says nothing to the server other than to order a drink and turn down her extra services. Can't tell if they're communicating sub-vocally... doubt the servers here have that kind of gear. Still, he hasn't shown me or anyone else in the bar the slightest bit of interest. Could be he's sure that he's far enough off the grid that he's got nobody looking for him here.

Not a bad assumption given the state of the known right now. It's total chaos across damn near a hundred systems. Long standing "second tier" galactic powers are vying for control of what was once the Cassad Empire and vultures are swooping in to glean the pickings of the once proud house.

Vultures like me.

The big guy takes a long swig, drains his cup in one downing then signals the server to bring him another. He doesn't look like he's expecting anyone to join him so I can wait until he gets good and "nice" before I move in. Not really sure if that'll make him more or less dangerous though.

There comes a ruckus from the far end of the room. A brief argument between two indo workers ends with one of them on the floor and the other laughing his ass off. I feign mild interest in the fight but my mark snaps his head in the other direction. Caught off guard I realize too late my mistake as I look to see what startled him.

It was a ruse and my backwater ass fell for it! My eyes jump back to him and the smug bastard is staring right at me. He's wearing a nasty "I got ya" smile and with one hand he beckons me over.

I had better do as he says 'cause with his other he's leveling one mean looking gun at me from under his table.

Buckin' Royal Guard…if I live through this I'll never underestimate them again.

Chapter Two
COMMERCE

I don't hesitate to get up but I take my time. Not sure if he'll fire off that heater here in the bar. Can't risk it; body armor I'm wearing is good enough for the minor weapons fire that the stick-up scabs outside in the lower city are packin' but not for much more. Can't see it clearly but it looks to have a decent enough power cell, which means it's energy based and more than he'll need to make most of me a memory. So I get the buck up and with my hands in the clear I make my way over to his table.

He gestures to the server and she slides a second chair over to his table. She's nervous, I can see, so I know she's the one who tipped him. Won't underestimate the wage slaves again either.

I try and adjust the chair to my advantage as I sit but with a quick tap of that gun to the underside of the table he lets me know he's on to me. The old guy grins, tight lipped and wide, spreading out that prickly stubble which sticks out like the quills of a scared daggerback. The surprise I felt from his getting the drop on me pales in comparison to the shock I get when he first opens his mouth.

"The infamous Pack Loren," he says. "...of the legendary 46th."

What the buck? How does he know who I am? Evidently the surprise on my face is apparent because the bastard laughs.

"What? Didn't think I could I.D. you that quick?" his voice is smooth, deep and slides out of his throat in that pompous Median belt accent.

"The Infamous?" I ask. "Legendary?" Sure, my old unit was pretty well known back in Arcadian space but why would anyone from the larger worlds have heard of us.

"Of course, Loren. You most of all" and his mouth stretches into an even wider grin, lips parting, showing his ink stained teeth. "You are Loren, right? The file I have details the loss of that eye and arm. Both regrown, I see, not replaced; my optics can tell. It's the corticolin bands just beneath the skin that give you away. So, you're Sgt. Pack Loren of Arcadias 46th Task Unit, who held their own against the Giaks and the Junns when the rest of that bit of space fell into chaos."

Hoofer-Fek. Nobody ever took notice of Arcadia and no one but Arcadians cared when the Giaks and the Junns tried to invade. What's he playing at?

"The Wars of the Blade raged all over," I say. "But our little piece of it never seemed to matter much to the rest of the known."

Somehow that smile grows even wider. "Maybe the hub-heads didn't pay too much attention, but when human soldiers from small worlds take down ten-foot-tall Giaks in unpowered combat...well, anybody who might have to eventually deal with that is gonna take notice."

I don't say anything to that. Can't tell if he's just glossing my finish or if he's speaking level. No reason for him to lie but the "admiration" has got to be fek.

With a sigh he leans back in his chair, seeming to relax a bit, but still keeping that gun on me. "And then there's you, Pack Loren..."

"I came here..." I try to cut him off but he just talks over me.

"...first a war criminal..."

"So say the Junns." I snap.

"...then a traitor..."

"I don't need a..."

"...an avenger..."

"I've got coin to..."

"The last I heard, Loren, you turned on your own unit" and with that his smile vanishes. There's the look of deadly intent I'd expected to see in the eyes of one of the Royal Guard.

I should just try and deal, after all that's why I tracked this bastard to the outer territories, to the Desolate Perimeter. But I can't help it; his little tirade on my personal history has me way off my game.

Which wasn't all that good to begin with.

"That's a lot of info on me. How long have you known I've been looking for you?"

After another swig of his freshly filled cup he answers. "Just about as long as it took me to order a drink."

"And you got all my stats just like that?"

"Oh no. I meant it when I said you and the 46th were infamous. Anybody in the merc game has looked up your unit ever since they started popping up throughout the known as hired soldiers."

That was true. Without a war most of my old unit had turned to being paid soldiers after we lost Arcadia. The memory bites hard…We lost Arcadia…

His eyes shine a bit as he watches my reaction. "I do wonder why you've been taking out your old crew. Maybe the betrayal of Arcadia wasn't your decision?"

I grind my teeth and somehow, I remember why I'm here in the first place. "I'm looking to make a purchase" I say.

His eyebrows rise. "You think I'm selling something?"

"You've something I want to buy."

"If you're thinking of hiring me out…I don't guard any-one or anything but myself these days."

Now I feel like I got some footing. "That's right; you were dismissed."

Those eyes flare for a moment then soften as the big man suddenly laughs. "Perhaps," he says with understanding in his voice. "Rumors and data bits are not to be trusted to tell the whole story."

"Perhaps."

"Then what does the 'infamous for perhaps no good rea-son' Pack Loren need to purchase from a 'Dismissed' Guards-man of the First House of Denir?"

I had hoped to make this offer from a position of strength rather than sitting with gun aimed at my poker. Really, I have got to get better at plan making.

"I would like to buy your armor." I say flatly.

"My armor? My battle Armor?"

"No sir," I explain. "Your Royal Dress armor."

For a long pulse beat I watch as his mind races trying to figure my angle. Not to worry, he'll never figure out what I'm…

"You're after Cassad."

Fek.

His palm slaps the table with such a clap that I thought the gun had gone off. Damn, I had underestimated him again.

"You've got to be kidding me, Loren" I wish he'd stop blurting my name out loud. "Cassad's Royal Guard is nothing like the Denir Royal Guard."

But he says it with just a bit of hesitation. Probably 'cause they were alike. The House of Denir was a Cassad house long ago, but the Royal Guard had been protecting the Cassads for longer than that. There were some very important similarities, such as the Royal dress armor.

"I'm sure you don't need it anymore." With that I very carefully reach into the folds of the Indo jacket I have on and pull free the small but brightly colored data card hidden within. As carefully as I can I place it on the table.

"If I even still have it…" He says as he picks up the data chip and examines it. "Well, look at that."

He still had it. The only question was; would he part with it? "Not much I know," I say indicating the chip.

"Not much," he agrees. "but QED certified Old Reg currency…damn you make it tempting."

I'll bet.

"And you have this with you here?" he asks with a tightness in his voice.

"I can get it to you as fast as you can get me the armor."

I watch what remains of the old Royal Guard wage war with the disgruntled and betrayed man he's become. The Denir had summarily dismissed their Royal Guard at some point during the last decade. A purge that had been a bit bloody according to…rumors and data bits. Still, the man had once been indoctrinated into one of the most fanatical military arms in the known. Getting his armor from him isn't going to be easy.

"Deal" he says abruptly.

Buck me… "Deal?"

"Yea. Surprised? Do you know what the Cassads did to us? To the Guard?" he asks leaning back into the chair. His face grows dark and his eyes stare at nothing. "We were…pillars…no…we were golden shields of light…protecting to the Lords of the universe. And we did not do it for prestige or crukin' coin!" he grows quiet for a pulse beat then adds in almost a whisper, "it was for love…"

There's a "click" and I know he's reset the safety on his weapon. He looks at me again trying to figure me out a bit more.

"What is this for you, Loren? The credits they're offering for Cassad is a symbolic gesture. No one expects him to be caught... killed maybe... in a planetary assault. But Cassad can't be captured and brought to trial. Your attempt for that ridiculous bounty is practically suicide. You want to die? Or...maybe you blame the Cassads for what happened to Arcadia."

"You said we had a deal. Where do we make the exchange?"

The big man lets out a big nasty hot breath and then cracks his neck. "You can bring the qed here."

"No. I may be slow, but I reboot quick. You OWN this bar."

He almost snickers. "On my honor I'll deal with you fairly, Loren. You bring that coin here and all is legit; I'll give you my armor."

"The entire set," I insist. "Intact and complete."

"On my honor."

Chapter Three
HONOR

It's raining by the time I make my way back down to bar, not that any rain drops actually make it down this far to the lower levels of the city. Instead there're several man-made "waterfall" conduits conducting the water down to the reclamation plants below. The walls of the building units run slick with drain water and there's a steady falling mist that drenches everything else sitting outside for extended periods.

Never the less I stop before I go in, considering this madness one last time. Without the need for a cover I came back to the bar in my flight suit, field jacket and virtual visor. It helps a bit against the sudden cold wetness.

On his "honor" he'd said. Don't trust honor...not one bit. Soldiers put their lives on the line for it in one battle, and then in the next you discover they never had it at all. Of course, the Royal Guard was a different animal. Most of them were born into the Guard, living for their Houses like most live for their god. But those fanatics were all dead, either killed in the purge or dead by their own hand when they found themselves out in the real known.

But this particular gentleman was indoctrinated through their regular armed forces. Still a fanatic but not as religious about those he guarded. Hopefully that works to keep him honest about this deal.

Before I can decide to enter the front is lit up in brilliant blue light. The entrance opens and out comes the Ex-Denirian Royal Guard flanked by a few well-armed employees.

"Were you having second thoughts?" he asks.

I take my time answering, letting him watch me look over his small army. My Virtual Visor covers my face from just above my eyebrows to just below my nose. With it on all he can see of my eyes are the two glowing holographic representations; ghostly, triangular patches of white light with no pupils, but they open and close in sync with my real ones. The visor also highlights some of the tech his squad is toting. One of them reads really high in the EM spectrum... might be a bogey... or maybe borged up. "No. Just wondering about the honor of the Royal Guard."

He snorts derisively. "You don't seem to have my qed."

"You don't seem to have my armor."

With another one of those nasty breaths the big man nods to one of his crew, who in turn walks back into the bar only to return a pulse beat later followed a huge, self-motivated crate. The Royal Guard opens the front of the crate and low and behold there sits his dress armor as shiny and polished as the last day he wore it. It's a pretty close match for the design the Cassad Royal Guard use. The armor gets passed down from Guard to apprentice I think so his set could be a few centuries old. He's taken care of it...and that worries me.

"Now how about you show me whatever it is you've got hidden under that holocloak."

He's good alright. Carefully I reach into my jacket and retrieve a small two ended remote. It's a simple little device, well-worn with chipped and faded white enamel that has two buttons that can be set to trigger multiple devices of various manufacture and function. I slide it around in my hand and depress the narrow-ended side.

Right next to me the ground shimmers and distorts until a pretty hefty cargo container can be seen hovering just off the ground. I reach down with one hand and pop the opening to reveal about two hundred and fifty thousand Old Regime Credits, all Q.E.D. certified and neatly stacked. It's nearly the sum total of everything I have left and it took me some time to get.

"Do you mind if I verify?" the Ex-Guardsman asks. I pull my own scanner from my belt.

"If you don't mind."

We step past each other without outward signs of worry or mistrust and I try to appear totally focused on my own scans as I have my back to him. I do notice however that the hired guns in his small little group are constantly peering about, no doubt looking for anything or anyone else I might have cloaked and waiting in front of this bar.

My scan completes first and I'll be damned…the old bastard just might be dealing fair. So I turn and wait for him to finish. Seems that after the purge the big guy has decided to check and then double check anybody he's dealing with. He scans every single qed.

"Looks good" he nods slowly but doesn't look satisfied. It's not the money… The QED certification, given by the Brython Currency Exchange, meant that the seven big wigs of the New Regime would still recognize the currency. So it was good practically from one end of the known to the other despite the war on the Cassads.

"Then I'll just be on my way."

"Just a second." He says and his little army produces a ton of small arms.

I flash a grim smile. "You're not reneging on our deal, now are you?" Something's off. His little gang of makeshift guardians look a bit unsure of themselves. They weren't expecting this it seems. What's the old guy thinking?

"I did a bit more research on you, Loren. Just trying to get past all the rumor and innuendo."

I drop the smile and ask again, "Are. You. Reneging?"

"Just wondering what your plan is for my old armor."

"Thought you had that figured out."

"More like," he hesitates and now I can see the proud face of the old Royal Guardsman peeking through. "How many of Cassad's Royal Guard are going to die in your attempt to bring him in?"

What the... his buckin' honor! How do I handle this?

"Uhh... not so many as you probably want."

His face goes blank. "As I want?"

"I know about the part they played in the dismissal of your Guard."

He stares hard, no doubt running every optical scan of me as he can, trying to see if I'm lying. But I'm wearing my Visor now, so this time he won't get anything and he'll have to judge for himself.

I jump back in before he can challenge my play. "Look, I'm not your payback for whatever it was they did. I'm going after Cassad and I need him alive, so I'm not risking going in chambered up to kill."

His face draws tight as he studies me for a moment, and then he looks back at the crate full of currency. "This a Doppler switch?"

"Yup." I say. As long as I'm in range of the crate I can blow it. Once I'm clear and gone...the switch deactivates. They're pretty common place so I'm sure he's not worried about it.

"Fine. Go." And just like that the deal is done. But I don't like the way he looks like he's still thinking.

I'm back to the port when I know the deal is going bad. It wasn't hard to find the three tracers he'd placed on the crate though I was surprised that he'd put none on the armor itself. Probably didn't want to compromise it I guess. What worries me isn't the crate; it's the little group of moles he has spread out at the port.

They're easy to spot; you can't turn failed salvage workers into clandestine spies. Edgy and looking over everybody traveling with cargo through the terminal, they evidently don't know I can holo-cloak the armors crate as easily as I did the credits. Looks like they're looking over everyone wearing anything like my visor. So I stow mine in my jacket next to my gun.

As I walk right past his ragged looking sentinels I wonder what happened that made the old guy change his mind. Maybe it was concern for Cassad's Royal Guard. Maybe he figured out I made up that part about them having something to do with the purge of his unit.

I reach the hangar where my ship is docked and find a little welcoming committee. Looks like at least one of his hired hands has got a decent brain; must've looked through the registry and took a guess at which ship was mine. There are seven of them, all armed but only three look like they're any good in a fight. I walk right up to them.

"This your ship?" I ask.

"Who are you?" the leader of the gang asks. He's little and holds his chin high with a clear chip on his shoulder.

"I'm Tagget, the Engineer you asked for."

He looks me up and down. "Where's your equipment?" he challenges.

"Uh…" I shake the tool belt I have sitting quite plainly on my hip. "Right here. Thought you weren't gonna be here. But you can show me where the problem is."

"I ain't the owner, backbirth!" he snaps and a few of his boys laugh.

"So…" I continue. "…you can't show me where the rad leak is?"

"Rad leak?" he asks and I point to the warning, flashing brightly on the holo terminal at the hangar hatchway.

"s'what I'm here for."

"Where's the owner?" he demands even as he and his guys step away from the hangar hatchway, one of them even bothering to shield his crotch.

I shrug my shoulders. "I don't know…salvage run? What's the problem? The leak getting' by the dampenin' wall?"

Again, he snaps, "I don't know! I ain't the rustin' port authority. Go fix it!"

I just shrug my shoulders again and step through the group of retreating thugs while trying to hide the growing smile on my face.

THUNK!

"Wha'd on styx is 'dis?" croaks the tallest of the thugs. I turn about and see him kicking a slightly wavering patch of air. The others all grow very interested in what nearly tripped their buddy.

Fek. The cloaked crate should've been closer on my heels but the damn power cell must be low. Would've switched to my own equipment but once I cleared out the tracers I saw no reason to give up the old guard's container.

"Hey. Didn't that guy the boss wanted have a…"

"GET H…" WHAM!

I take out the leader first with the hydro-spanner on my tool belt, despite his being the furthest from me. He drops like a Targo indigul and his crew fall into discord even faster than I'd have hoped. Of the rest, only two pull out handguns, both projectile weapons, which makes it better odds than I'd hoped. But as I pull my own NOK 37 handgun they rush me instead of retreat, actually providing cover for the armed buckheads. What on styx is he paying these fools?

I pop the gunmen with the clearest line of sight first but have to backpedal to avoid the wild swing of a long-curved blade that sinks right through the floor almost as if it was a holo. A Kendo blade? Where'd this fool get a Wars of the Blade weapon?

He's surprised he can't pull the blade free so I know it's not his. While he's yanking at it he gets two in his back from his panicky buddy.

Duck another swing from a stun baton. The Royal Guard must not be too deep in cred if he can't afford thugs with better weapons…

Duck.

Shoot.

…or who are smarter. Don't think anyone of them thought to call for backup. Good thing I shot the leader first.

Block.

Shoot.

Got the second gunman with that one. He drops and I get another one trying to recover his weapon. The last two are smarter than the rest or at least they wise up in time 'cause they're off and running. Don't know how long I have before they collect themselves and call the Guard to let him know where I'm berthed so I can't dawdle.

Still, no sense in leaving behind perfectly good weaponry...but the two handguns are Barron Inc. pieces of crap. Should've figured. The blade is fine though and I slide it up out of the floor with ease. Long time since I've seen a blade with a Kendo edge. It's pretty unremarkable; dao shaped...but no identifying marks or wrappings...no world colors. Might be older than the Blade then? The guy welding it was just a thug though, the blade never even whistled as he swung it. Wielding it requires a learned touch or you'll just end up getting it stuck in whatever you hack at. Idiot couldn't have known what he had; blade like this could buy him a small ship. Wonder how he came by it? Buck it...I don't have all day.

Through the hatch with my new armor in tow I step onto the hangar deck which sits cliff-side overlooking the white plains. The dark cloudy sky has just a hint of the approaching dawn so the silhouette of the far off Stony Mountains is just starting to emerge from the blackness. My ships running lights illuminate the hangar bay as I approach.

The hangar registry reads my ships name as: *Calypso's Lie*. Anybody close enough to read the emblem on her side would find it too burned and charred from rough entry to make out, but her real name is *War Child*.

I found her in the Targothian Graveyard, floating deep in the smashed-up flotsam, somehow, miraculously still intact despite the conditions there. She's a Mutt...M.U.T.T., a Multi-Purpose Utility Troop Transport. A holdover from the first space wars during the Great Age of Discovery. I'm not sure what duty she saw back then but I had to paint her new name over the faded original 'cause I couldn't sand it off. Some kind of animal glyph I think. Would've left her there to continue to sink deeper into the graveyard but I recognized the cete-armor. It looked like a wild animal then, spiky where impacts hadn't chipped off the new growth but the whole of it had withstood the pounding like a champ. So I claimed her and took the better part of two cycles rebuilding her, keeping her hidden from the raider gangs that worked the graveyard, spending almost every last bit of my coin to get her up and running.

I added the wings. Been in too many rough drops where an EMP or EMF strips away all power to not know that you'd better have decent mechanical hardware back up for your powered tech. I rebuilt three Tarkanian EMT engines and jammed two of them into the jet housings, keeping the third for a spare. Then I lucked into some Element G for the grav-well which meant I could do something few could; cross most of the known on my own without having to hitch a ride or even use a gate.

Of course, I keep most of this a secret as much as possible. Ship like this is worth its weight in lifetimes. I've had to protect *War Child* as much as she's protected me.

Her rear cargo hatch opens at my approach and I ascend into her belly with my new gear in tow. She's got a nice sized cargo bay which is mostly empty right now. Just some light ore that I can't unload cause it's overpriced and my, currently down, eight-leg walker.

I stow the armor beneath the floor of the bay in a pirate's hold and then make my way up to the command deck. With the grav-well off line the footing in the ship is a little precarious as *War Child* is constructed with the decks curving around the ships gravity center. Not a problem but it's a hassle when I'm trying to keep her specs of the grid.

War Child was originally designed for a three-man command crew at minimum or a wartime crew of about seventeen. She can transport seventy conventional soldiers or up to twenty heavy armored personnel. It wasn't hard for me to convert her to be piloted by one man but her command deck still held three stations. I really don't see the point in wasting the time on changing it; Ops and Tactical are still slaved to Primary. Besides the configuration is almost exactly the same as the Hawkbats I used to fly in the Blade.

I'm just strapping myself into the Primary control seat when my proximity alarm warns of pedestrian traffic. I check the ground feed and see the old Royal Guard, in full assault armor striding into the hangar with a bit more of his better armed employees in tow.

"LOREN! Power down your ship or I'll scuttle it right here!"

Ships sensors highlight why he even thinks that's possible. One of his men is leveling a pretty nasty piece of hardware at my ship; an armor piercing High Yield Explosive launcher. I try and gauge where he's aiming. It looks enough like he's targeting the cete-armor parts of the ship that I'll risk it.

A quick subvocal command and *War Child's* external speakers come online. "Thought we had deal?" I say. "Thought we both made out."

His men spread out around the hangar, ridiculously trying to surround my ship. Some are trying to find the cockpit, but War Child's canopy is now safe behind a two-meter-thick cete-armor shield.

"Deal's off Loren! I want the armor back! I cannot dishonor my fellow Guardsmen"

"Funny, I see your honor didn't get you to bring back the coin I dropped you."

"You power down and we'll work something out! You try to launch and I'll gut that ship… and then you!"

I check the angle on that HYE launcher again. Hmm…pretty sure. He'll likely target one of the engine housings.

"LOREN! Last warning!" The old guard is pointing his weapon at my ship. His armor battle armor doesn't look at all like the fighting armor of the Cassad Royal Guard. A couple of hundred years makes all the difference. Not sure he's got the fire power to do any real damage but he's more likely to know what he can hit to keep me on the ground. Even as I'm thinking I'm pulled down into the Primary Control seat as the grav-well powers up.

"Sorry, but all deals are final!" I say.

"You can't think your little plan is gonna work now anyway, Loren! Not when I let them know you've got my armor."

He's bluffing. No way will he come anywhere close to contacting the Cassad Royal Guard. They might not have actually had anything to do with his Guards purge but sure as styx ends they'll try and take his ass of the board if they learn where he is now. The Denir and the Cassads are not exactly allies at the moment.

Still…there's a risk. Don't want to have to kill the old guy but he's putting himself in my path. I can't help but to admire him for his sense of honor, as late in the game as it is. Damn it…

I start the launch and take her up…slow.

"FIRE!" I hear him order. There are two bright flashes; I missed seeing the other HYE launcher, and then two big explosions. *War Child* hardly even shakes as her cete-armor absorbs the blasts and reflects a ton of it back down into the hangar. I cut the hangar feed a moment too late and see the Royal Guard burned out of his armor.

I wonder if anyone'll give him the last rights he probably deserves. Wonder if there's anyone who'll honor his memory at all.

Chapter Four
DREAMTIME

I'm just about done pulling the Royal Guards dress armor apart when *War Child* alerts me that we've arrived at Hampton's Gate. With a groan I stand up from my work stool and take a look at how much I've done. The fancy purple and gold armor hung in the workshop bay like a macabre marionette, its innards open and exposed. It was harder to open than I thought it would be but somehow it still didn't take very long.

I trudge up to the Command deck and check the ships status. We're just coming up on the first of the outer markers, close enough to the gate that a check of the long-range scanner is warranted. Not much traffic coming in from this angle, which is good…, which is planned.

The trip here took a bit longer than it should have because I took put a deep, long dogleg in my flight course; needed to come into the gate from a vector that would match the course direction and time stamps in my fake log in case they're inspecting. Never know who's in charge of the jump gates these days with the Cassads falling off the map. The Junns took control of the gate at Cannius when the Giaks drove the Cassads out of the "Quad". The Protectorate Gate was nearly destroyed in the uprising at Sennal. The Amber Gate is being fought over right now by the Quaznians and the Norlans… don't know if that's been settled. The three big Gates; Scion, Alpha, and Maren are too big and too close to the heavily settled areas to be controlled. Still, with almost half the jump gates in jeopardy I've got to move quickly. Can't be on the wrong side of the known when one critical to what I'm trying to get done is blocked; I'm on a tight timetable.

Hampton's Gate is a good-sized gate that'll get me close to my destination with some time to spare. It's showing nominal traffic along my vector. Still a bit too far out for me to read what the ship types are so I sub vocalize a command to the ships Computer Ops Program to notify me as soon as transponder beacons are recognized.

Hopefully I can get through the gate without much problem. The long way to Cassad space would blow my timetable.

I tread back down to the workshop to get back to work on the armor, stopping along the way at my weapons locker. Going to have to test how well the old guard's gear holds up in a firefight.

My boots ring loudly on the deck plates. Wind screams across my armor pulling me toward a ragged, gaping star filled black hole. The entire side of the ship has been breached and is open to space. The launch bay is voiding air, equipment… ships… and men. We hit a null mine; a cloaked mine designed to breech capital ships, Giak design.

They'll be coming soon.

The wind dies. The bay is a vacuum now. I still hear the harsh ring of my boots on the deck vibrating through my armor as I race toward the breech. The rest of my Fire Team, what's left, races at my back.

No matter how hard we run we won't get there in time.

I see the bodies of flight deck personnel, having been blown out of the bay, flying away from the ship, some burned and charred.

I draw my Lance. My team pull their rifles.

We won't get there in time.

I don't want to take another step but it ain't up me.

I don't want to...see... but that don't matter.

The ship is listing. The null mine was one of three that we hit. The stars outside the breech spin as the ship slides off course.

A bright blue light fills the bay as the great western hemisphere of Arcadia rolls into view through the breech.

I want to stop.

I don't want to see it again.

I'm running, my heart beating hard in my chest in horrible anticipation. I want to turn away, I want to close my eyes but I can't.

I'm dreaming.

A.C.M. Training; Arcadian Combat Memory Training was the ADFs answer to the sudden blitzkrieg of the Wars of the Blade. It was pretty effective; a soldier like me could learn from the experiences snatched, post mortem, from the minds of veterans who fell in the opening conflicts. What took months of hazardous combat to ingrain could be implanted in just a few safe one-hour sessions. The training helped me to survive my tour with the 46th.

But... they never told us about the side effects. Forcing your mind to dream through an entire memory bucks up your head something wicked. There's Rem Jam, for one, or Black Sleep syndrome. But most suffer from Loop Dreams.

After enough training, you start dreaming memories. At first, it's the combat memories but soon you start dreaming your own memories... the most intense ones, which of course are usually the bad ones. Secondly, because it's a memory you can't change what happens. You can look around a bit more, maybe see something you didn't notice consciously before, but the memory plays itself out just like it happened in life; no selective perspective... no lying to yourself.

And third; you're lucid during the whole thing but unable to wake. Combat training needed to access your consciousness in order for you to gain the experience in real time. So now I dream, while wide awake, the most horrible things I've ever seen.

The entire rear port deck has been blown away. We're in high orbit over Arcadia and I can see almost the entire western hemisphere. Deep beautiful blue seas... verdant green forests...a jewel of a world. I wish I could say it was the last image I have of Arcadia.

It had been so long since I'd been home...

Shadows fill the breech... big shadows.

...Deep blue seas...

The shadows fly through the breech; their landing footfalls pound the deck plates so hard I can feel it through my armor.

...Verdant green forests...

My Tact-net flashes warnings of enemy weaponry at me.

Here it comes; a flash of light in high orbit that I see out of the corner of my eye. I glance once, sparing only that while I raise my Lance to fire on the enemy. Then another...

...down below on Arcadia.

It's only a wink of light. An impact on the southern continent, Embrezia. Only a wink of light.

I don't want to watch this.

Not again.

The C.O.P. pings me. It's enough of an electrical jolt to wake my sleeping body and pop my trapped consciousness free.

The chains holding the old guard's dress armor upright rattle as I shudder awake and I drop the small Cassad built rifle I'd been using to test it. Fell asleep trying to finish working on the old guard's gear. I'm soaked with sweat that I didn't work up during the project.

I hate dreaming.

Another ping. Time to get to control.

Chapter Five:
HAMPTON'S GATE

The space around Hampton's Gate is filled with ports, arrays and of course; traffic. Every gate is a hot spot for commerce. Ships making the jump are either going to or coming from halfway across the known most times. There are over five hundred major interstellar ports sitting in orbit of Hampton's, all offering all kinds of services to the weary travelers. And because this gate is one of the closest to the edge of the unexplored space there are a ton of settler convoys and scientific expeditions from just about every corner of the known. The G-Det is lit up like firefly mating season from all the traffic and each little bit of light in its holographic display has a corresponding transponder tag.

If there were any hostiles or even groups that I personally flagged then the G-Det would be pinging something crazy but it looks clear. Could be something on the other side of the gate but they're not likely to try and make the trip around; Hampton's is too big.

The gate itself is one of a unique pair, unlike the other gates in the known. Hampton's Gate is older than the Age of Discovery and was first found by Measure Hampton, a Cassad schooled physicist from some backwater world. She guessed at its existence when its sister was discovered in the inner realm. Bold as a bica she figured out how to access it and on her own, traversed the damn thing in a bucket of a ship to open up a whole other section of the galaxy and increase the size of the known by almost half.

The old broad, I think of her as old but I don't really know what her age was when she made the trip... the old broad must have had serious adrenal to even approach a rotating singularity let alone take her ship through it.

Hampton's Gate, here on the perimeter is a massive black "ring", a spinning, rotating singularity that's holds a wormhole open from here to the Dark Ring; an identical rotating black ring sitting in the inner realm. Doesn't really look much like a "black" ring; it's an open circular band of hot glowing gas that faces you no matter what angle you approach it from. The wormhole sits dead center and when you're close enough you can actually see the other side.

My comm-board lights up. A not so clear, pale blue, holographic image of an attractive woman appears above the old console. "Welcome, *Quiet Storm*, to Hampton's Gate. Please transmit your ships registry."

Good to know my new transponder is working. The fake Laplace plate cost me a bit but wouldn't work at all if I couldn't hide my real plate in the gravity well of the g-rock dead center of the ship. I transmit my credentials and wait. The greeting was automated and with the traffic at the gate there's gonna be a wait. I spend the time looking through the list of transponder signals broadcasting in the area while ignoring the constant stream of calls from traders, service stations and supply depots advertising their businesses.

There's quite a few of Cassad-space convoys coming through the gate now, no doubt trying to escape the tide of bloodlust running rampant through the inner systems. Without the Cassads' mighty Ziaran military to protect them, the inner realm is open to plunder. Only a few of them are still holding their own, but that won't last too long. One long convoy, just coming through the gate, is being protected by a Ziaran battleship that looks like it's on it last leg. Must have been a styx ride gettin' out of there.

Probably going to be just as bad going in.

I count seven different Cassad space convoys. Two Phaestus frigate convoys, five convoys out of Ngola that look makeshift and desperate. And there's one very well to do colonization convoy decked out with all the trimmings. Those ships are new and their transponders aren't registered, if they even have Laplace plates at all for a G-det to pick up. Looks like someone got their act together before the revolutionaries got too deep into the inner realm. There are probably even more exiting but the gate distorts every radiating field so I'm only getting a clear picture of what's happening on a small area of this side of Hampton's.

My comm-board lights up again. "*Quiet Storm*, please transmit your ships log, manifest and crew roster."

Not good. Could be standard now, what with the increased traffic, but it could also be bad news. I transmit the faked log along with the manifest of cargo I don't have hidden and my phony crew roster without delay.

Quickly I run through the rest of the ships showing up on my G-Det, searching for any that might also just be arriving from Rox822, which my fake log lists as my last port of call. I don't think there are any here. There shouldn't be any here; Rox is a good way farther away than Indo and my timetable had me beating any possible registered traffic coming from there by good margin.

An hour passes before I hear back from the Gate Authority. All the while I run through my options.

Hampton's Gate is too big for the Gate Authority to police in any effective way. Ships "Jump the Gate" all the time. But those ships either are desperate, have the speed to beat pursuit or have friends on the other side to beat the Gate Authority there.

I'm not desperate. Not yet. *War Child* still has her own grav-unit with a fat hunk of Element G. I can reach the inner realm on my own without the gate but that would take the better half of a cycle and the use of another gate. I don't have that kind of time.

War child is fast. She can hang with almost any ship her class or that has the firepower that she carries. But she's got no acceleration. If I wanted to jump the gate I should've starting pouring on the juice long before Hampton's was even visible. If I try it now I won't make it through before I'm targeted by half a dozen ships. *War Child's* armor can take some serious hits but if a system fails, like guidance or an engine, I could get caught or worse, fall into Hampton's event horizon and get "spaghettied" around the ring.

And last time I checked I don't have any friends… of any kind.

"*Quiet Storm*," this time the holograph is a young man, live not automated. That means trouble. "Captain Sivad, please adjust your heading and set sail to these coordinates."

I don't need to check the numbers; I already know that they want to me to fall in line for inspection. They're directing me toward a high traffic station with several ports and likely plenty of staff. "Sure thing G.A., but do you mind telling me why I'm being diverted from the gate?"

The hesitation on the kid's face is all I need to know it's bad. "Routine inspection, *Quiet Storm*. Please shut down your engines once you're in the pipe and open your nevron link."

Fek.

I adjust my heading but I'm just buying time. The kid looked apprehensive but not too charged up. That faked log cost me too much buckin' money for them to have found something wrong there.

If it's the log I'll kill Sticky.

Maybe they just think I'm running some contraband, which is par for the course these days. Might just be a shakedown…might be something more.

I check the G-Det again. No other ships are moving toward

my position, but some are falling into line for inspection. They'll be in position to target me if I comply. Still, it doesn't look like an ambush.

It just feels like one.

Fek! I need to get through this gate! I drop *War Child* into line with the inspection station.

"*Quiet Storm*, please open your nevron link."

"Roger that, G.A.; nevron link open," I say, for all the good it will do them.

Only takes them a few pulse beats. "*Quiet Storm*, we're having trouble accessing your ships command systems. Please stand by."

The advantage to having out of date, hodge-podge systems is that you'll always have an excuse for something not working right. No way they'll be able to connect to *War Child's* command systems, especially since I never networked them. It'll look suspicious but not too out of place for ships out on the perimeter. Now, if they think I'm merely carrying contraband then they'll tell me to dock it manually. But if somehow the old guard got word out on me then they'll send ships.

"*Quiet Storm*, we cannot establish a connection" the kid says without any further anxiety in his voice. "Prepare to dock manually"

I bring *War Child* right up to the dock and moor the ship without so much as a bump; don't want to give the Gate Authority reason to be overly aggressive. The port is big enough that the docking chamber could accommodate several ships her size, but because they couldn't gain remote control of her they had me line up *War Child's* rear hatch with their secondary docking ring. No problem, I make my way down to the cargo bay to greet them.

They're pounding on the rear hatch when I get there. Apparently, my docking controls are out of date too. So, I pop the seal and lower the hatch for them myself.

The G.A. came with a bit of force. There's one female in standard Gate Authority dress, carrying a data board, smiling and looking very officious and then there about ten others behind her; two in mech exos, the rest hiding arms… and no smiles.

"Greetings, Captain Sivad, to G.A. station Tortiv. Your automated review is done. Are your ship and crew ready for physical inspection?" The inspectors' manner is a bit of a contrast from the muscle standing behind her. Plus she's a looker; tall, lean and a good enough face job that I can't see the scars. They're disorganized… you don't run the muscle in right next to the distraction. That tells me that whoever's in charge of this facility didn't set up the inspection. Could be good news… or bad.

Hmm…what's the… oh yea, *"Quiet Storm's* a tight ship. We're always ready for inspection, Mrs.?"

"Ms., Captain. I'm Chief Donna Kirk. This is my inspection team." She says with a wave toward the muscle. She's good; hardly winces at all when she looks back at them. The exo gear the two deck-techs have strapped on are basic work units. But these have been racked; the power boosted and the response time doubled or tripled with incompatible servo units. Kinda gearing Pops taught me and Drez how to do for fun as kids. On our own we learned the hard way not to upgrade the power of an exo without reinforcing the frame.

"Well, let's get on with it. I don't want to be delayed too long."

"Of course, Captain." And she starts up the ramp with the muscle. I put on my best confused face and hold my hand up.

"Hold. You're not going to inspect without the proper gear?"

Now her look is genuinely confused. I see the muscle behind her get suspicious and fidgety.

"I'm sorry?"

"Well, as it states in my log; my crew is down with Rox-pox; nasty bug… highly infectious. Standard sterilization and air filters kill it just fine but you're gonna be inspecting the cargo hatches, engine accesses and the command deck. Can't be too sure that the scrubbers got to those areas."

"Rox-Pox?" asks the thick necked, pocked faced "inspector" standing on the ramp right behind Chief Kirk. He's wearing a tech vest with no under shirt, showing off his biceps which are pretty impressive if not stock and trade for a deck-tech.

"Yup. My Chief Engineer decided to get in some cheap binding while we waited for our cargo to get to port. Must have picked it up then."

"Do you mean Rozier's?" Kirk asks a little fearful, nearly dropping her data board. She should be upset. Rozier's or "Rox-Pox" hits women harder than men. You wanna see someone age two rotations in a week? Check out the Rozier's ward anywhere on the perimeter. Of course it's entirely treatable, but it requires a shipment of the inoculant or military grade nano-bodies. Neither of which the G.A. should have.

Or so my info tells me.

"What equipment do we need?" Biceps asks.

I have no idea. "Standard Bio-hazard wear. Standby testing terminal… the usual. You guys did read the log?"

Kirk is half-way down the boarding ramp. "I…I'll have

to…report this to my superiors…"

"Hold up, Donna!" Biceps has been eyeing me. "How do we know he ain't full of hoodoo?" and he takes a few steps up the ramp.

Pathetic; he's trying to test me and he's giving away all of their intentions. If they just wanted to shake me down then they would play it cool and try and wait me out. But if they want to…TAKE my ship then they want to jump in here now.

But their disorganized approach must mean that they don't have approval…or worse.

"Look," I say. "The cargo hold and most of the ship is just fine, I'm sure. Come on up."

Biceps actually takes a few steps up the ramp. The rest of the muscle is split with half backing up and the other half is moving toward the ramp. The Chief inspector is caught in between, on the ramp, her eyes wide.

"I should go check their log" she offers.

Biceps spits. "Fine! You," he points a huge finger at me. "You come out of there so we can…inspect…you're…ah…you!"

Biceps looks like he wants to pull a weapon, which I have no doubt he and his tiny little army have.

I slide my finger over the top side button of my remote.

Just then the bay alarm sounds. At the far end of the room a pair of doors open. Out walks a small group of men who look more the type to be running a Gate Authority inspection station.

"Hayland? Kirk? What on styx is this?" He looks young but as he gets closer I can see the streaks of gray in his hair and the washed-out color of his eyes. Unlike his chief, he's had real cellular repair work done, most likely to keep up physically rather than for the cosmetic side of it. With this crew of muscle-heads I can see why.

Kirk puts on her best smile and strides straight up to him. "Director Pile, we found some inaccuracies in this ships log and we…"

"And you what?" he snaps. "Thought I wouldn't know that ship was pulled into my station?" he brushes past her, knocking her data board from her hands. The man strides up the ramp right into Biceps face.

"Hayland?" he says through clenched teeth.

Biceps doesn't answer at first; he just looks over the rest of his buddies. I've seen this look before; he's checking their positions…about to go for broke. I turn the remote over in my hand until the button on the other side is under my thumb.

"You let that little…" Director Pile starts.

Biceps pulls the pulse gun he's been hiding from under his

jacket screaming wildly at the same time. I thumb the remote and the small hologram wrapped around the kendo blade disappears. There's a piercing, yet musical whistle that drowns out his little battle cry as I swing the blade. So loud was the whistle that everyone in the bay, those about to draw their weapons and those about to get shot, all stop and look, almost in time to see me return the blade to the holographic camo I drew it from.

Those biceps aren't as impressive when severed and lying on my ramp. Still…there's enough strength in that arm to squeeze the trigger two times, firing pulses out into the bay above his crew's heads.

The Director and his staff pulled their own weapons. I raise my hands as innocently as I can while the Director himself puts me square in his sights. Luckily there isn't a firefight. Kirk and her little shake down crew don't seem to want that kind of heat.

Of course that doesn't help me at all.

Chapter Six
GATE JUMPING

Here it comes.

"My crew found some very interesting discrepancies when we boarded your ship, Mr. Sivad."

Fek. Had I known I'd be held up using this alias so long I'd have made up one that sounded a little less buckin' ridiculous.

I'm sitting in the Tortiv's Visiting Crew lounge, which may not sound like I'm in their brig but there's no real difference. Director Pile's decision that would be, but it's the extent of his appreciation for keeping his head from being blown off.

"I'm not sure what you mean" I say. *War Child* is in lockdown mode. That means that the Command Deck, Grav-Well, Infirmary and any of the ships access ports are sealed. Those hatches and plates are also part of *War Child*'s cete-armor body. Doubt this station has anything that can cut through it. And *War Child*'s systems are, for the most part, incompatible with theirs so they're not hacking in.

"Well, your crew for one. We can't find any of them" Director Pile is looking at me pretty hard. Probably can't figure me out. I could be anybody with almost any motivation for going through Hampton's Gate. But I saved his ass and that's got him wondering.

"Crew is in medical quarantine. Can't be accessed until the Pox is out of their system."

"Right. That would be Roziers?"

"Like it states in my log."

"Yea. Well, I've checked with Rox822 and they're not reporting any Roziers outbreak." He's watching my reaction.

I'm not much of a poker player unless I'm actually holding all the cards. So I've just got to have faith in the fake log package I bought. Roziers is supposed to be a problem on Rox.

"That a fact?"

"That's a fact" he says with an almost pitying air, as if he's caught me in a lie.

"I did wonder how my engineer caught it. Seeing how the port we landed on was the only port on Rox… without a Roziers clinic." I mirror his pitying look right back at him.

He smiles. "So, your crew can't use the comms? Let us know they're alright?"

"Roziers requires a quarter cycle deep sleep session so the virus doesn't tear the body up while they recover. My Ops officer was supposed to be up now but the sickness must have advanced to where he decided to freeze himself."

Pile purses his lips in doubt. "So I have to wait three months to verify your story?"

"Actually, my Engineer will be up in only a few earning rotations but what's to verify? We're just going through the gate. Why the fuss?"

Pile looks at me for a pulse beat before answering. "The Inner Realm is in turmoil right now. The New Regime Coalition, the Cassads and a whole bunch of smaller war powers are grabbing what they can. We are monitoring gate traffic especially hard right now."

"Traffic coming out sure, but going in?"

"Going in even more so. We know citizens of the oba worlds are heading out here to escape the blood tide. But there are dozens of worlds out here looking to claim a bit of a stake back there as well; sending in mercs, weapons and supplies to whoever they can make a deal with."

"...Quiet Storm's not a supply ship." I almost forgot the buckin' fake name again.

"Not a big ship but you could carry specialized hardware easily enough. I recognized the cete-armor. Your ship could drop gear or men right onto the Cassad homeworld itself."

I laugh. "With our systems winking out the way they do we're lucky each landing isn't our last. You're kidding me, right?"

"You've just seen what the fall of the empire is doing to us even here. You think I'm kidding?" Pile leans back in his chair and continues to consider me. He could keep me here for the three weeks I lied about but something's off. He's in a hurry.

"With everything that's going on why are you trying to head into the Inner Realm then? Not the safest place for lone ships" he asks.

"You've read our log, Director; been a long tour out here on the perimeter, now we're going home."

He looks at me again then looks down. He's hard to read but that's supposed to be a sign of someone who's about to lie. "We're seeing some bad activity on the other side of the gate. You're gonna have to go another route."

And with that I'm escorted back to my ship.

My cargo bay is a mess. They dug into everything they could but they did not find the pirate hatches and they were not able to breech any of the areas on lockdown. They kept me in the lock up for so long that the battery in the holo-emitter failed. The Kendo blade juts up out of the bay plating right where it landed after I relieved Biceps of his namesake. Apparently, no one here knows how to pull one free once it's been embedded.

I even find my remote in the vent where I dropped it be-fore they took me into custody. Somebody went through my tool box though…looks like they grabbed my good set of calibrators.

Fek.

Takes me nearly a full wake cycle to square everything away; they actually pulled my walker off its rack to search it for contraband. I finally get the damn thing to hang straight when a very chastened looking Chief Kirk climbs *War Child*'s ramp.

"Captain Sivad? The Director wants to know when you will be ready to shove off. You haven't answered our calls."

"Somebody wrecked the comm line." I snap. "Can't access the comms."

She waits a bit longer while I stow away the lift-jack. Then she clears her throat. "It's just that we need the bay to continue inspecting…"

"Soon as I put my ship back together." With Pile flagging my ship, *War Child* will be tracked as far as their sensors extend. That's a good ways. No station around Hampton's will service her and every Gate Authority police ship will be set to fire on me if I make a gate approach. And they'll probably send a tracking ship after me until I jump. That means I'll have to leave Hampton's space, change transponders and then return to make a "run". Something that will cost me time and most likely buck my schedule.

So, I take my time, using the excuse of securing the ship to check the G-det and get a look at the situation around the gate. There are Dogon ships stuck at another Gate Authority port but the ships of the Khem are already on their way to the edge of Hampton's gravity well where they'll be able to jump to wherever they're going. They've got real money so I figure they must've paid off somebody.

My comm board lights up but it shows no incoming transmissions. Looks like the Gate Authority is transmitting coded messages… a lot of them.

They don't have "entangled" comms but my systems aren't good enough to break their encryption anyway. I doubt all this chatter is about me but that doesn't mean it's not trouble. I study the G-Det for a bit longer then run a passive scan on everything the gate isn't disrupting but I don't see anything worth worrying about. I take a quick walk back down to the cargo bay.

Chief Kirk is still in the Authority bay. She has a distant look in her eyes that tells me she's on a virtual line, either communicating with someone or just looking in on a transmission feed.

As casual as I can I walk down my boarding ramp and cross the bay to her. She doesn't notice me until I'm practically on top of her.

"Oh! Uh…"

"We're ready to make way."

"I…yes of course…" she stammers enough for me to start to worry.

"Everything alright?"

"You…" she plays with her data pad and in a pulse beat I see a green light flash on the bay status indicators set about the moorings. *War Child*'s been released.

"You can leave immediately, Captain" she says over her shoulder as she hurries from the bay. No sooner has she disappeared through the bay doors when klaxons sound and the indicator lights switch to bright red and pulsing. My remote is in my hand and I'm hauling ass back to my ship but there's no pursuit, no armed guard…whatever's happening, it ain't about me.

"STATION ALERT! SENIOR OFFICERS REPORT TO THE ANCILAR OFFICE. PREPARE FOR INCOMING HOSTILE CRAFT!!"

I slam the ramp controls and run like a treader for the command deck. The whole room is alive with warnings on nearly every holographic display.

It takes a pulse beat to squint through the mess in the G-det but then I see it clearly enough. A squad of fighter craft just came through the gate, guns blazing. Looks like they're targeting the Cassad ships. I pull up the comm-net; got to be something on there.

"There is no escape from the blood tide!" The holo lights up with the image of a man in fatigues and a beret. On his chest he bears the latest insignia that the so-called "Revolutionaries" are using; a Coalition patch.

Wonder how long you have to be in power before you're no longer considered a revolutionary?

I fire up the twin engines and more warnings sound. The alert must have reset the status of the dock release. *War Child* is still locked to the bay hatch. It'll be fine…the magnetic lock is connected only to her cete-armor.

There's a nasty whine as she begins to pull away from the station that only stops when their docking clamps snap. Every ship in the area is pulling away from the gate so I set my heading directly for it.

It's risky; a bad hit from enemy fire can send a ship into the event horizon. But the revolutionaries are so concerned with the Ziaran ships that they'll ignore my transponder until it's too late.

War Child is a fast ship, when she gets up to speed, but it takes a while. The engines burn pushing her through the procession of escaping ships and into firestorm of convoy ships under fire.

I have to take manual control as we get in close. The down side to hodge-podge systems is that you can't rely on the automated systems in combat.

Close enough now to worry about debris. I close the forward blast shield over the canopy and go to navigating off of the virtual holo display. Millions of kilometers close to hundreds of thousands and quickly to thousands and the space begins to get tight relatively speaking. We pass over one besieged convoy and then another. I'm thinking we're gonna go through without a hitch until my comm board pings.

"Quiet Storm, this is Prelate Gaston of the First Coalition Expeditionary Force. Reverse your course! Hampton's Gate is now under the control of the Coalition of Free Worlds."

He goes on to say that all gate traffic must be approved by the New Regimes Coalition. I laugh. In over a thousand years no one has been able to really control Hampton's Gate. The G.A.s control is marginal at best and only because the Cassads used a multicultural, multisystem task force to govern it. What makes the New Regime think they can do that when it they haven't even defeated the Cassads in twenty-two years?

War Child is gaining some speed now. Hopefully it'll be enough to shoot past the rebels on the other side.

Proximity alarms ring out; looks like the New Regimes Expeditionary Force is sending a little attention my way. Two Tyco fighters; Cassad design...probably Giak built... they're good ships but they lack the fire power to stop me from making the gate. Still it wouldn't be smart to let them know that too soon, they might send more at me.

War Child is made to fight in the nastiest of the nasties. She carries an impressive weapons package...most of which doesn't work worth a damn right now...and her main body in composed of cete crystal, one of the toughest materials in the known. She can take a beating. I charge the top mounted pulse cannon. It should be enough to keep them off me.

The pulse cannon opens up on the Tycos with nice accuracy. The leader's engines go dead in the first salvo and the second pulls off to avoid the same fate. *War Child* shrugs off their return fire like a champ.

Again, the Command Deck lights up with warning holos but it's just the proximity to the event horizon. I'm so close now that I can see the weird fishbowl eye of the wormhole showing the other side of Hampton's Gate. The G-Det is drawing a blank at this range but I'm sure there's a nice Coalition force sitting there waiting in ambush. Luckily for me they're expecting haggard refugees or docile cargo haulers.

Back to the auto systems for the trip through the wormhole; if the ship isn't lined up and traveling exactly perpendicular to the gate then she'll be pulled into the event horizon. The computer makes the adjustments to our course and I see that there wasn't much space between my ship and the gate to spare.

War Child drops into Hampton's and the perimeter fades and shrinks behind us. Ahead the Inner Realm blooms, opening like a weird black flower as we pull away from the Dark Ring.

"This gate is under the control of the Coalition. Stand your vessel down..."

Yea, yea. The New Regime has its little fleet spread out around the gate in pretty standard formation. Looks like Gunboats mostly...probably a battle cruiser and a capital ship on the other side of the Dark Ring, maybe more. But like I said; it's near impossible to control traffic on a gate this big. The dispersal of their fleet has them spread out too thin and most of their ships are in holding patterns around the various Gate Authority stations on this side. They're what's important. I just have to get *War Child* past them and out of the Dark Rings gravity well where I can pop the G-rock and jump the ship away. There's only one ship close enough and moving at the right angle to cause me any trouble.

When it's apparent that I'm not stopping they open fire.

The area is lit with particle fire, showing me their Commander's inexperience. His fleet is too close to the gate for particle targeting to be reliable. And indeed, the gunboats targeting is awful at this range. If I were intent on doing them damage and if I had some decent offensive weaponry I could probably take out the ship. Never the less I've got places to be.

I pour on the speed. More enemy fire crosses my flight path from aft. Looks like a couple of the Tychos followed me through the wormhole. My ship shudders a bit and the holo tells me that the pulse cannon is down.

Fek. Just got that fixed!

No way to fire back. I alter course enough that the Tychos will have to drag their route too close to the gate to fire effectively. Unfortunately, the new course lines me up nicely in the gunboats sights.

Another barrage of particle fire and this time *War Child* is hit hard enough to shake me in my seat despite the grav-wells inertial safeties. The holo lights flare with even more warnings but I ignore them and change course again. The gunboat tracks me, trying to force me into the reinforcements I'm sure are on the way. Can't let them corner me. Taking fire from one gunboat is better than getting hit by two...

War Child swings hard into the path of the New Regime ship. G-Det tells me it's a Cutlass class, Meridian; Cassad built. Good ship. The particle fire opens up again and *War Child* can't help but take fire. Again, the warning icons in the holo spin frantically but the cete-armor holds true until I'm past the gunboat and out of weapons range. Then the ship gives a horrible shutter.

BUCK! The starboard side engine blew...I check the holo and see the auto systems already attempting to compensate by slowing us down. Can't do that!

I jigger the power distribution and fire the port engine to max. Then I check G-Det... the Tychos are pulling back; they're not sure I'm toothless and don't want to pursue without back up. The gunboat is faster but she's got to correct her course before she can come after me and that gives me time.

But not much. With only one engine running, the gunboat'll be able to catch up and could be back in effective range in a little over five hours. *War Child* can't make a jump until we're completely out of the gates gravity well which'll take almost two days at my current speed and acceleration...which is crap.

I hop out of the primary control seat then head for the workshop and my mech gear. Can't risk troubleshooting the problem, I'll have to swap out the entire starboard engine with the spare. Never pulled an engine in under five hours while pushing C...but there's a first time for everything.

I crack open the suit locker and begin hauling out the EVO-wear.

Then I stop and take a breath
Halfway there.

Chapter Seven:
INNER TURMOIL

The gunboat and a few of its friends got close enough to fire just outside the edge of their effective range before I got the back-up engine to spark. They were still able to gain a bit but I made it outside the Dark Ring's gravity well and jumped with no problem.

First jump and I repaired the pulse cannon but couldn't fix the buckin' swivel mount. It'll only fire inside a very tight fifteen-degree field now. So, I point the thing aft as I'm more likely to be running than attacking. Wish I had more time to get it working properly but I don't.

Fourth jump and I finally finish with the Royal Guard's armor. Back's aching and my neck is cramping from squatting in front of its open innards for so long but it was worth it. Finally, something I plan actually goes the way it's supposed to. I hit the scrubber and take nap; Grav-well will be up for the eighth and last jump by the time I get up.

The stars wink out and pop back into view in different positions. I always marvel at how fast...what the buck?

The G-det shows nothing, but the damn thing always takes a pulse beat to catch up. What I'm seeing on the V-hud is from the weak visual feed. What I'm seeing is incoming.

I slap the manual control override and throw *War Child* into an off-kilter spin pulling her out of the path of what looks like a small freighter. We're not even past the freighter when another ship...a Cassad fighter cartwheels at us, spewing rads and out of control.

I pull *War Child* up thinking we're not gonna be able to avoid it but somehow, we miss colliding by what must be only meters. What on styx...

The G-det finally flares to life and fills with overlapping tiny points of light. The whole buckin' field is filled with ships! What the buck did I jump into? I plotted the jump for well outside Orun's kup-belt... well outside the anywhere where there should have been any traffic leaving the Cassad home star. But it looks like I jumped *War Child* right into the middle of a skirmish.

Staring at the G-det nearly gets me into another collision. Damn lucky...I know better than to get distracted when I override the autopilot. Even luckier still *War Child* hasn't been targeted by either side of this conflict. I chance another look at the G-det, trying to determine how on styx I'm getting out of this mess.

The first ships that the G-det is able to I.D. are the dead ones, as always. They're easier because their defenses are offline and they usually aren't moving as fast as the others so the G-Det gets a better look at them. Cassad ship...Cassad ship...looks like it's a major skirmish...

Or... or something else.

Very little weapons fire. And as my comms come online, suddenly there's lots of comm traffic; distress calls.

I pull *War Child* out of the path of another ship, more hunk of debris than space vessel now; it's a Cassad light cruiser damn near split in half. Behind that an even bigger ship, battle cruiser...holed by some kind of internal explosion maybe. And it gets worse.

There are ship I.D.s popping up on the G-Det now that aren't dead. Denir ships, Marajeshi fighters, Junn Ships...a few Giak ships and the list goes on. They aren't attacking each other, which is odd 'cause the Giaks are currently at war with the Junns. Instead all the capable ships seemed to be engaged in rescue operations. So who attacked them?

I lean forward and tap the icon of one of the ships transmitting a distress call. At once a pale gold holographic image of a woman, the ship's captain maybe, pops up.

"This is the Planetary Commonwealth ship the Confident Seven, we are currently under attack by Rebel forces and require assistance..."

Without listening to the rest, I tap another ships icon.

"...the Lagrange Miner, we are being boarded by Afan pirates..."

"...engines are dead. They're slaughtering the passengers! Please help us!"

"...the damn Stompers are pulling our ship apart! They're not letting us launch the escape pods! Oh no..."

Twisting in primary I draw the G-Det holo closer. The ships I thought were running rescue ops are actually pirating the ships. The Giaks are stripping ships down with the crew still alive inside, the Junns are running down fleeing ships like a pack of sulu, and the Denir are just riddling weakened ships with small arms fire to kill the crews.

The New Regime has already launched their surprise attack on Ziara; the Cassad home world. The comms are screaming with distress calls, all from Ziaran citizen ships. Looks like they're trying to flee the system. These running ships aren't military; they're civilian, trying to escape the assault of their home world. Now that the Empire is in its death throes the rest of the known is swooping in to pick the meat off its still breathing body. But none of the ships in distress are military. They're all commerce ships, industrial runners or passenger craft. The only armed ships are the long dead Cassad fighter craft which must have been trying to escort these civilian ships out of the system. With them gone the raiders are taking their time with the rest. There's no mercy being shown to the Ziaran civilians.

No mercy at all.

G-Det pings on a big ship, a passenger ship, riddled with hull breeches along its length. All about the ship, caught by its minute gravity, float the bodies of its former passengers. Whoever attacked this fleet made sure to kill them in this fashion…

…the so-called Blood Tide.

Still the pirates are not a real threat until they get a bead on me and only then if they decide I'm prey and not predator.

Or if I decide to intervene.

This is how it might have been on Arcadia at the end, at least for a while before…

I check the G-det and make sure I'm clear of incoming debris, then I begin checking ship I.D.s and one stands out.

Njaro Station; not a ship at all, but a massive space facility that orbits or rather WAS in orbit around Ziara. But right now, it's sitting in the middle of a field of dead ships, on the outskirts of the gravity well of the Cassad home world's system star, Orun. What on styx is it doing here?

Just as with the rest of the ships in this debris field I can see that Njaro is wrecked and derelict. Obliviously it was part of this battle but this could blow my whole plan. Buck! It's supposed to be orbiting the All damned Cassad home world!

The only reason I figured I had a chance to pull off this bounty in the first place is because I knew Cassad would head home after the invasion…knew that he would need to use the

Njaro to stage his retaking of the planet. Without it he'll just abandon the planet until he can come back later with a large enough force. One too large for me to grab his ass from.

I used *War Child*'s docking thrusters to maneuver into position to try a light sensor sweep of the station. The cete-armor plates covering the front of the engine housings part to reveal *WarChild*'s Broussard collectors and sensor screens. The G-Det hologram is immediately augmented with new information. Njaro's sub-light engines show evidence of having been running at high output. Could they have been trying to escape the system?

The Coalitions invasion should be in full swing by now. It must be a more horrible battle than I anticipated. Again, the "Blood Tide" ... most invading forces would have taken the Njaro by negotiation. Obviously, the near guaranteed slaughter of every Ziaran citizen found must have made the commanders of the Njaro desperate. They ran, with some help it looks like, but they couldn't make a jump...or "slip" as the station used the old Cassad slipstream tech.

The bodies of the inhabitants of the station begin to come into view. Njaro had been home to nearly thirty million souls. Whoever attacked the station didn't let up until they breached every compartment. All damn it... even the Giaks backed off of survivors when Arcadia was burned... but with the Cassads...

Never the less, I've got a job to do there may still be a chance. The wreckage of the Njaro may give me an opportunity I hadn't counted on.

G-det pings again; more pirates. They're crawling all over the massive Cassad station like ants. But these ships are not carrying or at least they're not broadcasting their transponders. Now that usually means illegals...unsanctioned by the Coalition, probably running salvage. But with the nature of the revolution in the inner realm it could be renegade rebels or even Cassad regulars turning on their own people. Privateers would broadcast their transponders to warn off challengers.

Quickly I check to make sure my transponder is offline and after adjusting *War Child*'s course, I cut the engines. Likely most of them noticed my jumping in but maybe they haven't pinpointed me yet and probably care even less. Now that I'm seeing them work there seems to be an air of cooperation; there are plenty of unarmed ships to go around.

Another set of pings and a small group of the ships specification flags pop up. Three of them; one's big, a cargo hauler maybe and it probably has the facilities to breakdown salvage. The other two are shuttle…no…fighter sized. They looked to be the ones doing the stripping…one is anyway…the other is his cover. But no scans come my way; none of them seem to have noticed me.

And that lets me know they saw me. No way they missed a ship jumping right into the debris field but with all the wrecks pitching back and forth and the other raiders breaking down ships they don't know whether I'm Ziaran or more raider competition. So they're playing at being unaware.

The stripper continues breaking down the wreckage from what looks like one of *Njaro*'s communications wheels while his cover continues making his security sweep as casually as he can. It's the cargo hauler that's really giving them away now. The captain of that ship thinks he can prep his engines without anyone noticing. He's either panicking or inexperienced. *War Child* must look like trouble to somebody in this group.

They've got a pretty old comm system 'cause I'm picking up quite a bit of their coded transmissions. I sub vocalize to the C.O.P. to run a decryption program but it'll take time.

I lean back heavily into the cushions of the Primary control seat. What's the play here? The station is drifting away from Orun. But it's sitting perfectly along the route Cassad should be coming in along when he gets here. I figured he would go to free *Njaro* first; it WAS in a good position to coordinate any attempt to retake his home world, has the facilities and resources needed but more importantly my recon indicated that it was his rendezvous point with some Ziaran agent. Now though… he might just pass it up and head in system if he arrives with more fleet left than he's supposed to have left after his tour on the perimeter.

What's the play, Pack?

I look at the huge station. It's mostly still functional for the time being, at least until the scavengers pull out its vital systems. But if I were coming in to stage a rescue of MY world from a bunch of rag tag rebels...

War Child's docking thrusters fire as we near the station. Better to pick one of big rings, a habitat ring, where the scavengers are scarce; they're not here to pick personal belongings. There's another nasty rupture right in the hydrogel shield and it's large enough for me to squeeze *War Child* in. We slide in easily enough, bumping a few odd bits of debris; small station cars...a few bodies that didn't get pulled all the way out of the station when the dome was breached.

These habitat rings were capable of sealing themselves even after sustaining multiple breaches. All known...how many times did they fire into it before those redundant systems failed?

I set *War Child* down on a park plaza near to what I hope is an access port to one of transport bridges. There's a lot of work to do here before his royal highness arrives; I need to get moving.

Chapter Eight
THE *NJARO*

Standard camouflage is too easily recognized by most ships sensors but a manual rig works just fine. It takes a bit to set it up but it's worth it. I finish hanging to last bit of camo netting just as a small flight of scavengers comes drifting by the breaches along this side of the *Njaro*.

They move smoothly, trying not to look as if they're looking for anyone in particular but sure as worlds turn they saw *War Child* approach. They can't be too worried about Ziaran authorities; I figure they probably just want to be sure they aren't losing too much to the competition. They run really aggressive high level rad scans. If there are any survivors in this part of the habitat ring that rad sweep just finished them off.

Buckin' vultures.

My rad alarms barely register the levels though as the camo rig reflects just the right amount back and sucks up the rest. It's fairly new so I'll get a few more uses out of it before I'll have to drop coin to get another set. The pirates glide on by and move on to scan the rest of the habitat ring. Time to get moving.

Now's not the time to take chances. Not sure how many have boarded the *Njaro* but it's possible though not likely that I could end up running into a few looters in the habitat ring looking for small coin or what not. And I'm not sure I'll have time to set up a good ambush sight before Cassad gets here so I pull up the plating above my pirates hold and lift out my Raptor armor.

Raptor armor; it's what made the 46th so damn famous. During the "Wars of the Blade" it gave mere mortal men a toe to toe chance against veritable titans. It isn't the best fighting armor by far. It lacks the firepower, strength and shielding of heavy armor units and the tech sophistication of the light armor units. It's modifiable like the special ops pieces but not upgradable like the newer units coming out of the major clusters. Never the less during the Wars of the Blade it was absolutely perfect,

Because when the big EMFs went up and all the lights went out the Raptor armor, with its primary power cell offline, kept going.

The weave beneath the fullerene plates is all "bio-mechanical" and gives the wearer augmented strength and speed that won't disappear when an EMP pops or even an All damned Dark Field. That makes it strong enough for an ordinary Arcadian to go up against a three and a half meter tall Giak and hold his own and even, if he's been trained, win more than half the time.

My set has hunter green paint on plates trimmed with gold that are locked onto a black bio mechanical weave. There's a chipped, faded "wing" insignia painted on the right shoulder guard for my old Fire Squad. Probably should have burned it off a long time ago to protect my identity but I always manage to not bother. Anyone who would recognize that logo is far, far away.

Without specific training the armor is too complex for someone to get into, even with help. I've logged thousands of hours in the armor however, so I can don the weave and lock on the plates almost subconsciously.

The bio-mechanical microfilaments, weaved into a thick membrane, comes to life around my skin, pressurizing and making the biometric connections like it was brand new. I slide the thinking cap up over my head and run through a quick diagnostic. I don't need the cap on to know that the armor is running at optimum. It's the one thing in my life that always does.

Again, I reach down into the pirate hold and this time I grab the helmet. The mandibles lay open and the winged visor is up waiting for my head. Instead I lock the helmet onto the back-shoulder plate while I get the rest of the Mission Package ready.

The wing housing, which is no larger than a field pack and looks like a natural part of the armor when on, takes a pulse beat to connect to the back plate. It's essential that all the command ports make their connections or the unit won't respond in real time to the thinking cap. Though the unit was designed to work manually and I'm more than used to it in that mode, I'm going to need my hands free for this op.

My twin carbide butterfly blades lock into place beneath my thigh plates, they're good micro-edged blades. Not as amazing as the kendo blade, but since I don't have a scabbard for that I can't risk carrying it.

The Sever 3030 hand gun and holster slide on easily enough around my waist. It's a good Ops weapon; fires "smart" rounds, specialty rounds or just plain old slugs that aren't affected by counter measures. Like my armor there's a strictly mechanical aspect to the firing mechanism that allows it to stay effective even under an EMF.

Next, I grab my M-11 rifle with the XR under barrel launcher. I'm not really that much of a full auto shooter but if you're alone against multiple targets you need a heavy auto weapon. It locks in at the small of my back just below the wing housing.

A few hand sized explosives including two EMP grenades. Don't like using them in sealed environments but since much of the *Njaro* is open to space anyway it won't matter.

Most importantly I set up the remote. Sweet little device I picked up during the Wars of the Blade. So complex…but so simple. I set the first function for the holo-imager. The second I rig to a dilapidated, obsolete plasma shield generator. It emits a small personal shield of magnetic plasma that acts like a personal heat shield for atmospheric entry. Also, it can stop small arms fire…from small arms made about five centuries ago. There was a brief window of time during the Wars of the Blade where armies tried using old mechanical projectile weapons. Our C/O was ready for this and issued us the shield generators. It burns pel crystals in an organic acid bath, works in numerous atmos and vacuum... smells like rotting eggs.

The generator snaps securely to my hip. I check the pel tank on the way to the hatch… I'm using qualt rocks instead because the shield shows up in the visual range a little better. They're processing just fine.

Without gravity the habitat ring is filled with floating debris that didn't make it out when the shield was first breached. The magnetic cells in my armor lock on easily enough to the stations walkways but I have to float across the park plaza where I landed *War Child* first. Microbursts from ports in my boots and gauntlets push me along where I can't get any tread. The debris knocks about, forcing me to identify every bit of it lest I let some scavenger get the drop on me.

There should be several ways to get to the stations core control levels from the Habitat ring. I find a couple of accessible railways but discount them. If someone is already in charge of the stations command center they'll know the instant I fire up the tram that I'm here. Instead I look for one that's already active…

…got one.

Just outside the industrial district there's a bit of activity. The district sits on several giant platforms that extend from the main habitat structure. The hydrogel shield that encircles the whole habitat ring shines with a bright amber glaze a few hundred meters away from the edge of the platform. Along the edge of the larger platform sit the industrial units, squat and wide buildings with skeletal spires rising up and through the far-off shield. That's where the scavengers are.

Looks like they're breaking into a fabrications complex. Smart move; between what's already been produced and the fabrications units themselves there's bound to be high value, easily moved loot there.

They're good. I know that without even seeing them in action. The tell-all is the fact that this little gang of pirates is multi-species. There's a human tech specialist breaking into the complex vault, a pair of long legged braiders running through the complex searching for more valuables... I see an Afan; a female braider, using a group of bogeys to load loot onto a hover cart. You can tell they're bogeys, androids that can pass for living beings, 'cause they're moving freight with mass way above normal Afan limits without exoskeletons. Then there's... what in the All?

They've got a damn Giak standing guard at the tram. A two ton...looks like four-meter-tall...humanoid from the Tri-Star system back in Eastspace. The big girl is wearing light armor, not that a Giak needs much more, and carrying a Warhammer rifle. That marks her as a vet. I should know; seen more than enough of them during my tour with the 46th. She's pacing back and forth inside the port in front of the two bridges that connect the habitat ring to the main station hub here; dual spokes on the main *Njaro* "wheel" as it were.

You can't get this kind of cross species cooperation without being successful, but I've never heard of a crew like this. Maybe this is some kind of quick hatched agreement by the pirates looting the *Njaro*? Or is this an established gang?

I don't see any tats or emblems. Nothing to indicate they work together other than the smooth and efficient way they're getting the job done. They must have worked together before. Bet my ship that they've got control of the Command Center as well then.

There don't seem to be any lookouts. Could be they've got the Command Center handling over watch so I've got to be careful and not stray into the station's visual sensor sweeps. Shouldn't be a problem; *Njaro* wasn't a military outpost after all.

Getting close to the tram isn't too hard. I find a small low hanging catwalk and make my way towards the port while trying to decide what exactly to do. I need to get past the Stomper and steal the tram without alerting their people in the station's Command Center.

The catwalk brings me directly underneath the port. I can't see the tram or the Stomper from here but there's got to be some way to access the bridge from the underside.

Right?

Been a pulse beat since I used the air foils but I'm not exactly gonna be burning atmo at a five times terminal velocity. The zero-G and the short distance should make this a piece of cake. I use the manual lever and the Raptor's wings extend from the back plate. Individual air foils project from the three sections of each wing frame. When folded you'd barely notice them in the housing but at full extension they have over a six-meter wingspan. My boots make no sound on the metal railing as I use it to launch myself into the air. The air foils work just fine in vacuum; they're low mass vanes filled with micro-counter weights that help to give an initial momentum boost at takeoff. It's not as effective as atmospheric flight but it helps get me to the bridge just fine.

The magnetic clamps in my boots and gauntlets don't work as well on the smooth duro-metal surface of the bridge. It's a slow, careful crawl I need to stay attached without drifting off. Makes it take forever to find an access.

"Daphon b'kayng." The Giak's voice booms in the tube, it's so powerful that it vibrates through the duro-metal to the audio receptors in my armor. She's communicating with the Command Center I figure; reporting the status of their little raid.

"PaQuashivence, berkerd. Monond sotond b'kayng."

Hmm...she just assured whoever she's talking to that everything was fine, I think. Been a little while since I was exposed to Giak without a translator but the last bit is a colloqui-alism; means something about the "ground" being stable. I'm not sure about the first part but pieces of it sounded familiar.

The only access I find is a good fifty yards further along the bridge. Who places a damn repair access this far out??

The only good thing about the distance is that the Stomper doesn't hear the panel pop open… or the hiss of the evacuating air!

FEK! Quickly as I can I climb into the tight passage and pull the panel closed behind me. I tune up the sensitivity on my armors audio receptors and listen. The Giak doesn't stir but I'm not worried about her having heard. It's her boss up in the Com-mand Center that would be getting a steady little alert on their status board about a loss in pressure on the bridge.

With the *Njaro* in the state that's it's in there should be a load of warning lights flashing now but whoever's running the show would be paying attention to where their crew was.

One pulse…three…six go by before I can hear the Giak mumbling into her comms. Now there's a sound I haven't heard in over five cycles…

Boom. Boom.

The Giak stepped off the tram and her powerful mag-netic boots stomped down the rail line towards my position. She'll cover the distance in a few beats. I grab the remote and hit the fat end. The holo-unit activates and I'm cloaked…hope-fully well enough to hide me from her sensors through the bridge floor. Still I draw my M-11.

Boom. Boom! Boom!

There are lots of ways to kill a Giak, a good number of ways to kill a Giak warrior but very few ways to kill a Giak vet. My mind races over the dozens of times I've squared off against one of these bitches.

BOOM.BOOM. BOOM!

They never go down easy. We used to say that dealing with the Giaks was like dealing with the truth; undeniable and painful.

The boots stop pounding on the bridge floor a few yards away. She can't have gotten my position…

Small explosions go off all around me. Weapons fire sound from every quarter. The whole bridge shakes so violently I'm thrown headlong into the tunnel wall. That's when I hear the old familiar drone of a Giak war hammer being fired.

What in the known?

The bridge shifts violently. Feels like the structure's stability has been compromised. In zero G it won't fall but it will swing in the direction the station is spinning.

More war hammer fire. It certainly isn't directed at me. Seems like someone else tried to get the drop on this crew. Someone who's never battled Giaks before because they got the first shot and didn't put her down. Now they've got a pissed off forty decimeter giant coming after them in the tight confines of the bridge.

Another explosion and the tunnel ahead of me opens in a blaze of fire and then collapses in on itself. I crawl forward to the damage and peer through ruined ceiling out onto the bridge. Smoke and floating debris obscure so much…

…but I can still make out the huge shadow of the Giak.

She's alternately firing and swinging that war hammer, banging out her attackers as cruelly as I remember back in the Blade.

I can see the shadows of her attackers. They move and fight as well as any I've seen but they've never encountered a Giak vet. She'll clear the bridge of them pretty soon.

And I can see him, standing tall in his royal armor, trying to regroup his men and direct a counter attack against the goliath;

Cassad.

Chapter Nine
THE LAST CASSAD

He doesn't stand a chance.

Maybe if they had critically wounded the giak on their first strike. Maybe if they had more men. Maybe if they knew what they were dealing with. Maybe if they had something they could hit her with big enough to get through that armor but like me they don't want to risk damage to the bridge.

As it is the Stomper is running riot through his men. They're Royal Guard… though they're not swathed in the Cassad family colors or displaying the Cassad family crest like I'm used to seeing. They're the best personal bodyguards in the history of the known. They've protected the Cassads for thousands of years and this Cassad for the entire bloody duration of the revolution. They're history is the stuff of legend. Their accomplishments so impossible to believe that most chalk it up to propaganda.

This is not their finest moment.

They've obviously never fought a Giak before.

You can't take them down with small arms fire. Even if you've got high caliber… or even armor piercing ammo, even after the rounds get through the mahbount plates they wouldn't have enough energy to penetrate the Giak's incredibly dense muscle. Tear up their skin all you want but the rounds never get to the squishy inside.

Even though high caliber weaponry might crack the armor unless you crack it and kill it in the same shot she'll just go even harder. And the wide area of the bridge is gonna get small real quick with a Giak swinging a five-meter-long war hammer. Close combat with a Giak is something you want to avoid.

Energy weapons take too much time to burn through the armor to try and use this close. The Stomper would just run you down and smash you into a nasty red paste that squirts out of your ruined gear.

Fragging it works. But again, the Royal Guard doesn't want to destroy the bridge. They may have to change their minds on that if they want to survive this. There are other ways to get to core control.

I'm almost mesmerized by the fight. Between watching the Guard operate, which despite not working is still elegant…still precise on an appalling level and watching the Giak battle, which brings back all too harsh memories. I almost forget I've got a stake in this fight.

"Fall back!" his voice booms through the tunnel. Good man, realize you're outmanned…well, kind of… and get the hell out of there before that Stomper brings that hammer down on your head.

If he runs now he can get…

But Cassad doesn't run. Even as the Royal Guard retreat back around him he charges the Giak.

Insane fool.

His guardsmen can't believe it either. So graceful before, even while getting clobbered, they twist and spin about awkwardly now, taken by surprise by his ridiculous move.

But he's not awkward. Cassad moves swiftly despite wearing magnetic boots. He sprints right at her, dropping the rifle he's been holding and drawing his side arm with one hand and a long blade with the other.

Down comes the war hammer. Cassad turns off his magnetic boots…

…scratch that, he and his guard have got to be using an artificial gravity system in their uniforms, still magnetic but more sensitive to the users' needs. You can tell by the way he just launches himself over the half ton block of metal and past the stunted armored head of the Giak.

He's not the first that I've seen do this to a Giak and I don't think it's the first time it's been done to this particular Stomper. Ready for it, she spins around…DAMN!... much too fast for something that big, bringing that war hammer with her. Cassad fires his sidearm right into her helmeted face, his aim true despite that hammer passing just over his head.

He'd turned those boots back on while aiming, firing and…the blade he had is no longer in his hands.

It's lodged in the back of the Giak's rear armor plate… right in the seam!

Cassad sprints again, around the Giak now still firing at her faceplate. His Royal Guard finally recovers and runs to join their…king or whatever, but a harsh barked order from him brings them up short. He intends to finish the Giak by himself.

Fool actually thinks he's winning.

I can see the nasty toothed fighting grin on her face through the guard in her helmet just before she spins abruptly the other way, bringing that hammer around in the opposite direction. Her turn is so sharp that her boots scrap along the ground despite the powerful magnets holding her to the deck. Cassad leaps to avoid the blow but the Giak's not trying to smash him. Instead she's firing the war hammer.

And she's a smart one. She's not aiming for Cassad.

His Royal Guard, caught flatfooted and out of place by his prideful order, are cut in half when the baleful weapon opens up. All damn… half of them dead just like that.

It's very easy to forget that hammer can shoot. After you've seen it hit a fellow soldier... smash a person into wrong, unbelievably unrecognizable mush… it can make you fear being hit by it more than being shot by it. Giaks know this… and they use it to their advantage.

I pop the safety off my M-11. Can't let the stomper kill Cassad. Don't know why they're already here; I should have had more than a work rotation to set up before they reached the *Njaro*…I think. Kept falling behind my schedule but thought I still had plenty of leeway. And where the buck is his fleet? No matter, Cassad is here with only a small force so this as good a chance to grab him as I'm gonna get. My original plan is blown to vacuum now but I've invested way too much just getting to this point. Loren, don't misfire now.

Before I can even begin to sight the stomper from beneath the deck I see Cassad make his move. He takes the advantage of the death of his men to charge the Giak again. This time he grabs the hilt of the blade he'd lodged in the Stompers armor. There's a small explosion; the blade must have introduced some kind of charge. Then, with a herculean effort, he pops a wide plate of armor off of the Giak's back, exposing the dark tattooed Giak warrior flesh beneath.

The maneuver cost him position though; she turns on him and swats him aside with bone crunching force. But the opening was enough for the surviving Royal Guard to take advantage of. They opened fire with smart weapons, every single round finding their way into the breach.

"ARROOO!" the Giak cried out and dropped the war hammer to the ground.

Smart weapons…they blew it.

The Stomper turns on the Royal Guard and I see the fire in her eyes. Fek… I've only got a few beats.

It's easier to push through the torn bridge deck than I thought it would be, gives me maybe the extra nano-pulse that I need. Without gravity it's gonna be hard to target her and my shot window will only be open for an instant. I jam the M-11 stock hard into my shoulder as I float in between the charging Stomper and the Guard.

Smart rounds fly around me as Cassad's body guards fire uselessly. They're not hitting the breech in the armor anymore and it wouldn't matter if it did. The Stomper's lost it from the pain and gone berserker; a state of hyper elevated violent rage. She'll attack and kill everything around her until the fury passes.

And the rage can only pass when there's nothing left to kill.

But there is one thing you can count on when a stomper goes berserker; the howl. She'll howl just once as she falls into the rage. Just once…for a few beats…

"HAAAAR…."

Her huge head slides across my sights and in the instant our eyes meet I plant one magnetized foot down and pull the trigger. I get two rounds out of six in her mouth. The big girl shudders and her body goes slack. Her momentum is arrested jarringly by the auto activation of her boots bringing her to a stop not two meters in front me.

Wow… last time I pulled that off I got smashed and ground into the plasticrete of a Crodun airstrip, but I still managed to take out two of them. At least that's what they told me when I came to.

The echo of the gun fire dies down and the bridge goes quiet for a pulse beat then I hear them behind me, the Royal Guard. My armors tact-net pops with warnings as I'm targeted several times over. Cassad is laying, twitching slowly to consciousness, down on the deck on the other side of the mound of dead Giak.

"Stand down, mercenary!"

Hmm? I expected them to fire on me immediately. Looks like cutting down that Giak for them is buying me a few moments. I'm actually gonna get a chance to see if my buckin' back up tactic will work.

I lower my rifle slowly and turn as peaceably as I can. There are six...no seven of them left. Big buckers too; they've been breeding these bastards for over a millennium and the smallest is at least quarter meter taller than me. Not many in the known that can look down on a native of Arcadia.

These guys get the best training, best equipment but today they look like they've been put through the ringer and it's from more than just the Giak beating.

Their equipment is mismatched and a few even look a bit piecemeal like they've had to supplement their gear on the fly. There are some pretty nasty burn marks on their armor from energy weapon fire. But they're still standing tall...and ready to fire on me with those very deadly Royal Elite rifles.

Good.

"Mercenary?" one of them says as she strides forward. Two others move to secure their fallen Minister.

Can't have that.

I reach down and pull the cord on the plasma generator. In a beat, a thin transparent pinkish bubble envelopes me. The Guard fire before the bubble completes itself but it doesn't matter; I'm moving and the rounds never reach me. The one who advanced on me catches two from my M-11 to his midsection then I send some more fire towards the two trying to get to Cassad.

They open fire on me in mass. The plasma shield bubbles and flashes with the multiple hits but I stay unscathed as the ammo veers off just enough to miss me. There's a pregnant pause in their attack and I can't help but smile at their confusion. Doubt they've encountered countermeasures so resistant to their weapons fire before.

And it gives me more than enough time to get to Cassad. His highness is still stunned and floundering from the Giak. I give him a quick tap and zap from the crowd control unit in my gauntlets to keep him sedate. More fire opens up on me from the Royal Guard. They're not too worried about hitting their king; little known fact: Cassad and his Royal Guard carry ancient counter measures in their armor to prevent them from hitting each other in case of tight skirmishes.

Damn it...I'm still smiling as their rounds bounce neatly off my plasma shield. I return fire and scatter them, not really trying to take them down but I need them off of my back.

Can't take Cassad back to my ship until I have time to strip him of whatever tracking devices he might have on him and I can't take him back into the industrial district because the raider gang has to be alerted to the fight now. That means using the tram and heading to the station core.

I haul the last king up and toss him over my shoulder. More of their useless weapons fire explodes around me as I get Cassad up onto the tram. The Giak had the tram on standby so it's nice and warmed up for me. Simple, standard Cassad engineered controls...I activate the tram and give the Royal Guard the courtesy of a warning shout before levering the tram up to full speed and bursting through their position and across the bridge.

A few more rounds of weapons fire chase us up the tunnel but it doesn't even harm the tram at this point. We're free and clear for a pulse beat.

I take a moment and look at the view of the central core of the *Njaro* through the transparent shield as we rocket closer. It's a shame; this was one of the greatest space facilities in the Empire...

...vultures.

Ah well...the sooner I disable Cassad's equipment the sooner I can head back to my ship. One EMP grenade, slightly modified, should do the trick. I send a few blasts of highly charged electron waves over Cassad and read the results through my tactical display. A few at a time his electrical systems go off line, even the pheromone particle emitter stashed in his boots shuts down. Using the slowly dying grid of disabled macro lines as a blue print I disable the rest of his counter measures and slowly strip him free of his gear. Oddly there are no subcutaneous or deep tissue implants… guess the Cassads are above such things.

I throw a standard tech jumpsuit on him and then bind his hands to his waist, one on each hip. Whew! That didn't take too…what?

The tram is speeding up. I look at the controls and see the ominous flash on the board indicating a remote set of commands. In almost no time at all I can see the dock we're racing toward at fatal speed.

FEK!

I try the EMP on the controls but there isn't enough juice left to fry the remote connection. There's no time to jury rig another grenade…

I grab Cassad and extend my Raptor armor's air foils. They catch the wind with a neck jarring jolt and we rise out of the tram.

Too much buckin' momentum! The tram crashes into the dock ahead of us by only seconds turning into a rolling ball of scrap. Metal shards fly through the air like shrapnel and I twist in midair trying to cover Cassad with my body.

We soar past the dock at breakneck speeds but the wings finally begin to slow us considerably after we clear the still tumbling tram. Can't maneuver for position…can't maneuver for anything other than a survivable landing as the Central Cores first partitions race at us.

We're still moving too fast! I curl around Cassad protectively and shield us as best I can with the wing foils as we slam through a guard rail first then into air car dividing wall.

UNG! The crash knocks the wind out of my lungs and in the pulse beat it takes me to recover I see that all I'm holding of Cassad is a bit of torn jumpsuit.

All damned… where?

"Lose something, Loren?"

What the buck? I look up and see a small gang of mercenaries floating in cover formation all around me. Cassad, still unconscious, is cradled loosely in the arms of a female soldier who is one of three of the mercenaries who are wearing armor… Raptor armor.

The female floats forward a bit tossing Cassad back to one of her mercs like a sack of grain. She lifts her visor and her eyes shine through with a wicked glimmer.

I take another breath, then; "Long time no see, Stepchild."

"Heh," she says. "Long time no see, Picker."

Chapter Ten
THE FIRE-HAWKS

They've repainted their armor, nasty splotches of dark red paint covering the old trim. Step-child is still wearing her "Heavy" package and is toting a MM 7&7. She's covered all the old 46th patches and insignias with the roughly drawn blazing fire emblem of the FireHawks merc gang. I supposed it's meant to look pretty dynamic but it comes off garish. Could be I'm just used to the subtle design I fought in.

The other two in armor I don't know, but I recognize the Raptor Armor easily enough.

"When the hell did you join up with the FireHawks?" Anger rises in my voice with every word.

"Join up?" she's smiling. "Picker, we STARTED the FireHawks."

"What?"

"Right after you bailed."

"You started a mercenary gang? Filled with Afans and All dammed Stompers? Using THAT emblem?" the fire bird logo was used by a pretty big merc army that operated back in Eastspace during the Wars of the Blade. They were a pretty impressive bunch… started by vets from some of the stronger Imperial worlds. But we pretty much ended them during the Blade so there's no way…

"…you started the FireHawks, Step-child."

"Oh yea…it's Phoenix now. And I never said I was the Duke."

"Phoenix…?" As casually as I can I take a look around trying to get a sit-rep. We're at the dock landing. It's separate from the main body of the Central Core. Cargo and people transferred here onto shuttles and made their way across what looks like a good hundred meters to the city proper. Below us there's a web of crossing gantries spanning down into the amber haze caused by the hydrogel dome. Armor's picking up the faintest bit of gravity here. If any of us float too far from the dock we'll start to drop.

They're clustered pretty close together… I don't see any back up…no overwatch that I can see. I glance at the other two mercs wearing Raptor armor and suddenly my gut tightens. I kick off from the wall and let the counter weights in the air foils straighten me up to face them. "These two are wearing the armor of dead men!"

She hesitates for a pulse beat and then shakes her head with a lot more venom than I'm expecting. "They've proven themselves worthy of wearing…"

"Proven what??" I point a gauntleted finger at the bigger of the two. "That's Yogger's armor, Step-child! Who is HE to be wearing that?"

The merc in question bristles a bit. But Step-child makes a dismissive gesture. "They are proven, Loren! Now what are you doing here? Who is this?"

Cassad lolls about in the arms of the smaller merc. If they recognize him…

"That armor needs to be interred with Yogger, Seph…how could you…"

"DON'T YOU DARE!" she screams and jets forward a bit. "You know…" her voice breaks only a little. "No…you wouldn't know; you left us so damn fast… what they did to the bodies of the 'traitors' we were bringing home before Arcadia fell.

"This way Baro gets honored…by those who know." She floats down toward me from her group and I lift my visor so that our eyes can meet. This close I can see the she still hasn't gotten rid of the old scars; one in the cleft of her chin and the nasty flash burn from a Junn plasma rifle still paints a dark brown "butterfly" across the copper skin of her nose and cheeks. I see the pain there and the same resentment I hold in my own heart. But it isn't enough.

"Boo-fek. Nobody should be wearing that armor, Seph. And who's armor is…" I stop myself as I recognize the battle damage pattern embedded across the wide chest plate and then the faint and poorly painted over "lightning" emblem on the shoulder guard.

"Recognize it, Picker?" Her eyes switched from pain to a dangerous anger in the space of a nanosecond.

"I do." I do…

"So, it's true?" she asks.

The memory came back easily enough. It's one of the top worst in the rotation of my lucid dreams. My throat goes tight. Showboat was…it had to happen.

Step-child floats ever closer. A few thick strands of her dark brown hair escape her flight cap and poke out of her visor. "We lost a lot of our people to the Blade…more at Dalius, but even more after. How many are yours?" Her eyes narrow to slits. I see it now; she isn't looking to avenge Showboat, she wants to take her still seething anger over Yoggers death out on me. This is just an excuse.

"I'm not here for this." I say. It comes out as a warning.

"I don't give a hot pile of fek what you're here for." Now we're so close our helmets are almost touching. "You're gonna pay for what you did."

"You don't mean Showboat." I say with challenge in my voice. "Or Half Head, or Bingo…"

I narrow my own eyes as I peer into hers. "or even Quick…"

"Quick?" That startles her. Good; I need her to know how much trouble she's in.

"No," I press on. "Who you want me to pay for is Yogger."

She starts to shake her head but I cut her off from answering. "But you really do need to think about the others first." I say. "Yogger died with honor. Sacrificing himself for his people…fighting with his squad at his side…saving our lives…but those others? They died in situations…very much like this."

I see a moist gleam in her eyes. Not sure if she's going to back off or come at me. I don't want to hurt her. Don't even want to fight her. She's saved my life more than once.

"You buckin piece of…"

"You need to be thinking about this little squad of yours… Phoenix." I snap. "Only thing you're going get here is a handful of dead mercs."

"Maybe you recalculate the odds here, dipper" spits the merc wearing Yogger's armor. "Dipper" is an Arenn term, sister planet to Arcadia. At least there's somebody in her crew whose people I didn't used to kill.

I make sure to keep my eyes locked with Step-child's. "You think your little gang here has what it takes? I know you were monitoring the bridge. You saw me take down your Giak. I'm still in fighting form. This is going to end badly for one of us but this does nothing for Yogger."

Step-child backs away from me. I let her go; if this goes bad I don't want more 46th blood on my hands. But she seems to be composing herself.

"I…I want to know who this is." She jabs a finger at Cassad. "And I want to know what kind of tech that is you used against that other merc crew on the bridge."

She's trying to save face for both of us, I think. I'll give her one but not the other.

"He's my business" I say. "But I'll give you the plasma shield."

"We're not letting this piece of fek go?" her squad starts to balk.

"We blew the tram to get him!"

"He killed Sieda." That objection spews from the vocal simulator perched on the shoulder of a particularly small merc. He stands just over a meter tall and covered from head to toe in EXO-combat gear. From his bow legged stance I realized he's Pan, a feral humanoid species from the Cerebus star system. Very secretive; they've managed to keep almost everything about themselves hidden from most of the known. Except for the Cassads, who had their foot on every world, no one gets cooperation from them. More points for the FireHawks.

"Not my intent to attack you." I say. Looks like Step-child doesn't run her squad with the kind of discipline we were taught in the ADF. One of her crew might decide to take it upon themselves to open fire prematurely. Can't tell which of them might pop first…they all look so damn jittery. Got to calm things down.

"Think we all should just let go what's past and move on from here." I say.

"You don't give the orders here." And the little Pan raises his weapon.

"No, I do." Step-child finally steps back up. I can tell from the way the whole crew is bracing themselves now that this challenge has been some time in coming. Not sure I want to get in the middle of this especially if the side I'm leaning to has Step-child on it. But then she says something that draws my gut tight.

"He's 46th," as if she were telling them I was part of their merc crew.

They all go silent. I don't. "What's this now?"

Step-child looks hard at me. "WE don't turn on our own."

I can't help but be curious. "Who's we?"

"Don't tell him fek!"

"Find your cover!" Step-child snaps. She stares down the merc in Yogger's armor again then looks back to me. "You only get that if you stand down and join up, Picker."

"Join up? Eat dirt with longnecks and Stompers? Not gonna happen."

"Then give me that shield tech." She floats forward and extends a hand. Her crew bristles a bit but remain in ranks. They must have all seen the plasma shield perform against the smart rounds. They want it but giving it to them is a big gamble I'm not sure I can risk losing.

Could be she thinks that my shield generator will give me an advantage in a firefight with them. So if I hand it over now she might just try and go at me.

Could be she's just looking for a way out for both of us.

All depends on how much she really blames me for Yog-ger falling.

I reach down and disconnect the generator from my hip, watching the small FireHawks Squad for the first signs of attack. They grow even more fidgety, but still look uncertain. Hopefully they at least wait for her to decide one way or the other.

I hold out the generator. Step-child looks it over without reaching out. I see doubt in her eyes.

"Looks a little like the bubble gennies we had during the Blade" she frowns. Of course, it looks like that because that's exactly what it is.

"It's not. Works a little better."

"Obviously. How?" she reaches out and takes the gener-ator. Her whole body shifts forward a bit as the mass of it sur-prises her; the qualt rocks I'm using weigh three times as much.

"Figure it out" I tell her. "Hand over my mark."

"He cost us, Phoenix" the Pan murmurs. "We should keep the man…take his armor…and his ship…and…"

"He's a point, Loren." Step-child says with an arrogant confidence. "Why shouldn't I just…"

"Cause you're not stupid, Step-child." I say as I give her a look I reserve for Junn pretty boys. But she's tough, 46th trained and tested in the Wars of the Blade, she won't fold now. This is going to go ugly. I've lost Cassad.

Before we hear the shot the merc wearing Showboats ar-mor and holding the unconscious Cassad is spun about from a long-range rifle hit. The next instant we hear the rapport and suddenly several more of the FireHawks take long range blasts.

The Royal Guard have made their way across the bridge.

Step-child ducks down and to her credit she's barking re-group orders even as she's hit herself. Her heavy armor handles the hits just fine but I see she's already struggling to plug in the plasma generator.

I really should warn her but I'm too busy trying to scoop up Cassad.

The last of the House of Cassad is tumbling head over heels down…down into a chasm of crisscrossing walkways, hit-ting a few but still falling none the less. I go full burst from my

M-11, toward the top of the docks, to get me moving in the opposite direction. Just a beat passes and as gravity takes over, I sweep the wings and shoot down after him. The lowest walkways should lead to the inner core. If I can get Cassad there…

Hot white tracers cut across my flight path to Cassad. A few of his highness' guardsmen must have come in ahead of their brothers. We're all in fast dives zigzagging past the thin walk bridges. They're coming in at an angle but in that Royal guard armor they've no real flight speed or directional control. I'll get to Cassad first so they're trying to cut me off with sporadic fire.

It costs one of them; not paying enough attention to his own flight path the guard slams into a cross bridge dead center.

Our speed picks up as the gravity in this section is almost at one full G. We're falling faster and so is Cassad.

Fek! More cross fire from the Royal Guard. I raise my M-11 and send back rounds, hitting one nicely center mass and sending him, careening, into a cross bridge rail hard enough to lose his weapon.

Ahead of me I see Cassad hit a relay antenna, spin and then head directly for a particularly wide bridge. Just moments after he slams into it, my boots come down on the same walkway harder than I anticipate, forcing me to catch myself. My rifle hits the ground, pops out of my grip and spins away down the bridge. I sprint after it and toward Cassad but more tracer fire tears up the plasteel plates around me. The bridge shudders as another of the Royal Guard lands hard in right in my path. His foot stomps on my errant rifle and with a grin; he levels his own weapon at me and pulls the trigger.

Can't help but to enjoy the look on his face as every shot veers wide of hitting me. I pull my Sever and return fire with much better results putting him down with torso shots until he falls away from the walkway.

I take a look around. The rest of the Guard seems to be engaged with Step-child and her little squad of looters. She's not doing so well herself, having taking more hits than she should have trying to depend on that useless plasma shield.

Time to go.

I recover my weapon and then walk over to Cassad who looks… well at least he's still breathing. I rack my M-11, keep my Sever in my gun hand and toss Cassad over my shoulder with the other. Without looking back, I haul ass across the walkway and into the corridors of the central core of *Njaro* where I can lose anyone trailing us.

Almost done.

EPILOGUE

I fasten the holo-emitter to the binding bar behind Cassad's neck. He's still unconscious but now only due to a sedative that won't last too long. I checked him out in my small med-bay and despite all he'd been through Cassad is going to be just fine. Well until his trial anyway.

So I position him, upright, in the cargo bay, locked into a prisoner binder. Then with the remote reconfigured, I depress the button on the wide end and the crystal clear and life like image of a large cargo container shimmers into focus hiding Cassad completely. He'll wake in a hazy darkness, unable to see where he is.

That done I return to the workshop. This time I have my own Raptor Armor up on the rack. Hardly any damage to speak of, a few plates could be reset but that's all. I check to see that the inner emlin alloy I pulled from the old guard's armor is still in place. It's doubtful that the Royal Guard will catch up to me before I turn Cassad over to the New Regime but "just in case" is what wins the argument.

Long ago the Cassads used the emlin as a safe measure to make sure that their own personnel would never be hit by friendly fire. Over the years that alloy got forgotten by most and was only used in the old ceremonial armor and perhaps in the Royal armament of Cassad himself for purely traditional reasons.

But the weak point in the weaponry was still there, hidden in their secret history, just begging to be taken advantage of. The smoke screen of the plasma generator was a fail since one of the Guard clearly saw his rounds veer off target after he fired on me when I didn't have it but at least it bought me enough time to get Cassad.

His fleet never made an appearance in system. Could he have lost it out on the edge of the known? His men looked beat up enough. Guess the money I spent getting Ziaran transponders was wasted. Maybe Sticky can get a good price for them.

The FireHawks sent out encrypted messages with 46th code keys attached but I ignore them for now. With any luck I won't be in the merc game anymore so I won't be running into them again.

C.O.P. pings and I head for control. *War Child* has made it out of Orun's gravity well and can make the jump now. Time to get paid.

KING'S COURT

BY

HOWARD NIGHT

From the personal log of Spiro Walsh, Nazerian Abatan Security Command Officer 3rd rank during the Trial of Cassad the day after the Reading of the Charges.

"You know everybody went on and on about that visor the Merc who brought in Cassad was wearin'. That visor with those damn holographic ghost eyes. But I was there, down on the arena floor after the first attempt on Cassads life failed. The Merc had his visor knocked off and had just taken out four of those assassins by himself when we finally got to them. And his and my eyes met...in that moment before he realized I was friend and not foe. Let me tell you; I found myself wishin to the Almighty that he'd put that visor back on, cause catching his eye... it was like being stared down by an all-beast..."

Chapter One
NEW BEIA

New Beia, formerly known as Esara, the one-time capital of the Sumatran Republic, is now the official home world of the New Regime. Coalition forces forged their agreement here after the start of the Wars of the Blade.

It's a standard terran class world, terraformed long ago to meet human requirements.

The Median Belt became their first an easiest won battleground during the revolution; there was hardly a shot fired. Most of the worlds here were long tired of Cassad rule and when the outer territories made their first push the New Regime took full advantage and "liberated" the sector.

It's a blue and white world…lots of cloud cover…heavily settled so there's very little natural vegetation. I expected that I'd be directed to one of the orbiting stations but as I approach my contact sends me a comm.

"You're directed to the Nezerian Tower, Abatan city. Landing protocols are being sent to you now." Her holo comes through clear and it's the first time I get a look at her face. She's a lot younger than I thought or at least appears to be, pretty too.

"Nezerian Tower," I sub vocalize to the C.O.P., the Computer Ops Program, and the G-Det holographic display zeroes in on the landing site. The tower is…quite a site. Built on the foundation of the Nezerian Mountains, which are some of the biggest mountains in the known, the Nezerian Tower is one of the tallest planet bound structures ever built. The upper levels extend past New Beia's troposphere and into the mesosphere where they connect to trans-orbital elevator lines of several low orbit space facilities.

And it's big; the tower has the mass and size to host ten different cities within its walls each with a population of a few million citizens. It's so big that it has three different space ports, the biggest at its base but the other two were actually built on the upper levels.

"Abatan City Space Port" my contact confirms. The highest-level city, the highest-level space port… ok. I begin my approach and drop my ship, *War Child*, into the atmo.

Damn…the tower is big! I could probably make my way there without instruments.

I lost my Brython escorts not too long after passing through the gate but soon picked up some fancy, fresh built, New Regime gunships to watch over me. They're probably crewed by a mix of officers from the member groups of the Coalition. This close to their capital though I doubt there'll be any trouble.

Still…I keep my ports open.

"Seventh Seal, this is Abatan Port Control, you are marked on approach. We understand you have the stick?"

"Roger that, Abatan. I have the stick."

The Nezerian Tower grows and grows as *War Child* gets closer. Buck me it's big! Each city of the tower lies in a cup shaped ring, each one smaller than the one beneath it, though I can only see the top two for the clouds. All of them are connected by massive tower pillars that maintain the shape and stability of the structure. I can see the port; it hangs insanely over one side of the Abatan City ring. Who on styx had the engineering ability to design that?

Abatan City lies just under the "cap"; the upper most levels where the Towers control is located. It's the smallest city but it's also the New Regimes Coalition council's headquarters. I can see the fanfare from three clicks out; looks like they know Cassad is on his way.

I follow the landing protocols and circle one time around the tower. Flags from the different members of the New Regime pepper the tiers and spires of Abatan City. There are swarms of air cars racing about, a few following my progress as *War Child* closes on the port.

Even the port itself is bigger than I'd thought. It's got three levels, any one of which is large enough to land my ship in. As it is I'm directed to the center level. Makes sense; it's protected a bit from an orbital strike or even just prying eyes.

There's a massive welcoming committee waiting for me at the landing circle. Soldiers, armored units and of course the dignitaries all jammed into the small service corridor surrounding the port. I extend the landing legs and, just for show, cut the hovering jets a good ninety decimeters off the ground. With a crash, *War Child* comes down hard; scattering the deck techs like mice. She's a brick of a ship, the hull and most of her structure is cete-armor which makes her tough as anything in the worlds but not too pretty. She's an old drop ship so she's got impressive looking, albeit mostly empty, gun ports. A nightmare from wars centuries ago, I found her drifting in a graveyard and rebuilt her to her former glory. Well…maybe not her former glory…fek…anyway I got her running.

"Nice landing, Seventh Seal." I forgot my contact was still on the open comm. I throw her a smirk and a wink, which, translates as one of my "ghost" eyes winking out on my visor.

"So…" I challenge. "I still don't see my money."

"You'll get paid, mercenary. All of the known is watching now."

Yea. Wouldn't do to see the new lords of the known reneging on their agreements. Nevertheless… "I'm sure. Meet me at the forward hatch…alone."

She balks but I cut the comms. It's getting tight now…that small crack of light that's my way out is getting thinner and thinner.

I strip off the armor first. Coming through the Median Gate to get here was a dangerous mission and I threw on my Raptor armor in case *War Child* suffered catastrophic damage. But now that I'm planet-side I figure if this goes bad now it won't help me.

One last check on the "package". In *War Child*'s prep bay there sits a rather innocuous looking stack of cargo containers. I retrieve the small cylindrical remote from my equipment pack and tap the button on one end. The camouflage holographic containers shimmer and fade revealing a man bound to a restraining bar and locked in a control collar. A bit overkill maybe but he managed to free himself before and nearly killed me so now I'm not taking any chances.

He is the king of the known after all.

Catching Cassad was more fortuitous opportunity than bounty hunting prowess but I got it done regardless. It took most of my resources, all of my skill and tore up my ship in the process. All of that for a massive amount of qed that would put an end to my mercenary days. Better be worth it.

Cassad can only stare back me now, which is good, don't want him causing trouble this close to the deal getting done. I tap the remote again and the holo shimmers back up.

My contact should be at the port by now so I throw on my flight suit and field jacket then check my visor and head to the forward hatch.

Chapter Two
THE ADVOCATE

"STANDARD INOCCULATION SUITE UPLOADED," the C.O.P. tells me as my prep for the New Beia ecosystem completes itself. "VIRTUAL INTERFACE UP-LOADED."

There's a roar when I pop the forward hatch followed almost immediately by a sigh of disappointment when they see it's only me coming down the ramp. Just stepping over the safety rail at the edge of the landing circle, my New Regime contact makes her way over to meet me followed by two smaller females in Coalition colors. Her dress is…formal; long, wide sleeves that cover her hands, gold flecked tunic and some kind of headdress. Whoever she is she must work in an official capacity with the Coalition itself and not merely one of the member worlds. She has a confident walk. Can't tell if she's flaring for her superiors, the crowd or maybe even just for me.

"We've got Coalition Special Guard on their way to take custody…"

I ignore her as she goes on about the transfer procedures and take a moment to take in the port. The air is almost…sweet. We're too high for them not to rely on some kind of atmo generators but the port is an open deck. Must take a bit of power to continually pump in O2…and heat. It should be freezing but it feels like a mild day…like fall on Arcadia…

I've been to New Beia before but nowhere near the Tower. Too many procedures and official gauntlets to run through. Planet hopping among the more developed worlds is a headache that just isn't worth it if there's no cred bump. But now I'm a special visitor with all the privileges extended to a diplomat.

The view out of the hangar is amazing.

The mob awaiting Cassad is huge. For the most part they're New Beia citizens but there are plenty of offworlders too. The virtual posts floating through the crowd are from literally hundreds of different worlds. My visor is picking up all kinds of sensor sweeps and recording waves. No doubt a lot of them are trying to get an I.D. off of my image and bio-signature. Good luck; my flight suit masks my bio-sig and my visor actually projects a low level holo over the exposed portion of my face just outside the visible spectrum...makes a computer I.D. impossible.

I turn and look over my contact. She's got no virtual post but her two friends are sporting glowing Coalition ID tags. I don't see any bags; I don't see any crates... "I don't see my money."

"Now is not the time to..."

My ghost eyes narrow as I peer at her. "Now isn't the time? Lady, this is the buckin' transaction!"

She falters a little bit and then composes herself quickly. "You will be paid" she insists. "You do understand that very few thought it could actually be done. That anyone would be able to..."

"Is this where you try and tell me you don't have the money?"

Her face drops a bit. Oh fek... "The money is being gathered as we speak."

From her body language I thought for a pulse beat that she was about to tell me they didn't have it. But Sticky assured me they did in fact have that money...had so much coin now that the bounty shouldn't have been a problem.

"Good. I want it in..."

"It's being gathered..." she cuts me off.

"When will it be here?"

"There is still the matter of the trial" she says.

"Which has nothing to do with me."

"Mercenary," her voice rises in frustration. "...the bounty is being held by the only faction that the Coalition trusts to hold the money; the Nth Consortium."

Nth Consortium? The name is familiar. "And it's being brought here now?"

"No" she says. "You will receive your payment once there has been a conviction."

My eyes flare. "You expect me to sit here and wait for you to stage a trial? It took you twenty-three years to knock this family off the throne; I'm not waiting while half the known queues up to spit in the eye of the Cassads."

"It will not be a lengthy trial!" she argues, once again glancing to the crowds. The activity around the pad and in the corridor beyond is increasing. I can see banners; virtual, holographic and real, approaching... could be dignitaries. And there's a group of security officers, armored, headed our way.

"You've got to be kidding me." I mutter.

"You WILL be paid. I swear..." she hisses. The security group looks to be another Coalition force; some of the member groups are represented.

"Your word is no good. You're not getting Cassad till I get the coin" I tell her.

"And what will you do, Mercenary?" She's talking harshly but in hushed tones. For some reason she doesn't want them to hear us. "Try and take off? They'll blow you out of the sky. You've no choice."

"Wanna bet?" I'm bluffing. I'm bucked.

The Coalition Security group slows to a stop not ten paces off. Their commanding officer, ID'ed by her floating virtual badge, looks to be a Denir, decorated in war if that braid on her shoulder means anything. She's wearing light battle armor, all spruced up in its ceremonial configuration for this little show. Quickly she looks me up and down, lingering only a little on the NOK 37 resting on my hip.

"Prim Locasta of the Coalition of Free Worlds. Nezerian Security Command," she announces herself. "Ready to take Minister Cassad into custody."

Out of the corner of my eye I see my New Regime Contact signal to one of her assistants. Then she quickly turns and addresses the Security officer. "Prim Locasta, it seems there's been a bit of a miscommunication."

The Prim narrows her eyes at that. Behind her the banners begin to emerge from the crowd. First to enter is a Daliun Delegation, riding in open air cars and waving to a mesmerized crowd.

"Adila Eboro…you're the Advocate?" The Prim addresses my contact. "Fine. I was told Cassad's presence on this ship was confirmed."

Advocate?

"He has Minister Cassad," my contact, Eboro, assures her. "The miscommunication is about how we proceed with the exchange of custody."

"Then I will clear that up." The Prim steps forward. "This port, for all the commotion, is secured. You may bring Cassad down here. Now."

Horns sound. Behind the Daliuns another delegation walks in, or rather, floats in on personal hoverpads; the Brythons. The Ambassadorial royal family comes in with plenty pageantry and plenty of 'bots. Unlike many in the known the Brythons prefer their droids look like machines rather than mimic beings. They walk stiffly besides the royal carriage while carrying the royal crest and royal pendant. They're all such royal…

"I said 'now', mercenary." The Prim takes another step forward.

The "Advocate" is watching me intently. She doesn't want me arguing with them about the money. Why?

"The Minister remains aboard my ship until we square things up." I say. The Prim studies me with enhanced eyes. She'll get nothing through my visor.

"Square things up?"

"There are…security concerns." Advocate Eboro, interrupts. "Despite the Coalitions protocols there is worry about Cassad arriving fit for trial."

"Really, Advocate?" the Prim glowers at her.

"I want Minister Cassad," The Advocate starts with just enough hesitation that I can tell she's making it up as she goes. "…the Minister will be sequestered here for the duration of the trial."

Uh oh...

"Here?" the Prim looks over my ship like she's looking at a pile of bicafek. *War Child* isn't a "sleek" ship by any means; she's bulky and shaped like a brick with two huge engine housings on either side. The hull is all cete-armor, a rough crystal that grows like crab plate. I added the tritansteel wings which don't quite match the hunter green pallor of the armor. "That is not acceptable."

"As Advocate for the Accused I..."

"This is NOT acceptable." The Prim steps forward boldly and points at me. "Bring Khalid Cassad down at once or you will be taken into custody as well."

Looks like I'm not the only one bluffing. Without a nevron lock on my ship they can't access it without force. Any attempt to tear into the ship, they've got to know, will end up killing Cassad.

I growl. "Not until I'm...

"I have been given custodial powers!" The 'Advocate' cuts in, stepping in between me and the Prim. "And I am not satisfied that the safety of my charge can be guaranteed if he is moved from this ship."

"Your custodial powers extend to the trial itself, under the watch of Security Command, in our own facility. Bring him down." The Prim takes a look over her shoulder. Seems she just as aware of how many eyes are on us.

"We will," The Advocate states very loudly. "For his arraignment first thing next sunside." Then without another word to the Prim she sets off across the landing circle to meet the nearing delegations.

The Prim looks to me, opens her mouth to speak, and then stops to look over her shoulder again. She watches as the Advocate addresses first the Daliuns, then the Brythons.

I eyeball her too. Whatever she is telling the Daliuns they're taking it stone faced but accepting it. She moves on to the Brythons where the Ambassador begins nodding as if he expected whatever it is she's telling him.

Amazingly, the Daliuns begin gathering up their little parade and head out of the terminal. Prim Locasta mutters a curse and heads after the Advocate, trying to chase her down before she gets to the Quaznians who are just entering the landing pad.

Another wave of scans washes over me. Vid drones float just beyond the landing pad taking in every bit of data they can and transmitting it to every corner of the known. At least they're trying; the New Regime has a fek-load of counter measures passing through the air so I doubt the drones are getting more than grainy 3-d vid. Still, I double check the visor to make sure my own personal countermeasures are up. Don't want my specs on anybody's most wanted list.

The Quaznians get loud, their voices carrying across the landing pad as they expressed their objection. But the Advocate doesn't back down and from the body language of the Prim it seems she may have even gained an ally.

This goes on for a while with each delegation, as they arrive, all taking their turns at being directed away. The last few all look to have been given the heads up but even so one or two put on a show for the masses.

Finally, it's done and the Advocate and the Prim head back over to me.

"It's been agreed that Minister Cassad will remain aboard this ship for the duration of the trial." Advocate Eboro is again looking at me intensely. She doesn't want me to balk in front of the Prim.

"I must first verify that Cassad is actually on this ship." The Prim is giving me the dark eye now.

"Of course." I say then pointedly give her a look over. "But you're not coming aboard my ship with all the hardware."

The Prim twists her lips up knowingly. Then, to my amazement, she begins taking off her armor right there.

"Uh…" The Advocate is as startled as I am.

The armor seemed to me to be ceremonial and of a light class but she does not so much take it off as step out of it, leaving it standing on its own behind her. The Prim steps out of her armor, nude save for a thin pair of black bottoms.

My visor takes in her body, trying to sift through the counter measures in the air to see what security tech she has left without her armor. But all I can see is how lean and muscled she is, the soft sheen of her light brown skin and the telltale scars of a soldier. She's seen battle and she's proud of it. I'm glad the ghost eyes of my visor don't have holographic pupils; else wise she'd see how hard I'm staring at her dark nipples.

"I've no hidden weapons, mercenary." She says.

"We'll see." What my visor can't pick up here *War Child* will be able to detect in the airlock. "And you?"

The Advocate looks a little aghast. "I most certainly will not, mercenary! I…"

"Then you can wait right here until I come back with a portable scanner." I tell her. Her eyes move quickly from me to the Prim fast enough that I almost miss it. She doesn't want her alone with me…or with Cassad.

"Wait…" she grimaces then begins to remove her ceremonial garb. Fek…this isn't what I had intended; escorting two naked women into my ship…with the whole buckin known watchin'. There's a collective uproar from the crowd around the dock.

But Advocate Eboro has more modest undergarments on. Her hair beneath that headdress is set in long locked braids, each set in uniform rows over her head. There aren't any battle scars but she does have some skin art over her arms and legs…probably more beneath her thin top and bottoms.

Somewhat relieved I nod and lead them into the forward hatch where *War Child*'s security sensor suite launches its check to ferret out any serious threats.

And just in case...

"What's that?" The Prim asks as I pull out a modified EMP grenade.

"Exactly what it looks like." I tell her.

"You're going to fire off an EMP right here in your ship?" she asks incredulously.

"Raise your hands."

After a pulse beat she complies and I fire off the modified EMP in short, directed bursts and watch as the last of her subcutaneous hardware is taken offline.

"Clever, mercenary" she admits, but there's a low level of anger behind her eyes; tells me I just ruined something for her.

After running the EMP over Advocate Eboro, who was carrying no hidden electronics I let *War Child* check them over again.

No bioweapons either. Or at least none that register with *War Child*'s latest update. So…hopefully there won't be any surprises.

"Just follow the yellow guide." I tell them indicating the running lights that line the walls of the service ways through *War Child*. Set that up before I landed; don't want to lead them through my ship, don't want either of them behind me.

Of course, this is proving just as distracting. The Prim is in outstanding shape and her skin, despite the crisscrossing scars, shines like cocoa milk. Can't help but watch the muscles in her back work as she walks. It's cold in the ship…I bet her nipples are rock hard.

The "Advocate" isn't a fighter. That much is clear; she's more ample than I would have thought after seeing her jump me in the graveyard. It plays nicely as she tries to keep up with the much taller Prim.

"Here?" The Prim asks. We've made it all the way to the hatch sealing the Prep Bay. I take another moment, trying to act as though there was something else distracting me.

Been too damn long…

"Pull the latch." I tell her.

Clearly, she's not worked aboard a ship designed to beat EMFs because she pushes every indicator light like they're buttons. Then she figures it, turns the large latch and pushes open the hatch.

The Advocate slips past her to get into the room first but as she gets halfway across the bay she realizes that the yellow indicators ended back in the corridor. She looks quizzically about the room, the cargo containers, my eight-leg-walker and then turns to me as the Prim joins her.

"Where is the Minister?"

"Where is the PRISONER?" the Prim corrects her.

I pull the remote from my jacket pocket and press the small end. The cargo containers shimmer then fade, revealing Khalid Cassad, son of the now dead emperor Ose Cassad, strapped to a restraining bar.

The Advocate actually bows. "Minister Cassad."

The Prim spits at his feet, onto my deck plating. "Cassad. At least it looks like him."

Cassad simply stares back at the two.

"You're using a control collar on him?" The Advocate sounds almost aghast.

"He was…disagreeable." I tell her.

"I'll need a genetic sample to confirm his I.D." The Prim says but she already seems convinced. From the way she's staring daggers into Cassad's eyes she's clearly got something personal against the man. Not sure what that could be. The Denir are the leaders of the Kujiunga Na; one of the founding members of the New Regime. But word on the Hub was that their own defection from the Cassad empire was simply a matter of business and, save for the purging of their Royal Guard, not terribly bloody at all. The Cassad embassies in Denir space had been allowed to pack up and leave. They even took in defectors themselves.

"Not a problem." I walk over to my work table, retrieve a sub-dermal surveyor then toss it to her. The Prim inspects the tool but since they're fairly simple she's quickly satisfied that it's not rigged to give her a false sample.

"Thank you, mercenary," she says then grabs Cassad by his jaw, raising the surveyor with the other hand. "Well, Cassad…"

"You will not!" the Advocate moves faster than I do and grabs for the Prim. But she's not a fighter and the Prim tosses her across the room easily.

It's enough of a delay that I have my gun out and jammed into the Prims temple before she can drive the surveyor into Cassad's head.

"I was not going to kill him," she claims. "Just take a little flesh and cruk his perfect face."

244

"Liar!" The Advocate scrambles to her feet. "She wants vengeance!"

"I'll have my…" the Prim starts when I cut them both off.

"I don't care!" I take the surveyor from her clenched hand. "But nobody's damaging the merchandise until I get paid."

Eboro freezes at this, her eyes darting from me to the Prim. But the Nezerian Security commander just snorts at me, and then returns to glaring at Cassad.

So I toss the surveyor to Eboro and she steps in between the Prim and Cassad.

"Apologies, Minister, but it is necessary" and as gently as she can manage she applies the subdermal surveyor to his shoulder. Cassad doesn't flinch, mostly because the control collar is set so high he can only move his eyeballs.

He's not getting loose on my ship again.

Done, Adlia turns and slaps the surveyor into the Prims hands. "Satisfied?"

"No," the Prim tells her. "Not until he pays for his crimes."

"Then we're done here" I tell them and lead them both back to the hatch. The Prim is fairly bouncing with excitement while the Advocate seems greatly subdued. At the hatch she takes my arm.

"I need to speak with Cassad privately."

"When I'm…"

"I'm his Advocate," she insists. "I need to prepare him for his trial."

The Prim laughs but doesn't seem to care one way or the other. "We will verify Cassad's I.D. but I'm sure it's him. Prepare that murderer all you wish, Advocate; he will die as surely as worlds turn." And she walks down my ramp and steps back into her armor, the distinct look of anticipation on her face.

"I must have time to prep him and I'll need to council with him during the trial." Eboro says.

"But you can't get me my money until it's over?" she takes a step back and I realize I'm practically snarling.

"When he's convicted you will be paid."

"Seems to me, as his 'Advocate', you'll be working against that" I confront her.

"His conviction is assured, as the Prim was so delighted to point out. The trial is…a show for the Coalition." Eboro's eyes shade over as she speaks.

"Then what's the point of making me wait?"

"What is not known to everyone in the coalition is that there are two different factions that will pay the bounty depending on the outcome of the trial. This is something you would do well to keep to yourself. First, there are those that want him dead, they will foot the bounty if he is sentenced to be executed."

"And?"

"And there are those that want him imprisoned…sentenced to unspeakable punishments and indignities for as long as he can be kept alive. It is they that will pay the bounty for that conclusion."

I can't tell from her demeanor which fate she preferred or which would be better for me. Not that it mattered; I was going to have to sit through a trial either way. But maybe…

"Then a show of good faith."

"How do you mean?" She looks almost affronted.

"A down payment. Twenty-five percent." No way will she go for that, but I need to try.

"I don't have access to that kind of money."

"Then I'm sure I can find one of the members of the New Regime who would like to take him off my hands for about that much."

"Doubtful."

"Guess I'll have to see for myself." I watch as she grapples with a choice.

"I can…I can see your ship refueled…and four hundred thousand New reg…" she stammers a bit.

"Not good enough. Ten million…Old reg." I say.

"Ten?? No, I couldn't…and in Old reg? Maybe five hundred thousand…"

I hit the door controls and grab her arm, moving her outside the hatch.

"Ok! I can get you one million. But not for a few rotations," she says without much certainty. One million...won't even cover all the repair work *War Child* needs.

"Next sunside. Or I start making inquiries." A weak threat but she looks to be buying it. Still, I can't help but to be curious.

"And how did you become his Advocate? You don't seem to be Ziaran born, one of the First One Million."

"I am Akanman," she says quietly. Never heard of them. "May I council with Cassad?"

It's not like I have a choice. "Get your clothes first. It gets cold in the Prep Bay."

Chapter Three
BACKDOOR

I monitor the Advocate's meeting with Cassad from Primary. Even with the Control Collar settings at minimal he doesn't say much. Eboro seems to be pretty candid with him about his chances, which doesn't seem to affect him one way or the other. Unless she's talking to him in code she's actually prepping him for his trial.

So, with one eye on the monitor I do a little recon research. First, I check the Nezerian atlas for the layout. They're going to hold the trial in the Hall of Kain, a converted reconstruction of an ancient sports arena. It's big but not nearly large enough to fit all the representative caucuses from the New Regime. They'll likely be broadcasting the trial on the Hub and thus to every corner of the known.

And since I'm not gonna let Cassad out of my reach until I'm paid that means my image will be broadcast across the known as well.

Fek, should have counted on that. Of course, the merc that caught Cassad is gonna find himself the object of much interest. A quick check of my visor shows me it's working just fine. It ought to keep my face from registering on any vid or sensor scans. My flight suit will do fine for keeping my bio-signature private as well.

I hope.

Movement on the Prep bay monitor catches my attention. The Advocate is trying to get my attention. "What is it?" I say over the comm.

"Your ship's systems are woefully archaic," she complains. "We are done here. I need to return to make preparations for the trial."

She fills me in on some of the details of what is going to happen, balking when I tell her Cassad will never leave my side and that I'll be using a control collar. Eventually she relents as we get to the forward hatch.

"The Reading of the Charges is tomorrow. They will come for him first thing sunside."

"First thing, after I get the down payment" I confirm and watch her go.

Almost home…only the hard part left.

Not halfway through last watch *War Child*'s proximity alarms ring a half a beat before the Port Admin sends me a transmission. Looks like someone wants to parlay. I check the ground feeds and see a small delegation approaching the fore of my ship. Blue, white and silver colors… Daliuns.

Hmm…

I don my flight jacket and visor and head down to the foreword hatch, along the way gathering my Sever and the remote. My comms are pinging with their hail but I take my time, don't answer and just pop the hatch when I'm ready.

There are six of them; three men, three women. Two of the males are "Pretty Boys"; the genetically altered soldiers the Junns sent against the rest of my home star sextor, the Quad, during the Wars of the Blade. They're not in armor but I've seen and killed enough of them in combat that I can pick 'em out of a crowd.

The other male and one of the other females look like auxiliary staff, probably just there to assist. One of them is carrying a Junn banner, emblazoned with the "House" crest of the Junn family they work for. I don't recognize it but I'm only familiar with a few. The last two women are decked out in more impressive "house" regalia, so they must hold some higher status. Like most of the Junn reps these two have gold hair and blue eyes, all added, I'm sure after reaching their representative ranking.

I walk across the landing pad toward their group who has stopped at the pad rail. Dock security is keeping other onlookers back by the port entrance but they let these guys through with no escort; the Junns have pull. Before I'm halfway across the pad I turn and point the remote back at *War Child*. One press on the small ended side and there's a notable flash along the sensor lenses on the front of the engine housings and an audible chirp.

In case anyone decides to try something funny.

"Greetings." The two females say in unison when I get to the rail. "We represent the House of Derai. We are House Speakers, Cherlander"

They pause for a moment where I'm sure they are expecting me to introduce myself. I cross my arms and wait.

The two of them continue on in unison, not fazed by my silence. "Our patron, Lord Lan Derai, seeks an audience with Minister Cassad."

I expect there's some kind of offer coming so I don't bother saying anything just yet. Instead I spend the time running passive scans over their group, trying to see what everyone, especially the two Pretty Boys, are carrying. But the counter measures in the air are blocking everything.

"You would of course be rewarded for your assistance in this manner" the two House reps say together.

"Fifty million," I say. There's no chance that any one Junn House has that kind of money to spare or that they would even part with it if they did.

The two Reps smile those pretty white smiles at me despite what must be a very disappointing response.

They don't know me…can't know that there's no deal they could ever offer that would make me work with them… with the Junns.

"The same amount as the bounty for Minister Cassad?" Again, they speak in unison. Even their facial expressions are in synch. Never seen this before…I wonder how they're connected.

"We seek only a very limited audience with him before the trial."

"Fifty million, QED certified and I don't care what you do with him." They don't have the coin.

"There must be something else that we can…"

"You can't pay fifty?" I ask.

"It's just that fifty million is certainly not commensurate with a brief audience with your prisoner."

"Then walk away."

"If you could just see…"

"Now" I growl. "Don't come back." And I turn and walk back to *War Child*. To their credit they don't try and argue anymore.

I watch their delegation make their way off the landing deck on my ground feeds. Wonder what the Junns want with Cassad? Sticky had no intel on them one way or the other when it came to whether they needed or wanted him to make it to trial. The Cassad Empire has a few worlds left but nothing that would make them a more attractive ally than the rest of the New Regime. Unless they believe the minister has some family secrets hidden away.

Which he probably does.

I cut to the Prep Bay feed and check on his highness. Cassad is still bound. Good.

Chapter Four
THE FIRST GRAND COUNCIL

First thing sunside they come; Coalition Security Command lead by Prim Locasta. Vid hover bots fill the golden air just beyond the dock terminal, hovering above a throng of onlookers and beyond that, in the air just outside of the city proper, New Coalition gunships patrol throngs of ships trying for a good sensor peek at Cassad. No Coalition delegations outside today; they're probably already at the Hall.

I head down to the Prep bay where the Advocate, who came aboard earlier with the good faith money, and Cassad wait. She took off the tech coveralls I had him in and now has him decked out in his...royal attire. Wonder how that went with the control on?

"They're here."

"Fine" she says and steps aside to allow me to release Cassad. And I do, but not before manually turning his control collar up to the top levels. Can't risk slaving the unit to my remote cause I've already used up the two slots.

"He can't have that on during the trial" she warns me.

"Not while he's testifying" I correct her.

She looks like she wants to balk but with everything she's going up against today she's probably deciding to let this battle go without a fight. I walk Cassad through the ship to the foreword hatch just to make sure the collar is working. With it on and leveled up Cassad can only manage a slow, even walk. He's had the best Cassad training and led Cassad forces out on the perimeter of the known, I'm not going to risk moving him while he's free to use that experience and training against me.

There's a deafening roar when we exit the ship. The crowd is finally getting their look at the captured leader of the Empire that ruled them for almost a thousand years. The roar is a mix of cheers, boos, and various chants that fight over each other to be heard.

My visor alerts me to all the attempted sensor sweeps as they wash over us. So many but they're probably canceling each other out as much as the ports security measures are. These things are trying to send vid feeds to the entire known. Gonna be famous... fek.

The Prim and her security detail meet us at the bottom of the ramp.

"Remove the collar, mercenary. We have our own."

Before I can tell her to take a swim down styx the Advocate speaks up.

"We will be using our own personal security tech during the trial. You wouldn't want anyone to worry that his testimony was compromised?"

The Prim twists her lips into doubt then nods. "Fine. But he will wear no collar during his actual testimony."

"Of course. Today, however, we are only hearing the charges" Eboro points out. "Please lead the way."

Nezerian Security surrounds us and I try not to look uneasy, try not to look like I'm worried at all about the hundreds of things that can go glitch right now.

We're taken to a hover platform, I climb on after Cassad and the Advocate follows. It's wide enough only for two more and the Prim and one Nez SeC officer join us. The rest of the Prims security walks beside the platform as we float out of the port and onto the main concourse.

The crowds of New Beia citizens and of course Coalition visitors from across the known have been cordoned off, providing the platform with a wide path. The barriers don't hinder the roar as we pass by. The collective power of the rage in their voices vibrates my skin under my flight jacket. Styx...I could've charged a qed a look and made the fifty million on my own.

The Tower feels even bigger now that I'm in it than it did on approach. I can't even see the other side of this city level for the huge towers that fill Ataban proper. But I can see the Hall of Kain, looming ahead of us. Over the two huge front doors stands a colossal statue of the legendary Kaine, god of the Esari long ago. Or something like that. The bowl shape of the Hall is only broken by the four towers at each corner. The towers look down onto the main arena floor where the trial will take place.

Fool's gold for a sniper.

"Do not worry, mercenary." The Prim notices that I'm eyeing the towers. "My security measures have taken everything into account, including the Four Fathers. But only an amateur would attempt to attack from there"

The Four Fathers; the towers. Most assassins would avoid using them as their perch because they're way too obvious. But from my time in the 46th, I learned to always look out for a way to do the very thing that everyone else thinks is impossible. There's a sniper, I once knew, that would have found a way to get up there, take the shot and then get out without getting caught.

But since she's dead…

"So how did you catch him, mercenary?" The Prim asks. She's been watching me, evaluating me most likely, and the entire way here. I don't think she expected me to be around for this long after delivering Cassad.

She and I probably think more alike than not.

Still I don't answer her; instead I turn to give her a ghost eye glare.

She just smiles at that. "The whole known is going to want to know about you mercenary. Better get used to the questions."

No. The whole known might want to know about the merc that brought in Cassad, but Pack Loren and he don't have to be the same person. Soon as I'm paid I'm fading into the black.

Horns blare when we arrive at the steps to the Hall, just at the feet of Kaine. I thought it might be time to move but the platform simply slides up the steps, maintaining its level angle all the way to the top. That's where we disembark. There's a contingent of Coalition security at the entrance to the Hall, along with a few officials. The Prim greets them with a bit of ceremonial flare. She announces to the arrest of Cassad and asks for permission to present him to the court. The Coalition has only been around for a little more than two decades and a lot of these ritual practices are just a mix of the differing cultural practices. So they come off a bit labored and awkward.

The huge doors to the Hall of Kain open and we stride in, making sure not to move faster than Cassad can step with the collar on. The lobby of the Hall is filled with the lesser dignitaries of the New Regime all standing behind a literal line of Coalition security personnel.

These low-level ambassadors and adjuncts aren't prudish about letting Cassad know what they think. They shout curses and threats. They cajole and ridicule him as he passes by. There are insults and gestures I've never heard or seen. The Cassad's presence on Arcadia was minimal to say the least. No one even noticed when their embassy in Market city evacuated before the Giaks launched their last attack. They'd never been much of a political factor. So we never harbored the kind of anger for the Cassads that I'm seeing here. There are more than a few dignitaries with tears in their eyes they're so angry.

"Security point" the Prim announces. We arrive at the entrance to the main part of the Hall. A red cloaked guardsman carrying what looks more like a pike than a rifle steps forward and looks us over.

"No weapons or military grade tech beyond this point. No recording or transmission devices allowed in the Hall." His voice is electronic so he might not be human beneath the garb.

"Prim Locasta, head of Nezerian Security Command," the Prim announces herself. "Special dispensation has been granted to my detail for the purposes of the trial."

"Noted, Prim Locasta. However, HE, is not a member of Nez SeC." The guard points the long pike in my direction.

"Advocate for the accused, Adila Eboro." Eboro announces herself. "This man is a part of MY security detail. He will accompany Cassad at all times."

She looks back at me standing next to Cassad. "And he will be armed."

"That is not acceptable, Advocate Eboro. This man is not a registered citizen of any Coalition world. His identity is unknown and - the Guardsman looks me up and down then settles on my visor - his tech is of unknown registry as well."

The visor isn't anything unusual, it's just old. "Special measures to insure the success of this trial," Eboro tells him.

There's a moment where it's obvious that the Guardsman is receiving instructions from someone. Then, "The mercenary must register his identity with Nez SeC," he or it says finally. The Prim looks over her shoulder at me and smirks.

"Well, mercenary?"

Eboro speaks up again. "His identity will remain secret. The mercenary..." I can tell she's thinking on the fly again. "...and his team are still engaged in locating Cassad targets."

Good one. It may even help to insure I'm paid properly. The Guardsman again waits for instructions. Then, "You are cleared to enter the Hall. You will keep your weapons holstered for the duration of the trial. You will engage in no scans of the delegates or their guests. Please proceed forth."

And they step aside as the big doors open. The cries that erupt out of the Hall overcome those of the crowd outside. I would have thought that the real royalty and dignitaries would have comported themselves with a little more reserve but this is out of control. As we enter the Hall the audience members in the stands surrounding the entrance are not only screaming worse threats than those outside, but they're throwing debris as well.

Security Command did a good job of relieving them of anything more dangerous than rolled up programs and paper service trays though, so it's mostly garbage that's hurled at us. That and... spit, but the stands seem to be beyond that reach at least.

"You die today, Cassad!"

"...of my ancestors, Cassad, finally!"

"Murderer!"

"For one thousand years of oppression!"

Once beyond the stands we make our way to the center of the Hall. The old arena floor is set apart from the stands by a wide and deep trench. From what I can see the walls down in that trench are lined with ancient barred prison cells. There are some haggard and beaten faces staring out of those cells; Ziaran citizens and officials all waiting for their inevitable fate.

I can smell blood.

Above us the Hall is open to the star filled sky. It's an illusion; the bottom of the top level of the entire tower hangs above us. The walls of the arena are so high that the Abatan city skyline is hidden, so we can only see the Four Fathers, the holo field and the sky cars floating high above trying to get live vid. They had better be careful; there's a pretty strong null field stretched across the top of the arena. At least that's what I read.

We step across the trench by way of an ornate ivory bridge and into the soft black sand of the arena floor. No…not sand really, small glossy beads so smooth they slide easily under foot.

It'll be hard to run on.

They've set up two small bunkers; one for the accused and one for the prosecution. Each has a raised platform on the top. That's where Cassad, and I, will be standing during the trial. It's only now that I'm starting to rethink whether it's really necessary to for me to escort him everywhere.

Ugh…I'm absolutely sure that if something happens to him before he's convicted I'm not gettin' paid. Just a little while longer, Pack…

The Prim and her detail stop at the bunker entrance. "We are not allowed inside. Only Cassad and his Advocate…and her team I suppose." I can barely hear her for the crowd but I get the point easy enough as she and her people leave.

We step inside. The bunker has three rooms; the main room with a platform that must raise the accused to the dais on top, there's a small alcove with a table and chairs then in the back, there's a lavatory. Along the wall of the larger main room is a one-way window. From here we can see pretty much the entire Hall, the Prosecutors stand and Grand Council of the Coalition balcony. There are two rows for the council; one, the largest, for the representatives of the member worlds of the New Regime, spans the entire circumference of the stands. They sit above the main stands that are filled with citizens of those member worlds. Above them all, in smaller but shielded suites, the seven members of the Grand Council watch. The top powers of the Coalition who were the most responsible for the fall of the Cassads.

I can see the Kujiunga Na suite. The largest of the luxurious viewing boxes, it was given to them not only because it was the ex-Cassad ambassadors who were key to the start of the rebellion against Ose but because there were so damn many of them. Sitting prominently in the center of the group is the Denir representative, bare-chested and adorned with a single white jewel of some kind nestled snuggly between her breasts. I can't remember her name and my visor can't get a read on her ID because of the security waves running through the hall...good thing that works both ways.

The din of the crowd is abruptly cut as the bunker door closes behind us.

"How long?" I ask. Eboro turns and fixes me with a dark stare.

"Ah! Mercenary! He who knows and sees..."

"Until the charges are read?" I clarify.

"Oh...well, there will be a long procession as the member world representatives are brought in one at a time."

"All the member worlds?" I mutter the question, not really needing it to be answered. This could take all sunside.

"There is no corner of the empire...the Coalition I mean, that would dare miss this." The Advocate removes her ceremonial shoal and walks Cassad to the table and chairs in the small conference room. Stiffly, he sits; the control collar limiting his movement adjusts slowly to new commands, as it is designed to do. She then tends to him, seeing to his comfort while at the same time informing him on what was to come.

I take the time to run passive scans over the inside of the bunker. The research I found on the Hall of Kain seemed to indicate that the bunkers were designed to deflect active scans and keep out snooping hardware. All in order to keep the games here played honestly. It made for the perfect Advocate chambers during trials.

There's no spy tech in the bunker, at least none my visor can detect. Eboro does not seem to be concerned with potential listeners but that could just be due to the inevitability of a conviction. She goes on to Cassad about the trial.

"I have had been given a list of witnesses who will speak on your behalf..."

"That will not be necessary. No one need risk themselves testifying for the Empire in front of the rebels." That's the most he's said since he escaped the load bar.

"Minister," Eboro says softly. "Those not willing to testify have already been...executed."

Cassad thinks for only a moment then points out, "They would have been executed immediately after regardless."

"Not necessarily, Minister. I can guide their testimony, gain them leniency." Eboro produces a small personal Hub connect and lays it on the table. The disc is small enough to fit in the palm of her hand but projects a wide holo-field that becomes her workspace complete with three wide visual fields and a small conventional key field on the table. From where I'm standing I can see the dossier holos of the first two witnesses.

"The Subjucarious of Special Operations will be one of the first to testify on your behalf, Minister." Eboro expands the holo of the man and raises it above her workspace. The Subjucarious, or S.S.O., was an older Ziaran citizen, his thick mane of braided hair was whiter than grey. The holo of him was recent as his face was swollen and bleeding from the beating he had already taken

Cassad shows no reaction to hearing this. The S.S.O. was more the day to day administrator of the home world so most Ziaran citizens saw him far more frequently than Cassad himself. But from everything I've seen Cassad must have known the man very well.

The Advocate goes on about the witnesses but my attention is drawn away to the arena stands. They're clearing a path through the dignitaries…the member representatives are being brought in.

Drums sound and are followed by a low and driving horn. The arena goes dark as all lights move to one corner of the room. Fanfare sounds and out come the banners of the first rep.

"Xioung, Heavenly Sovereign of the world Appogoi!" The small man is dressed in a red and gold armor of an ancient style, his face covered in a grisly mask and his head crowned by a wide helmet. Xioung wore a ceremonial sword on his hip inside a long and curved scabbard. I've never encountered anyone from Appogoi before but I don't have to have in order to know that this is not the actual man himself.

The real Xioung would not be alone, without a court or security so it's a bogey, probably hard cased and not holographic. Likely it has its very own entangled comm node so that the real "Heavenly Sovereign" could see and even feel the experience in real time. Xioung takes his time finding his seat along the representative balcony, stopping to acknowledge the rabid crowd of the arena.

More horns and drums sound. A second set of banners, this time neon holographic projections of the flag of the people of Tennace, one of the more technologically advanced civilizations, floats into the room. Behind it walks out another bogey; no...this one's definitely a holo as she's transparent and has wings. She's likely the head representative of their Corporate Council.

"Director Suri 'a Velne, of the world Tennace!" is announced. She takes her time as well, using her fake wings to pretend to hover above the crowd. How long is this gonna take?

"Last time I checked there were more than one hundred worlds in the Coalition" the Advocate says. I had not meant to ask the question out loud. "And as the Cassads fall new worlds are added to that."

So we wait as world after world is represented. The Norlans, The Nth Consortium, the Jemsa Overmind and more and more. The Brythons actually sent a real person to represent King Brython, but then I missed seeing his courts entrance as the Major Council members were seated before we came into the Hall. The Brython viewing suite is to the immediate left of the Denir suite. Almost as big but filled with more bots than actual people...damn; now that I really look the Brython rep and his wife might be the only people in the suite.

The lights flare again; the Quaznians sent actual people as well and...so did the Daliuns.

Junn Lord Lan Derai, strolls in with security and with his wife whose name is drowned out by the crowd noise. They stand a good two heads taller and a hands width thinner than everyone else. They're almost as pale as my own "ghost eyes" so they stand out a bit even from the other outlandish representatives. They're dressed in Daliun royal blue, white and silver robes and both wear silver crowns that frame their faces down to their chins in an intricate lattice. The Junns are bold for a small world; allowing an ambassador to hold their council seat instead of Lord Junn himself. I stare at them for the remainder of the introductions, wondering how hard it would be to get a shot off that would actually make it across the room.

The representatives have been seated and tucked in good when the petitioning governments are announced; worlds that want in or are being asked to join the New Regime. First up...All damn.

The ground shakes. The tunnel entrance from where the reps entered goes dark as something big blocks the running lights. In they come, three of them, big ones...Giaks.

Swathed in battle dress, that nasty dark blue Giak armor, they stomp into the arena. Each is at least forty decimeters in height, twice as big as me and as wide at the shoulder as they are tall. Their footsteps can be heard across the arena and must be shakin' up the bodies in the seats on that side of the hall 'cause the Giaks are an easy two thousand kilos a pop. These bitches aren't wearing their helmets so those mangled brutish faces are glaring out at everyone from behind thick locks of hair for all the known to see. Their rough reddish skin is covered in dark grey tattoos which mark them as being from one of the most prestigious of all the Giak "mounds".

No way they petitioned the New Regime to join. The Giaks are too prideful and they're still at war with...well everyone. Maybe it was the Coalition that did the asking. I look back across the stands to the Junns but I can't quite tell if their faces are so pinched because that's just their usual look, or if they're upset at seeing the one group that's been keeping them from taking over Eastspace being treated as guests here. And they wouldn't be alone; most of the known have only seen Giaks on vid or holo. Seeing them live and in person can be...overwhelming. There are gasps of shock and terror at the sight of them and more than a few in the stands actually make to bolt from their seats.

The last Giak to enter the room is an officer. You can tell because though just as tall, their body proportions are a lot closer to human and a lot more feminine. Officers wear war helms that completely cover their faces and I was always told no one's seen what they look like.

But looking at those massive thighs…who would want to?

Wow. The New Regime must want the Giak shipyards pretty bad. If they're allowing them into the Coalition what's going to happen with the Junns? Will they have to give up the Cannius Gate which they're barely holding now?

Not sure if that's good or bad for Arcadia.

Of course, there is no Arcadia.

Chapter Five
ARRAIGNMENT

"BRING FORTH THE ACCUSED!"

The Advocate, Cassad and I step up onto the platform. To my surprise it does not lift us to the top of the bunker. Instead, the entire bunker lowers itself around us. The ceiling above us shimmers and melts away. Far above, in the false New Beia night sky, New Coalition gunships have joined the party of sky car vid hounds.

Once again, the crowd erupts as the bunker slides down into the black sand, disappearing from sight as we are revealed. The chants begin again, this time they seem to have come to a consensus on what to scream, outshouting Cassad's introduction.

"SHAO, SHAO, RAHN!"

"SHAO, SHAO, RAHN!"

"SHAO, SHAO, RAHN!"

"It means, 'Die tyranny'." Eboro explains though I can barely hear her.

The other bunker has receded into the sand as well. Standing across the arena from us now stands the prosecution. Three New Regime reps, two men and a woman.

"The Woman," Eboro says to Cassad. "is the Valian Conin, Advocate General. She represents the Median worlds, a coalition within the Coalition.

Conin displays Coalition colors, all in a long dress that trailed along the ground. Her head is adorned with a tall, wrapped headdress about which small colored lights orbited. The skin of her face was drawn tight giving her the appearance of having been chiseled from a solid bar of onyx. Her eyes were alight and on fire as they peered across the arena floor at us…at Cassad.

"The fair skinned man is Lord Jon Edins, Brython. Speaks for the Coalition worlds in the vast empty between the smaller clusters."

Between the small clusters included the Eastspace…the Quad. Why would the Bythons claim to be representing those worlds? The Brython haven't made any move on the Quad or tried to implement control. At least not yet.

Lord Edins is a small but hard looking Brython. His dress is a sharp contrast to the Conins, as it's far less ceremonial; a simple black suit over white underdress. His eyes are covered with dark, archaic glass lenses set in frames perched on his nose. There is a small gold crest on the fold of his jacket. My visor zooms in and shows me the shield, split into two sections each bearing an animal. A ram on one side and a winged serpent on the other.

"The last man is the most dangerous" Eboro warns. I turn my attention to the darker man who stands to the fore of the others. His dress is…odd. It's…oh I get it; he's dressed like a Cassad Official except the colors of his trim are like that of the New Regime.

"Onted Galvin, First Equal of the Grand Revolutionary Council," Eboro says. "He's been executing the Cassads in trials all over the known."

Galvin's eyes are on our bunker. If they were filled with the anger and fury that's pretty much standard in the room then I wouldn't be worried. Instead there's a cold clarity in his eyes and a solid unwavering readiness in his stance. He's not just standing in front of the others; he's standing…apart, as if he's not bothering to follow the protocol of the New Regime trial process… as if his own agenda takes priority.

The "First Equal" is also carrying a blade. It's ceremonial, long, curved and clearly lethal. The way his hand rests on the hilt makes it clear as open sky to me; he intends to kill Cassad himself.

"Executing Cassads?" I ask.

"Yes. Anyone who's had any position in the Cassad administration" Eboro tells me. "Very public and very brutal executions."

"What's the position of the First Equal?"

"Consider him…the 'Hand' of the Coalition. Broad power and responsibility, he executes their will" she says with a hint of fear in her voice.

Fek. The more I look at Galvin the surer I am that he'll bring that swords edge to Cassad as soon as he gets a chance. What's he got to lose? The crowd here would go wild and the Coalition Council would be satisfied collectively. I can't let him near Cassad.

"What's his responsibility during the trial?"

Eboro looks at me then and follows my ghost eyes to Galvin. "He will question the witnesses and of course he will attempt to question Minister Cassad."

Galvin doesn't have another weapon that I can see. If he's only carrying the scimitar then maybe all I need to do is keep him at a distance. "He'll make a play at Cassad if you let him get near."

"He wouldn't dare. There are too many council members who want this trial played out" she argues.

"If you let him near Cassad…he will kill him."

"Then…" Eboro turns away from me and says over her shoulder, "Protect your bounty, mercenary."

The chants of 'Die tyranny' die down as the light in the Hall rises just a bit. The Coalition Council is illuminated softly in golden light. Then three beams of light swirl through the arena, passing over the crowd, the three Coalition prosecutors and us before settling on an even patch of black sand.

The patch slowly shifts as something beneath the sand rises. Another bunker…no wait, a tower, as black as the sand, pushes its way up to stand a good ten meters high. The top splits like an egg, the walls falling away and down to the arena floor where they sink into the beads and disappear. Standing on the top of the tower now is a woman wearing a bizarre spiral shaped outfit that was more sculpture than dress. She holds her hands out to her sides with her palms facing up and stands on one leg with the other bent so that her foot is resting just behind the knee of the first. Her face is decorated with a very convincing holo-set giving her leonine features.

"The pall of oppression has been lifted!" the lion lady speaks. "The reign of the tyrant family has ended!"

The crowd roars its agreement and applauds. I can still hear threats against Cassad being called out.

"For one thousand cycles Cassad has plagued the galactic proper with their self-proclaimed right of sovereignty. Their thousand-cycle dominion has been one of torture, theft, slavery and genocide."

The arena rumbles. I notice a small icon flashing on the HUD of my visor and sub vocalize a command to check the virtual audience. This trial is being broadcast across the known but more than that, just as most of the New Regime council is only here in virtual form, so are many other spectators throughout the known. Virtually, there are billions of citizens in the stands, their holographic representations overlapping each other so much that they're just one nasty multicolored moving blob with flashes of pumping fists and angry faces. I could set the visor to only show certain holos…I could see those holos from the quad only if I wanted…or even…

"Here now stands the Cassad. The LAST of his line! The LAST CASSAD!" the lioness waits as the crowd loses it again. "Come forth any who accuse the Cassad of crimes against their worlds. Come forth any who lay claim to his wretched life!"

From the other side of the arena, out of a tunnel much like the one the Council entered from, emerges a small group. They step onto the sand, four of them, Virogens; one of many peoples that had been conquered by the Cassads. Their world was once called Viro, and it was supposed to be a pretty nice agricultural planet. Still is, though now it's called Zuna and the Virogen people are down to their last few hundred living in orbiting reserve stations above the planet itself. These four men are all lean and sallow, like most Virogen I've seen. Their worn, outdated utility flight suits are ill fitting and have been patched with sealant tape.

The Virogen stand in the spotlight now for all the known to hear their story.

The First Equal steps away from the other prosecutors and marches across the arena toward the Virogen. I notice that the light that follows him is a slightly more reddish gold than the light that remains on the Brython and the Advocate General.

"Identify yourselves" he commands the Virogen.

Of the four, all men, the tallest speaks up. "I am Petrov Musinovic, Chief of the Watch, Solar Enterprise, Zuna..."

"You mean, 'Viro', do you not?" Galvin corrects him.

"I...yes...Yes, Solar Enterprise in orbit of our home-world Viro," the man corrects himself hesitantly. I wonder if the New Regime has actually allowed the Virogen back onto their homeworld now that it's been liberated.

"And what," Galvin asks. "charges do you lay against Cassad?"

The Virogen all look directly at Cassad. Musinovic points a long boney finger at us. "The Cassad took our world. They invaded and imposed their sick law upon us. Their Empress denied our ancestors the very right to have their own children! They forced us to breed with them; a privilege they called it, but we soon realized that we were being slowly exterminated. Those who defied them were 'quarantined' to the orbiting Colony stations. Our numbers have slowly dropped for the past four centuries..."

"First Equal," Eboro interrupts the Virogen. "If we could please simply hear the charges."

Onted Galvin turns around like he's been assaulted, his hand on the hilt of his sword tense and tight. He steps sharply in our direction a few meters and if he'd been reasonably closer I swear he would have walked right up to us. As it is he stops almost midway.

"How dare you, Advocate?" he says, his eyes wide with anger. "The Virogen may be a small member of the Coalition but they deserve to face the accused. They, as well as any who have suffered at the hands of the Cassad, deserve to let the worlds of the universe know their story!"

The crowd goes wild and the very air shakes. The First Equal speaks with a genuine passion that I've rarely seen in a politician. He believes in this.

Eboro, to her credit, does not cower to the thunder of New Regime storm. "I agree, First Equal. We will no doubt hear the story of the Virogen when you present them to testify. Today, however, they must simply present their charges against the accused."

The First Equal, Galvin, stares at the Advocate for a long tense moment. Then he draws his sword and points it at her. "You speak with Cassad bravura, Advocate. How long have you been in their employ?"

Eboro shudders slightly at this but answers quickly and confidently. "I am of the Akan, First Equal, and I was set to this task by the Coalition of Free Worlds Council itself."

"You are the Advocate of the Cassad..." he's shouting now but Eboro raises her voice as well.

"Have them present their charges or remove them from the court, Prosecutor!"

Wow... I'm impressed.

The crowd boos. The chants of 'die tyranny' start up again. Some are screaming, accusing her of being a Cassad. Even more flaming debris falls onto the black sand. Unnoticed to most, the First Equal dips his head slightly; he's talking to someone on a subvocal channel.

"Virogen!" he shouts, and the crowd dies down. "Cassad's snake is correct."

Boos arise again but the First Equal shouts it down. "You will be given the chance to testify. The worlds will know your struggle, your pain and the triumph of your return to your home world. I swear it."

The crowd is somewhat mollified by this though I sense they're anticipating a long and satisfying trial.

"Please, my Coalition colleagues, present your charges." Galvin almost bows.

The Virogen hesitate and look to each other. Then the tall leader, Musinovic, speaks up.

"The Virogen charge the Cassad with…Murder…"

"MURDER!" The crowd repeats each charge as he lists them.

"…theft…"

"THEFT!"

"…and geno…ATTEMPTED genocide!"

"GENOCIDE!!"

And so it goes. World after world is brought in to list their charges against the Cassad Empire. Most of the charges are similar of course but there are a few special charges. The Tennace charged the Cassad with technological oppression; stifling the growth of their knowledge base. The Jorean accused the Cassad of exploiting their planets natural resources to the point of rendering it uninhabitable. There were charges of "crimes against humanity" and "crimes against nature".

The Brython accused the Cassad of crimes against the cathol god and of hiding evidence of his existence. The multi-cultural crowd does not respond as heartily at that.

After almost half a solar day of this, a small but unusual group takes to the arena floor to bear witness against Cassad; children.

Small, very meek looking and dressed practically in rags. They enter the bright light for all the known to see. Gasps and cries come from the arena stands at the sight. These kids could be from practically any world in the known…they could be Arcadian.

The First Equal addresses them without the overbearing tenor which he's been using all day. "You are the Nerum of the moon Gaspara?"

The children all nod.

"First Equal, with all due respect, we have already heard from the Gaspara representatives," Eboro points out. Did we? I can't remember.

"With no respect, Advocate Eboro, I tell you that we have not heard from the Nerum people. They are a separate group, self-governing on the moon of Gaspara before the Cassad imposed their wicked law. They deserve to be heard now."

"Are we going to subject children to the stress of a trial, First Equal?"

Galvin turns, fixes Eboro with that "I'm going to cut your head off" gaze and says; "Unfortunately, due to the Cassad, these children are all that's left of the Nerum."

Hmm...yea...Cassad is dead.

The First Equal addresses the kids again. "Children of the Nerum, please state your charges against the Cassad."

The children huddle together, their eyes wide with fear. The First Equal finally puts that sword away.

"Please, children, don't be afraid to speak for your people. You are safe here from the Cassad, safe under the protection of the Coalition of Free Worlds."

The first child to speak is a small brown skinned girl; her hair tied with bright red barrettes in twin braids one on each side of her small head. Her eyes are big, wide and crescent, like dawn on a new world but sad. She can't be more than four Arcadian cycles old. So small is her voice that the amplifier doesn't pick it up. Another child, a taller boy, whispers to her and she tries again.

"My mommy is dead" she says. The crowd cries their sympathy. The First Equal bows his head. Even Eboro has her hands clasped over her heart.

"Your name, child?" Galvin asks her.

Her tiny lips barely part as she speaks. "Ceri."

Another kid, an even smaller, lumpy haired boy, steps forward and speaks up in soft voice. "We...we don't have any food."

Ok...even I want to kill Cassad now. The arena cries again, this time there are several pledges to take the kids in.

"Children..." the First Equal is looking back at Cassad. "Even children were not to be spared under your rule. How many? On how many worlds?"

He turns back to the kids. "It is my understanding that your parents, the last Nerum tribe, sacrificed themselves so that you could live."

They all nod. The girl in braids speaks again. "My mommy said she had to go away. For us to be ok."

"Your mother," Galvin says, "must have loved you very much."

"She said the Ca-shah..." she mispronounces Cassad and looks back to the other children. "They made our food bad."

I sneak a sidelong look at Cassad, but with the collar on it's hard to tell if he's affected by this.

"and made our rain bad..." tears fall from her wide eyes.

There is open sobbing in the stands now. Eboro drops her hands and addresses Onted.

"First Equal, surely this is not..."

"Have you no sense of compassion woman? Let these children speak!"

After a pause the big-eyed girl goes on. "She said they had to go away to make us better...so that we...would be better..." the other kids are wiping tears now.

"Yes, child, they sacrificed themselves for you. And it was not in vain, I promise you." The First Equal looks truly moved.

"And the Ca-shahs have to go away now" her little lips curl in a horribly sad pout.

"This," The First Equal points to Cassad. "is the last of the Cassads, child. And he will go away...forever."

The kids' heads all snap in our direction so suddenly that it's a little unnerving. "He's got to go away now," the girl says and the others all nod and all of them... all of them stop crying.

"I've got to stop this." Eboro mutters, marches off the pad and heads across the arena floor in the direction of the Council. She won't have any luck; this is the show they all wanted.

The Advocates movement is noticed by the First Equal but he continues with the kids none the less. No one seems to notice how dark their gazes have gotten. "He will child. Cassad will pay for what was done to your parents. I will see to it... personally."

"Now" she insists.

"Yea," says another of the kids. "Now!"

There's actually a soft kindness in the First Equals eyes now. "He is not going anywhere, children. The Cassads have taken away many mothers just like yours across all the worlds known. We all have a right to…"

"Now!" the little big-eyed girl finds her boldness and the others back her up.

"They must go away now!"

"Now!"

A little caught off guard the First Equal tries to quell them. "Children, please, do not…"

But the girl begins marching across the sand toward Cassad. "He must go away!"

The First Equal, arms outstretched to stop her, moves to block her path. "No child, this is not the way…"

"NOW!!" whoa…her voice gets suddenly deep. Her mouth opens wide…too wide; her jaw descends far enough to fit a gourd in!

There's the disgusting sound of flesh ripping and suddenly the girl expands. It looks at first like she's exploding on the inside but she's still moving…and changing! Her chest pops right out of the ragged shirt she has on, a nasty bulge of muscle and a riot of ribcage that grows impossibly fast. And her legs swell with even more muscle and her feet elongate until she is standing on her toes.

The kids' arms balloon as well, with ugly bone protrusions bursting up out of her skin at her elbows and shoulders. One immense arm swings and catches the First Equal, surprised and off guard, under his chin. He's sent flying across the arena floor and lands in a splash of black sand.

The other kids are transforming as well. Each changing from a small timid little innocent into a hulking three-meter-tall beast.

And they all have eyes on Cassad.

"NARRRGH!" they bellow… and charge.

Chapter Six
THE CHILDREN OF NERUM

They gallop at us on all fours with such ferocity that the black sand kicks up several meters in their wake. Their roars echo across the arena and the crowd responds with a collective gasp. Some kind of meta-morphs but transforming faster than any I've ever heard of.

Three…four…five…with at least one more behind them that I can't see… "Run Cassad!" I scream. The bunker will never rise in time and security in the arena itself is nonexistent due to the various treaties.

But I'm still armed.

I whip the NOK 37 off of my hip, sight down the lead beast and try not to think about how it had been a toddler just a pulse beat ago. The gun bangs against my palm after each squeeze of the trigger.

The first round hits it square in the chest in a spray of blood that the thing hardly notices. The second tags it a little father up where its clavicle should be and still the transformed girl rumbles across the sand at us. What the buck are they made of?

The next shot I put into her forehead. The NOK 37 hits with good enough stopping power that her head is thrown back forcing her to stumble and fall. But no penetration; skulls are too damned thick! Should've brought the Sever!

I reset and target the next the beast, sending every round to its cranium. The first misses but the next two catch it in the jaw and temple causing him to swerve and stumble to the sand as well.

The third leaps over his fallen playmates. Training takes over for a pulse beat and makes me target him center mass. Two shots wasted; he just ignores them.

Fek! One of the first two is getting back up even as I reset and pop another three rounds at his head. He drops but they're all getting closer…this ain't working!

But it's too late to change tactics. I sight the big girls head and force her to stop again, switch targets once more and bring down the fourth.

I can see three more behind the first group bounding on the sand. Too many and too close now, I'm gonna have to make a break for it. But I turn and see something I'm didn't expect.

Cassad…walking.

The All Damned control collar! He can't move any faster!

"NAHHRGH!" the roar is right behind me and I spin hard, drawing my kendo blade at the same time and leading with gunfire. One shot, right into the eye of the beast almost on top of me. The furenium bullet doesn't explode out the back of the dense skull, instead, after rattling around inside, it pops out the other eye. Almost at my feet the thing drops into the sand.

I reset and target the next, not daring to hope for another shot that good. Still I manage head shots and get it turned a bit. It's enough that it won't maul me and as it passes by; I rip the kendo blade through its leg, severing it completely.

It drops and I'm targeting the next of them, trying the same strategy; head shots, get it turned, then use the Kendo blade. This time the head shots fail to push the thing it off its course and I have to sidestep to avoid the blind swipe of a clawed hand. Though off balance I'm still able to take its head off with one swing of the kendo.

Another howl and I turn and sight the next Nerum.

WARNING: SABERNOK 37 FURY ROUND COUNT: 05

The warning flash distracts me enough to allow the mutated kid to dodge me and go for Cassad. I'm forced to turn my back on its buddies while I track it and pull a spare round cap from my belt. I sight the big thing but its back is filled with rolls of muscle and sheaths of bone. There's no shooting through that, damn it!

I throw the kendo blade. It spins end over end, singing a shrill song and leaving a trail of vapor behind as its single molecule lined edge, now glowing, rends the air. It sinks deep into the monsters back, right into its spine. Already turning back to rest of them I hear it hit the sand rather than see it.

Fek! I duck to avoid another clawed swipe and fire rounds into the bone covered knees that are right in my face.

Something gets through because the beast drops nearly on top on me. With a grunt I shove the thing away and before it can get its bearings I jam the muzzle of my NOK against its neck and pull the trigger. Blood splashes over my visor and blocks my vision.

So I fire blind where I think the next one is coming from. Drawing my gloved hand across the holo-glass of my visor I sweep off the blood in time to see a wall of muscle and bone before it barrels into me.

"Wuff!" I don't resist, letting the thing knock me back across the arena. My still tender ribs howl at me but don't break, yet. The sand is surprisingly soft to land in but hard to get a footing on. So I can't spring back up. I settle for firing from off my back. Now I target knees and ankles, the narrowest parts of these things, hoping I can hoopty the rest of them.

One down…and another before the others retreat and sprint around…trying to outflank me. But now that I've got them off of me I should be able to hold them long enough for the Nez SeC to finally respond.

Just as I'm lining up another shot along the sights of my NOK, the Nerum I'm targeting leaps up, twists in midair and dives into the black sand as if it was so much dark water.

What in the known?

It disappears completely. And his buddies follow suit; all of them diving into the glossy black sand, their clawed hands digging faster than my eye can follow and they're gone…just like that.

WARNING: CHEMICAL EXPLOSIVE DETECTED!

The warning flashes across my visor. How on styx did someone get a chem bomb in the arena? A primitive one too for my old visor to detect it when the New Regime did not. I follow the flashing warning icons to the source. The beast, the first one I managed to stop by cutting its leg off, it's still crawling after Cassad; it's the source of the warning. Ah buck; A bio-bomb!

I sprint after Cassad, who's walking with as much speed as he can muster with the control collar on. The All damned sand shifts under every footfall…kept the Nerum from charging me faster than I could respond but now it's slowing me down.

There's no point in killing the Nerum anymore, the bomb is likely to go off no matter what at this point. Never the less I snap off a shot at her head as I pass by, might be enough to slow her.

Might be the pulse beat I need to get Cassad to safety.

POOSH! One of the Nerum beasts explodes up out of the sand right next to me as I run. It rakes a clawed hand across my shoulder as it flies up over me and then back down, claws digging insanely fast to slip it beneath the sand again. The other Nerum beasts begin bursting from the arena floor like gulfish bounding from the sea. I'm firing left and right now, catch one in mid-leap and send him sprawling away. But the others are hot on my heels at this point and my visor flashes two more bomb warnings. Fek! I thought they dove beneath the sand to escape the bomb but...

WARNING: CHEMICAL BOMB READS AT CRITICAL MASS!

Where on styx is Nez SeC?

POOSH! Hot fire rips across my leg as I'm tagged by another slash of those claws.

Cassad has nearly reached the bridge at the edge of the arena. The crowd on that end of the floor hasn't even moved. They're watching everything as if it were another All Damned sporting event here in the Hall of Kain.

POOSH! I shoot the next leaper down and have to jump over it when it tumbles to the ground in front of me.

WARNING: CHEMICAL BOMB DETONATION IMMINENT!

Finally, I reach Cassad and grab his arm. Instead of pulling him up onto the bridge I spin him hard and hurl him into the trench.

POOSH! Another Nerum beast bursts out of the sand behind me, clawed hands extended. It's got too much momentum for my NOK to stop it...

WARNING: SABERNOK 37 FURY ROUND COUNT: 05

...04...

03...

02…

BOOM!!!

I'm hit by a wall of black sand, lifted up and hurled across the trench. The ledge of the cell wall catches me in the small of my back and I drop down to the prison level in a limp heap.

A pulse beat passes and I'm not sure where I am or what I'm doing…the trial…Cassad…the Nerum! One of the beasts must have blown itself up but was still beneath the sand …only reason I'm still alive.

Ugh! Lost my visor…fek…lost my NOK…can't hear a thing over that ringing…

"CRA-SHAH!!" Heard that! There's another Nerum perched above me on the edge of the arena floor. Its eyes are on Cassad who lay still against a prison cell gate.

Down to my last weapons, I pull the twin ferron carbide butterfly blades from the hidden scabbards in the back of my jacket. They're micro edged, not as sharp or as durable as the kendo but the first couple of strikes will be just as effective, if I can get any hits in.

The Nerum leaps down a little shakily; looks like the blast did a number on it as well. Can't let it recover!

But a wave of dizziness washes over me as I rush at it. Can't stop… got to get at it before it can kill Cassad.

"HA!" I drive the first of the blades right into its neck just where it meets the boney shoulder. The Nerum tries to shrug me off but I don't let go of the blade so it rips its way free and blood sprays in gushes.

I spin and drive the other into the monster's gut but get the angle wrong. The blade only cuts the skin, stopping dead when it hits the dense muscle.

"NARGH!" it cries. One clawed hand reaches out and shoves me away. My ribs…feels like two of them actually, wail again but it doesn't feel like they broke. I stumble across the trench and slam into the bars of a cell. Another Nerum, this one burned and missing an arm, lands next to the first. They both ignore me, look to Cassad and move toward him.

I climb to my feet and rush them from behind. So intent on getting to Cassad the Nerum closest to him doesn't even notice when I shove a blade straight down through the top of his lagging buddy's head.

The blade gets stuck in the tough bone and I'm so glitch that I don't let go. I get dragged down to the cell block floor with the dead Nerum.

The last of them, at least I hope it's the last, closes on Cassad. I can't get there in time...I can't...my NOK!

Just a meter away, I dive for the gun and roll to a kneeling stance. But the bucka's got its back to me. All I can see are the thick shoulder plates and bulbous knots of muscles.

"Nerum!" I shout. But the creature ignores me and raises its nasty clawed paw to rip Cassad open.

Then I see the bright red beret in the tufts of scraggly, wire hair jutting out of its cranium.

"C-Ceri!"

The misshapen head turns at once and our eyes meet over my gun sights. It's...hers are so big...like dawn on a new world...

The NOK 37 bangs in my hand twice. The first shot was the killer; right in her left eye. The second smashes into her forehead and sends her falling backward over Cassad.

There's a crash behind me and I twist, gun first, to find Prim Locasta and her Nez SeC officers landing in the trench. From somewhere on the floor behind me I can hear the tiny warning chime of my visor sounding.

WARNING: SABERNOK 37 FURY ROUND COUNT: 00

It takes me a moment to lower my gun.

The Prim walks up and looks past me to Cassad, who's pinned beneath the Nerum but clearly alive. She then looks me up and down, nodding appreciatively but when our eyes meet she hesitates a bit.

"There's a common saying, mercenary; 'better late than never'."

"Bitch, the fight is over. What the buck do you think 'never' means?"

Dark Universe

Choices
By
Milton Davis

Wapiganapo tembo nyasi huumia. (Swahili)
When elephants fight the grass gets hurt.
-Swahili proverb

Clarence Mbeki watched the proceeding on the vid with his family in stunned silence. Sarafina, his wife, sat beside him clinging to his arm. Toby sat beside her, his mouth hanging open as the close-up Khalid Cassad's battered face filled the holospace. Jamila, the little one, paid no attention. She was fully into her floating blocks, humming a tune as she pushed them to and fro. Clarence glanced at her and smiled. She was the luckiest of them all. She had no inkling of the events taking place. He was determined to keep it that way.

Toby faced him, the fear in his face stabbing Clarence like a knife.

"What are we going to do, baba?" he asked.

Clarence smiled back at his son. "This doesn't concern us, son. We're little fish. I doubt anything will change."

"But you work for the regime!" he countered.

"Like I said, son, we're little fish. Don't worry us."

His head buzzed. He left the room and went to his study.

"Hello?"

"Beki, it's Mark. Are you watching this?"

Clarence closed his eyes then took a deep breath.

"Yes Mark, I'm watching it."

"This is crazy, man! What are we going to do?"

"Calm down, Mark. We're not going to do anything. The rebels got what they wanted. I suspect everything will get back to normal soon."

"Not for us," Mark argued. "We worked for them!"

Clarence took a deep breath before answering. "Like I said, Mark, don't worry about it."

There was silence between them for a moment. Mark was a worrier. Clarence could imagine him pacing his condo right now, rolling a stylus between his skinny fingers.

"Look, Mark, I got to ...."

"Have you called Celone?" Mark cut in.

"No, why?"

"She's not answering."

"Maybe she's not home."

"Neither is Terry or Pausa."

Clarence throat tightened. "So, what?"

"Don't be naive, Clarence. You better start making plans. They're coming for us. They're coming for us."

"Mark, I got to go. I'll see you in the office Luneday."

"I hope so. I really hope so."

Clarence disconnected as Sarafina entered the room.

"Is everything alright?"

Clarence smiled at his wife. He saw the worry in her eyes.

"Everything's fine, just Mark being paranoid."

Sarafina crossed the room then took his hand.

"I think you're taking this too easy, baby."

Clarence rolled his eyes. "Not you, too?"

"You work for them."

"We all do one way or another." He sat on the bed then pulled her beside him. "What are they going to do, kill all of us?"

Sarafina didn't answer. He wrapped his arm around her waist.

"Look baby. They got what they wanted. Cassad is theirs and all that goes along with it, which is us. After a few weeks of parading around Khalid they'll give their cronies all the good jobs then go home."

His wife snuggled against him. "I feel sorry for Khalid. He's a good man."

"How do you know that? He's the oba's son. All those folks have blood on their hands."

He kissed her on the forehead. "Come on; let's go back to the room. The kids are going to think we're having sex."

Sarafina punched his shoulder.

They did make love that night. There was desperation about it, as if it would be their last time. Clarence lay awake long afterwards, Mark's words spinning in his head. By the time morning came he was still awake staring at the ceiling. He cut off the alarm before it went off then trudged to the bathroom. He was done shaving and showering when Sarafina joined him.

"Round two?" she whispered.

Clarence smacked his hand against her wet bottom. "I wish."

Sarafina had her way, making him late. When he arrived on the 110th floor of the Imperial Archives Teresa, Pausa and Mark waited in the office, relieved looks on their face.

"Nobody told me we were having a party," he said as he entered.

Teresa pounced on him, hugging his neck tightly.

"We thought they got you!"

He slowly pried her away. They had a thing once before he met Sarafina and she was constantly looking for reasons to rekindle it.

"I'm fine. You need to stop listening to Mark."

Mark stepped forward. "Really?"

He handed Mark a sheet of paper.

"What's this?"

"It's a memo. There will be a meeting at 12:00 noon. A New Regime representative will be addressing all the Imperial Archive employees. We're not to engage in any work activity until the representative arrives."

Mark pushed past his cohorts then sat at his desk.

"So, we have a meeting."

"This is how it starts," Mark said.

"So how many revolutions have you experienced, Mark?"

Mark glared at Clarence.

"That's what I thought. Okay, listen up. Go back to your desks and play whatever games you have until noon. And don't worry. Everything will be fine."

The trio sulked out of his office. Clarence shook his head. He switched on his comp hoping to catch up on some personal work when the screen flickered, replaced by a New Regime symbol. Soon afterwards it was replaced by the beautiful but stern woman's face, her cocoa similar to Sarafina's.

"Clarence Mbeki?" she said.

A chill went through him. "That's me."

"I'm Rosalinda Chalms. I'll be your N.R. liaison. I'm due to your office at noon, but I'd like to speak to you personally before my arrival."

"Where are you?"

"At the Palace. I'm sure you know the way."

Clarence swallowed. "I do."

The woman smiled. "Good. I'll see you at 10:00?"

"Yes, ma'am."

"No formalities. Just call me Rosalinda."

"Yes...Rosalinda."

She smiled again and the screen went blank.

Clarence moved mechanically as he gathered his things then left the office.

Teresa, Pausa and Mark pounced on him.

"Where are you going?" Pausa asked.

"To the Palace."

Mark froze. "I knew it. I knew it!"

"It's just a meeting, Mark. We'll discuss it when I get back."

The three looked at him as if that was a remote possibility. As he entered the elevator, he thought the same.

Clarence stepped on the taxi grid and a vehicle eased from the programmed traffic then stopped before him. He sat then waited as the toll box synched with his credit chip.

"Where to?" it asked.

"The Central Palace."

Instead of taking him immediately the taxi remained still. A hand print grid emerged from the dashboard.

"All personnel visiting the Central Palace must submit to security scan prior to arrival. Please place your hands on the grid and look forward.

This is new, Clarence thought. He placed his palms on the grid then sat still as his eyes and hands were scanned.

"Identity confirmed."

The taxi door shut and they sped to the Central Palace. Clarence had little time to contemplate his situation for the Palace was only a few blocks from the Archives. A young woman with mocha skin and pale brown eyes was waiting for him when the taxi door lifted, dressed in a pale blue suit, the color of the revolution.

"Mr. Mbeki, welcome to the palace," she said in a contralto voice. "Miss Chalms is expecting you."

Clarence followed the aide through security and into the palace. He was too nervous to take advantage of his first visit to the magnificent structure. Mark's words kept running through his head as the aide led him down a corridor lined by doors on either side. Clarence suspected these were the former servant quarters but he couldn't be sure. They finally stopped before double doors at the end of the hall.

"Go right in, Mr. Mbeki."

The doors slid open and Clarence entered. The office was sparse. A large desk rested before him, a floor to ceiling window forming the wall behind it. Two chairs sat on either side of the desk at angles.

"Clarence?"

A hidden door opened in the wall on his right and Rosalinda Chalms entered the room. Her blue suit fitted her curves sensuously, matching the playful smile on her face. But Clarence knew better. This would not be a good meeting.

She shook his hand then gestured to the chairs.

"Please, sit."

Clarence chose the right-hand seat and Rosalinda smiled.

"I would have chosen the left seat. I'm left-handed."

"Force of habit," Clarence croaked.

The aide entered with a tray of coffee. She made Rosalinda a cup then offered one to Clarence.

"No thank you," he said.

"Coffee is not the preferred stimulant here," Rosalinda commented. "I believe kola nuts are popular."

Clarence nodded. "They are."

Rosalinda pursed her lips then shuddered. "Too bitter for me."

She leaned back in her chair.

"Let's get to it, shall we. There are going to be major changes in your department. I called you here because I'll need you to handle the fallout immediately after my visit."

Clarence relaxed a bit. They weren't going to kill him.

"What kind of changes?"

"We're reassigning all single employees to nonessential positions in the capital. It's our belief that people without obligations are more susceptible to negative persuasion."

Single people. His entire team. Clarence cleared his throat.

"How soon will the replacements arrive?"

Rosalinda smiled. "That easy, huh? No protests? No defense for your team?"

"Would it make a difference, ma'am?"

"No, it wouldn't. Archives contain sensitive information. We can't afford to have people we can't trust with access to it."

"And you can trust me because I'm married." Clarence said.

Rosalinda's eyes narrowed. "We can trust you because you have more to lose."

Rosalinda took a long sip. "This victory was hard won, Clarence. We did this for you, us, the entire Known. But these are delicate days ahead. Everything we fought and died for could be lost by a simple mistake. We won't allow that to happen. You won't allow it to happen."

"I understand," Clarence said.

Rosalinda smiled. "Good. I'll see you in a couple of hours."

Clarence took the cue and left the office. The aide waited for him outside the doors. She escorted him to a waiting taxi that sped him back to the office. Clarence's entire body shook. He wrapped his arms around himself, trying to bring the shaking under control. He opened his mouth and a sob escaped.

"Oh my God!" he managed to say. "Oh my God!"

It took Clarence the entire taxi ride back to compose himself. By the time he stepped onto the side walk he had some semblance of control. He took a deep breath before entering the building then taking the lift to the Archives floor. The lift door parted and he strode to his office, his outer countenance hiding the emotional tempest raging inside him.

His team was on his heels as he entered his office.

"So, what happened?" Mark almost shouted.

"We discussed details of the meeting," Clarence answered.

Everyone looked at him expecting more.

"Look guys, I'm not at liberty to share. Rosalinda will explain everything."

"Bullshit!" Teresa spat. Her exclamation rattled Clarence. Out of the three of them Teresa was the most calm and level-headed.

He took a deep breath. "Look, this is what's going to happen. The three of you are going to be assigned..."

"Oh Jesus!" Mark found the nearest chair the plopped down. He jammed his hands between his knees and rocked back and forth.

"I knew it. I knew it! They're going to kill us."

Teresa and Pausa gave him desperate looks.

"Nobody's going to get killed." At least not now, he thought.

"The Coalition has deemed the Archives a highly sensitive area. They want to reassign anyone who they feel will be a security risk."

"You know what that means," Mark said.

"Actually, it puts you out of harm's way," Clarence said. "Your replacements will be married personnel."

"Oh my god," Teresa said. She reached out and touched his cheek. "I'm so sorry, Clarence."

Mark stopped rocking, "Why are you sorry for him? We're the ones in trouble!"

"Stop worrying about your own ass and think for a minute," Teresa retorted. "They're moving married couples in so they can use their families as a veiled threat."

Mark looked up. "Jeez, Clarence. You got to get out of here, man. You got to take your family and run."

Clarence let out a desperate laugh. "Look. I didn't tell you anything, okay. If anyone else asks you what we talked about, don't say a word. Now go back to your desks."

Teresa gave him a sad look then left. Pausa just stared for a moment and followed. Mark was the last to leave.

"There is a way, you know," he said.

Clarence's eyes narrowed. "A way to what?"

"A way to run." He closed Clarence's door.

"There's a way off the planet. Some of the Empire is still controlled by the Cassads. The Regime is claiming victory but that's not quite true. They could get you and your family out."

"We're not going anywhere," Clarence replied. "Everything is going to be fine."

Mark looked away then back to Clarence. "I'll be gone by the end of the week."

"What?"

"I've already paid for it. It was damned expensive but it's legitimate. It's too late to get on my shuttle but they have regular runs for now."

"Go back to your office, Mark. I don't want to talk about this anymore."

Mark started to open his mouth but stopped.

"See you at the meeting," he finally said.

Clarence waved him away. He sat at his desk and began to think.

Rosalinda and her team arrived just before noon. Clarence set out a vid cast and everyone gathered in the large conference room. They crammed toward the rear of the room as if awaiting execution. Clarence stood in the front, occasionally glancing back at his coworkers, his eyes meeting Mark's. He turned away then forced a smile to his face as Rosalinda and the others entered the room.

"Greetings everyone!" she said. Her voice was warm and soothing, her smile bright and generous. She was very good at what she did. Clarence could sense the tension ease in the room as everyone shuffled about, returning her smile.

"I am Rosalinda Chalms, the new head of Archives. I wanted to come personally to introduce myself because I've heard so many good things about this team. Clarence is well known and admired, but we all know who really does the work around here."

The others laughed. Clarence managed a chuckle. Rosalinda gave him an approving smile.

"As in all transitions there are always changes," she continued. "I've studied the Archives department for some time and determined that many of you are working way below your pay scale. You deserve better. So over the next few days we're conducting interviews to find our shining stars and place them in departments where they can prosper. Clarence will be the point man for this process, but all reassignments will be approved by yours truly."

The tension increased. Rosalinda seemed to sense it and countered it with another one of her brilliant smiles.

"This is a new day for us all; a better day. The Coalition is dedicated to destroying the ingrained nepotism that plagued the Empire and replacing it with a democratic process that creates opportunity for anyone with the right skills, no matter what their lineage."

Rosalinda nodded to her assistants. They tilted their heads, a distracted look in their eyes. Moments later the elevator doors opened and servers rolled in tables of simmering food and drinks.

"So today we celebrate!" Rosalinda said, striking the pose of a game show model.

They were hers now. Everyone swarmed the tables, indulging in the feast. Teresa, Pausa and Mark were the last to join the festivities, each one of them glancing at him before taking part.

"Those three are your friends," Rosalinda said in his ear. He jumped. He didn't notice her approach.

"Yes, they are," he replied.

"You told them."

"Yes, I did."

"I would have done the same."

He turned to face her. If they hadn't had that conversation hours earlier he would have thought she was attracted to him from how she gazed at him.

"You are a good man, Clarence," she said. "Don't let your goodness bring you to ruin. No more leaks, okay?"

Clarence nodded.

"Good. Now make a plate. This was expensive and I don't want it to go to waste."

He watched Rosalinda saunter away then join everyone as if she'd known them for years. He pulled up a chair then sat. A stabbing pain hit his stomach and he hurried to the men's room. He just reached the stool before he threw up.

"Everything okay in there?" Rosalinda said.

"I'm fine," Clarence called out.

He heard the door open then the clicking of heels.

"I'm going to need you to be stronger that this, Clarence," Rosalinda said. "We have hard choices to make."

'I'll be fine," he said.

"I hope so. Come by my office tomorrow after work. I can help you."

She closed the stall door then left. Clarence made his way to the sink and cleaned himself up. He made up his mind. As soon as he got home, he was going to call Mark.

When Clarence arrived home that evening he carried on as if nothing was amiss. He played with Jamila while Fine prepared dinner, and then carried on a lively discussion with Tony about the finer points of calculus. The family watched the vid as they always did, then he put Jamila to bed while Sarafina took a shower and Toby lost himself in the Loop. After the children were sleep he shared a glass of wine with Sarafina then they made love until they were too sleepy to continue.

But Clarence couldn't sleep. Rosalinda's face appeared in every moment his mind wasn't occupied, telling him those same words over and over. There was a noose around his neck, a noose made of his loved ones that could jerk him off his feet any minute.

"Fine," he whispered. Sarafina squirmed about but didn't answer.

"Fine", he said louder. She didn't move.

Clarence eased out of the bed then picked up his phone from the dresser. Mark's face appeared in the screen.

"Look Mark, about that..."

"Run we talked about tomorrow?" Mark finished. "Good! I'm glad you decided to finally get in shape. We can run after work. Make sure you bring something comfortable."

Mark hung up. Apparently, he thought the phones were tapped. A few days ago, he would have dismissed the thought, but his world was different two days ago.

The next morning in addition to his lunch Clarence packed a pair of running shorts, his old running shoe and a t-shirt. Sarafina looked at him with a smirk.

"You're going running?" she asked.

"Yeah, Mark and I."

Her face became serious.

"Okay, then. Have fun."

Work was normal, with the exception of the Regime observers looking over everyone's shoulders. He kept his conversations with his friends to a minimum and focused on business. At day's end he went into his private bathroom then changed. Mark met him in the lobby.

"I hope you can keep up," he said.

"I'll do my best," Clarence replied.

They walk across the street to the park then jogged.

"So Mark, tell me..."

Mark shook his head. Clarence remained quiet until they were a good distance from the office building.

"So, are you in?" Mark asked.

"I'd like to ask a few questions first."

"No questions," Mark replied. "Either you're in or you're not."

"So I'm supposed to just jump in without knowing who these folks are? You know I don't work that way."

"You know me, right?"

Clarence nodded.

"Then you know them. Are you in or out?"

Clarence shook his head. Mark frowned.

"Teresa and Pausa are in. The three of us will be gone before the end of the month."

Clarence stopped running, stunned by the news. "You're quitting?"

Mark kept running. "No, we're just not going to show up one day. If we quit they'll know what's up. Sorry Clarence. I don't want to die."

Clarence began running. "Me, either."

Clarence went back to his office to freshen up and dress. He took a few minutes to close up a couple of searches then headed for the door. His phone chirped before he could exit.

"Clarence," he answered.

"You're working late," It was Rosalinda.

"Ah, yeah. Went on a run after work."

"Running. You look in good shape to me."

"Thank you." Clarence felt his hands trembling. It was enough having her hover over his work. Having Rosalinda physically attracted to him was unnerving.

"Are you headed home now?" she asked.

"Yes."

"Stop by my office on the way. We have a couple of things to discuss. I'll send a car."

"Sure thing."

Clarence hung up the phone then sat hard. He wasn't prepared for any of this. What the hell was he supposed to do? He picked up the phone, put it down, and then picked it up again. He pressed the code.

"Hi baby," his wife said.

"I'm going to be a little late. Rosalinda wants me to stop by her office."

There was silence for a moment.

"Is everything okay?"

Clarence shook his head. "I hope so."

The car was waiting when he exited the office. The ride was over too soon, the walk to her office he didn't remember. He was sitting before her desk when he realized he was the only person in the building other than Rosalinda. She emerged from her private bathroom as perfectly put together as ever.

"Thanks for coming, Clarence. I wanted to share some news with you before tomorrow. I'm trying to keep you in the loop. The first transfers have come in."

She handed him a printout. Clarence scanned the sheet then froze. Three names stood out; Mark, Pausa and Teresa.

"I hope you're not too upset," she said. "Your friends were determined inadequate for the new duties the Archive will take on."

"How would you know that?" he said, his voice tight. "You never worked with them."

Rosalinda sighed. "You know this works. It's a paper-work decision. The computer can't see personality."

"I can't run the office without them," he said.

"They'll be replaced with more capable people. Better now than later, don't you think?"

Their eyes met. She knew.

Rosalinda smiled then rubbed her stomach.

"I'm hungry. How about joining me for dinner?"

Clarence stood. "Can't. My wife has dinner waiting at home."

Rosalinda pouted. "That's too bad. Another time maybe?"

Clarence forced a smile. "Maybe."

He headed for the door.

"I think we should be friends, Clarence. It would be better for both of us," Rosalinda called out.

"I'm sure it would," Clarence replied. He hurried out of the building and into a taxi. By the time he reached his home he was hysterical.

Clarence ran up the walkway. His hand shook as he placed his palm against the door. To his horror the door opened. He rushed inside, running from room to room calling out his wife and children's' names. No one answered. The energy left his body and he fell to the floor and began sobbing.

A firm hand gripped his shoulder.

"Mr. Mbeki? Please get up. We need you to come with us."

The words meant nothing to Clarence. His family was gone.

"Mr. Mbeki. Get up please. We don't have much time."

"Just kill me here," Clarence answered. "Get it over with."

The hand shook him.

"You have it all wrong, Mr. Mbeki. We're the good guys. We're here to take you to a safe place. But we haven't much time. The authorities are on their way and they don't work for us."

Clarence sat up, wiping his face. He looked at the person looming over him. It was the taxi driver.

"Please come with me, Mr. Mbeki. We have to get you off Ziara."

Clarence hesitated. "How do I know you're telling me the truth?"

The man smiled. "You don't. I can tell you that your friend Michael contacted us after your run. Apparently, he was being watched, for no sooner had he disconnected with us did Regime agents pick him up. That's when we knew he had to act fast or we would lose you, too."

The man stood. "Please Mr. Mbeki. We have to leave now."

Clarence stood then trudged behind the man.

"Where's my family?" he asked as he climbed into the taxi.

"They're safe," the man replied. "That's all you need to know right now."

"What the hell do you mean safe?"

The man looked into the back seat. "They're off planet, probably on their way to an Imperial planet by now."

Clarence gripped the seat rest. "Which one?"

"I don't know," the man replied. "My job is to get you to a ship. Once you're off planet you'll get more information."

Clarence slumped in his seat. This was a nightmare come true.

"What do they want with me?" he said. "I'm a nobody. This war has nothing to do with people like me."

"It has everything to do with people like you," the man said sharply. "Did you think you would go along as if nothing happened? The Empire is crumbling, Mr. Mbeki. Everything that made sure your life was calm and peaceful is gone."

The man kept driving until they were out of the city. Soon they were bordered on either side by ruined buildings. The road became ragged so the man switched to hover mode. Huge ships lay in ruins about them, some still burning weeks after being destroyed.

"Where are we? What is this?" Clarence asked.

"This is Accra," the man answered without looking back. "This is the war."

Clarence looked at the devastated city in silence as the driver cruised over the ruins. All this time he thought Cassidy had been spared, that the takeover had been peaceful. The war was 'out there', not in his backyard.

"The rebels didn't overwhelm Cassidy like the other planets," the driver said. "It was too valuable. Still, they had to neutralize certain areas to secure the planet. So they did it from the inside."

Clarence looked at the driver. "How? Who on Cassidy would betray the Cassads?"

The driver laughed. "See, the Empire refused to believe all its regents were in on the rebellion. They would embrace anyone who came to Ziara and professed their loyalty. All they were doing were opening themselves to the coup de grace. Once the rebels discovered how to hack the A.I.'s it was as good as over."

"Hack the A.I.'s?" Clarence shook his head. "No, no. That's impossible. The A.I. are programmed down to the chromosome level. It would take years to hack just one, let alone millions. You would need..."

"A quark key," the driver finished. "And they have them. They got them from right here. From your department."

Clarence shuddered. Who in his department would reveal something as secret as a quark key?"

"Anyone would for the right amount of money." The driver answered him as if reading his thoughts. "That's how it happens, Clarence. A bunch of insignificant decisions finally add up to one deadly blow. And that's how Accra got burned...and Kanem...and Orleans...and Louisiana."

"Stop it," Clarence said. "When do I get to see my family?"

"I don't know," the man said. "A different team was assigned to them. It's best you don't know where they are for now and vice versa. If either of you were caught you might tell where the other might be."

Clarence's fear slowly turned into anger. "You have no reason to keep me away from my family, unless you're using them to manipulate me."

"You know things we need," the driver confessed. "You'll be more cooperative if you have a reason to tell us what we know."

"You're no better than them," he spat.

"Of course, we are," the driver said. He turned and flashed a smile at Clarence. "We're the good guys."

The taxi reached a fairly clear area then landed.

"Get out," he said.

"What are you talking about?"

"Get out!" the man shouted. "My job is done. Someone else will pick you up here. Tell them what they want to know and you'll be reunited with your family in a safe area. The Empire still exists."

"How do I know you're telling the truth?"

"You don't. But you don't have a choice."

Clarence stepped out of the taxi. He wrapped his arms around himself as the vehicle lifted then sped away. As it became a dim light in the distance another light appeared overhead, growing with every second. The stench of burned plasteel and flesh made him shiver as they light grew brighter. As the light began to hurt his eyes he realized he never had a choice. One way or another he would work against his will. He once thought the war was at an end. He realized now that it was only just beginning.

THE FIRST DOOM
BY
DAVAUN SANDERS

*The entire Known watched spellbound as the last heir of
the Cassad lineage stood trial for the 'crimes' of his family.
Broadcasts reached from the Core to the edge of the Known.
The universe was changing before them, swirling into a mael-
strom of uncertainty. But for a few, the woes of the Empire were
insignificant. For one man in particular, the key to existence lay
in the expanse of the Unknown. He just needed the right crew to
get him there...*
　　　　-Samake, djele/historian. From the Cassad Chronicles

Kyria Grazheen faced down every hollow-eyed stare in
the mess hall as she flexed her hand, ignoring the pain lancing
through her knuckles. Over fifty women and men surrounded
her, former Cassad crew bound by nothing but a shared desire to
lash out over their fresh despair. She knew their pain, but sympathy in the Known served a mercenary worse than swallowing
a handful of irradiated rounds.

"That's the last warning you're gonna get." Kyria's
brown gaze settled on the man at her feet. He cupped a hand
over his jaw, glowering up at her through a puffy eye. He had
the good sense to keep his mouth closed while she spoke, even if
it meant swallowing a little blood.

"One more fight in this outpost, and I'll shut the broadcast down myself. You can listen to it in orbit like all the rest."

The scowls deepened as more of the surveying crew set to rush her. Behind them, Shuster's hand slipped under the bar. Kyria gave a slight shake of her head. He kissed his teeth in exasperation, refusing to budge. Perfect. The man's grip rested on worse than the mess hall's poisonous ale.

Kyria winced, flexing her fist again as one of the Cassad elbowed past his crewmates to face her. Veins bulged along his muscle-bound neck. "You Arcadian vermin act like you're the-"

"Ah, finally." Kyria pried the tooth out of her knuckle with a grunt. A few drops of bright blood oozed out, spattering on the mess hall's grated metal floor. The surveyors' angry mutters died out as Kyria peered down at the stocky man; an Element G dispersal engineer by the smell of him. "You were saying?"

"Our survey lasted a decade, Arcadian." The engineer drudged up some civility as he helped his friend to his feet. "We've finally returned from the Unknown to find civil war? Half our worlds under this New Regime? And there's a trial of the emperor-"

"I don't care." Kyria tossed back the cracked incisor. The first man gave her a gap-toothed snarl as he snatched it from the air. She held in a smile. "And this 'Arcadian vermin' has seen worse than you've ever dreamed. The broadcast stays on. Don't make me get up again."

Kyria returned to her empty table without another word. No charging boots followed. The surveyors were already hunkering back around their cold metal tables as the trial dragged on. "The Cassad ravaged our home world!" the latest witness wailed. The feed of Emperor Khalid Cassad's trial had echoed through every hall of the Efalus Six outpost for days-thanks to some blindspliced audio ports hacked together by a well-meaning engineer from an orbiting ship. Kyria intended to thank the woman personally if the feed kept working up these crews. She couldn't blame them too much, though; the young emperor's New Regime captors had crafted quite a spectacle.

"Khalid deserves a thousand times a thousand deaths for all who've endured Cassad butchery in the Known!"

Reverence, anger, satisfaction and disbelief rippled through the surveyors' expressions; sometimes all squeezed onto one person's face. People from some deluded worlds still venerated the Emperor of the Known as a god. They were easy to pick out; eyes bloodshot and unblinking. But if their beliefs held any spark, Khalid Cassad would not wear chains-And Kyria Grazheen's credits would be worth more than a handful of steaming fek.

She downed her last shot of Cloudspittle and set the empty glass beside a neat row of three more, just as chipped and empty as the Cassad surveyors around her. Shuster's disapproving frown drifted over the heads of the surveyors. She leered at him, ignoring how the vile drink licked away the skin inside her windpipe. He snorted, muttering to himself as he rummaged through his stock of Roofcutter, ink and Ziaran wine. Kyria didn't care, so long as he brought over something strong. She would take a few days with a hoarse throat over the dead woman's voice blooming back to life in her head.

Gotta take a stand somewhere, might as well be here. But this is gonna hurt, rookie.

Too late. Kyria squeezed her eyes shut, willing the voice away. A sudden microburst hit the entire mess hall, rattling the airlock behind her table. She would be first to go if the seals failed.

The trial feed cut out, prompting curses all around. Irritation flashed through Kyria as she massaged her temples. "Next person to mouth off gets their ass worn like a sandal, and I'm walking all the way back to..."

Her words died off as she opened her eyes. A burly man stood before her, wearing a Cassad officer's uniform like nothing she'd ever seen, an angular cut of blue bordering on black.

"You lost?"

"I was just about to ask you the same question." The lilt of the man's baritone betrayed a heritage from the interior Known, maybe even Ziara itself. He held an irritating air of self-assurance, though he didn't look down his nose in that pompous way Kyria had endured from other capital-bred officers. Meaty palms, steady gaze, but definitely not military-technician over-seer, maybe?

"You hold the most potential of anyone upon this entire planet, I suspect," he said. "Yet you serve the least use so long as you linger here. What a puzzle you've become."

"You have no idea." Kyria's implanted warden tech signaled no passive scan alerts, yet the Cassad officer's cool, dark eyes dismantled and reconstructed her in a blink. Most of the surveyors eyed him more warily than Kyria, and he hadn't even drawn any blood. She shifted, suddenly tense. *Is this a sniffer, doing Loren's recon before he comes gunning for me?*

"I'm right where I need to be."

"As are we all." The officer nodded to himself, like he had picked over her secrets and pocketed the most promising. "I'd like you to serve as a crew chief aboard my vessel." He extended a hand. "My name is-"

Kyria laughed in his face. No way had this bumble gaff meant to mark her for an assassin. "Best get back to orbit, Cassad. Outpost overseers don't like recruiters much."

The officer lowered his hand, thick eyebrows rising. His surprise deepened as Shuster chose that moment to shoulder in front of him.

"Found you one last bottle, Grazer."

Wiry and lean, with smooth ebon skin and a clean-shaven head to match, Shuster looked the officer up and down as though he meant to start a fight himself. He knew he'd never do more than take the chill off the worthless insulation job in Kyria's bunk for a night, but he still enjoyed testing his limits at the worst possible moment.

The Cassad officer smiled back pleasantly, earning Shuster's frown.

Kyria took the Cloudspittle with a nod of thanks. "Send a round to that table I just broke up." She poured a bit over her knuckles with a grimace, surprised the wound didn't hiss. "But don't tell them it's from me."

"You sure?" Shuster asked.

"I'm sure. People don't respect the birch in one hand if they see the sugar in the other." She glanced at the surveyors whispering quietly among themselves. Smallish people from Pacifica; men and women of all stature and shade from the Reach, unmistakable Euphrates folk-who knew how their double irises made others squirm, but didn't hesitate to stare. Even a few Marajeshi sat among them, with freckles sparkling like emerald powder on their brown skin.

Some of the surveyors had undoubtedly been drafted by the Cassad, while others joined to earn higher citizenship tiers. None of it mattered now that the empire had fallen apart. Allegiances lived and died in the surveyors' eyes as they waited for the trial feed to resume. *It's like watching the Known crumble all over again.*

"Get that damn blindsplice synced again, too," Kyria grumbled. "And make it two rounds."

The officer opened his mouth, but Shuster barreled right over him.

"Sure, sure. Might as well spend all those creds you saved up while they're still worth a damn." He sighed at her swelling hand. "Get that looked at. By Parunja's Drift, next time use your volt knuckles! You're not made of alloy, you know."

"Life would be easier that way." Kyria snorted and poured herself three more shots. "Another bottle of this fek you're passing off for swill will scour out the soft parts soon enough."

Shuster's eyes twinkled. "Let's hope not."

The officer cleared his throat. "I'll order a double of level-three Ease, if that's not too much-"

Shuster laughed in his face. He strode off to pour Kyria's credits into other people's sorrow. The officer's expression remained cordial as he plopped himself down at her table.

"My name is Amadi Zele."

Kyria blinked as he hefted the bottle of Cloudspittle and sniffed it experimentally. "First time outside the Known?" she asked dryly.

"Indeed, but my work demands nothing less. I'm close to the truth of a Dark Age myth, hidden for millennia. This last voyage will-"

"That's supposed to impress me? Myths come and go. One is standing trial in New Beia right now."

"Quite true." Zele scratched his mustache thoughtfully. "Tell me, how long did you work in Targotha?"

"Who said I-" Kyria's hand snapped reflexively to her shorn scalp before jerking it back down. The blue stubble screamed of her stint in Tar City and its notorious pollutants. *At least I stopped sweating blue.* She glared at the man irritably and downed another shot. "You're from the explorer vessel that just put in. Hope you're not planning to stay in orbit long with the way you're hemorrhaging crew."

"We depart as soon as you're ready to come aboard." The man's lips quirked. "I'm an Averator of the Cassad Empire."

Kyria nearly laughed in his face again. "The former Cassad Empire. What in the Known is an Averator?"

Another microburst slammed into the module, forestalling his answer. Some of the surveyors glanced Kyria's way. She noted the disappointment in their eyes when the airlock held.

"You've never heard of Carigine Pelson? Darius Berden?" He sighed at Kyria's unimpressed shrug.

"Just you."

"Small wonder the empire is collapsing," Zele muttered, carefully pouring for himself. "I gather you're in need of credits, and I'm in need of your skill set for a survey of my own. Deep into the Unknown."

"You don't know a damn thing about my skill set." Kyria snatched the shot back from him and downed it, suppressing a shudder. Deep surveys meant cryosleep and free reign for the dead woman in her head. "Besides, I'm under contract with a freighter due here in two weeks."

Zele rubbed his chin. "I could always requisition your service, though I'd prefer you join us of your own volition."

"Please. Any Cassad order you whip up means absolute fek," Kyria retorted with a grunt. "There are no rules in the Unknown, especially now."

Zele sipped his Cloudspittle and immediately spit it out. "I rarely miscalculate this badly," the Averator murmured as he stood. "Efalus Six is about to become...unpleasant. With the level of training you received in the Forty-Sixth, I'm surprised you didn't notice sooner."

Kyria's smirk evaporated as she bolted to her feet. "How did you know-"

The hair on the nape of her neck stood up an instant before the proximity mods in her cortex went off. A static hum filled the stale air as a Brython Knight of the Realm clanked into the mess hall. The massive robot resembled a torion tank with legs, covered in a pocked, gray composite wrought in cruel angles and forged for death. A double barreled repulsor cannon rested atop one arm, and the Knight wielded a long-handled purge blade, a nasty weapon designed to maim and scar in offering to the Cathol god.

"Oclorious the Redeemer bears witness upon this system." The robot's swiveling receiver node bore a mocking resemblance to a human head. Twin data relays glowed a piercing blue; resembling dead, burning eyes.

Lost your edge, Grazer. Kyria's hands slipped unconsciously into the volt knuckles hidden in her pocket. She laughed at herself-even with her pick of weapons, her exposed flesh stood no chance against plate armor a half-meter thick. She tensed as the Knight's scan paused briefly over her military implants, but it swept on, searching for someone who mattered. Shuster earned an additional scan of his own, but his hands stayed on his drinks.

I'm going to show you what it takes to be a leader, the dead woman promised.

The Knight's grating, unnatural voice approximators pierced the air, coldly fervent. "The Efalus system is now under the blessed protection of the Cathol, and the righteous glory of the New Regime. Stand by for conversion and reassignment. You may rejoice."

No one breathed as Oclorious stilled, calculating the new lives of everyone within the room, assigning them to posts within the New Regime without so much as an interview. The surveyor that Kyria confronted earlier bristled. Every Marajeshi went rigid in affront. They hated Brython folk and their robots with a passion that Kyria envied...but none of them were soldiers. The Averator stared at the Knight with a stupid look on his face, as if he were chewing his tongue.

"Stop that," Kyria warned him under her breath. "You'll get us all killed."

"What?" Zele asked innocently.

"You've got a palate swiper. You keep sending messages back to your ship, that Knight will cut it out of your mouth and expel the rest of us out of the airlock!"

Averators were apparently intelligent, for he ceased at once. "Time to depart, I think. Conversion has never suited my purposes. I'd need a few days to design something that can overcome a Brython warship. May the Known be kind, Arcadian."

"Wait." The Averator's words bounced through her head, settling upon a realization. "You're an explorer. You didn't say anything about weapon tech."

Zele ignored her, peering up at the room's audio port. "Just a little tweak..."

Oclorious jerked out of its proselytizing scan. "Command priority override." A table of surveyors scrambled clear with a shout as it rumbled straight for Zele. The metal table squealed free of the floor, pulling apart before the Knight's steel-plated legs.

"I told you!" Kyria snapped, backing away with a snarl.

"Averator Amadi Zele." The Knight's blue orbs burned down at the Cassad. "Priority asset level status confirmed. You are hereby ordered to convert."

The Averator flicked open a handheld device Kyria had somehow missed before. His eyes glittered in triumph as he took in the surveyors' stunned expressions. "Until the All is Known and stars are dust!" he shouted. "May Cassad forever stand!"

Zele tapped his device, and the mess hall's audio ports crackled back to life. Chaos filtered through the trial feed, explosions, screaming and weapons fire. A Hub relayer's panicked voice reported over the tumult, but his words were unbelievable.

"-that is confirmed-it's the Njaro! A space station under Cassad control has attacked New Beia! The former emperor is missing-but his mercenary guard is reportedly in a firefight with-"

Oclorious halted as a ragged cheer overcame the mess hall. The Knight swiveled crisply. "Heathen parameters actuated. New convert protocols are now active."

Kyria barely noticed. Her blood ran cold at mention of the emperor's mercenary guard. "You would be in the middle of that, Loren. Whatever keeps me out of your sights."

The surveyors grew emboldened in their cheers, no longer cowering from the Knight of the Realm.

"The emperor lives and fights! Khalid!"

"All else is dust!"

Cold sky to hot core, Efalus Six had rediscovered an unfortunate, unflinching loyalty to the Cassad Empire. Kyria edged away from the inevitable slaughter pit. "Averator, this is one nice pile of fek you've-" She gaped, searching the room. Zele was gone.

Kyria turned to bolt herself, but the dead woman's voice stopped her. *Whatever you do, don't die alone, rookie. Not while people are depending on you.*

"I know!" she snapped at it. Kyria caught Shuster's eye and very deliberately held up her volt knuckles. He licked his lips and nodded, reaching under the bar.

A handful of the bolder surveyors surrounded the robot, jeering. Bottles broke against the Knight's blue orbs. "Reassessing threat parameters," Oclorious pronounced.

"Hey, Pacifica." The surveyor Kyria had kicked around turned back to her. "No hard feelings, all right? If you want some payback..." Kyria slid one of her last two knuckles across the table. His face lit up as he caught it. "May Cassad forever stand."

"Thanks, Arcadian." Air whistled through the gap Kyria had opened in his teeth. She almost felt sorry for him as he slipped the volt knuckle over his fist. A jagged orange arc flashed from the thin metal strip. The weapon might damage the robot's optics, but he'd never get that close.

"Reassessing threat parameters," the Knight's dead voice boomed out. "Fifty percent complete. All converts must kneel in fealty. You may rejoice."

She edged for the closest hall. Shuster pulled out an ugly black tube, his prized reverse polarity destabilizer, and set it regretfully on the bar. Kyria grabbed a Marajeshi woman and pointed the weapon out. "Weeks' worth of charge will cook some Brython circuits. All yours."

The woman didn't hesitate. She strode straight for the destabilizer with murder in her eyes.

"Reassessing threat parameters. Ninety percent complete. Hostile targeting sequence engaged. You may lament." Kyria burned her boot treads hauling out, with Shuster a step behind.

"We can barter passage," she said breathlessly as they sprinted down the drab halls, straight for the docks. "I can pilot the outpost hopper."

"Passage where?" Shuster demanded. "Do you know how far it is to the next shipping lane?"

"We'll figure it out, we always do. If there's a Brython warship in orbit this whole outpost is-" Kyria stopped in her tracks. "You!"

Amadi Zele strolled just ahead, arms folded behind his back. He turned expectantly. "Ah, Arcadian. You've reconsidered my request?"

"You...you stirred up those poor fools just to slip out of there." Kyria whistled. "That's some frigid fek, Averator."

"I could remove myself from the gaze of that lumbering embarrassment whenever I wished," Zele replied. "Your compliance required more...how did you put it? Birch and sugar?"

Shuster made a strangled sound, and Kyria's face burned hot. "You're insane," she spluttered. "There's no guarantee anyone comes off this rock alive, now!"

"Yet here you stand unscathed. I learn quickly, Kyria." His smile never reached his eyes. "There are no rules in the Unknown."

Kyria spun as the whine of the Brython Knight's repulsor cannon cut the air behind them. The surveyors' shouts for the Empire turned to screams. Zele didn't even blink. "I'll triple the credits of your prior contract."

"I need something more tangible," Kyria shot back. "I have project specs. And I want passage for my friend."

Sweat broke out on Shuster's brow at Zele's skeptical appraisal. "He has your skill set?" the Averator asked doubtfully.

"Even better," Kyria said. "He can cook."

"Very well. Agreement in principle." Zele wore the smug expression of a man who always got his way. "The same rate suffices?" Shuster bobbed his head, dazed at the exchange.

"Good. We'll discuss your...project aboard my ship, Arcadian. There's no time left to waste."

The man strode off with new purpose in his step. Zele's single mindedness intrigued Kyria just a pinch more than it unnerved her-but if not part of his crew, she was either converted or dead.

"You just negotiated rates with a Knight at your..." Shuster swallowed. "Thanks for throwing me in the deal. I guess the Cloudspittle didn't eat away what's left of your heart."

"Might be easier that way," Kyria replied softly, squeezing his hand. For a moment, she thought it better to take her chances with Oclorious the Redeemer than Amadi Zele. "Watch yourself. He's Cassad."

"Then why help him?" Shuster murmured as they followed. "Even if Khalid survived the trial, he can't stop the Brython and Marajeshi from carving up the Empire, not unless he's got a secret fleet hidden somewhere. The Cassad are done."

"I guess I have a thing for lost causes." Kyria fingered the remaining volt knuckle in her pocket. "He's out to change the Known...and we don't have a choice."

"What do Averators do, anyway?" Shuster stared at Zele in awe. "Make their own credits?"

Zele glanced back with that knowing smile. "No," he said, his dark eyes glittering. "But we do make history."

***

"His ship is a klick out from soft dock range." Kyria had insisted on taking over the hopper's controls, despite the protests of Zele's pilots. A single look from the Averator silenced them. She let the thrusters out and the Cassad shuttle leaped through cold space. "Anything on the Brython?"

Shuster slid in beside her without a word, eyes fixed on the gravimetric radar. "I don't see her on g-det. Instrumentation's not tracking through the rock's penumbra."

"Keep looking. That Knight's next move is to send out proselyte drones after it's christened the outpost."

"Anything in the Known you don't know how to fight, Kyria?" Shuster muttered.

Looks like it's just you and me, milkrat.

"I can think of at least one," Kyria muttered. She glued her eyes to the tactical display, but the dead woman still stirred.

The better they know you, the worse you can hurt them.

"Do you like my ship?" Unfettered pride rang in Zele's voice. "Her name is the *Dubious*. I designed her myself."

Shuster cleared his throat. "She's, ah..."

His hesitation made Kyria glance up, only to hold in a groan. A sensor array of two offset dishes swallowed the ship's forward hull, with the most exposed observation deck she had ever seen perched just above them. Four arrayed cylindrical modules of uninspired, high tensile alloy joined the observation deck to the rear drive component and Element G transverters; five Cassad Ajuka-class burners-grossly overpowered for its mass.

"See-through is what you're looking for." Just looking at the *Dubious* made Kyria feel naked. It was not only ugly, but useless in a fight. A better named ship didn't exist in all the Known. She twisted to arch an eyebrow at Zele.

"You don't believe in armaments? Hull plating?"

"Some turrets would fit nicely in place of that observation paneling," Shuster muttered, shaking his head. "No shield batteries. We're safer in this hopper. No taking her through atmo, either. Can you imagine the shear?"

"Attacking an Averator's ship even accidentally was once punishable by death." Zele's frown deepened as he took in his pilots' worried expressions. "Already you're enhancing my outlook, Arcadian. Are you also knowledgeable in such areas, Mr. Shuster?"

"Me? No. I can do the welding, if it comes to that. But Grazheen's full of useful-"

Kyria's elbow to his ribs shut that line of thought down. Shuster grunted, clamping his mouth tight.

"You wanted a crew chief." Kyria relinquished helm control to the hopper's autarchic drive. "That's what you've got."

"Certainly," Zele replied. "I'm quite confident you will pass my executive officer's appraisal."

Kyria stiffened. "Now there's an eval? You said you needed me!"

"I've found it providential to bow to others' talents on the rare instances when they supersede my own," Zele explained with a shrug. "I hope to bow to yours as well, Arcadian."

"Fair enough," Kyria muttered. As if Zele weren't an odd enough breed, now she had to tie bootlaces with her teeth through a fek-eating grin for some puckered-ass Cassad officer? She glanced over to share a sneer with Shuster, but the sight of the man trying to chew a hole through his lip ebbed away her anger.

Play nice with the Cassad, or learn to rejoice for the Brython.

Shuster stopped his fretting to gawk through the fore window. "What the..."

Kyria glanced up as the nearest cylinder of the *Dubious* rushed into view, too fast. "Fek!"

A docking bay door split open to receive them just before the hopper slammed into the Dubious's hull. The craft eased to a gentle stop before Kyria fully braced herself. She gaped out at the ship's dock, filled from wall to wall with a viscous, clear gel. "A wet dock? These are experimental!"

"Only the best for my ship," Zele beamed. An overhead hatch hissed open, and he immediately climbed the ladder out.

One of the pilots smirked, a diminutive man with crested locs and gray eyes. "Experimental is a fluid word around here, Arcadian." He extended his hand to Kyria and Shuster both. "Name's Julet."

"I'm Ellin." The second pilot added in a drawl that marked her from Indo, along with the triangular fortune scars on her smooth cheekbones. "Welcome to the family. Better get moving while you're still a priority."

"Lead the way." Kyria licked her lips and nodded encouragingly at Shuster. She counted her steps all the way to the operations deck, a spherical room offering a view of the surrounding space on every axis. The dirty blue glow of Efalus Six shone through the clear composite under her boots.

So it has some value, she conceded. Like standing in a room-sized HUD display. Still too easy to wipe out the entire command with one clean shot. The configuration reminded her of the glass cages the island Premiers used to fight chameleon sharks on Pacifica.

Enough operation ports for ten crew surrounded them, but only a man and woman stood among them, hunched over a single tactical display.

"You know we're the last ship in orbit, waiting for you." The man expanded his arms, and the deck display shifted to zoom on the Brython warship.

Kyria's throat went dry. The long, irregular hull brought to mind an armored viper. Turrets protruded from the ship's underbelly, while fission stacks on top outgassed factory waste directly into space, leaving dark stains on the gray hull.

"I'll never fully understand your fascination with introducing random elements into our mission. We could do entirely without these Brython." The man took in Kyria. "Who is this?"

Zele smiled warmly at the man, an expression as fond as he had held for the *Dubious*. "Paki, my executive officer, meet-"

"Kyria Grazheen." She strode forward and extended a hand. Youthful, with dark hair perfectly edged and a strong grip and confident air, Paki didn't act elitist at all. Kyria resisted staring at his shocking orange eyes-she didn't care what obscure world Paki might hail from, and needed to make a good impression here. "Pleasure to-"

"He's not the executive officer," the woman next to Zele straightened. "I am."

Oh, fek. Kyria drew a measured breath. The woman wore a Cassad uniform cut similarly to Zele, and a tight cord kept her dark hair pulled tight. Kyria cleared her throat. "Averator, I thought you wanted-"

"Remiliat Dumasani is the most intuitive person I've ever met," Zele interjected, scratching his mustache as he peered at the Brython ship. "Rem, Kyria's agreed to be our tactical officer, and will surely-"

"That's also my position," Remiliat interrupted. Her bearing screamed military background-and a well-disciplined one-which somehow made her more irritating.

Kyria shot Zele a reproachful look. "You told me crew chief on the surface."

"My duty again." Remiliat shook her head. "Averator we needed an astrometric technician!"

"That task is within my purview, I'm afraid." Paki added, offering Kyria an apologetic shrug. "You'll find that titles are rather indefinite within this curious existence we call home."

Fresh knots formed in Kyria's shoulders. "So I'm learning."

"You may stay." Remiliat's curt address made Shuster jump. "I can stand no more of Amadi's experiments on our palates." Kyria only earned a contemptuous glance. "But you serve no purpose here-nor anywhere, if the stink on your breath is any indication."

"Perhaps I miscalculated," Zele sighed, motioning Paki to one of the consoles.

Kyria strode past Remiliat, reaching for Zele's arm. "Now wait just a-"

"You are voiceless here, Arcadian." Remiliat's hand rested on Kyria's shoulder with a sister's familiarity. Kyria's legs simply buckled beneath her. Only reflexes honed by her years in the Forty-Sixth saved her from falling flat on her face.

"Don't touch me again." Kyria rose slowly, masking her shock over the woman's mystery attack. Her warden tech hadn't even gone off. "We can trade nerve clenches all day, after I'm paid."

Shuster groaned. Zele and Paki exchanged a long look, but neither moved a muscle.

Remiliat's fists clenched. "We don't need you, and furthermore-"

Alarm klaxons sliced the air. The observation deck's main display flashed red.

"The Brython warship is firing projectiles," Paki said calmly.

"Well...evade!" Zele spluttered.

"Not at us, sir. At the planet."

A white flash in the stratosphere drowned out the HUD's red warnings. The murky blue atmosphere of Efalus Six began to dissipate from a point on the equator like a spreading sore, revealing the barren rock of the surface at hundreds of kilometers per second.

"By all the Known," Shuster whispered.

Kyria's throat tightened at sight of it. *Almost as bad as home.* Her eyes stung, but the others were too riveted to see her blink away the tears.

"An atmospheric bomb. Reclamation." Zele's brow drew down. "The outpost equipment is still of use to the New Regime. They're consolidating their reach on the edges of the Unknown."

Remiliat muttered an oath and strode back to her console, hate glistening in her eyes. "What waste. Paki, get us out of the-"

A high-pitched squeal brought Kyria's palms over her ears. "Cassad vessel," Oclorious' voice grated through the space. "Cease propulsion and-"

Paki's hand flicked over the nearest console and the Knight's voice cut off. "I abhor the Brython," he muttered. "Plotting our course to-"

"You'll stand a better chance of erasing a fixture on our g-det if you plot an inverted jump point out of the system,"

Kyria cut in. "Might lose a few weeks from your destination, but I'm pretty sure you don't want that warship following us."

Paki paused. Remiliat's eyebrows raised, and a grin split Zele's face. *You're not this person anymore*, a voice cautioned, but Kyria pressed on. "Of course, I'm sure you've thought of that already," she added dryly, matching Remiliat stare for stare. "I can show you, unless you still mean to send me back down there."

Remiliat's jaw worked soundlessly for a moment, but a look at the oncoming warship sealed her decision. "Do it."

Paki made room at the console, but Kyria folded her arms. "Personal armor created per my specs, Averator," she said. "That's my pay."

"Intriguing." Zele's response was immediate. "Done."

Kyria strode to the console and began dropping in coordinates. "You see it now?" she asked Paki. "A short vector on the Z-axis. A Knight of the Realm's decision engine is based on probability percentages. If you split the difference between your intended coordinates, and factor in a heading in the opposite direction-"

"There's no way to derive our true destination. They cancel each other out." Paki gave a slow nod. "Most impressive, Arcadian. I can finish the rest."

Kyria stood aside. *One friend on this heap, at least.*

Zele's satisfied look had returned. "Allow me to show you the rest of my ship."

"You have more important things to prepare," Remiliat interjected. "Please, the both of you. Follow me."

Zele shook his head ruefully, but held his silence. There was nothing to do but follow Remiliat off the deck.

Shuster's hand tightened on Kyria's wrist for an instant then slipped away. "Thank you," he whispered. "Could've been us down there."

They'd both lost friends on Efalus Six, the first place on the edge of the Known that had tried to fill the planet-sized void in Kyria's heart. Now it was more like dead Arcadia than she could ever wish. Kyria silently cursed the Brythons for the reminder of what she had lost. What she had failed to protect.

Remiliat made terse introductions among the remaining Cassad crew; over thirty bleary-eyed men and women just as grateful as Kyria when the *Dubious* lurched under their feet, signaling that Paki had evaded the Brython warship.

"Most of the ship is devoted to experimental space, particle density analysis and the like," Remiliat said, casting Kyria a hooded look. "The Averator has the tools on hand to fulfill your...request. What do you need armor for?"

Oh, just to fight off Pack Loren, the merc who captured Khalid Cassad himself. He's hunting me and the rest of the Forty-Sixth down, and I'd like a fighting chance for the day he shows up.

"You may run this ship for Zele," Kyria said. "But I deal with him for pay."

"Secrets lead short lives aboard the *Dubious*, Arcadian." Remiliat spun on her heel. "Inoculations are required for our mission. Come."

"Careful, Grazer," Shuster whispered. "I'd bet a week's pay she's from Atunbé. I've heard...stories. Don't mess with her."

Kyria shrugged, she'd never heard of the world. "Wouldn't dream of it."

They followed Remiliat dutifully into a medical bay, a sparse room with no dedicated personnel-not even a field robot for surgery. Shuster sighed as Remiliat motioned him to stand on a dark, rubbery tile inset into the metal deck.

"Pathogen scanner," she explained.

"I'm not Marajeshi," Shuster muttered.

"Can't remember the last time a ship actually took me through proper protocols," Kyria said. She inhaled from a delivery mister, a cone-shaped device bristling with wires and tubes that suspended from the low ceiling. The cold spray tasted like fek and clung to her throat.

Remiliat frowned at her. "The Averator was working on a master inoculation in his spare time." She proffered an identical mister to Shuster, who regarded it suspiciously. "Never know what infections await upon any new world, let alone the

Unknown." Her eyes rested on Kyria. "Time for us to sleep now."

Kyria nodded with a casualness she did not feel. "Lead the way."

The crew quarters were lined with long metal nightmare tubes, cold and black. Remiliat began to strip wordlessly. Kyria's gut knotted up. She suppressed a shudder and followed suit.

"Looks like we don't bunk together this time," Shuster whispered. "How are you going to wake up if-?"

"I'll be fine." Kyria flexed her stiff hand as she sidled up to the nearest tube with a tight jaw, aware of Remiliat's eyes on her. Shuster beat her to it, making a show of settling down inside, buying her time. His face was still lined with worry as he watched Kyria through the glass. A puff of relaxant frosted the tube pink, and he was out.

"Surprised you're bedding down with us," Kyria managed as she clambered into the next tube. Her skin pebbled at the cold steel.

"I spend enough time with Paki as it is," Remiliat replied. "Cryo is a welcome respite from the chaos of the Known."

"Good thing we're bound for the Unknown, then."

Remiliat didn't match Kyria's smile as she stared down at her. "You're not fit for the Averator's mission. His vision. He doesn't see it, but I do. You are a broken woman, Arcadian. You've let others down before, and you'll do the same with us if the opportunity arises."

A snarl curled Kyria's lip, but bile stirred in her stomach, too. "You don't know me at all, Remiliat."

"Perhaps. Sweet dreams, Grazer."

"What did you call me?" Kyria's voice went shrill, equal parts furious and frightened. The cryo tube sealed shut, reducing her lunge to palms pressed on the glass. What level of leachware did this woman possess to pull Kyria's call sign-and *where* had she pulled it from?

Remiliat gazed through the glass, her face like a woman viewing the corpse at a stranger's wake before finally turning away.

Kyria's chest grew tight. Her breathing shallowed. The prompt on the glass before her queried for dream inhibitor or stimulator, and she made her selection. Orange mix misted into the tube, stinking faintly of artificial lilac and denatured Element G. She pressed tightly into her palm as the inhibitor took hold.

The synaptic trip circuit embedded there failed to fire.

Way to go Grazheen, you broke more than that guy's tooth! Kyria lost consciousness, plunging into an all-encompassing darkness where the dead woman laughed softly and patiently loaded her rounds.

***

"Raids are the best, rookie." The dead woman's words echoed in Kyria's head, the same as they had a hundred times before. A thousand. Kyria feared it was the only dream she had left. "Especially against close foes. The better they think they know you, the worse you can hurt them."

A full squadron of strangers in outdated assault armor surrounded her, jouncing in their restraints as the dropship hit Junn atmosphere. The Arcadian soldiers' worn metal exoskeletons whirred and clicked as software synced and weapons went live. Kyria felt their gazes through eyes that weren't hers. She felt the lips of another woman bare in a wolfish smile.

Finally, one spoke, too smooth-faced for this mission. A boy in a flying tomb. "Captain, who are you talking to?"

"The milkrat rookie who's getting the honor of experiencing my memories one day," the Captain fired back. Kyria never once saw Shalexa Mercible's face in her dream, though she knew it like her own. "You heard about the memory training?"

"Yeah, heard about the drooling test subjects and procedural inquiries." The sergeant beside Mercible snorted on cue. "You just wanted an excuse to talk to yourself, Cap. Command will never push it past the experimental phase-"

"Mark my words, it'll be standard ops," Mercible interrupted. "And my memories will only go to the top of the class. Real keepers. You hear me, rookie?" Kyria felt Mercible's gloved knuckles rap against her skull. "I want a personal invitation to every medallion ceremony you attend on Arcadia. All of my family sitting here with me, too-so remember their faces. Take care of us. Good seats."

The boy's eyebrows climbed. "You're crazy, Cap!"

"Just now figuring that out?"

Mercible's squadron laughed. Kyria despised the unfeigned fondness in their eyes-a dead woman did not deserve such loyalty. Mercible dropped her voice low, just for Kyria. "Don't worry about them, milkrat. I'll show you what it takes to be a leader. I'm gonna make you famous."

One of their pilots twisted in his chair, the whites visible all around his dark eyes. "Seven birds to our left! We're breaking off the-"

The cockpit erupted in fire. Orange and blue flames licked over the squadron's exoskeletons, setting uniforms alight and blackening their flesh beneath. Mercible screamed as her metal ident-tags seared her chest.

The dropship lurched, plunging into freefall. Mercible's voice came to Kyria's ears. "Report! Who-"

"Captain!" The kid's shrill voice cut her off. Long flames curled over his thighs. He struggled against his seat restraints. "We're breaking apart!"

"You stay in that seat, you hear me?" Mercible bellowed.

The kid ignored her, panicked and blinded by smoke. Kyria watched helplessly through Mercible's eyes as he pulled free of his seat restraints, slapping at the fire. The kid hooted as the flames winked out in a last howl of wind, flashing a relieved smile. His face disintegrated as one last burst of Junn flak tore through the dropship.

The dead woman blacked out in the crash, but Kyria never did. All was still, for a little while.

"Kid?" Mercible asked. Nothing. She opened her eyes, grimly assessing her squadron. All dead, bodies shredded by flak or debris. "Looks like it's just you and me, milkrat." She looked down and whistled softly to herself. "Gotta take a stand somewhere, might as well be here. But this is gonna hurt, rookie."

No. Please, Kyria thought. *I can't.*

A contorted piece of steel hull girding pinned the Captain's thigh just above the knee. Her left leg had twisted around so her heel jutted up where her toes should be.

"I know what you're thinking, rookie," Mercible said with a low laugh. "But it's just flesh. It can be replaced. All a question of pain tolerance."

Mercible grunted as she struggled to yank her Lance free of the nearby debris. The weapon hummed to life, its long blade vibrating dangerously. Kyria wanted to claw her eyes out, but the dream forced her to drink in every detail.

Mercible hissed as she set the Lance's blade across her thigh. Blood bubbled and smoked where it touched the hot metal, boiling away from it. "Whatever you do...don't die alone, rookie." The captain spoke calmly through her gritted teeth. "Not while people are depending on you. Not like this. I forbid it."

***

Kyria awoke with a start. An alarm chimed faintly in the cryo tube. The frosted glass hissed aside. She clambered free, but her legs immediately buckled and the steel plated floor greeted her with a cold kiss. Kyria lay there until the trembling stopped and sensation returned to her legs. A light blinked behind the skin of her palm-her sleep mod had finally kicked in. She'd never had to use it in a cryo tube before.

You hear me, rookie? It's just a leg. You can make a new leg out of the medallions I'm going to get for you. Kyria never spoke the dead woman's name; it only encouraged her to stir. *Now pay attention. Exo-armor can process your new equilibrium better than you can if you lose a limb. Don't fight the balance when-*

"Bad enough I replay it when I'm awake, too," Kyria muttered. She stood, thankful her legs held.

A glance at the open cryo tube's chronometer surprised her. She'd slept just over two weeks; half of their expected flight time. Shuster's measured snoring came loud enough to crack his tube open, but Kyria checked on him anyway, brushing her palm on the frosted glass. *I'm keeping more of my crew alive than*

316

you, Captain. Her argument cheated on numbers, but even a frail truth held some comfort.

Remiliat slept peacefully as well, the first time Kyria had seen her without a scowl. The woman was beautiful, in a fragile kind of way. The only thing missing from her repose was a drill wrench buried in her chest. More *Dubious* crew filled the cryo tubes, except for Zele and Paki.

Kyria rifled through the crew lockers, grinning wryly as she slipped on a standard Cassad suit, much too tight for her tall Arcadian build. She tugged the collar, and the auto seam unspooled more fiber at the shoulders, crotch and hips. Tight enough to show off enough muscle to discourage cowards-while giving anyone else exactly zero handholds in a fight-but still loose enough to breathe.

Kyria laced up her old boots, slipped her remaining volt knuckle in her pocket, then set off to find Zele and explore the rest of her latest home. The *Dubious* had a straightforward, clean simplicity that she grudgingly grew to respect, every surface covered in polished blue composite or steel. Several of the metal doors she passed bore titles she did not understand.

Time Density Acceleration. Amaurotic Matter Conversion. Propriosense Enhancement. Independent Neuron Synthesis. Not even a passing curiosity slowed her pace. Every last room sounded like trouble.

The Averator held a private room close to the observation deck, as Kyria suspected-a typical feature of Cassad design, demonstrating the rigid hierarchy of power. Zele added his own flare to the display; brightly lit panels on either side of the door glowed red: *Caution. No entry without Averator approval.*

Kyria tapped an entry request. The door sprang open without even a summons chime, revealing an impressive room with glossy white composite on every surface. All manner of tools hung from the ceiling, from a shipwright's plasma welder to a medic's laser scalpel-along with a dozen more Kyria could not fathom. The Averator stood with his back to her, humming to himself.

A foul stench snaked into her nostrils, worse than a circuit fire in a waste disposal node. "Zele?" Kyria managed to cough out, holding a hand to her mouth.

The Averator turned away from the broad central work table, staring straight through Kyria as he ambled to one of the smooth white walls. He wore the exact same officer's suit-two weeks' worth of wrinkles left no doubt, though that didn't account for the room's reek. A half-band of coppery metal rested above his ears like a Tar City scrap merchant's circlet. The components scattered across his table made Kyria's heart leap against her ribs.

"You've been working on my armor this whole time?" she asked eagerly. The dark alloy framework of his design looked too smallish, like it would shatter if a Giak warrior backhanded it. "That's supposed to go toe-to-toe with Raptor armor. If you read my specs right you would-"

"Now where did I put that binding protocol?" Zele murmured to himself as he paused, staring at a blank white wall.

Kyria frowned. Surely the man did not sleepwalk. She stepped past the door's threshold, raising her voice. "Zele, did you hear-"

The panel before him abruptly slid out of the wall, draped with a mass of gray flesh. Fluid sloshed on the ground, slopping over the Averator's boots. Tiny points of light glowed pink among the tissue, which looked like a tray of starved Sentrian bloodworms woven together in a thick mat.

Unbidden thoughts and images poured into Kyria's head, all laced with Amadi Zele's probing voice.

Where is it?

Pain flared at Kyria's temples as symbols and equations flooded through her mind's eye.

I must take into account the Arcadian's existing implants. Such an intriguing puzzle. An interface must be designed so there is no cognitive overlap.

Kyria staggered back with a cry, clutching her head.

Her specifications are imperfect. Much better if I design a new alloy, to withstand a higher stress load. What looked like molecules appeared in her mind's eye, torn apart and reassembled a thousand times.

Yes, yes-excellent! These binding protocols will ensure that molecular cohesion is fully-

Her heel caught on the threshold and she spilled back in the hall. The door whisked closed. The flood of information immediately ceased.

Kyria dry heaved so hard that her ribs ached. Her brief interlude with the Averator's chaotic thoughts had even stunned the dead woman into silence. *Ever stop to wonder if there's a good reason you've never heard of an Averator, Grazheen?* Kyria staggered upright. Raw terror fueled her sprint through the empty halls. *He's Cassad, after all. Bred from the same strain as the monsters who thought up the ELE weapon that destroyed Arcadia-only smarter, clearly!*

Kyria ignored her first impulse, to wake Shuster and break into the arms vault together. That made no sense, two weeks into the Unknown. Instead she retraced her steps to the hopper that first brought them aboard. If the Averator proved as insane as she suspected-or Remiliat acted on her disdain-a hopper at least gave Kyria a flash exit if this job went wrong. But only once they were back in the Known.

The hopper floated silently in the wet dock, half-submerged in the Averator's impact gel. Kyria boarded and pried open a control juncture between the pilot's seats. A relieved breath escaped her as she studied the network. Even Cassad ship design reflected their strange blend of ruthlessness and compassion. The *Dubious's* safeguards undoubtedly possessed hack sentinels to prevent incursion bombs and leach-ware from crippling its systems. Yet the hopper owned half as many security features; part of the Cassad mandate to make such craft simple enough for a child to steer if necessary-which meant Kyria could commandeer it with a few mods.

She tersely started reconfiguring base code. Another trick she'd learned from the dead woman, when Mercible hacked the downed dropship's CPU to steal enough power to charge her assault armor.

The better they think they know you, the worse you can hurt them.

Kyria held down her bile and finished the work. She entered the next bay to repeat the operation and stopped with a groan. This wet dock held no hopper, only a massive, transparent reclamation tank filled to the brim with briny water. A pang of guilt stabbed her. Stealing one of the two remaining hoppers consigned half of the Cassad crew to their deaths should they ever truly need to escape the *Dubious*.

"An eyeful of his experiments, and they'll all come with me." Kyria baled at the smell as she drew closer, like meat gone slick with decay. "What else are you hiding, Zele?"

A dark shape swirled up to her in a rush of fetid water. A data pad set into the glass flickered on, but Kyria ignored the white script flashing across the screen. Her fists clenched at the sight of eight powerful tentacles covered with toothy suction cups, each connected to a bulbous green body. *The Averator's studying a bilking irlon!*

The creature's dark skin emitted a series of flashes, sinuous shapes that twisted and rippled, melting into orange, yellow and pink. A meter-thick tentacle burst from the tank, snaking down to loop around her torso.

"What in-"

Kyria's grasp slid right off the irlon's skin. She pounded helplessly on muscle strong enough to bend steel. The tentacle abruptly released her.

"Should've ripped me apart while you had the chance!"

Kyria whipped out her volt knuckle, set it to max damage and heaved it. The metal flashed orange as soon as it hit the surface. White froth churned the brine around it. The irlon rushed her again, spraying water across the bay. A tentacle whipped out at Kyria and the air left her lungs. She hit the ground with a grunt, rolling to a rest near the bay entry.

The door whisked open to reveal polished boots. Kyria peered up at the science officer, staring at her with his orange eyes.

"Rem predicted you wouldn't sleep," Paki said, striding past her as Kyria hastily rose and snapped to attention. Water pooled around her boots. "An alert signaled me of a power disruption. What's happened?"

"Damn thing tried to kill me." Something about the man sat wrong with Kyria as he stopped beside the tank, staring intently into the water.

"I highly doubt that." He waved dismissively for her to relax. "We've no use for military protocol here, Arcadian. This creature is-"

Water slopped over the edge as the creature surged for the glass. "Look out!" Kyria shouted.

A tentacle looped out, ensnaring Paki as it had Kyria. He peered at her reproachfully, as if the tentacle drooped over him were natural as a uniform.

"There's nothing to fear. Consider this...a handshake."

Paki frowned at the blisters along the motley green skin before his face. "Amadi should've considered the avarice an Arcadian might bear for distant cousins of-"

"That thing isn't irlon?"

"No. His name is...unpronounceable in our language. Their ship was found in the Unknown." The tentacle peeled away from him delicately and submerged again. The creature retreated into the murk.

"Perfect. There's fresh fek to step in on every meter of this ship, isn't there?" Kyria edged forward as Paki pressed his palm on the glass. Dim orange flashes emanated from the furthest corner of the tank.

"You've wounded our guide to the Stack, Kyria. Badly." Paki shook his head gravely. "He's twice offered course correction to steer us clear of the irradiated zones of this nebula."

Kyria's blood ran cold. "These things are not to be trusted. I'd never have come if I'd known."

"It's of little matter if you wished to leave us now," Paki said. "There are no shipping lanes near our coordinates. The Averator almost jettisoned another of our hoppers to make room for more experimental space, but we've just enough room for our crew if escape pods become necessary. Zele holds his work above all, but cares deeply for everyone's welfare aboard the *Dubious*."

"That's comforting." Kyria flushed, unable to meet Paki's gaze. "You've been awake the entire time too, haven't you? Do you spend your free time in some meat locker like the Averator?"

Paki stiffened. "You entered his study?" At Kyria's nod, his eyes widened. "Never go in there again, do you understand? He's developed an organic perception array, to store data and prioritize different reason problems. Including your armor."

"You're saying he's built a...an extension to his brain?"

"His own personal hive mind. It allows him to go without sleep, among other things. The organic projections would drive anyone else quite mad."

Kyria's mouth went dry. *His own personal bilking hive mind. This is the man building my armor? Who plans to change the Known?*

Paki straightened at another set of irlon flashes in the water, brighter and urgent.

"What is it?" Kyria asked.

"We're nearing the Stack, a week sooner than projected." Paki hesitated as he turned back to Kyria. "I must wake the crew. You realize I must also report this incident to Zele and Remiliat. Answer me honestly...are you a spy for the New Regime?"

"No," Kyria muttered. "I just...made a stupid move."

"Our allegiance to the Cassad hinges on Zele's mood, but until he says otherwise, you will consider this a Cassad ship. Please do not attempt to kill any more of our essential personnel, Kyria. The Averator believes your skills will be important to his mission, but Remiliat has no qualms about your expulsion."

"I still haven't been assigned any duties here," Kyria retorted. "I'm no scientist, and your only crew problem is numbers."

Paki shrugged as he walked out. "I trust his acumen. Even on those disastrous occasions when it fails us."

***

Zele ordered his entire crew to the observation deck as soon as they shook off the cryo fatigue; apparently some Cassad tradition that he insisted on that hailed back to when they were still conquering the Known. Kyria suspected the way the Averator's eyes flashed as he conferred quietly with Remiliat and Paki did not bode well for her at all.

Shuster ambled over to where Kyria stood alone, shoving a plate and cup into her hands. "You make it really damn hard to stick by you sometimes, you know that?"

"I know." Kyria sipped her water, wishing for something stronger.

"I've yet to meet an Arcadian who's over what happened to your world. It was on you and the Forty-Sixth to protect it, so that makes you twice as twisted up."

"You gonna rub the training dreams in my face, too?"

"No, but thanks for cinching my argument." He smiled across the deck as he spoke. The Averator nodded back graciously. Shuster had managed to rig the ship filtration system to infuse their water with carbon bubbles, and even added some spice to the special rations Zele had set aside for his impending triumph. That was Shuster's way; he made friends wherever he went.

"I'm doing the best I can, all right?" Kyria found her hands shaking. "By all means, you can go and-"

"You're not going to finish that sentence," Shuster cut in roughly. "You gotta heal, Kyria. You're scared to take charge of anything, especially your own life. Saving up credits, designing some damn armor in case Pack Loren himself comes after you? I get it. Just make sure you remember to take it off after Zele builds it, okay?" One of the crew began fiddling with a heating gauge on the food trays, and he stomped off. "Damn it, get away from that! You want to lose your eyebrows?"

"If Zele builds it," Kyria murmured.

The trio of officers broke their meeting. The Atunbé woman flashed Kyria a ghastly smile, folding her arms expectantly. Zele strode right up to Kyria, and she faced him squarely. The scattered Cassad crew stilled expectantly.

"Arcadian-"

A proximity alert forestalled him. The deck's massive viewscreen revealed the last dusty contrails of the nebula, dispersing to reveal a dense carpet of Unknown stars. Zele's lips quirked in an almost smile. "Fortuitous timing. Unless you hacked my ship's sensors along with the hopper?"

Kyria's tongue caught in her throat. "I-"

"Nothing in the Known occurs without an Averator's knowledge," Zele said mysteriously. The effect was wasted when he pulled at his mustache, staring eagerly at the data streaming across the viewscreen. "That rule holds especially true aboard my own ship."

Kyria shrugged. "Good thing for me we're in the Unknown."

"Time will tell, Arcadian. We'll speak soon enough."

A gentle lurch signaled the *Dubious* dropping out of its jump. Kyria felt foolish looking through the viewport like the rest of the crew, as if the King of the Known was going to ride out of the star's center with a chariot and handful of figs to greet them.

"Three worlds in this system. Preliminary telemetry indicates...they share the same orbital plane." Genuine awe cracked Remiliat's voice. "They essentially form the points of a triangle around the parent star. Equilateral."

"Perfection," Zele breathed. "Undoubtedly inhabited." He turned to the crew, giving Kyria a wink as his baritone swept through the observation deck. "Most of you hail from worlds where the Cassad Empire built monuments to their greatness. Before us lies a star system unlike any other-one that is constructed. There are three stars in this formation, perfectly aligned on the galactic axis, according to our guide; this is the centermost of them. You each bear witness to possible evidence of a precursor to the Cassad Empire, an intelligence in power during the Dark Age. We're here to determine the truth of this."

Astonished whispers filtered through Zele's crew. "But there was nothing before the Cassad," Julet muttered in disbelief. "That's what the lesson masters taught us in academy."

Kyria exchanged an impressed nod with Shuster as she sidled closer. "By the All," he said. "Sure is something, if it's true."

"A piece of history," Kyria whispered. She could not remember the last time she'd felt eager for anything more than a bottle of Cloudspittle, or another chunk of credits stashed aside for her armor. She wanted a place in this mission, somewhere. "It'll shake the Known if it's true."

They looked on silently as the *Dubious* pulled closer to the Stack's central star.

"You did it, sir," Paki said to Zele, his fingers flashing over a data pad.

"We did it," Zele corrected. "This is a monumental step for us all. The Known's greatest discovery and my second greatest achievement." Zele clapped the younger man on the shoulder. "Now the real work begins."

"Averator..." The tension in Remiliat's voice drew everyone's gaze. "Data is coming in from the sensors. The worlds may have been inhabited once, but there's nothing there. They're desolate."

"What?" Zele snapped. "That's unacceptable. We're not at a proper range to-"

Alert klaxons cut him off. Warning lights bathed the observation deck in red. Trajectory lines transposed over the black of space displayed on the forward monitor, converging on a point orbiting the star.

Paki frowned at his display. "There's another ship out there. The star's corona shielded it from us before."

"What?" Zele snapped his attention to the nearest console, face suddenly slack. Cold sweat clung to Kyria's back as Zele's hands flew over the controls. "Determine the origin at once! If the Brython somehow..."

"Pinging it now," Remiliat replied.

Alarm quivered in Kyria's gut, too loud to ignore. "Stop. There's no telling how it will-"

"Already done." Paki looked between Remiliat and Zele, concerned. "Shall I prepare jump coordinates should it prove-"

"Calm yourselves. There are no signs of activity." Remiliat's expression promised words for Kyria later. "It's derelict, Averator. We'll ask the irlon after he's...recovered, to be certain."

"Thank the Known," Zele breathed, straightening in relief. The deck's display reverted to the green of normal scans as he made soothing gestures for the crew's benefit. "Apologies for the excitement. We'll begin active scans of the nearest planet and determine landing sites for our remote drones by the end of this ship cycle. Attend to your work stations."

None of the crew moved an inch. Kyria tensed as Shuster shuffled forward, clearing his throat.

"With all due respect, Averator-the *Dubious* isn't a Cassad ship any longer. Half of us are stragglers, and a few of us are homeless after Efalus Six."

Kyria never saw Paki leave his station, but he suddenly stood before Zele and Shuster as though he felt no need to bother with the intervening space. He faced down over two dozen crewmen with no trace of alarm in his orange eyes. "You'll be paid as agreed," he said in cool precision.

Remiliat settled into a stance beside Paki, face clouded in fury. "Arcadian, I'll see you expelled into that star's corona if you've intended mutiny this entire-"

"I had nothing to do with this!" Kyria threw up her hands, shooting an accusing look at Shuster. She stepped between both groups. "I can't believe I'm saying this, but I want to see this mission through!"

Shuster stared at them all before breaking out into a huge guffaw. "By the Known, that isn't...this isn't how it looks. I'm sorry. What I meant to say is, for all intents and purposes...we're a mercenary crew. We've no itch to captain-except maybe Kyria. I don't know if we'll ever understand what we're doing for the Averator out here, although I'm sure it's important."

Zele arched an eyebrow. "What a relief to know you don't intend to murder us in our sleep for the simple act of hiring you. What are you suggesting?"

"That ship out there...by derelict law is salvage." Most of the crew nodded in agreement as Shuster continued. "There's a cut of that for all of us, in case Cassad credits go to fek. Kyria's getting something solid in payment. Why shouldn't we?"

"I retain all data and tech," Zele said immediately.

Kyria jumped as Paki strode to a terminal and began inputting commands. *The man is bilking fast.*

Shuster shook his head doggedly. "That's the most valuable-"

"For research and with final say." Zele bulled right over him. "Basic mechanism of the ship, pods, scrap, munitions, Element G-the ship itself, if any of you are qualified to pilot it-are yours after my sweep."

"We split rights to the tech," A Marajeshi crewman called out. "If you go sell it off to-"

"The highest bidder?" Zele laughed. "The New Regime, who may kill us all for our trouble? Or the Cassad, with empire credits that may not be worth a bottle of Cloudspittle by the time we return?"

Zele swept his gaze over the crew. Kyria was not the only one to flinch before the man's sheer intensity, and she chastised herself for not seeing the danger there before. "Make no mistake. I am of the Cassad. But if the upstarts of the New Regime supplant the empire entirely, my work will go on. I've no time to be a... ship monger. Take it off to the Targothan Graveyards after I'm finished with it, for all I care-if you make it that far."

Shuster looked around, and saw nothing but nervous nods of agreement. "Fair and settled." He spat in his palm and extended it.

Zele peered at him with a bemused look. "I think not. Paki?"

"Crew salvage terms updated." The first mate returned with a data pad. "Agree here."

"Your duties are still required of you," Remiliat added coolly. "Any digression, and that ship will be your new home, whatever its condition."

One by one the crew shuffled forward to the contract. Kyria earned a reproachful look from Paki as she came up last. "You are surprising, Arcadian," he said. "You profess an interest in our mission in one instant, and then concede to a petty salvage squabble in the next. For one who has lost so much, wouldn't-"

"I never leave credits unclaimed," Kyria replied. She caught the Averator's eyes as she extended her hand to verify the salvage terms. "There's no guarantee you've found what you think. And this doesn't affect our original agreement."

Zele nodded, suddenly eager. "I've given much thought to your particular puzzle, Arcadian. Once we've completed this survey, I'll be happy to show you my-"

"A ping just came back," Remiliat announced, frowning intently at her station. "Data encryption is processing. Cassad most likely, but it's not recognizing our handshake. There's a name, at least. *Desecratia.*"

Zele's eyes went wide in shock. Shuster swore under his breath. Remiliat looked at them in confusion. "I've never heard of such a ship."

Kyria's palm tingled above the data pad. She jerked her hand away too late. Officially bound to the salvage agreement, she let out a defeated laugh. "Don't fathers read to their daughters on Atunbé?" she asked. "It's one of the Three Dooms."

***

Kyria zipped up her incursion gear back in the crew quarters. Shuster sat silently before the locker next to her, watching her dress when he thought she wasn't looking. "Let's get this over with. Paki's leading the salvage appraisal. I've got the feeling he doesn't take kindly to tardiness."

Shuster stared at his boots. "I'm not going with you. Zele's orders."

Kyria stopped. "What?"

"We drew straws. Some are headed over, but most are helping prep for the planet survey."

"I didn't get to draw straws!"

"Come on, Grazer. Is there any doubt where you'll end up in this kind of stuff?"

"I should clout you."

"Wouldn't be the first time." Shuster grinned. "Bring me back a souvenir." His face grew serious when Kyria didn't return his smile. "Don't tell me you've bought into this talk about the Doom. It's a cradle fable!" Shuster stood, pacing as Kyria laced up her boots. "A stupid rumor the Cassad let drift around the worlds they conquered to keep everyone in line. *'Revolt in the night or spit at the Cassad, and a Doom will take flight with a chastening rod.'* As if a battle platform could just show up in orbit. We gobbled that doctrine whole as kids before we even knew how gravity wells worked!"

"Normally, I'd agree with you." They exited the crew quarters for the wetdock. Kyria cursed herself for the seventh time for leaving her remaining Forty-Sixth gear behind on Efalus Six. "Except there's a ship out there named Desecratia orbiting one of Zele's precious rocks. Did you see the pre-specs? Battle platform doesn't even come close...it's a true-to-death siegenought! Do you know what a ship like that will mean to the Cassad? To the New Regime? The Averator's right-salvage for that thing is a death sentence. The minute you make it back to the Known, people will tear it apart. And we'll be caught in the flak."

"Leave the siegenought aside for a minute." Shuster shook his head. "The stuff Zele's saying, about the Dark Age...maybe it's enough to get people to look at the Known in a different light. Stop the war, even."

"The war's bigger than any one person," Kyria said with a sigh. "I don't trust him, either-so quick to insist on the tech rights. He's Cassad. If that ship's what it's supposed to be, we're better off steering it into that sun."

"Not before I get paid," Shuster grumbled. "Besides, there's no way to be sure it's a Doom."

Kyria stopped short. "There might be."

She abruptly changed direction, hurrying down a different corridor. Shuster followed hesitantly as Kyria led him back to the bay set aside for the irlon. His scowl deepened as the door whisked aside, revealing the irlon's tank. "Is that...you trying to get me thrown out of an airlock, too?"

"Just look out for Paki while I-"

"Bilk off, Kyria." Coldness settled into Shuster's eyes, one Kyria knew well from her own reflection. "You're losing it."

"Shuster-"

He abruptly marched off. Kyria kissed her teeth in frustration, but made her way into the bay. Tentative pink and white tones issued from the water's shadows. Kyria typed her phrase into the glass's data pad. *What do you know about a ship at the Stack?* An overhead light flashed her query into the water, mimicking the irlon's strange visual language.

Kyria waited. "Come on, you slime-eating cephalopod!" The water remained dark, betraying not so much as a ripple. She moved off with an oath. A splash touched her ears, and the nape of her neck sizzled hot. She yelped and spun around. The irlon had thrown her volt knuckle at her!

A burst of orange light issued from the water. The anger drained out of Kyria as she read, worse than if the irlon grabbed her, the same word over and over again as the irlon flashed.

Death.

"Should've converted with the Knight, Grazheen." Kyria pocketed her knuckle and hurried to the wetdock.

* * *

The Desecratia's dark hull stretched for kilometers, a slim frame of cruel angles with turrets and missile arrays covering every available surface. Kyria swallowed as the hopper fell under the ship's shadow.

A yawning cavity dominated the central mass. Angular metal protrusions surrounded it, so the fore and aft halves resembled an array of wicked eagle talons grasping for each other without quite touching. The ship appeared whole despite such a bizarre configuration, as if its designers had chosen against giving the siegenought a heart.

Paki studied the HUD wordlessly, not offering a single word of confidence as his salvage crew gaped through the hopper's portholes. The siegenought accepted the hopper's softdock query. *So even if it's not Cassad origin, it responds to Cassad protocols.* Kyria didn't know if that was a good sign or not.

The outer ship clamps hissed into place. Kyria's stomach lurched as Paki immediately strode for the airlock. "Shouldn't we prep our gills?" she asked. "No guarantee of atmo in there."

Paki blinked. "Of course, Arcadian. A good precaution."

The other crewmen stole grateful looks at Kyria as they helped each other loop the emergency breathers around the necks of their dark blue incursion suits; lightweight composite that proved tougher than it looked.

One of the Cassad latched Kyria's gills into place without asking. "Glad to know one of us is actually trained for this work," he murmured gratefully.

Kyria shrugged and checked her Pacifier H22, a standard Cassad shock trooper's rifle. The others had chosen lesser sidearms, either afraid of the smart rounds or too stupid to know it was the best weapon. "That's why I'm here..." She cast about for the Cassad's name. "Julet."

Julet blinked as she deftly tapped new configurations into the Pacifier's guidance defaults, then clicked on her suit's atmo gauge, wrist mapper and threat filters. Fresh readouts poured over the clear faceplate of her helmet.

"You realize I'm sticking to your hip through this, right?" he asked, mimicking her.

"Watch out for yourself, Cassad. My hip pocket isn't the best place to be."

"Says who?"

"Says Arcadia."

Julet's smile slipped as the airlock hissed open. The crew followed Paki through the airlock without a hint of precision. An automated rail cutter stationed in a cross corridor could wipe them all out without even burning through fifty rounds. Everyone except Paki, at least.

He led them swiftly through the derelict, a warren of halls that suddenly opened into cavernous terraces full of workstations, or ran past micro-arcologies of stacked crew quarters. Kyria never let up her tension for an ambush, and refused to remove her gills despite the solid atmo readings. Ellin left hers on, but Julet and a few others removed them after a taste of Paki's pace.

"Forget the armaments," Julet whispered, rubbing his hands together as if the credits were already issued to his account. "Imagine what we'll pull off the Element-G needed to jump a ship of this size?"

"Who told you to holster?" Kyria asked curtly. Julet grudgingly pulled his weapon back out.

"Three of them, you know. The Dooms." The brick-shaped Euphrates-born mercenary that the crew called Perk nodded thoughtfully. "The Cassad never let more than one stay in the Known at any given time. Too much of a threat."

"Hey Paki, you mean to search the whole thing in a day?" Ellin called out.

"If I must," he replied. "The sooner this is complete, the sooner we pursue our real work on the planet's surface."

"Likely this ship already razed the planet," Perk said. He snapped his jaw shut when Paki frowned back at him.

"Pace up and chatter down," Kyria said. "I don't want to see your shadows' lips move, clear?"

The ship was massive, and searching it at Paki's tireless clip soon had Kyria sweating. She had never seen an actual battle platform, except for study back in military school. The All-damned siegenought dwarfed the specs she remembered-it rivaled some jump gates in size. *Someone's gotta be checking on it, for it to maintain sync orbit. But who? I saw in Zele's eyes, he didn't even know it existed.*

Paki suddenly halted before a black metal door, rigid as a Marajeshi seeker wolf that had just sniffed out an edible blood type.

"What do we got?" Kyria asked. A panel inset into the steel wall had been retrofitted over an older panel, glowing faintly with a Cassad code dialect she'd never seen before. "Paki, talk to us."

"Research and advancement." A few quick taps and the door responded. Julet, Ellin and a few others jumped as a metallic screeching echoed down the hall.

"Guide rails must be rusted out," Perk offered.

Kyria ground her teeth as Paki entered with no deployment orders, not so much as checking his corners. The man acted like he was invincible, or else utterly convinced the ship was abandoned. The crushing emptiness of the *Desecratia* had made them all overconfident.

They entered a monstrous room with a ceiling high overhead. A long row of research bays marched away from them, some sizable enough to hold the *Dubious* itself.

Paki's lips pressed together as he took in the space. "We must conserve time," he announced. "Arrange yourselves into pairs. We may not be able to strip all the available data of a ship this size, so research takes first priority."

Kyria bit her lip as the others began to split up. Julet approached, but Perk nudged her first. "Looks like it's you and me," he said with a leer.

Normally Kyria would leer back, but their commanding officer's stupid orders had her tense. "You remember the way out of this bilk hole?"

"I remember how much I liked watching you put those gills on, squish."

Squish? "I've never been to Euphrates." Kyria decided his lips made up for the double iris. "You'll have to tell me what that means when we finish up here."

"Easier to show you. I like that hair, think I'll call you Blue." Perk paused for a moment. "Unless the cook is..."

"He's Zele's crew...not mine." Kyria gave a bitter laugh, and Perk shrugged.

"Thought we were all Zele's crew."

The salvage team spread out. Paki ended up with a sour-faced Julet, who entered a bay directly across from the entry.

Kyria motioned Perk to a bay that looked nearly barren. No ominous tools-or Averator's spare brain matter stuffed into the walls. Just bare workspace and terminals. All perfectly clean, just like every other meter of the ship.

"Pretty boring," Perk mentioned grumpily.

"Exactly why I picked it," Kyria retorted. "Boring usually means alive."

Perk nudged one of the displays. Kyria swore as an axial grid powered on. A miniature hologram of the *Desecratia*-rendered down to its rivets-rotated silently before them. "Why'd you do that?" she snapped. "You stupid, botch-eyed-"

"Downright ghoulish, she is," Perk marveled. He waved a hand through the intricate hologram. Flesh sizzled, and he pulled it back with a yelp. "Every bit of this ship is made for pain. We didn't even see the bomb bays on the way in-look at those soul rakers. Ordinance like that will turn mountains into mass graves. You see anything like that on Arcadia, Blue? I'll bet you did."

"Careful, Euphrates," Kyria said, typing into the interface. "You'll never get a kiss like that."

A simulation ran. Dark light pulsed in the middle of the *Desecratia* hologram, a pulsing vortex that crackled and licked at the ship's hull. Finally, a black point spread from the siegenought's hollowed middle, yawning open until it consumed the ship.

"By the All..." Kyria's jaw dropped. The hologram winked out, replaced by a data stream that confirmed-

"What?" Paki's demanding voice bade her to turn on leaden feet. "What did you find?"

"This ship has a self-destruct," Perk said blankly. "Some Doom it is. Not sure why Blue is all spooked."

"Thought we tripped it," Kyria lied.

Paki took in her quivering knees. "I'll take over here," he said. "The next bay over may interest you, Arcadian. Some sort of experimental armor compound. For ship plating, I believeperhaps we can use it to allay your concerns about the *Dubious*."

Right that moment, not even a custom build of Raptor armor would stop Kyria's gut from clenching. Perk was too stupid to realize what the *Desecratia* had just shown them. Paki immediately restarted the simulation as they left him. He would soon understand why this ship truly was a Doom, and undoubtedly report it to Zele. Bile licked the back of Kyria's throat.

By the All, if the Cassad were evil enough to build some-thing that can do this, I'm glad they're on the cusp. A new determination settled within her, exhilarating and terrifying. *Some worlds will get it worse than Arcadia if any of this tech gets back to the Known. I can't trust Zele to do what's right.*

A sudden scream echoed through the research wing. Julet sprinted straight for them, his eyes wide around as bell-fruit. More of the crewmen ran right behind him.

"That shriek come out of you, Cassad?" Perk's lips curled in amusement.

"There's a damned irlon in one of those bays!" he shouted. "It just rose up, like-"

"Everyone to me," Paki commanded, striding into the main thoroughfare between the bays.

"You heard him, form a rank in case it's hostile." Tightness rippled through Kyria's shoulders as the salvage team pulled back together.

"Friends of your guide?" Perk asked Paki dryly. "Too bad Blue tried to cook ours up for dinner, or they could talk."

"Shut up," Kyria snapped.

"Perhaps," Paki replied, peering into the poorly lit bays. "Keep your weapons holstered for the moment."

The squad finally formed a line, although one ragged enough to make Kyria grimace; and get any squad leader in the Forty-Sixth stripped of their rank and sent to scrape hulls in a vacuum.

Perk looked a question at Kyria. She nodded. They wordlessly took flanking positions on either side of the Cassad line, positioning themselves behind the nearest bay walls. Ellin and one other started to mimic them, until Kyria held up a hand.

"Stay there!" she hissed. Idiot Cassad. Best drilled shock troops in the Known-except for Marajeshi diamond reavers-but their auxiliary personnel were helpless. Hopefully they didn't manage to shoot holes in their incursion suits.

Paki stepped forward, one hand open. "We mean you no harm," he called out. How the man expected to speak with an ir-lon was beyond Kyria. A series of flashes from the darkness made her jaw tighten.

"You understand that? What's it saying?" The flashes were nothing like she had seen from Zele's guide. The colors were off, sickly green and an eye-wrenching blue; they pulsed through rigid geometric shapes fast enough to make Kyria's eyes hurt. A looping tentacle whipped forward, pulling a nightmare body behind it.

"Get back, commander!" Kyria shouted. More of the creature's legs slithered out, covered with bristling suckers that screeched against the metal. The irlon slid forward at a drunken rate, deceptively quick. Paki stared at the ceph's flashing body, transfixed and unmoving.

I want a personal invitation to every medallion ceremony you attend on Arcadia. The dead woman snapped Kyria out of her trance. She trained her Pacifier on the irlon, just where the legs met the body.

"Hostile target identified!" she shouted. "Open fire!"

The mishmash of weapons drilled into the creature. Julet and the other Cassads' low-level energy stunners slowed it. Kyria's first shot took a leg completely off at the base.

"No!" Paki screamed.

Perk and all the rest ignored him. The Euphratian's ancient sonic driver peppered the ceph with charged pellets. One specialist in Raptor armor would have laughed off the entire volley, but this irlon was exposed, except for a silvery sheen that covered the bulk of its squid body-nothing resembling armor.

The creature dropped with a wet shriek, tentacles splaying and whipping about until it finally lay still. Blood and darker ink oozed over the metal gridded floor. Julet whooped, and the other Cassad lowered their guns with nervous laughs. At least until they noticed Kyria and Perk. They hastily snapped their guns back up, despite Paki's scowl. The man had never drawn.

"It is quite dead, Arcadian," he snapped, planting himself in their line of fire. "The communication it attempted was-"

He stopped. The creature did not quite stir, but its body somehow sagged, as if a last gasp before dying shuddered through the dark flesh. "It's still breathing," Perk called out anxiously. "Maybe we can-"

336

A sense of wrongness tugged at Kyria's gut. "Irlon don't breathe."

Sooty mist filled the air around the creature, shining and glittering silver wherever the muted light of the science bays touched it. Kyria backed away on instinct.

Perk grunted. "Smells worse than a fungal reclamator. That's a new one." He glanced at the rest of them and jerked as his eyes settled on Julet.

"What?" the Cassad frowned at him.

Kyria edged closer to check him out, then glanced at her threat filters. "Anyone else reading a rad leak in here?" she asked. Paki blinked, and the rest shook their heads. Kyria eyed Julet cautiously. "You're browning by the second, my friend."

"This is some joke because I've never shot a stunner before, right?" Julet smirked, wiping his cheek. Kyria's eyes widened. A pale streak stood out where his hand had touched. He gaped at his hand in horror. "My faaaace..."

His words ended in a high-pitched shriek as his face continued to darken. Not a radiation burn. Pinpricks of blood squeezed through his pores.

"Plague." The word escaped Kyria's lips.

Perk cupped his mouth protectively. His bearded skin sloughed off up to the cheekbones, like the bloated peel of a too-ripe moonfruit. Kyria would never kiss those lips after all. Perk staggered to her, holding out the bloody mass of flesh and hair and skin in his open hand. "Bluuueee..."

Kyria puked, even as she staggered back out of his reach. A scream tore out of her lungs as her skin prickled. She felt as though every drop of Cloudspittle she had ever swallowed had leached through her pores and set on fire. She took two strides forward and unloaded smart rounds until the irlon's body resembled a ruptured cyst of blackened pus. The strange mist continued to disperse.

Paki dropped to the floor, his entire body lost to convulsions. Cassad howls filled the Desecratia. Ellin clawed at the gills around her neck, they were filling with crimson. "Arcadian, help me!"

Kyria tore her eyes away. "Back to the ship, crewmen!" She risked a shout, fearing her tongue might drop away. "Move!"

A few of the Cassad tried to comply, but bent in fits of screaming as the gills cleaved right through their cheeks, their necks. *They're all gone.* Kyria lurched into a run.

"Kyria Grazheen..." Paki struggled to rise, reaching for help. The irlon's poison cloud now drifted through the air with purpose-by the All, it was settling on Julet and Perk! Their bodies twitched and danced like they were infested by Targothan spark lice.

Remember their faces. Take care of us.

Kyria cursed and grabbed Paki's arm. A relieved sob escaped her when his skin held fast. He weighed enough to make her spine pop, but she was Arcadian. She hefted him to his feet. "On your feet, Paki! I can't carry you the whole damn way!"

His mouth opened, but no words came out as Kyria dragged him through the bay doors. A ship alarm peeled through the *Desecratia's* halls.

The promise of death helped Paki find some balance. He stumbled less and ran more. Echoed memories of the crewmen's screams chased Kyria all the way back to the hopper. *We're Arcadian*, the dead woman admonished. *We don't leave family behind.*

"So much for salvage," Kyria whispered. Her hands shook at the controls. "Tell me you're all right."

Paki's orange eyes only offered a vacant stare. Kyria considered expelling him from the hopper's airlock. He had seen the *Desecratia's* true nature. She bit her lip as the hopper shot back to the *Dubious*, and Paki watched her decide whether to kill him or not. She reluctantly decided against it. Better for a superior to explain why everyone on the salvage team was dead.

***

The *Dubious's* bay doors didn't budge as the hopper drew close. Kyria began to sweat as a console flickered on to show Zele's scowl and Remiliat's intense stare.

Kyria preempted them. "Everyone's dead, except me and Paki," she said. "Some sort of biological countermeasures. Paki's still reeling from it, or he'd tell you himself."

"A *biological* contaminant? That would mean-" Remiliat's eyebrows climbed her forehead. "Replay the events exactly!"

"We're not sick. The hopper swept our vitals clean. We're wasting time. That ship is dangerous!"

"Yes, yes," Zele said soothingly. "Give us a moment to think this through."

The channel abruptly muted. Kyria wiped a hand over her scalp in frustration. Her eyes widened at sight of the glittering blue flecks on her palm. Hair follicles. Stained blue from Tar City, like indigo powder from a spent smart round. *Am I sick?* She licked her lips, glancing back at Zele. No way they had seen that on the monitor.

Paki gazed at her silently, working his mouth open and closed as if rediscovering his tongue. Kyria held a finger to his lips. After a moment he repeated the gesture. He doesn't want them to know how messed up he is either, she thought bitterly. *Hair falling out and a trauma mute...what a pair we make.*

The monitor's audio flicked back on. "Upflash your mission data," Remiliat ordered.

"You'll get it all when we're aboard!" Kyria shot back.

Remiliat snarled in exasperation and turned to Zele. "If you would just allow me to-"

"Absolutely not," he said firmly. "Kyria, this is not the time to be secretive. I've trusted you a great deal, and now you must reciprocate. I don't take what's happened to my people lightly. We're from every corner of the Known, but we're family."

A knot formed in Kyria's chest as she decided to believe him. "Listen to me. The siegenought is more than a ship-that maw in the center? It's a fully functional jump gate. We both saw the simulation." She swallowed and glanced at Paki. His orange gaze offered no guidance. "What's worse...it can jump right on top of a damn planet. They were looking for ways to beat the gravity well threshold, and this ship does it. No ship in the Known can do that."

"Intriguing." Zele rubbed his chin. Remiliat at least possessed enough sense to look ready to throw up.

Kyria watched the Averator closely as she chose her next words. "So what do you propose we do with it?"

"Permission to board, Averator." Paki's voice grated out, making Kyria jump. "We're fully capable of returning to duty. Quarantine the wetdock if you desire additional safety precautions. We have much more to report."

Zele and Remiliat exchanged a long look. "Arcadian," he said quietly. "What do you advise regarding this ship?"

Kyria did not hesitate. "Destroy it."

"I had sincerely hoped you thought along that course," Zele said.

Kyria gawked at him, speechless. *He's not a monster. And he's relieved I'm not a monster.*

Remiliat cleared her throat. "However, we cannot lift the quarantine upon the ship until we understand what happened to our crew. You understand."

Paki inhaled sharply. "Sir, this course of action is a mistake. I do not believe-"

"Paki, you are ill-suited for such a task," Zele interrupted, colder than Kyria had ever seen him. "Kyria Grazheen, you are hereby promoted to the rank of executive officer and second in command. This new mission takes all precedence over the Stack."

"Sir?" A lump rose in Kyria's throat. The hopper's console flashed green. She affirmed her helix signature, once again signing her life away over a Doom. "The *Dubious* could never even carry enough ordinance to dent the siegenought. It needs to be destroyed from within."

"Very well, Arcadian. We'll await your instruction on how we can be of assistance."

"I'm sorry I was offensive with you earlier," Remiliat added abruptly. Her attention shifted to Paki, and her demeanor returned to the frost Kyria knew so well. "Crewman, assist your superior however she requires. Understood?"

Paki's eyes flashed. "Yes, sir."

Remiliat and Zele exchanged a long look before the monitor winked out. *Never visit a grave twice*, her father had told her as a child. Every muscle in Kyria's back tensed as she turned the hopper back around. "No hard feelings, all right?"

Paki's face remained still as he stared at the *Desecratia's* shadow. "A mistake on my part, soon rectified."

Something about his voice forestalled Kyria's reply. *Think, Grazheen.* Zele and Paki shared a genuine protégé relationship from what little she had seen. Why all but disown him now? And Remiliat, practically acting like she had served with the Forty-Sixth! *I'm sorry I was so offensive with you.*

Everything fell into place. The bizarre behavior, the refusal to let them board. Paki. Zele wanted to split her away from Paki. *To keep him from me, or me from him?*

Kyria chose a softdock well distant from the first one they had entered. Once again, the hopper locked into place. "We go together this time," she said to Paki, checking her Pacifier. "Watch each other's backs."

The airlock hissed open. He strode out without replying. Kyria hurried after with a scowl. "Listen, a field promotion doesn't mean you're out of the family, I've just got more experience..."

Her words drifted off as they exited the softdock. The siegenought's warning klaxon had ceased, but Kyria's warden tech alerts were all screaming at her. "The ship's powering itself up."

"Yes." Paki's voice floated back to her down the hall. "Counter insurgency cycle, and jump gate sequencing."

Kyria aimed her Pacifier and squeezed. She didn't need to know how Paki knew that; only that he shouldn't. An electric flash pulsed around Paki as the smart rounds took him in the ribs. He slumped forward, but didn't drop.

"Oh, fek." Kyria swallowed as he turned around. Glowing orange wires dangled out of the exit wound under his right pectoral muscle. Fluorescent blue coolant leaked down his ruined incursion suit. "You're an All-damned android?"

"I am not the construct Paki 8HN-1C." Kyria's remaining rounds opened blue plumes in his chest, but Paki didn't even break stride as he rushed forward to grasp her neck. "I am as far above him as he is above you."

Kyria's jaw creaked as her sight faded, but no words came.

"This ship is death," Paki said. Coolant dribbled from his lips, staining his precise goatee a dark blue. "I will escape to the sector of origination. You will help me find the Known."

"No..." Kyria said, struggling vainly in his grip. Her entire body shook, but not in terror of the cold intent in Paki's orange eyes. She was not afraid to die. Only to sleep.

***

Kyria's dream ran free through her mind, a psychotic old friend that had finally popped the last seam of a dementia coat. She drifted in and out of consciousness, struggling to wake up. A faint awareness of Paki clung to her, dragging her limp body by the ankle deeper into the *Desecratia*.

Whatever you do...don't die alone, rookie. Not while people are depending on you. Not like this. I forbid it.

The sear of the Lance cutting through Mercible's leg jerked Kyria back to face the dream. They howled together as the captain's femur gave way with a loud crack that echoed through the wrecked dropship. The remaining flesh sliced away easily, still impaled on the dropship's innards.

Mercible lost herself in a gibbering moan. She clenched her teeth, and it was time for the second leg. The dead woman's sobs deepened, pouring into an all-consuming loss that consumed her and Kyria both.

"There, that wasn't so bad. Gonna miss that blood. Gonna need it. We're Arcadian. We don't leave family behind." The captain tapped adjustments into her wrist-nav, calibrating the exo-armor to account for the lost weight. "Think they'll give me a medallion back on Arcadia, rookie? For walking without legs?"

The dead woman's mutterings poured through Kyria's dream. Her breath grew ragged as she teased out her armor's new mass ratios, glancing from time to time at her severed legs. "Still with me, milkrat?" she whispered. "If I can do this, you can do anything. We held off on the stims until now for a good reason. On your feet."

Mercible plunged the cold needle of a medical stimulant into her neck. A cry tore from her throat as she surged to her feet. The exoskeleton trembled for a moment, syncing to her new equilibrium. The captain took a step forward, closer to where the dawn of a Junn sun shone through the shattered cockpit. "Time to get back in the fight, rookie."

***

Kyria lay face down on a cold metal floor. Her eyes adjusted to the dark, and a scream bubbled in her throat. Perk stood before her, horror and pain etched within his double irises. Nothing of his lower jaw remained, and a dry rasp poured out of his exposed gullet. Kyria scrambled back, retreating into one of the research bays.

"All damned, Perk," Kyria said softly. "I'm sorry you're awake in there."

"Kyria Grazheen."

Paki's voice echoed above her. The android turned from a monitor at one of the upper research bays and simply stepped off the catwalk into thin air. He plummeted ten meters to land upon the floor with a clang and spray of blue coolant.

More shapes emerged from the *Desecratia's* shadows. People in various states of decay with threadbare clothing and skin dry as fallen leaves, putrid irlons with missing tentacles...and the dead survey team of the *Dubious*.

My crew.

Julet's haunted eyes regarded her from a face covered with swollen dark blisters. Ellin and the others watched her too, all dripping and decaying; their incursion suits the only thing holding their organs and bone together in some bizarre mockery of life.

"What...are you?" Kyria hissed, recoiling as Paki traced his fingers along her bare scalp. He rubbed his fingertips together thoughtfully.

"Unanticipated chemical variance prevented integration," Paki said. "Memory archives indicate-"

"-variance originated from Known location, Neolon City, Targotha." Julet stared at Kyria in horror as his lips moved without his consent. "Study and threat management given priority status upon-"

"-successful integration." Ellin finished. She stepped forward, dark blood thick and viscous within the gills still secured around her neck. Whatever controlled Paki, controlled the rest of them, too. "Preparation for next integration-"

Kyria edged further into the bay. She didn't need to hear any more.

Paki frowned after her. "Do not resist, Kyria Grazheen. Your form is needed to leave this place. Expansion is imminent."

Expansion? The siegenought rumbled again, and Kyria understood. *By the All...the ship is in a jump countdown!*

Her crew members flanked her, jerking and lurching into a semi-circle around her. Their rotting voices assailed her with cold reason. "I must be free of this place, Kyria Grazheen," Julet croaked, dried blood cracking around his lips. "Before expansion. Endless void. I must return-"

"-to the Known." Ellin finished.

Perk reached for her arm with a dry hiss.

"I'll be All damned if that happens!"

Kyria chambered her leg and drove her heel at Perk's sternum. His ribcage caved in around her foot with a snap of emaciated bone. Congealed organs slopped to the floor as she pulled her boot free, slick with dark blood to the knee. Perk didn't even drop. Silver flecks streamed out of the ragged wound in his chest, swirling through the air toward her.

Picobots, Kyria realized in horror.

"Do not damage your portal, Kyria Grazheen." The voices of Paki, Ellin and Julet came to her as one. "I have need of it, to carry all of me."

"Not that I can stop you." Kyria lunged for the closest thing at hand. Her fingers closed around the experimental hull armor, a plunger filled with murky liquid metal. "But I'm damn sure not staying here to be another blood puppet!"

Paki darted forward with a sickening burst of speed. "You will damage yourself beyond functionality if-"

Kyria's hand closed on a plunger, full of metallic, blue-green goop-nice and toxic. She stabbed it into her gut. The picobot cloud drew back instantly. Kyria coughed and smiled weakly at Paki. "You'll never get off this heap. I hope it jumps into a star!"

Kyria jerked as pain radiated from her stomach. A thousand pinpricks of raw current clawed along her spine, pondered over her organs and ignited every pore of her skin. She doubled over with a shriek as the viscous metal leached into her body, scouring her nerve by nerve.

Kyria writhed in pain, vaguely aware of rough hands grabbing the collar of her incursion suit. The android's disgusted voice came to her after a moment. "Your portal is still of use, Kyria Grazheen."

"No," Kyria whispered. A high-pitched hum sounded in her ears. Her body hurt, but the stuff did not feel like dying-she knew that sensation from Mercible. She had only managed to scramble her sync ware.

The sound of the *Desecratia's* jump countdown thundered out around her, in a language she had never heard before. Above all the noise, the dead woman's words drifted back to her. *Not like this.*

Paki set Kyria down on a flat work surface and held her firmly in place as the three meat suits clustered around her. Perk, Ellin and Julet opened their jaws, disgorging a rush of picobots. Pity and relief shone in their eyes as they collapsed one by one. The air grew thick with silver specks, a roiling cloud hovering over Kyria's face. "By the All..."

Not like this. I forbid it.

Kyria clamped her jaws tight, but Paki pried them apart as the cloud descended for her face. She spit and gagged, clawed at his grip. The bots poured down her throat, skittering down her nasal cavities, spilling into her lungs; her tear ducts. Her heels drummed the table.

The high-pitched hum in Kyria's ears suddenly ceased. A new voice pierced her fading consciousness. *CASE SYSTEM ACTIVE. SUBVERSIVE MEASURES DETECTED. EXECUTE COUNTERMEASURES?*

She stared defiantly up at Paki. The voice did not come from him; she knew it in her gut. She felt it there.

Not like this.

The thought did not come from Mercible. Kyria recognize it as her own. Her throat barely grated out the word.

"Execute."

Whatever entity controlled the android frowned. "You-"

A shudder flared through her skin like nettles dipped in sunlight. Paki stepped back as Kyria shone blue. Her skin, her teeth, her bones-every part of her surged with raw current. She rose with a scream of agony.

It's just flesh, the dead woman comforted Kyria. *It can be replaced. All a question of pain tolerance.*

Picobots spewed from her mouth as she hacked and spluttered, finding breath as electricity coursed through her body. Black smoke streamed from her incursion suit.

CHARGING. The disembodied voice ripped through her consciousness again. A cascade of picobots fell from her mouth in glittering streams as Kyria staggered to her feet. They did not rise back into the air.

Paki stared at her in shock. "You have...lessened me," he hissed.

The android's fist flashed out, faster than Kyria could react. She saw her own blood spray on Paki's face before sprawling across the floor. She knew without looking that he'd done more damage than her own kick had to what was left of Perk. She attempted to breathe, and felt air suck through the wound in her chest.

COMPRESSION IMMINENT, REPAIR PROTOCOLS READY. EXECUTE? Kyria worked her jaw but no words came out. How could she, with her ribs folded in on themselves? *LIFE*

SYSTEMS BELOW THRESHOLD LEVELS. OVERRIDE INITI-
ATED.

Her chest rippled as jagged fragments snapped into
place. Cartilage molded itself around the healing bone, securing
it. Skin knitted before her eyes.

Paki lunged forward.

THREAT RESPONSE INITIATED.

Kyria's fingers glowed a brilliant blue. She grabbed in-
stinctively for the android's torso before his hands closed on her
throat.

Paki's lips peeled open in a wordless howl. Waves of
picobots fled from his nose, ears and mouth. The blue of his
coolant intermixed with their silvery sheen. The android toppled
in a limp heap.

Kyria held a hand to her mouth, but the bots just hovered
in the air around her. Another warning alarm boomed through
the siegenought. *The jump countdown.* Kyria made to run, but
Paki's outstretched hand stopped her.

"Wait."

"Paki?" Kyria said cautiously. "It's out of you now? The
plague?"

"Not a plague. An artificial sentience. Like nothing in
the Known. It's evolved independently...consuming older generations of itself for centuries. It is vast." He coughed. Coolant
dribbled down his lips. The orange of the android's eyes had
dimmed considerably. "You must return to the *Dubious*. The
evolution sequence will complete in moments."

Kyria tightened her fists. Her knuckles glowed blue,
translucent. "I can destroy it. We can steer it into-"

"No!" Paki looked at her urgently. "Destroy the *Dese-*
cratia and you lose any link to finding the other Dooms. *Reck-*
oning. Penance. They must all be dealt with."

"All forsake me," Kyria muttered. "I can still get you out
of here. Zele can repair you, right?"

The android shook his head. "Too much risk. Help me
before it overcomes me again." Paki reached up calmly to peel
skin away from his temple. Brown bits and pieces dropped to
the ground in damp flakes. The cloud of picobots pulsed around

them, surging dangerously. Kyria grimaced as she finally revealed the coal-colored metal of his skull. He tapped a panel
above his ear and removed a small diamond memory node. His
orange eyes flickered as he handed it to Kyria.

"Give the Averator this data." Paki winced as picobots
slipped into the holes in his chest. "Your new abilities...are
stored within it as well. You may be the only one who can physically withstand this...vastness within me. CASE Armor: Critical
Anatomy Subatomic Enhancement. I imagine it is quite painful."

Kyria allowed herself a smile as Paki lurched to his feet
with a grimace. "Pain I can deal with. What about-"

"I'm no longer in full control of my systems." Paki's
words poured out in a rush. His fists clenched and unclenched.
"I've hidden Known data, but I don't know how long my safeguards will last. You must run now, Arcadian. I cannot stop another regression. Run before I end you."

"All bless you, Paki," Kyria whispered.

She took off in a dead sprint for the hopper. The swarm
of picobots darkened the air around her, but didn't veer too
close. The echo of Paki's footfalls soon pursued her, faster than
Kyria could ever hope to run.

CHEMICAL METABOLISM CONVERSION, EXE-
CUTE?

"Fek," Kyria muttered. The CASE armor had yet to let
her down. "Do it!"

She lurched forward as fire braided her muscles. Her
legs churned, eating up meters of deck as the Desecratia's cold
halls blurred past her. A last sharp corner turning to the hopper
came too quick. She careened off the wall with a grunt, crying
out as her arm shattered.

She punched in the door override and rushed into the airlock. Kyria's heart thudded in her chest, the hopper door opened
with agonizing slowness. "Come on, come on!"

Finally, she passed through, only to gape in amazement.
Zele and Remiliat stared back at her uncertainly, in the flesh,
their faces lit by Kyria's blue glow. The airlock cycled shut

behind her. Remiliat licked her lips and slowly trained a Pacifier on Kyria's chest.

"Your skin," she breathed. "What in-"

"It's me, move it!" Kyria shouted. "He's right-"

A thud on the airlock made them all jump. The reinforced porthole revealed Paki's ruined face. Kyria shouldered past Zele and took the hopper's controls. "It's not him. He's been co-opted by some kind of AI. We're leaving."

"This cannot be," Zele whispered.

"It must be." Kyria tossed Zele the android's memory node. "For the Known."

Zele caught it, and his face crumpled in recognition. Outside the hopper, Paki's lips moved soundlessly. Rem flicked a switch. The android's words flooded their audio ports. "I've partitioned my higher faculties, but the vastness will soon overrun it, Averator. Kyria performed admirably, you were wise to select her."

Zele staggered to the airlock, his hands trembling on the glass.

"Shut yourself down," he whispered hoarsely. "We can scrub you once..."

Kyria and Rem touched eyes. Kyria slowly shook her head. No. Rem did not interfere as Kyria pulled the hopper away from the *Desecratia*.

Zele spun back to them. "Stop! What are you doing?"

"I'm taking command," Kyria said softly. "This is still my mission."

Zele pounded on the airlock in frustration. "Paki, do as I say! Shut yourself-"

The android shook his head with an effort. "I must say goodbye now, Averator. Watch over each other. I will try to reason with it."

"Paki, *no!* I just need time to calculate-"

"Find the other siegenoughts...before I do."

Zele recoiled as the remaining expression leached out of Paki's torn face. The android studied them a moment, orange eyes flashing. He gathered himself to kick off the hopper's hull.

Zele cried out as Paki floated back through cold space, toward the *Desecratia*.

Kyria slumped with a sigh. "I tried to bring him back, Averator. I'm sorry."

Zele opened his mouth to speak, but the HUD's sudden flashing stopped him short. Remiliat peered at her console. "It's jumping."

Kyria wheeled the hopper around. She had to see this for herself. The hollow in the *Desecratia's* center crackled with energy. A light engulfing orb sprang to being in the hollow, expanding to swallow the ship in a void so dark it twisted Kyria's eyes. The stars grew visible once more, but the siegenought was gone.

Gravity waves shook the hopper, strong enough for Kyria to grip her seat. Shuster's worried voice crackled over the *Dubious* link. "Are you guys all right?"

Zele stared bleakly into the darkness of the Unknown, listless. Remiliat eyed him worriedly.

"We're all right, Shuster." Kyria swallowed, staring at her skin with a sense of wonder and fear. The blue tinge had faded away to reveal her deep brown. *Am I really?*

"Grazer! You made it!"

"More or less." Kyria flexed her arm experimentally. The bones were no longer broken. Her bruised knuckles from a few weeks ago no longer hurt. A cold fear snaked through her stomach. She couldn't feel anything. "Stand by."

Kyria cleared her throat. "Your orders, Averator?"

"The Stack still awaits us, I suppose," Zele said quietly. "Nothing great is ever obtained without loss. Or so I've been told."

"Agreed," Remiliat said over her shoulder.

Zele pulled uncertainly at his mustache before finally meeting Kyria's eyes. "I... was hoping you'd stay with us, Arcadian. Help me recover my android in one piece."

Kyria's answer was immediate. "Only if it means I get to fly that Doom into the nearest star." She spat in her palm and extended it.

The Averator's eyebrows rose, but he grasped her hand. "We're in agreement. Of course your armor will be complete before we return to the Known." Zele said quietly.

I'm gonna make you famous, the dead woman promised.

Kyria looked down at her hands again. "I'm not sure if I need it anymore."

"We'll find out soon enough." Zele took the seat next to Remiliat and synced Paki's memory node. "Let's see what we can learn about this vastness."

THE QUEST

BY

HOWARD NIGHT

The mighty House of Cassad was besieged, invaded and gutted. Its splendor laid out in horrific ruin across burned and crumbling Ziaran hills. Deep beneath the sacred grounds the ravagers rooted through long forgotten treasures, ancient relics and hidden secrets. The New Regime professed themselves a more benevolent ruling power than the fallen Cassads. But were they wiser? The Cassads had not hoarded those treasures for themselves. They were protecting the Known from the harbingers of the apocalypse.

> *-Samake. Cassad djele/historian. From The Cassad Chronicles*

THE FALLEN WORLD

The landscape rolled beneath them as the shuttle flew over the great continent. Ziara was a kaleidoscope of contrasts; beautifully architected, sprawling cities of gold and glass stood proud in some provinces while devastated, burned out apocalyptic nightmares were all that remained in others. One vast uninhabited region, a loping plain divided by the river *Eze*, was filled with deep lush grass on one side and impaled by the smoking hulk of a Cassad battleship on the other.

"The *Mlinzi*." Rayne stated grimly. The small balding man was particularly unremarkable but his voice carried the strength of command. He was not speaking directly to the pilot or the other passenger of the shuttle. Instead his intonation of the ships name was his way of issuing some respect as well as regret. Once before he'd seen the ship, in space and looking much more impressive. As Captain of his own ship then, he and the *Mlinzi* commanding officer had managed to negotiate a cease fire during the early years of the New Regime rebellion so both ships and a fleet of civilian craft were spared a firefight. The war record for the *Mlinzi* was clear that it was one of the deadliest ships in the Cassad fleet, the commander need not have been so diplomatic with Rayne but the safety of the Cassad civilians had been the priority for the *Mlinzi*.

But there would be no negotiating with the newly ratified Coalition, many of whom blamed the Ziara civilian populace as well as the Cassad rulers for the tyranny of the empire.

"Yes, Captain," the pilot answered in a stoic electronic voice his face also did not bear the same grim look of the Captain. As a matter of fact, there was no expression at all on the solid smooth blue face plate of the mostly mechanical man. From his durasteel toed feet to the tips of his three fingered artificial hands there was little evidence that he was anything other than an android. "She was downed two days ago by the 3rd Coalition Expeditionary Force."

"Two days, Commander WSE?" Rayne asked, pronouncing his pilots name as "Wise". "Two days and she still burns?"

"She was a fine ship. She and her crew will be remembered." The deep voice of the rather large and well-armed man seated further back in the shuttle almost echoed. Ukudumo was the Chief Tactical Officer of the HMS Lexington. He joined this small team to provide his captain with his personal security presence.

"Will she, Chief?" Rayne peered over the dichotomous landscape, to the burning cities as well as the gleaming ones. "Or will our Coalition rewrite the history files?"

"That has already begun, Sir." Commander WSE answered. "The Coalition is reporting the invasion of Ziara as a 'rescue' from the Cassad Royal family."

"Rescue?" Rayne snorted. "I doubt that's how the

citizens of Ziara would put it."

"And yet it was necessary, Sir, the Cassads were an empire of tyranny." Ukudumo declared.

"And will our 'new regime' be any better, Chief?" Rayne grimaced as the shuttle passed yet another downed Cassad battle craft.

"We're receiving an incoming transmission..." WSE reported. "Coalition Ground Command is ordering us to turn back."

Rayne sat up and manually activated the communications program at his console. "Coalition Command, this is Captain Sumner Rayne of King Brythons Ship; the *Lexington*. I am here as SIR Sumner Rayne and I am responding to a summons from Sir Vance of Have. This is official Knight of the Realm business sanctioned by the Prime Cathol and the Lord Cane himself."

The communication terminal remained quiet. "Is it possible Sir Vance did not clear this with the Coalition?" Ukudumo asked.

"Possible...but Vance was on the Strategic War Council that planned the attack on Ziara." Rayne told them. "As a Knight he would have taken part in the attack itself."

"I am detecting no Brython transponders at coordinates you provided." WSE reported. "Could they be in error?"

"Sir Vance makes few errors," Rayne told him. "And you wouldn't detect any Brython transponders either. His personal transport is in orbit. He arrived with the Coalition forces."

Finally the communications terminal came to life. "Shuttle *Pythea*, your flight path is confirmed and clear. Please do not deviate as there is still heavy fighting in Abolese city."

WSE acknowledged the flight path and then turned back to Rayne. "Sir Vance did not land with his own crew, Sir?"

"Sir Vance is not with the Royal Space Service. He is of the clerical order."

"A priest?" Ukudumo asked. "How can a priest be a Knight? A tour of duty in combat is required for all sworn in isn't it? The clerical order is sworn to peace."

"Many of the current standing Knights have come

from the clerical order. Though most never took their vows, Sir Vance is one who has." The Captain explained without going into all that was required to be knighted. As well-known as the knights of the realm were in the known there was much about them that was kept from the public.

"We are in view of our destination," WSE reported. Ahead of them, lit by the slowly rising sun, lay the huge grounds that were almost a city unto itself, the Cassad compound... the Royal estate...the home of the Cassad Royal family for almost a thousand years.

THE MARSHAL AND THE GIANT

Before them lay the wide cliff side city of the Cassad Royal palace. Like the world itself now, the palatial city was a jumbled mix of wonderfully crafted buildings and plazas as well as charred ruins and craters. On the western side sat the biggest crater, filled with smoke and surrounded by a ring of ruined earth. The main palace stood still towering, on the eastern side facing the morning sun.

Only today the suns golden rays were blocked by a massive structure that the shuttle could not fully see because of the Tower itself.

"It seems that someone has set a cruiser down on the actual palace estate," observed WSE.

"That's too large to be an R.S.S. cruiser," Ukudumo corrected. "It's almost the size of a battleship...what is it?"

The shuttle flew about the palace tower until they too fell into the shadow of the immense...

"That is not a battleship," WSE decided.

"It's...that can't be a..." Ukudumo shook his head in amazement.

"It is," Rayne confirmed and his face grew even grimmer. "An Eoten; a
war mecha. It seems as if Sir Hershey has received the call as well."

The shuttle slowly circled the huge black machine as it began its landing. The Eoten was a monstrous, bipedal war mecha and it was quite literally kneeling down on what was once the Cassad palace memorial square.

Its massive landing struts were designed to make it digitigrade; meaning it walked on its "toes". Now its legs were curled down so that it kneeled on one with most of its weight while the other kept it stable. From the crushed and obliterated remains of palace building beneath it and the blast scoring across the grounds, Rayne could tell the ship had landed here, not walked. The top half of the Eoten resembled more of a ship, with clear bridge and engines housings. Covered in battlements and guns one might think that it took a large crew to operate the ship. Yet Rayne had never seen nor even heard of anyone crewing with Sir Hershey. Still, how could one man manually operate it? All the systems necessary to run a cruiser or battleship were active in the Eoten as well as the systems needed to make it walk on those legs, or grab with the long mecha arms he knew were now curled up beneath the top half.

"I've seen vid of the old war mecha," Ukudumo was leaning so far forward in his seat to get a look that Rayne could feel the man's heavy breath on his neck. "They became obsolete almost as soon as they were deployed."

"Those mecha were not designed as this one was. Sir Hershey's Eoten is more battleship than walker."

"How did he commission such a ship?" There was just the slightest hint of envy in Ukudumo's question.

"You will have to ask Sir Hershey."

Just as the shuttle landed in the shadow of the Eoten, another vehicle rolled up into the devastated grounds.

"An ED9 entry drop rover." WSE reported. It was an armored eight wheeled vehicle with twin gun turrets on the front and the rear. Its ten-foot wheels negotiated the ruins easily and soon enough it pulled up in front of the shuttle.

"Its markings indicate that it is from the KBS York," WSE accessed the files deep in his repaired brain. "Under the command of Commander Marshal...DAME Marshal."

"Another Knight?" Ukudumo asked.

"So it would seem," and Rayne headed for the ships lock.

Commander Marshal was an intense looking woman. She wore the combat armor of a royal marine, save for the helmet which was racked on her back so her dark red short cropped hair flitted in the rising Ziara winds. Her dark skin was far richer in color than the last time Rayne had seen the woman, a sure indicator of her travels to worlds farther away from the pale Brython home star.

She was flanked by two crew members, one a small diminutive woman, jet black hair with sharp, intelligent eyes who also wore combat armor although it looked far more scientifically specialized having only small arms racked on her hip.

The other was the more profound. Almost nine feet tall, Rayne had seen few Giak warriors outside of Eastspace but here one was decked out in scarred and pitted gray armor.

"Sir Rayne," Marshal greeted him. "It's been awhile."

"Exactly five cycles since I apprehended you for crimes against the Prime Cathol... Dame Marshal."

"Yes, a necessary deception in service to all of Brython as I'm sure you've been made aware." Marshal matched Raynes grim look.

"And yet I see you here with a Giak warrior," Rayne walked right up to the group and stared up into the eyes of the large Giak. "...known to raid Brython colonies in the desolate perimeter. Yes, I recognize you, Tabal."

Marshal stepped in between the two. "An undeserved reputation, Captain. Tabal has been a member of my crew for some time now. She's served the Prime with distinction."

"And has she?" Rayne turned to the small dark-haired woman. "I am aware of your history as well, Dr. Toshima. As well as your leanings toward heresy."

"My crew are my responsibility, Rayne. Worry about your own, the tin man looks like he's about to piss a bucket full of lubricant."

Whether he was insulted or not, WSE's clear smooth face plate remained impassive. He'd been called worse since his return to service by those who believed there wasn't a man beneath the layers of cybernetic prosthesis.

"I received the call the same as you did. Sir Vance is well aware of my crew roster. So, if it really offends you feel free to not answer the call of a fellow knight." Marshal ran her gauntlets through her short hair and waited.

Rayne looked as if he were going to argue further but stopped himself and simply turned to the Cassad palace doors. "The call will be answered."

And the two groups proceeded to Cassad tower, to the huge glass opening at the base of the last house of the Cassads.

Inside the immense lobby of the tower they were greeted by Coalition staff many of whom looked to be administrative workers and not soldiers. The great room was more like an amphitheater with a wide long set of stairs descending to the main floor. The walls and floor were all richly colored red wood and clear glass. The corners were oases of tropical plant life from around the known. The clear Ziara sky could be seen through the skydome over the great room so natural light flowed in so clear it was as if they were standing outside.

And there were bodies and blood everywhere.

"Sir Rayne?" A tall woman dressed in contemporary business attire made her way to them, stepping over bodies as she did. "I'm Kathy Estarh, Managing Director for Palladium Enterprises engaged by the Coalition of Free Worlds to help re-settle this world for introduction into the new regime. We've been expecting you."

She bowed neatly to Rayne who merely nodded. Then she turned to Marshal and pointedly avoided looking up at the Giak warrior Tabal.

"Dame Marshal? It's an honor. Would you all please follow me?"

"I take it Sir Hershey is already meeting with Sir Vance?" Rayne asked as he fell into step behind the woman, walking next to Marshal.

"Ah...well yes, although...Sir Hershey...I guess that all Knights of the Realm have their...unique characteristics." She told them. They made their way into the palace tower, finding even more bodies and destruction among the finely crafted furnishings and wall art.

"Have you...uh...have either of you ever visited Ziara before?" Their guide asked while gingerly stepping around and over pools of blood.

"Never." Marshal stated stepping through a large pool without worry. "Hardly ever got to work in Cassad territory it's been shrinking so fast recently".

"Once," Rayne stopped at the edge of the drying blood. He looked about and noticed that the rest of the Coalition staffers were not engaged with clearing the bodies or checking for survivors. They were not medical staff, soldiers or even police. Each seemed instead to be cataloging the palace; registering each piece of art, equipment and any surveying damage with pretentious headshakes.

"...before Brython joined the Coalition." He stepped around the pool of blood as well and the group continued on.

"Well it's a mess but we'll get this world up and running again... better than before, now that the Cassads have been stopped."

Rayne noted the lack of Coalition bodies among the fallen and with some horror, the number of non-combatants killed. The Cassad family home was not a high priority target and should not have been taken with such extreme force.

They rounded a corner and the hall opened up into a sunlit lobby. There were mini hover cars lined against the wall and bubble pods waiting to zip passengers up the many floors into the tower.

But Estarh did not lead them to either of those. Instead she walked them away from the palace proper and down a wide side corridor that got increasingly narrow and battle worn until it ended at an obliterated section of wall, still smoldering from being ripped open by some type of weapon.

"When did the fighting here end?" Marshal asked watching as her Giak crewman stepped through the opening without needing to duck.

"Forty-eight hours ago. My team arrived earlier today.

But this damage here..."

"This was Sir Hershey's work." Rayne finished for her.

"Yes," Estarh nodded clearly upset. "It most certainly was."

Marshal looked at the damage curiously and was forced to jog a bit the catch up to the group as they rounded yet another corner. "What did he have against the wall...oh."

They group stopped as they found themselves in a service work shop, usually only meant for the staff. Hunkered down in the room, a swath of damaged work benches and tools strewn about in its wake, sat a heavy armored combat walker.

"He clearly could not fit." Rayne explained.

"Please, Sir Rayne," Estarh asked. "If you could appeal to Sir Hershey to refrain from bringing the tower down on us all."

"There is little chance of that," WSE answered. "Cassad Tower is a Category 8 structure, there is little Sir Hershey could do to compromised the integrity of the building."

Just as he finished telling them Sir Hershey took a rumbling step forward. The top of his armored mech ripped through the ceiling substructure and a few hundred kilos of debris rained down.

Everyone, including Marshals crew and the Palladium staff looked to WSE who simply answered, "At least, that is the report filed on the Brython Security HUB."

The mechs feet ground loudly on the ferrocrete floor. It was a bit slower than most armored combat units but clearly a lot harder to bring down. Right now, its path through the service area was blocked by some very insistent Palladium executives trying to keep it from further damaging the building.

"STAND ASIDE, PEASANTS, THIS BUILDING WILL BE RAZED FORTHWITH, THESE MEAGER WORK-WAYS AS WELL AS THE TOWER ITSELF."

The sudden boom of his voice startled the Palladium staff into backing away. The mech took yet another step forward and the room shook.

"Sir Hershey!" Rayne shouted. Despite the noise of the mechs step and the screams of the staff it was enough. The mech stopped and swiveled its top half around.

"This is Sir Hershey?" asked Marshal. "He walks around in a mech while outside of his mech battleship?"

"SIR RAYNE!" The armor plates on the front of the mech opened in segments revealing a transparent shielded cockpit. Never the less the occupant of the mech was still shrouded in darkness. "I SEE YOU HAVE ANSWERED THE CALL AS WELL."

"Sir Hershey," Captain Rayne looked about the room and the clear damage that was done. "Would it be possible for you to exit your armor just this once?"

"FOR THIS PLACE, RAYNE? TO PROTECT THE HALLOWED HOME OF THE CASSADS, RAYNE? I THINK NOT."

"Well the corridor looks like it just gets tighter, Sir Hershey." Marshal stepped forward and asked in a sardonic tone, "This might be a stupid question, but why can't you just proceed on foot? The building has been cleared for two days."

"MIND YOUR TONGUE, FELLOW KNIGHT; I AM NOT TO BE QUESTIONED LIKE SOME FIRST YEAR INFANTRY CADET."

"She has a point, Hershey," Rayne was losing his patience. "The way forward will not accommodate your...vehicle."

Even as he spoke, Rayne received a transmission over his personal com-link. Instead of responding he nodded to WSE, who activated his internal comm and sent a query.

"The LEXINGTON is reporting that the *X1* has just entered orbit of Ziara," WSE told Rayne. "And is sending a shuttle down."

"The *X1*?" Rayne asked a little shocked.

"Problem, Rayne?" Marshal, too was receiving information from her ship, the York.

"It seems as though Sir Galace has received the call as well. The *X1* is in orbit as we speak," he announced.

The room became quiet as the two other Knights verified this new information. Rayne broke the silence with the question that was now burning in them all.

"What could Sir Vance have found here that would

warrant five Knights of the realm let alone the Captain of the most powerful ship in the Brython fleet?"

"Make that six Knights...at least," Marshal said her hand cupped over her ear. "The Lost fleet has entered the Ziara system."

Rayne snapped his head to WSE who immediately relayed a call to their ship. Chief Ukudumo walked up to Rayne's side and subvocalized a private communiqué. "The Lost Fleet May destabilize the law and order the Coalition is attempting to keep in this system. We may need to be ready to evacuate if its presence causes problems."

"The Lexington confirms that the *Mediterranean* is in system but not the entirety of the Lost Fleet." WSE told them.

"Six Knights of the Realm? When was the last time so many received a call?" Rayne asked no one in particular. WSE answered anyway.

"Brython Historical files indicate that the last gathering of Knights responding to a Call was in 782 KBT. Two hundred Knights were called to Brython to secure the throne from Lord James of Hush."

"So the Knights don't get together for parties?" Marshal asked. Rayne remembered that Marshal's induction into the Knights was quite unusual and had been kept so secret that she did not even have a knight to patron her in. He was not surprised that she knew very little of their history.

"The Knights gather at least once every five cycles but seldom do Knights send a Call for aid. Even more rarely does a Knight send a Call to another Knight...and for Sir Vance to send a Call to SIX of us..."

"WHAT COULD WARRANT SUCH A THING?" Hershey asked.

"What the hell did he find here?" Rayne asked...again to no one in particular.

HOLY KNIGHT

For the next hour the group waited there, Rayne and his crew patiently pacing, Commander Marshal and her crew left to tour the Tower but managed to return before the next Knight arrived.

Sir Hershey still remained in his armored mech.

"From the battleship *X1*," Estarh announced. In walked two Brython Fleet personnel, a tall blond female with very pale skin and a shorter man with dark, olive skin and a thick graying brush mustache; "Commander Caprice Long and Captain Franklin Galace...SIR Galace."

The three Knights greeted their peer but it was Rayne that Galace first spoke to.

"'is wou' ma'e six of us 'en, Rayne?" Galace had the thickest accent of them all; a deep, halting cadence with almost no stress on his consonants. He was from Brythons second colonized star system; The Cold Star.

"Indeed, Sir Galace. There has yet been no word from Sir Vance as to the purpose of his call."

The tall Commander Long spoke up. "If I may?" At Galace's nod she continued. "Since the *Wars of the Blade* lost the Cassads their shipyards many have been anticipating the eventual attack and liberating of their home world."

"Yes, Commander?"

"The most popular discussions always center on what secrets the Cassads still had in their possession. Particularly those artifacts that allowed them to take control so fast after the Dark Age."

Galace managed a slight "hmm" but Rayne frowned. "Yes, I've seen and read the many conspiracy theories myself. Many on the subjugated worlds want to believe that the Cassads had some special X factor that gave them the advantage after the Dark Age. Anything from believing that Ziara was not plunged into darkness as was the rest of the Known, to tales of brokering deals with advanced 'aliens'. I'm sorry, Commander, but the most likely explanation for the thousand-year reign of the Cassad Empire is that they were simply better than everyone else at conquering."

Galace added another "hmm" that could have meant anything while Long pursed her lips and stood her ground.

"Never the less, Sir Rayne, there are bound to be

several items of interest in the Cassad treasury or in their classified files."

Commander Marshal laughed. "Bigger they are the harder they fall and the Cassads still have a long way down. Whatever is in the mystery vault can't be too special, or it would've saved their empire."

"It was special enough for Sir Vance to call us all in."

"But we're not at the Vault, Sir Rayne," Commander Long pointed out. "Sir Vance has led us here, to the Cassad home."

"Where the hell is Sir Vance anyway?" Marshal asked.

There was the sound of footsteps in the corridor and soon another of the Palladium staff announced; "Sir Thorion, Admiral in command of the 7th Fleet."

In walked a group of hardy looking Royal Marines surrounding their equally hard looking Admiral. Thorion had leathery, pock marked golden brown skin and his face set in what could have been a permanent frown. He regarded the group for a moment, his eyes lingering over them all until Rayne again broke the silence with a greeting.

"Sir Thorion, we did not expect you for some time. We were told the *Mediterranean* only reached the system an hour ago."

Thorion nodded as he shook Raynes hand and answered in a deep gravelly voice. "It has. I arrived in a gunboat over half a day ago. Bringing my ship earlier might have only caused a panic." He looked again about the knights, nodding to Marshal and Galace then glaring at Sir Hershey.

"How many of us were called?" He asked.

"Sir Vance deemed it necessary to call five of us. But what purpose..." Rayne began to answer when a clear young voice cut through the room.

"Actually I called six of you."

They all turned, Sir Hershey ripping through the ceiling again, to the darkened entrance of the corridor beyond. In it stood a small man, young, barely an adult with sandy colored hair. He wore the black tunic and ankle length robes of a priest, even sporting the common order white collar... though the ceremonial sword he had strapped across his back and the gun holstered on his hip said that he was much more.

Rayne strode past the armored Hershey and greeted the young man with a deep and respectful bow. "Father Vance, it is good to see you again my friend."

"It is good to see you as well, Sir Rayne. Thank you for answering my call." Then the young man turned to the rest gathered there. "Thank all you."

Marshal twisted her face up in doubt. "This...kid...is a Knight of the Realm?"

"Sir Marshal has only been recently knighted," Rayne explained, glaring over his shoulder at the Dame. "And has yet to learn the proper respect we knights have for one another."

"Respect aside," Thorion growled. "The 7th Fleet is awaiting my return. What could possibly have been so important you called us, Vance?"

The young man smiled serenely. "Rest assured, Sir Thorion, I have not called you all in vain. If you will follow me I will explain on the way."

Then Father Vance turned to face Sir Hershey. "I'm afraid, Sir Hershey, you will have to abandon the confines of you armor in order to answer the call."

The big mech reared up. "THERE IS NOWHERE YOU CAN GO THAT I CANNOT FOLLOW." And he pointed a gauntlet bearing cannon at the opening to the rear corridor.

"SIR HERSHEY!" the other knights cried out. Father Vance simply took three steps and placed a hand up on the cannon.

"That is not the way, Sir Hershey," he said calmly. "Now hurry and join us, the Lord has set us to a most serious task."

There was a click and a loud hiss...then the front of the mech opened up and out leapt a large man...wearing yet more combat armor. This black set was similar to Dame Marshals but bulkier and Hershey was wearing the helmet.

"Very well," Sir Hershey rumbled with considerably less boom. "As God wills it."

"You've got to be kidding me." Dame Marshal

muttered.

Father Vance looked about the group. "I'm afraid from this point on only the Knights I've called will continue on."

Some nodded but others, "My crew has my complete trust. They go where I go." Dame Marshal stated.

"Yes," Rayne agreed reluctantly. "You must trust my crew as you trust me, Sir Vance. I would not have brought them or my ship otherwise. Very likely you called on me because I am a Knight that commands a ship of the fleet. Whatever this calling is for it will involve my crew as much as myself."

Admiral Thorion nodded in agreement and Captain Galace gave another, "hmm".

Father Vance smiled knowingly. "Of course, Sir Rayne, my trust in you extends to your crew through your trust in them. The same for you all. However, I would not have called all of you here for anything less the most serious of circumstances. As Brython knights you already bear the responsibility of the safety of the Realm, the Crown and the execution of God's will. What lies ahead of us should only be taken on by those whom can bear that weight. I expect that all of you will brief your crews after we meet...but I will leave it to you to decide whether or not to share the task with them. You may decide that they should not be so burdened."

There was some balking from Thorion's people and the giak, Tabal, but eventually the knights followed Sir Vance on without them.

The pathway was dimly lit and appeared to be yet another service corridor.

"Can you tell us now what you have found here, Sir Vance?" Rayne asked.

"The Alaafin's vault of course, Sir Rayne," Vance answered.

"Thought the vault was at the Imperial Center?" Marshal asked.

"Yes," Vance nodded. "The Cassad Vault is in the Imperial Center, but the Cassad Alaafin's Vault is here, beneath their ancestral home."

"Ose's vault?" grumbled Thorion.

"A more personal collection," Father Vance explained. "Treasures and secrets handed down from king to king, from parent to child. The archive dates back at least five hundred years before the end of the Dark Age and there are items in there..."

The corridor turned and opened to what looked like a simple unbarred door. Father walked up to the door and opened to reveal a very small storage closet filled with metal storage boxes.

"...items in there that look old enough to have been constructed before the Dark Age began." Father Vance stepped into the room and moved a few of the boxes around. Rayne watched closely but the young priest did not open any of the containers nor slide any away from the wall to reveal anything of note. After a moment, Vance stood back, looking satisfied with the new arrangement.

"They took great pains to keep this location a secret, even from themselves," he said then closed the door. Before any of the knights could ask him anything a loud hum began to emit from all around them. Then a very noticeable vibration rose up out of the very flooring in rhythm with the hum. There was a loud snap and then the entire corridor floor detached from the walls and began to drop.

They found themselves on a floating platform that was slowly descending into a cavernous underground complex. A small control console folded up from the platform floor in front of Sir Vance who keyed the device on and laid his fingertips onto its smooth surface. By sliding dimly lit icons about on the panel he was the able to guide the platforms descent.

There was very little light but Rayne could see enough to tell that the cavern walls were lined sporadically with rectangular man-made housings. They were large, big enough to store a several one-man fighters.

"I've lost contact with the surface," Thorian reported.

"Yes," nodded Father Vance. "This subterranean cavity is somehow cloaked from scans. I believe there is something in the rock itself that scatters radiating waves. We will not be able to communicate with anyone until we return."

"How far down does this go?" Dame Marshal was leaning over the side of their platform, shinning her light down into the darkness.

"I have not yet descended to the bottom," replied Sir Vance.

"So the entire vault has not been secured?" Sir Thorion asked with anger in his voice.

"No," Sir Vance admitted matter-of-factly. "And yes, there are still dangers and Cassad security measures that need to be bypassed down below."

"And where are your men, Sir Vance?" asked Captain Galace. "Are they securing the vault or..."

Sir Vance shifted his hands on the controls and the platform began to level out its flight path. "I came here alone, Sir Galace. I do not have a command of my own."

Their platform passed very near to one of the rectangular housings, close enough to see that housing was embedded into the cavern wall itself.

"These are... cargo containers." Rayne realized. "Old...very old...there is rust on them...they're made of steel and iron."

"Steel and iron are common place in the known, Rayne," Dame Marshal corrected. "That doesn't make these old."

"Untreated steel and iron on space worthy containers? Look at the oxidation. No, Dame Marshal, these containers are older than the Cassad Empire...they predate the Dark Age."

"Correct, Rayne, I see Terropology is still your passion." Sir Vance made another adjustment and the platform leveled off completely. They passed container after container until finally Vance stopped them in front a one container along a row of dozens.

"You've only been here for a few days, Sir Vance," Sir Thorion addressed him. "But you sent your call months ago. You did not discover this by accident. What intel did you receive?"

"I've been on Ziara for almost a month, part of a covert group meant to help with the assault of the planet. I discovered this vault the day before yesterday." Sir Vance told them.

The platform lowered itself beneath the container and they could see the open underside. After lining itself up beneath it the platform rose into container, locking in and becoming a simple floor. They group of Brython Knights found they were once again inside a nondescript corridor ending in an airlock.

Sir Vance strode forward and engaged the airlock. Sir Thorion stepped forward and insisted, "Yes, but you were lead here by what information? This vault is enormous, why this one particular container?"

"This is the container I was lead to, Sir Thorion," Sir Vance said with a strange calm.

"What lead you here, Sir Vance?" Rayne was curious as well.

Sir Vance engaged the airlock and with a hiss and a metallic clank, it opened. He looked at the Knights over his shoulder. "The same thing that lead me to call you particular Knights for this mission."

Dame Marshal nodded, "The Prime Cathol, right?"

"Of course not, Dame Marshal," Sir Vance frowned only a little. "I was lead here by God."

THE BLACK VISION

Sir Vance led the way into airlock, unlocking the secondary door and passing through without hesitation. Rayne started to follow when a strong hand gently pulled on his shoulder. "Yes, Sir Thorion?"

Thorion looked past Rayne to be sure Sir Vance was still moving on before speaking. "He was lead here... by God?"

Rayne nodded seriously. "As Knights we often embark on tasks given to us by the Prime Cathol based on his sacred communication with The Lord our God. You know this Sir Thorion."

Dame Marshal was leaning against the container wall. "Sure, the Primes interpretation of Gods will but Vance ain't the Prime Cathol, he's just a priest."

Rayne looked at the rest of the doubting Knights. "The

Prime Cathol, himself, was a Knight of that order before taking on the post. As was the Prime before him."

"Long before my time, Rayne," Marshal snapped. "None of the candidates for the next Prime are Knights now. Vance ain't got that status."

"And he is the last of that order of friars, Rayne," Thorion pointed out. "I have serious doubts that he was guided here by the Lord."

Rayne fixed them all with a steely gaze. "We are here now, fellow Knights. Answer the call." And he stepped through the secondary airlock.

The airlock opened into a larger hallway filled with stairs that widened as they descended toward a soft golden light. All about the stairs were strewn broken metal husks, most were one to three meters wide. Their insides were exposed, belching out smoke and sparks over live wires that had spilled out on to the floor like the innards of disemboweled animal carcasses.

"Watch your step, please." Sir Vance warned them. "They are all deactivated but may still bear volatile weaponry."

"Hover drones...old...but security class. Someone came through before we did." Dame Marshal noted. "Took them all out."

"No one has been down here since the reign of Claudia Cassad," Sir Vance corrected her. "I dispatched the drones."

Sir Vance continued on down the stairs but the other Knights all paused to consider the ruined machines. Rayne watched Marshal kneel down and examine one.

"Small arms fire took this one out..." She moved down a few steps to look at another. "This one by something bigger..."

Sir Thorion walked down to look over her shoulder. "Plasma...the same type of weapon equipped by the drones themselves."

"They attacked each other?" Rayne asked.

"More like..." Marshal looked about the staircase, taking in the angles. "They got in each other's way trying to get at their targets."

"Possibly," Thorion agreed. "They are extremely old."

"Possibly," admitted Rayne. "But the platform that brought us here seemed to function without sign of age."

"Sir Vance has no command," Thorion stated. "Who destroyed all these drones?"

Rayne knelt down and looked closer at the sheered open armor of a drone. "He did…this one has been torn open with a kendo edged blade."

"What?" Dame Marshal asked with doubt. "That sword on his back?"

"I am open to other theories." Rayne stood and moved down the steps.

They all hurried to catch up to Sir Vance who had reached the bottom of the stairwell. It ended at a broken bridge spanning the gap of a man-made cavern with smooth but rusting metal walls yawning dawn far below them into darkness. There were other bridges they could see, likely from the other cargo containers but none connected to each other. And there they found an even larger number of wrecked drones, some of which were clearly larger and more lethal models. Sir Vance made his way across the bridge without hesitation, using the body of the largest drone as a makeshift walkway to cross the gap where the bridge was broken. Again, his fellow knights paused to consider the evidence of a massive battle but this time, after only a quick look to one another, they continued to follow him.

There was a door at the other end of the bridge. It was bent horribly and open enough to allow them to pass through and into a lit chamber.

There Sir Vance finally stopped and the other Knights took in the room. The walls were lined with what could have been life pods, the closest were two cubic meters in dimension but there were larger ones further back in the room. On the side of each, facing into the center of the chamber, was a smoky white circular lens almost a meter wide.

Dame Marshal walked up to the nearest one and peered inside. "Is that...an actual book?"

Sir Vance nodded. "Yes, but more importantly, a very specific book."

Marshal leaned even closer almost pressing her face

onto the glass. "It's written in old Arabic...the...'Koran'?"

"Correct. And there is a copy of the bible not three vaults down." Sir Vance was beaming. "A bible...from nearly a thousand years BEFORE the Dark Age even began."

Galace gave another "hmm" but Sir Thorion let his frustration out. "Are you telling us you called five...no SIX Knights to escort a copy of a book you already have back to Brython? Sir Vance I..."

"The sacred word of our Lord is no mere trifle, Sir Thorion! Watch you're your tongue!" Sir Hershey bellowed.

Rayne raised his hand sharply. "Sir Hershey, please! These vaults have not been opened," and he pointed farther into the chamber. "But that one has."

A nondescript pod, no different than the others, did indeed sit open further into the chamber.

Sir Vance took an apprehensive breath, the first break in his otherwise serene composed countenance. "While I do find the discovery of the bible most important, I have not called you all in vain."

Now Sir Vance took slow deliberate steps across the chamber toward the open vault. "It was the hand of God that led me here..." He explained. "A vision unlike any that I have ever had. I was...embraced by the vision, body and mind. I saw...felt, really, a great breaking that reverberates across all that is. Like a sharp blow to the spine of the universe."

The Knights followed Sir Vance, slowly, allowing him to maintain his distance and lead them to the far vault. They took the opportunity to peek through the glass panels of the vaults as they passed them by.

"Something has happened that can affect everything we know. Something fundamental to the universe itself." Vance said.

Inside one vault, Rayne spied what he thought was an embryonic storage container. Though he could not make out the writing on the label, the red color was clearly a warning against opening it.

"I then saw the darkness of the star field split to reveal a great but fading eye, cast with a great sadness. The split brought down the stars and a great darkness fell over every-thing." Vance's voice carried far in the chamber and echoed back at them.

Galace paused at one vault to examine the desiccated remains of a humanoid torso. It did not appear to be a standard human body to him nor had he any idea what humanoids it might even be close to. Though its thin, pale gray skin was ee-rily familiar.

"Hmm," he muttered.

"Then the ground beneath me hardened and shifted. Steel turned to rock, rock turned to sand and sand into fire..."

It was an old style holographic star chart that caught Sir Thorion's attention. He had traveled the known extensively and could not identify any part of the map.

"I saw myself, bearing the arms of a soldier, but fallen into pieces before a massive lock. My face was filled with des-pair." Vance neared the open vault and stepped into a harsh beam of light coming from within it.

Hershey paused at a vault only once. It was filled with several bricks of translucent material, stacked like precious metal. A small red laser from Sir Hershey's helmet attempted to pierce the glass; a small scan but the vault would not yield its se-crets...yet.

"I bowed to my own fallen body and held my own head before me. Its eyes were dark and hollow but its mouth opened and closed as if trying to speak." Vance told them.

"An Ubesi orb," Dame Marshal uttered in surprise. "That's an Ubesi Orb." Rayne turned to see her staring into a wide vault, hands pressed to the glass. Inside a gelatinous sphere floated, bobbing up and down softly, its shaped wavering slightly. It was metallic in color and reflected Dame Marshal's eager face back at her.

She pulled at the edges of the vault. "Ung! How do you open these things?" she demanded.

"What's an Ubesi Orb?" Sir Thorion asked.

"No one knows," Rayne told him as he walked over to get a better look. "Several have been reported found throughout the known but no one has ever actually produced one for examination. It's a myth."

"Wrong, Rayne," Marshal spat. Her hands wound their way around the vault looking for a catch or panel to activate the door. "We've found three...goddamn."

"Three?" Rayne asked incredulous. "I've never seen any reports of any Ubesi Orb being found."

Marshal nodded grudgingly. "All information on the orbs is kept secret. I shouldn't have...Ung! How do these things open, Vance?!?"

Suddenly they were all bathed in harsh light. The Knights turned their attention from the floating orb to Sir Vance, who stood by the open vault and had turned its opening toward them. Inside on a small tee, sat a shimmering odd shaped cone of white, powdery material.

"What is this?" Sir Thorion demanded.

Sir Vance continued his vision tale. "After a moment of trying to understand what my own head was telling me, the world about me transformed and I found myself standing here on Ziara, its world burning and being overrun."

The knights drew closer and could see that the shimmering effect on the powder came from tiny flashes of light, intermittent and random. Sir Hershey took a step back. "My systems detect 'Dark' Fusion...in that vault... in the open. How is this possible?"

"I fell through the earth into this very chamber..." Sir Vance went on. "Though in my vision only this vault stood without ruin. Inside was not this surprising collection of Hyperion particles, but the broken end of a black key."

"Hyperion particles?" Several of the Knights exclaimed but it was Sir Thorion that stepped forward. "Not possible, Sir Vance."

Rayne was more willing to believe. "Hyperion particles would explain the 'Dark' fusion Sir Hershey detects."

Sir Vance lowered his head and continued telling of his vision. "As I reached for the black key I heard a terrifying voice call to me. I turned to see my broken body, haphazardly cobbled together and limping toward me...reaching out for me. My head spoke and I heard the voice again and it said; 'one turn and the wolves return..."

"Hyperion particles do not exist for more than a billionth of a nanosecond." Sir Thorion argued.

"Nor can they be...gathered as there is no force known that can affect them." Rayne agreed.

"Yet, there is 'Dark Fusion' taking place in that vault." Sir Hershey stated.

"...two turns," continued Sir Vance. "begins the unmaking..."

"How can we be sure those are Hyperion particles?" Marshal asked.

"We'll need a specialist...although, as I understand it, there is no one who has ever done more than theorize their existence." Rayne wondered.

"M' Chief Scientist 'an 'onfirm 'is." Galace stated.

Rayne looked to the Knight but Galace said no more. Then Sir Vance, head down, finished his vision.

"...three turns and all will be forsaken."

THE QUEST

"What is the meaning of this vision, Sir Vance?" Sir Hershey asked having dropped to one knee.

"Perhaps we should focus on what we know to be..." Sir Thorion grumbled but was cut off when Sir Hershey turned on him.

"Perhaps, honorable Knight, you should return to your fleet of damned souls if you cannot silence yourself when the Lord's wishes are being revealed to you!"

Sir Thorion was not cowed by the armored Knights outburst. "Are you sure, Sir Hershey? Are you sure this is a message from God?"

"Sirs..."

Rayne tried to calm them down.

"There is no doubt in my mind, Sir Thorion, save for my doubt in your faith in God." Hershey walked right up to Thorion and stared down at him through the hard metal plate visor in his armor.

"Are you sure in Sir Vance? Your faith in God's word only extends in your faith that Sir Vance is correct in his vision. Visions are notoriously fallible. Like those that interpret them.

"You dare?" Sir Hershey raised a gauntlet.

"Enough!" Rayne shouted. "We are Knights of the Realm and we will work together as such!"

He turned to Sir Hershey. "The Prime Cathol and the Lord of Brython Knighted everyone in this room. You will respect that Sir Hershey."

Then he turned to Sir Thorion. "If it were not for Sir Vance we would not have discovered this chamber. You will heed what he says."

The room went quiet as both Hershey and Thorion turned and walked away from each other. Then Rayne turned to Sir Vance. "You selected this group of Knights with purpose didn't you, Sir Vance?"

The priest did not nod but answered, "Of course each one of you has talents that are of need."

"I thought so. Confirmed when Sir Galace stated that his Chief Scientist had the means of confirming the Hyperion in that vault. What would you have the rest of us do?"

"There is much we must all do. My vision indicates that the Hyperion is but one part of a larger danger. One that could destroy the known."

"Hyperion in a state like this," Thorion was standing in front of the vault, staring hard at the clumped particles. "Might be indicative of an unknown universal force at work."

"Hmm," Galace agreed.

"A newly discovered universal force will shift the balance of power in the known." Marshal stated. "Why didn't the Cassads use it?"

"Perhaps...when first discovered, they realized they did not have the means of safely exploring its potential." Rayne surmised. "Then...the vault was somehow forgotten."

"During an unexpected death of a Cassad king maybe," Marshal agreed. "So knowledge of its existence never passed on?"

"Possibly..." several agreed.

"There are five of you and five tasks that must be completed." Vance explained. "I will need to speak to each of you individually."

Father Vance left the vault with Sir Hershey first, seeking a private place to give the knight his mission. Rayne was relieved; had the young knight not done so on his own Rayne would have insisted that Hershey be counseled first to send the combative knight on his way as soon as was possible.

Like the others in the chamber, Rayne took the time to examine the contents of the vault. He gave the rows of pods another tour but stopped next to Sir Thorion and the pod containing to relic holographic star chart.

"Have you figured out what this map charts, Sir Thorion?"

"Yes," nodded Thorion. "It's the home system star chart...charted out to fourteen light years."

Rayne looked at the map with doubt. "Sir Thorion I'm afraid that's not possible. This map shows less than fifty stars within fourteen light years of Brython..."

"Not Brython, Rayne. This is a star chart of Earth. Man's original home system."

Rayne looked again. "How can you tell?"

"The three stars dead center..." he indicated by placing a pointing finger against the glass lens. "Their color codes and positions match the old files of Alpha, Proxima... and Sol."

Rayne looked closer. "Perhaps. Sir Thorion, but there is no verifiable data on anything other than those three stars. This could be anywhere in the known."

Thorion grimaced. "With everything thing else in this vault? No Sir Rayne. We are looking at a map to Earth."

Rayne considered for a moment and looked about the map. "It's a rudimentary chart at best. I recognize no other significant celestial objects. And there are no reputable charts from before the Dark Age to compare it to."

"There are on Brython...in the Hallowed Sea."

"That is rumor, Sir Thorion," Rayne corrected. "Nothing more."

"I've seen the charts myself," Thorion asserted. "This could be what we need."

"You mean your fleet, Sir Thorion?"

But the knight said no more. He only continued his thorough examination of the chart inside the pod.

Eventually Father Vance returned but Sir Hershey did not. The priest made his way through the chamber to the two knights.

"If you would please excuse Sir Thorion and I, Sir Rayne?"

Rayne nodded, "Of course," and stepped away to a discreet distance. He tried to examine another pod but he could not help but his attention kept being drawn back to the Knight and the priest. Father Vance and Sir Thorion were not engaged in conversation for as long as Rayne thought they would be, taking into account how long it took for the priest to return from giving Sir Hershey his task. When they were done speaking, Father Vance showed Sir Thorion how to disengage the entire pod from the wall. It was equipped with a working hover pad which allowed the knight to push it easily from the room.

It was the pod with the ancient star chart inside.

Rayne grew restless as Father Vance talked to the other two knights one by one. Sir Galace was sent on his way with a pod as Sir Thorion had been; the Hyperion particle pod as Rayne expected. But the conversation Father Vance had with Dame Marshal got loud...on her end.

Rayne watched as she marched Vance over to the pod with the alleged Ubesi Orb floating inside. She clearly wanted to take the pod but the priest was adamant. As she stormed from the chamber Rayne wondered if she had, in fact accepted the task.

"Dame Marshal did not seem pleased with her task," Rayne stated plainly as Father Vance walked up to him.

"Among the many knights, which are a very eclectic group, she stands out. The Prime Cathol was against her being knighted."

Raynes eyebrows rose at this. "I was unaware of that. It was the Prime Cathol himself that told me of her mission. He seemed to have full confidence in her."

"Not at first, unfortunately. Dame Marshal is not as tied to the Brython kingdom as most knights but she will complete her mission I have no doubt."

"And what is it, Father, that you would have of me and my ship?"

"It is not my will, Sir Rayne, but the Lords. The task is set before you from the Lord our God."

Rayne nodded grimly. "And what is that task?"

"Yours will be the most difficult, Sir Rayne," Vance admitted as he turned and indicated for him to follow. "You know of the prison planet Deggar?"

"Of course," Rayne nodded. "It was taken by the Coalition during the *Wars of the Blade*."

"Not quite, Sir Rayne. The Coalition was given access to the prison only after an uprising. When the support the facility needed to maintain its security was compromised because of the *Wars of the Blade*, the Nth Consortium took control."

"The Nth Consortium?" Rayne had previous dealing with the organized criminal organization. "I did not know they had taken Deggar."

"Yes. They have been...auctioning off Deggars prized prisoners ever since."

"You want my ship to go to Deggar and retrieve a prisoner?"

"No," Father Vance shook his head and came to halt before a softly lit pod at the very end of the vault. Rayne peered inside...

...and saw nothing.

"It's empty."

"Not always..." Father Vance said in an offhand way. He stared into the lens as if waiting for something. After a long moment his face became grave. "Sir Rayne... in my vision, I saw your ship at the prison world."

"I have never been to Deggar. Nor, do I believe, has the Lexington during her service."

"You will go to the prison planet; the Lord has shown me this."

"For what purpose?"

"...I do not know."

"Then, if it is the Lords will, I will take the Lexington to Deggar. This does not seem to be so difficult a thing, Father."

The priest continued to stare into the pod for moment more yet still there was nothing there. Then he turned to face Rayne and his eyes were very dark.

"The known is about to unravel before us. Mankind may fall back into darkness, into a pall of death not seen since the Dark Age. In my heart I know the only way to stop this is to complete the quests the Lord has tasked you with. You must go to Deggar, Sir Rayne."

"Yes… if the Lord wills it. Yet…without knowing why we are there…"

"Whatever you find there. Sir Rayne, remember you're a Knight of the Realm. That should be enough to guide you."

Rayne nodded gravely then firmly raised his chin. "I will, Father. The Lexington and her crew will do their duty."

"Sir Rayne, of that I have no doubt but I must tell you, Captain, in my vision, your ship never returns from Deggar."

AUTHOR BIOS

Milton Davis (*Landfall, The End of the Known, Choices*)

Milton Davis is a research and development chemist, speculative fiction writer and owner of MVmedia, LLC, a small publishing company specializing in Science Fiction, Fantasy and Sword and Soul. MVmedia's mission is to provide speculative fiction books that represent people of color in a positive manner. Milton is the author of Changa's Safari Volumes One, Two and Three. His most recent releases are Woman of the Woods and Amber and the Hidden City. He is co-editor of four anthologies; Griots: A Sword and Soul Anthology and Griot: Sisters of the Spear, with Charles R. Saunders; The Ki Khanga Anthology with Balogun Ojetade and the Steamfunk! Anthology, also with Balogun Ojetade. Milton Davis and Balogun Ojetade recently received the Best Screenplay Award for 2014 from the Urban Action Showcase for their African martial arts script, Ngolo. His current projects include The City, a Cyberfunk anthology, Dark Universe, a space opera anthology based on a galactic empire ruled by people of African American descent, and From Here to Timbuktu, a Steamfunk novel.

Malon Edwards (*The Quiet Black*)

Malon Edwards was born and raised on the South Side of Chicago, but now lives in the Greater Toronto Area, where he was lured by his beautiful Canadian wife. Many of his short stories are set in an alternate Chicago and feature people of color.

Penelope Flynn (*Initiative on Euphrates*)

Penelope Flynn is a child of the 70's a southerner by birth but has lived in the south-central U.S. for the past two decades. She writes speculative fiction focusing on horror, science fiction, fantasy and erostasy and in any combination of those sub-genres. She has branched out into digital illustration with the ultimate goal of translating prose spec fiction projects to graphic novelizations and/or animated projects focusing on epic stories with diverse characters. Penelope has studied screenwriting and comic book scripting. She is the Editor of OTHER SCI FI Magazine, the host of Discussions From the OTHERHOOD, the podcast for OTHER SCI FI Magazine and the author of The Renfield Chronicles.

Howard Night (*King's Hunt, King's Court, The Quest*)

Author of "The Serpent Cult" and Co-editor of Dark Universe: Interregnum Speculative Fiction Books, Howard Night loves setting his characters in warped versions of his hometown of Philadelphia and neighborhood; Mt. Airy. His current novel, King's Bounty, is set in the Dark Universe.

Ronald Jones (*Monsters of Eden*)

Ronald T. Jones is a time traveling, dragon-slaying, starship-piloting, galaxy-renowned science fiction writer and all-around adventurer. He is the author three novels: Chronicle of the Liberator, Warriors of the Four Worlds, and Subject 82-42. He has written a host of short fiction, ranging from science fiction to fantasy to steampunk. His works appear in the following anthologies: Griots I and II, Genesis I and II, Steamfunk, Sci fi Talk's Tales of Time and Space, and Tales From the African Diaspora. When Ronald is not writing, he is busy in his extra-dimensional laboratory constructing advanced AI capable of administering the sprawling domain of his galactic empire.

Balogun Ojetade (*Once Spoken*)

Balogun Ojetade is an author, master-level martial artist in indigenous, Afrikan combative arts and sciences, a survival and preparedness consultant, a former Communications and Asst. Operations Sergeant in the U.S. 7th Special Forces Group (Airborne) and a priest in several Afrikan spiritual traditions.

Balogun is Master Instructor and Technical Director of the Afrikan Martial Arts Institute, which has branches in the Unites States, England and Ghana, West Afrika and Co-Chair of the Urban Survival Preparedness Institute.
He is the author of the bestselling non-fiction books Afrikan Martial Arts: Discovering the Warrior Within and The Afrikan Warriors' Bible and eight novels, including the Steamfunk bestseller, MOSES: The Chronicles of Harriet Tubman (Books 1 & 2); the Urban Science Fiction saga, Redeemer; the Sword & Soul epic, Once Upon A Time In Afrika; a Fight Fiction, New Pulp novella, Fist of Afrika; the gritty, Urban Superhero series, A Single Link and Wrath of the Siafu; the two-fisted Dieselfunk tale, The Scythe and the "Choose-Your-Own-Destiny"-style Young Adult novel, The Keys. Balogun is also contributing co-editor of two anthologies: Ki: Khanga: The Anthology and Steamfunk.

Finally, Balogun is the Director and Fight Choreographer of the Steamfunk feature film, Rite of Passage and co-author of the award-winning screenplay, Ngolo.

DaVaun Sanders (*The First Doom*)

DaVaun Sanders has resided in Phoenix, Arizona since 2002, where the local spoken word community fostered his passion to pursue writing novels and screenplays. The World Breach series began as a dream vivid enough to play like a movie trailer. Deciding to write the debut novel took some time, as it wasn't part of "The Plan," but when the housing market collapse forced DaVaun's small design firm under in2008, he decided to step away from architecture and plunge into writing full-time. He's currently loving every minute as an indie publisher. DaVaun is a proud husband and father of twins.

DaVaun's first novel, The Seedbearing Prince: Part I, has reached as high as #1 on Amazon's genre lists for Science Fiction and Epic Fantasy, and remains a perennial favorite in the top 100 downloads. His short screenplay "Vault of Souls" won the Grand Prize in Phoenix Comicon's 2014 Short Script Competition. A scene from the short that was produced by Rangelo Productions and shot in Phoenix by Director Kevin Phipps debuted at a 2015 Phoenix Comicon panel.

DaVaun's most recent release is The Course of Blades, the third of six books in World Breach, and he is hard at work on completing Dayn Ro'Halan's epic adventure.

K. Ceres Wright (*A Tryst That Cuts Both Ways*)

K. Ceres Wright is the author of the cyberpunk book, Cog. Her short stories, articles, and poetry have appeared in Hazard Yet Forward; Genesis: An Anthology of Black Science Fiction; Many Genres, One Craft; 2008 Rhysling Anthology; Diner Stories: Off the Menu; Far Worlds; and The City Anthology

The conquest of the Known was a complex operation. For some planets, the Cassad arrival was considered a miracle, as the technology they brought with them lifted the worlds from Stone Age like conditions. For others, the Cassads negotiated alliances that would soon be betrayed. For others still, such as the Brython Theocracy and the Alien Worlds, it was all out war. In each case the Cassads prevailed due to their technological advantages, tenacity and deep resources. Soon most of the Known worlds were under Cassad control. Administrators selected from the One Million were placed in control of each world; each world was required to pay a 'rehabilitation tax' which paid the cost of the Cassad technological innovation. Soon the Known worlds possessed comparable technology but the payments were still required. This was the time of the Cassad Alifia, The Cassad Peace, which lasted for approximately one thousand years.

DARK UNIVERSE: THE BRIGHT EMPIRE

Coming April 2018 from MVmedia!

CPSIA information can be obtained
at www.ICGtesting.com
Printed in the USA
FSOW03n0546070318
45164FS